HERON ISLAND

HERON ISLAND

a Dade Wyatt mystery

R.A. Harold

Station Road Press
Montpelier, Vermont

Heron Island
R. A. Harold

Published by Station Road Press
Montpelier, VT 05602

Cover photo and author photo by Wayne Fawbush

ISBN 978-0-9831609-0-8

for Wayne, *sine quo nihil*

CHAPTER 1

The boat gliding southeast from Heron Island to the Vermont shore might have held a courting couple out for a Saturday excursion, the woman reclining under a lacy parasol in the stern, the man pulling steadily and evenly on the oars.

"But, Mr. Wyatt, surely I can persuade you to join us for the ceremony?" Mrs. Van Dorn's tone was half entreaty, half protest.

The oarsman paused, the lines of his arm muscles softening. His dark eyes met her china-blue gaze.

"You're very kind—but I promised Mr. Dodge a game of chess when I get back, and he is so rarely at leisure." A slight, apologetic lift of one shoulder. "One wants to be a good guest."

She leaned towards him, letting the shade of her hat-brim deepen the blue of her eyes. "I'm sure Warren would understand—don't you want to see the new steamer?"

It was a perfect midsummer afternoon, the sky blue as a flag, dabbed with just enough cloud-fluff for decoration. Tiny wavelets danced on the surface of the lake's darker blue. The *Vermont III* would be the largest steamer ever launched on Lake Champlain, and there was to be a band concert in Burlington afterwards.

Wyatt bent again to his oars. "I'll hope to have a ride on it before the summer's out. I'm sure you and Mr. Van Dorn will have a fine time."

The rebuff stung, though gently delivered. It almost spoiled the small victory of getting more than ten words out of him after a campaign of five days, an effort that must end with her husband's imminent arrival. She settled back among the silk cushions and let her gaze wander from the honey-colored ribs of the Adirondack boat, rolling slightly from her movement, to the play of muscle along Wyatt's shoulders and arms.

A week's sun had bronzed the cheekbones of his long face, and with the thick, dark mustache bracketing a wide, well-shaped mouth, he could pass for a pirate, or a lawman of the Wild West. Her mind's eye pinned a sheriff's star on his collarless white shirt, replaced the boater which shaded his eyes with a gray Stetson.

The Van Dorns often socialized with the Dodges back in the City, but this was their first invitation to Dodge's private island with its newly built Camp. Her husband Gerald, a genial, portly merchant banker at Morgan's, was to join her by train from New York. The company of Mr. Dade Wyatt, mannerly but laconic and thereby fascinating, had driven all thought of Gerald from her head. But the object of imagination and curiosity was not yet to be drawn out, and the shoreline was fast approaching.

"You will be here for Mr. Roosevelt's visit, won't you, Mr. Wyatt?"

The President had accepted an invitation to Heron Island for a few days in August, drawn by the promise of bird watching in the cool Vermont air and by a generational debt to his host, Warren Dodge, whose late father, a pulp and paper baron turned Congressman back in the eighties, had been a moderating influence in Roosevelt's brash political youth. The Van Dorns, along with the Dodges' Vermont friends, the Webbs and the Fisks, had been invited for a midsummer stay, and would later be guests for the great occasion.

Roosevelt's visit was the last thing Wyatt wanted to talk about. A specialist in security and investigations, he had come to the island at the insistence of his friend Dodge to survey arrangements for the President's stay. He was joining the party for dinners as a fellow guest, but disappearing for much of the day to scout nearby islands and bays in the Adirondack boat.

Milly Van Dorn had done him a favor, Wyatt reflected, by requesting conveyance and presenting him with an opportunity for close observation. He watched her push back a strand of auburn hair and fan the faintest dew of moisture from the exquisite bow of her upper lip. It occurred to him that, like many rich men's wives he'd known these last few years, she might be inclined to other favors …

"I guess I'll be back in August," he said slowly.

"I suppose he'll have to bring a lot of guards with him, won't he? After that whole—*debacle* in Buffalo—I can't imagine how they could have let that happen, can you? Hiding his gun-hand under a handkerchief! Shouldn't someone have spotted that?"

It was Wyatt's turn to be stung, and far worse. In the two years since the McKinley catastrophe, for which no one but himself had attached blame to him, he had stuck to such low-stakes assignments as nosing out labor organizers in Dodge's paper factories and keeping watch on agitators in crowds for political speeches. Dull work compared with his prior life, but as much as his frame of mind could manage these days.

He'd failed once, and that failure had shattered a nation. And now Dodge wanted him back on the front line, this time to protect a man he revered as a reformer and as a commander. He could barely stand the thought of putting himself at such risk again.

He shook off the haunted vision and brought his gaze back to his companion's. "And Mr. Van Dorn—he'll be able to join you then too?"

"Unless Mr. Morgan has him off on one of his—acquisitions." There was the faintest curl of the cupid's-bow. "Though I dare say even he would have to excuse Gerald for a visit with the President."

"Good for business, I should think."

"I suppose so. I find business talk so tiresome, don't you? But then I don't even know what your business is. Perhaps it's fascinating to you."

"I don't suppose anyone's business is fascinating to anyone else," Wyatt parried. "You've met the President before?"

"Well—no, not really. Gerald knows him, of course. But you must know him—Mr. Dodge told me you were in the Rough Riders! What is he like? I confess I'm dying to meet him. He sounds so bold. So manly. It's all I could do not to tell my girl-friends about it. But they said we mustn't, for security reasons and so forth." She gave a little shrug and rolled her eyes. "As if anyone I knew would be a threat to him!"

"I guess you can't always tell," Wyatt said.

She frowned at him and pursed her lips. "Good heavens, you're not suggesting—"

"Oh, not your girl-friends, of course, but—servants, for instance, overhearing things. We, ah, don't always know what their outside interests are."

Her eyes flickered away for an instant, but she cupped her chin in her hand and gave him the full strength of her blue gaze. "I dare say you're right. What with being positively *over-run* with foreigners these days—I do love the new Camp, don't you? It reminds me of the Webbs' place in the Adirondacks—" Her backwards look brought into his line of vision a profile that could have graced a cameo.

The roofline of the shingled lodge was dropping out of sight now, the cliff-girdled island with its verdant lawns and copses of poplar and young maples receding with each stroke of the oars, the low hills of the Grand Isle peninsula blurring to gray-blue beyond.

"You've spent time with the Webbs?"

Dr. Seward Webb, an eccentric New York millionaire who had married a Vanderbilt heiress, had just built a railroad across Lake Champlain that joined the southern tip of Grand Isle to the mainland. Webb had hosted the President at Shelburne Farms, his hackney horse-breeding estate on Lake Champlain, the previous summer.

"We've known them for ages! Well—three or four years. I count Mrs. Webb as a friend—the doctor's rather reclusive— oh, I don't mean inhospitable, just quiet, he couldn't be more gracious—Gerald had something to do with financing one of his railroads. And we met the Fisks last summer—such a delightful couple!"

Wyatt remembered that Roosevelt had been addressing a Republican gathering at the Grand Isle mansion of Nelson Fisk, the former Vermont lieutenant governor, when he'd received word that McKinley had been shot. Another sting of painful memory…

He watched the rosy color ebb from Milly Van Dorn's cheeks as she lapsed into silence. In her flower-trimmed straw and dotted-swiss muslin, she was a picture for Sargent—no, it was far more personal than that. She was having the same effect on him that the smell of bread wafting from a bakery has on a man who has not realized until then that he is hungry. Her cheerful prattle, which might in other circumstances have irritated him, seemed all of a piece with the sparkle and wink of the waves, the gossiping breeze bending the crowns of trees on the shore. He let it blow aside the veil of melancholy which had been closing in on him, felt in himself the desire to respond.

Through half-lowered lashes, Mrs. Van Dorn watched Wyatt's arms keeping the boat's pitch-and-roll barely perceptible as they drew towards the Vermont shore. He was too lean and muscular for a man of her class, where corpulence was a badge of success, and he didn't seem much interested in the doings of society. Though his hair was still dark and thick, with barely a hint of gray at the temples, there was something in the set of his face—not lines, really, except for a few light crows' feet she could see when the sun flashed beneath the brim of his boater—something that betokened the experiences of maturity, of one past some prime. Perhaps not even a physical prime, but a prime of the heart, of the affections…

The Webbs' carriage would take Mrs. Van Dorn to Burlington, as they had arranged earlier in the week. She strained forward, wanting to have first sight of the boat-tunnel under the Sandbar causeway.

"Have you known the Dodges long, Mrs. Van Dorn?"

"Oh, indeed! About five or six years now." She lit up with his renewed attention. "Shortly before I married Gerald, we were invited to their box at the Metropolitan—so that I could be inspected, you see, and—"

"—I dare say you passed!"

She felt his smile melt something in her core. "Are you fond of opera, Mr. Wyatt? I adore Puccini! Gerald thinks he's sentimental—I can't think how he'd know, he's sound asleep halfway through the first act..." she wrinkled her nose and shrugged, trailing a diamond-dewed hand in the water.

"I'm told his *Tosca* was splendid—"

"Oh, it was! So—grand, so passionate! But there's something...terrifying about *Tosca*, don't you think?" She shuddered. "Killing for love. I could never do that."

"What about dying for love?" Wyatt's eyes were intent on her face. She looked quickly away with a little laugh.

"Good heavens! Not that either. All I meant was—I prefer *La Bohème*. Poor Mimi! Have you seen—"

"No. I haven't." She saw something in him shut down, shut her out. The causeway was drawing closer, and she couldn't bear to let him slip away.

"Forgive my asking—is there a Mrs. Wyatt?"

"There was, once."

He looked away, but she caught the shadow that passed over his face. He had paused in his rowing and she could hear the water drip from the oars.

"I'm sorry."

"No need." He forced a smile. "It's been a long time."

"How strange that a—such a *cultured* man as you should be alone." She leaned forward, her face intent on his.

"Lot of that in the world." He began to row again. "Wise to get used to it," he added, surprising himself with so disingenuous an addition.

"Oh, pray don't say that!" She held up a hand in protest. "One mustn't cut oneself off from life. One must turn to—to the comforts that friends can give."

He looked over his shoulder. There were figures on the Sandbar causeway, waving at them, two black horses hitched to a yellow-wheeled wagonette behind them.

"It seems your friends are waiting for you already."

"Do let us be friends, Mr. Wyatt!" She let a dimpled smile lighten the intensity of the plea.

Wyatt took a breath, returned the smile and plunged in his turn. "I should like that—naturally."

"I could tell when we met that you were—a sympathetic person. How wonderful that we shall have a few more days on the island—to get to know each other better. And pray don't worry about Gerald!" she waved a dismissive hand. They were closing in on the shore, where their voices could almost reach. "He's not the jealous sort."

She strained forward and shielded her eyes. "There's Mrs. Webb, all in white—and those must be the Fisks." She pointed to a slender, dark-haired man with a neat black beard and a tiny, plump currant-bun of a woman standing next to him, both smiling and waving at them. "Oh, look! Dr. Webb came as well. They said they would all come, if it was a nice day, but I was afraid they might just send the carriage."

"You'll be in good company for the ride to Burlington, then. I'm glad."

After the Burlington concert, the Van Dorns and Fisks would sail back to the island on the Webbs' steam-yacht, *Elfreida*. Dr. Webb, a compact, red-bearded man with gold-rimmed glasses, wore a yachting cap and a nautical blue blazer. He climbed down onto the rubbled causeway and shouted a welcome. His wife Lila hovered behind him with an anxious smile, the breeze ruffling the white silk flowers on her elaborate bonnet.

"Do be careful of your footing, Seward dear—be sure Milly's got a good grip on your arm. How kind of you to bring Milly to us, Mr. Wyatt!"

Wyatt glided in along the bank of the Sandbar and threw Webb a line. Mrs. Van Dorn rose, steadied against the boat's rocking by Wyatt's hand at her back. She gathered her skirts and, taking the doctor's waiting hand, stepped gracefully out of the boat. She thanked her ferryman with a soft-eyed smile, wondered why she was left with the feeling that Mr. Wyatt had learned more about her on their little voyage than she had about him.

CHAPTER 2

Having escaped further entreaties to join the concert-party, Wyatt rowed back north to the open lake south of Heron Island. In the ripeness of mid-afternoon, the breeze had died and the lake was mirror-still. It was as if he were rowing in the air, the world below him all sky and clouds, the oars dipping and rising like the wings of a great bird. An outdoor concert would have been a pleasant thing at that, on such a day. But it would have been carrying the pretense of equal footing farther than he thought proper.

The Adirondack boat glided through the water, sun warming its cherrywood spars and gunwales to a tawny red. Its hull was wide enough for a carry-yoke and for rowing cross-handed, slim enough to slice fast and silent through the water like a sharp blade through silk. A beautiful thing, light enough to portage on a strong man's back...he could buy one of these boats with his savings, leave New York and its memories, build himself a little cabin and set up as a fishing guide...the island came into view, a dark smudge rising out of the lake.

He came around the lee and reflexively looked for the blue heron he'd once seen fishing below the southern headland. Not there, which didn't surprise him. You never saw anything marvelous or beautiful when you were looking for it. Beauty had come to you in its own time and on its own terms...*nothing pleaseth but rare accident...* Shakespeare's Prince Hal had been his favorite role in his acting days, the enigmatic rogue all irreverent ne'er-do-well on the surface, all cold-eyed killer underneath...

At the top of the bluff Wyatt spotted a figure, and not unlike a heron at that: his host's son Jeremy, a lanky college boy with a thatch of red-blond hair flopping over his brow. Hands thrust deep in the pockets of his white ducks, collarless shirt open at the neck, he was gazing in the direction from which Wyatt had come. When the guideboat crossed his line of vision he waved and nodded north towards the dock, turned and dropped out of sight below the brow of the cliff. As Wyatt pulled the boat in, Jeremy caught the line tossed to him and secured it neatly to a cleat.

"I don't suppose you've got time for tennis today." There was more than a hint of petulance in the tone. "Father says you're playing chess with him."

Wyatt followed Jeremy up the gravel path towards the ice-house and the guest cottage. The boy stopped suddenly and turned to face him.

"I hope you and Mil—Mrs. V. had a nice ride."

"A lady like that can't help but be pleasant company." Wyatt waited for more.

"I don't mind telling you—I wish she'd stayed back," Jeremy blurted. "Uh—I mean, I can't paint when she's not here— I've been borrowing her paints and things—and I forgot to ask her if it was all right. Before she left with you."

Wyatt sat down on the steps of the cottage. "Didn't I see the two of you painting yesterday, over in the flower garden?"

Jeremy reddened but managed a smile. "I was helping her with the composition. She's good, you know—she was trying to get that big blue cluster of lupines in the foreground, with the lake. She says my work reminds her of Sargent. Maybe she's only being friendly…"

Wyatt scanned the eager young face. "You are talented, Jeremy. Anyone with half an eye can see that."

"I wasn't fishing for compliments. Or looking to be patronized."

How sensitive a boy of twenty could be, and how foolish. As though the two of them were rivals for Milly's regard. Jeremy was her stepson's roommate at Yale, more likely, Wyatt thought, to be an object of maternal indulgence than amorous attentions.

"You should have brought your own paints. Are you afraid your father wouldn't like it?"

"The only thing he cares about is owning more paper companies than Grandpa did. Having an artist for a son—it's not what he has in mind for me, I know that." Jeremy sat down abruptly on the step beside Wyatt. "But painting is the only thing I care about!"

The only thing, perhaps, Wyatt thought, *but not the only one.* "Have you ever talked to your father about it?"

Jeremy stared at him and snorted. "Oh, really, Wyatt! How on earth would you start a conversation like that?"

Wyatt stood and looked down at him, curled up around himself on the step like a snail evicted from its shell. "Show him some of your work. What he values is people who are good at what they do. I think he might surprise you."

"Our house in Manhattan is full of paintings. Pa's got taste, I'll give him that. But his own son—I don't think he and Mamma think artists are quite respectable."

Wyatt grinned. "If they're any good, they probably aren't. Look, would it help if I broke the ice for you? Brought it up with him?"

Jeremy rose and took a few steps up the elm-lined path, hands dug into his pants pockets. He turned back, his cheeks aflame. "Thanks, but I'm old enough to fight my own battles." He stalked up the path to the house.

Wyatt stared after him. Until now, he'd only seen that passion on the tennis court, where the son shared Warren Dodge's competitive streak. Some primitive rage would rise in him, turning his pale cheeks to flame as he swung at the ball, smashing serves with the precision and ferocity that had won him a spot on the Yale 'varsity. Wyatt enjoyed their contests. He could play up to his best without the concern he so often had about humiliating a patron or employer.

It would be too bad for the boy to spend the whole summer as he was doing now, moping around after Milly Van Dorn. This would be Jeremy's last summer here, Dodge had told Wyatt in a tone of uncharacteristic wistfulness. It was a dull place for a young fellow. He'd be better off with his friends in Newport or Cape May. But Augusta hadn't wanted to let him go just yet. That, Wyatt reflected, might have been a mistake.

He found Warren Dodge and his steward Alexis Germain squeezed into the small wine cellar below the kitchen, next to the Camp's wood supply. Though a man of average height, Dodge looked small in the shadow of the slender, olive-skinned Germain, a mixed-blood Creole from Louisiana. He scanned the labels of the bottles Germain was handing out to him, quickly setting aside or rejecting Germain's selections.

"Hullo, Wyatt, back from ferrying? —we had some Romanée-Conti in there somewhere, last I looked."

"We've only got a few left." Germain squatted down to a low shelf and extracted a dusty bottle, which he wiped with a linen towel as he handed it up. "What did you want to do about Marcel's trout?"

The island's off-season caretaker had proudly presented Germain with the results of a morning's fishing in a grass-lined creel. Dodge looked up from the label he was reading. The afternoon sun caught a raw-boned face with pale blue eyes, ruddy skin, wavy reddish-blond hair only now beginning to thin out in his late forties.

He nodded towards Wyatt. "He knows the whites better than I do."

"Haut-Brion?" Wyatt offered. Germain shrugged and nodded.

Dodge went back to the label. "How much did he soak you for, for those trout?"

"They're beautiful fish," Wyatt said. "I saw them in the kitchen."

"Could've gone out myself and caught them, if I'd wanted to take the time."

"It's play for you, work for him," Germain shot back. "We're lucky he brought them here first."

"But he takes advantage. You know he does. What about that wine?"

"I'd go with a Meursault. Lot of butter in that almondine sauce." Germain rose to his considerable full height.

Wyatt scanned the label of the bottle Germain was holding and reactivated a perennial topic. "When are you going to lay in some of those Californias?"

Dodge's nostrils flared. "*Et tu*, Wyatt? When they start winning medals."

"Be too late by then." Germain gave Wyatt a conspiratorial wink. "Man that knows how to play the market like you, you get in on the ground floor—"

"You and Wyatt are the wine experts. All I know is pulp and paper. Get him to stake you."

"But you're the one with the money. I could cut you in—" Germain cocked an eyebrow. Dodge stared back, but the corner of his mouth twitched upward.

"And then you make a fortune and leave me? Why would I want to do that?"

"Fair question." Wyatt bent to pick up the bottles Germain had pulled out.

Germain laughed. "Don't suppose I would, if I was you. Got the Pol Roger chilling, by the way."

"Good." Dodge held out his arms for Wyatt to load them. "Mrs. Van Dorn likes champagne."

"What about Mr. Van Dorn?"

"Gerald? He's not particular. If she tells him he likes it, I'll wager he will."

Wyatt followed Dodge up the cellar stairs with an armful of reds, the movements of Dodge's wiry body as lithe and efficient as a catamount's. Wyatt shared his friend's passion for tennis and chess, his disgust with the wallowing in food that swelled so many of his colleagues to elephantine proportions. Like his father, a shrewd Yankee mill owner who had founded a pulp and paper empire on bargains and good timing, Dodge valued only two things in the business game: competence and results. Associates like Germain and Wyatt, who delivered on his expectations, found him generous; those who failed him received no second chances. But he had refused to listen to Wyatt's self-flagellation about McKinley's death.

"I wasn't there, so I can't judge. If you blundered that day, which I doubt, you weren't the only one. Besides, you've got a chance to make up for it. Make sure Roosevelt gets here and nothing happens to him while he's on my island."

Simple enough, surely. Wyatt deposited the wine bottles on the kitchen table and crossed the dining room to the front verandah, which faced Grand Isle to the west. Stepping onto the herb-thick grass, he let the warm air waft the scent of crushed thyme into his nostrils. Behind him, Dodge came down the verandah steps and stopped to gaze at the blue-black expanse of the lake.

Germain stuck his head out of the screen door and nodded in a vaguely northeastern direction. "Miz Dodge was just asking where you'd got to."

"Wyatt, set up the board, will you? I'll be there shortly."

Indoors, Wyatt inhaled the sharp scent of varnish from the Douglas fir matchstick paneling that ribbed the great room. Trophy heads from the late elder Dodge's study gazed serenely from the beams: bighorn sheep, mountain goats, African antelopes, a pensive moose. They contrasted oddly but not unpleasantly with the urbane rose and white satin stripes of the lounges, divans and armchairs. Beyond the dining room, divided from the great room by a massive stone fireplace, lay the galley pantry, where Germain was icing down bottles of Meursault in a copper-lined cooler.

Germain was a trophy of another sort, a sepia-skinned aristocrat lured away from his French Quarter restaurant and his longtime mistress by an offer of astounding generosity after

Dodge discovered him on a business trip to New Orleans. He ruled the Dodge household off Park Avenue in the City, as unchallenged as a medieval abbot.

"Boat came from Burlington Grocery while you were gone," Germain called from the pantry. "Got a few crates of ripe strawberries to wash and sort through. You want to help till Mr. Dodge gets back, it'll be worth your while."

Strawberries were a weakness of Wyatt's. It occurred to him that Germain knew that, along with a lot of other things one wouldn't think Germain could know. He delved happily into the task, gently shaking the wooden crates into the kitchen's deep sink, watching the plump red berries tumble over one another.

Dodge found his wife on the north verandah arranging roses in bowls. Chestnut-haired, still handsome at forty-five in a dress of striped cornflower blue and white, Augusta had the kind of looks that would turn mannish and florid as she gained weight with the years. To him she would always be the belle of twenty he'd married.

"It's time we got Amy out of long hair and short dresses," she greeted him.

"She'd rather trousers, I think." Dodge leaned against the porch door watching their daughter, fifty yards away, scramble over the rocky neck between the main island and the wooded headland where gulls, cormorants and swallows roosted. "Our little surprise," as Augusta often referred to Amy, was an odd, abrupt child, unlovely and intelligent, the dark bang across her forehead always in need of a trim, all long limbs and still flat-chested as a boy, though she was past fourteen.

"Do you think Dr. Webb will really come this time?"

Dodge took the abrupt change of subject in stride. "He said he would, didn't he?"

"He's said that twice before and not appeared. Lila keeps mumbling about his poor health, but I wonder if perhaps we're not—ah, not—"

One side of Dodge's mouth curled up. "Up to the Vanderbilts' standards?"

"Well—since you put it that way." She turned her head away.

"It's what you were thinking. I don't know why you think we've anything to worry about on that score."

"I've never known Seward to be ungracious," she said hastily, "It's just that he doesn't seem himself the last few times we've seen them. I wonder if he has a nervous condition. Neurasthenia, perhaps."

Dodge waved a dismissive hand. "I wouldn't know anything about that." They re-entered the house by the door of a screened dining porch.

Augusta centered a bowl of roses on the long refectory table in the dining room. "Do you think it was quite wise to set Milly on Mr. Wyatt?"

Dodge pretended to bristle. "Shanghaiing him was entirely her own idea. Besides, Wyatt can look after himself. He seems to have come back unscathed."

Germain and Wyatt were on the fourth crate of strawberries when Dodge returned. Germain was frowning at a newspaper that had lined one of the earlier crates.

Dodge snatched a berry from Wyatt and popped it in his mouth. "What's that?"

Never seen this before," Germain said. "It's all in Italian." He snapped the newspaper open. On the masthead, a long-haired Herculean figure spread his arms below the jagged capitals *Cronaca Sovversiva*. "*Subversive Chronicle*, I'd guess. Looks like an anarchist or socialist rag of some kind." He peered at the small print on the masthead. "Published in Barre. That's, what, fifty miles from here? It's the inaugural issue, from three weeks ago."

"Who's behind it?" Dodge asked.

Germain passed the paper to Wyatt, who leafed through it. "The articles aren't signed. Carlo Abate's listed as the editor. Sculptor, as I recall. One of the anarchist crowd I was looking out for when the President came up to Montpelier last fall."

"You came back up last year?"

"Wilkie—the Secret Service chief—wanted some extra muscle. I rounded up a few local fellows and put them in the crowd. Seems this anarchist lot in Barre had shot the police chief a couple of years back, damn near killed him. The White House men weren't sure what to expect. Nothing, as it turned out."

"Because they took the precaution of hiring you, *mon vieux*," Germain said.

Wyatt shrugged. "Didn't see much evidence of the prime suspects we'd heard about. A lot of quotes here from Luigi Galleani. Name mean anything to you?"

Dodge took the paper from Wyatt and scanned the inside front cover. "One of those dago bomb-throwers, isn't he? The one they ran out after the silk strike in Paterson. Went on the lam to Canada, is what I heard."

"I'd best check up on these Burlington Grocery men," Wyatt said. "Galleani's a Propaganda of the Deed man—you're right about bomb-throwing. And Barre is close."

Dodge grunted. "This would show up when I'm trying to get the President here."

"We're forewarned. And there's no reason to think any of this crew—" Wyatt tapped the newspaper with the back of his fingers, "would know about your plans."

Germain frowned. "Odd coincidence, this turning up in the strawberries, *n'est-ce pas?* And look here—this chart. I don't read Italian, but it's not that far from French. It's got Umberto and McKinley and a lot of other crowned heads. Looks like a list of assassinations."

Wyatt angled the paper to let the sunlight fall on the page. "Attempts. If this were baseball, I'd say they were batting .300. You're right, though, we'd best be cautious. I'll have to pay a visit to the grocery warehouse, see if I can track this to its source."

CHAPTER 3

Months later, after everything was over, Wyatt would re-member that Saturday on the island as a sort of prelude to the Fall, a last afternoon of innocence. The boating-party had arrived from Burlington on *Elfreida*, accompanied by the members of a string quartet lent by the Webbs, as the sun lengthened the elm-shadows and deepened the greens on the lawn.

"Mrs. Fisk!" Amy Dodge came running across the causeway onto the dock, in a clatter of arms and legs. She threw her arms around Elizabeth, who hugged her and got on tiptoe to kiss her on the forehead.

"Amy, dear, how you've grown!"

"I've just found the most perfect clutch of eggs, I think they're cormorant's, will you come and look tomorrow?"

"Let Mrs. Fisk get herself settled before she makes any more social commitments," her father said, ruffling Amy's dark hair. She brushed his hand away.

"Cormorants' eggs?" Gerald Van Dorn turned back towards Amy, his whiskered pink face alight with interest. "What an exciting find, my dear. I should very much like to see them."

"Would you really? I didn't know you were a birder. How wonderful!" Amy smiled like a sunrise scattering clouds. "You must come with me—first thing tomorrow."

Bands of fair-weather clouds turned vibrant rose over the slate-blue Adirondacks, the sinking sun blazing molten copper in their midst. On the great screened porch where the string quar-tet had set up their instruments, serenades and divertimentos in minor keys put the boating-party, now in decolleté silks and evening suits, in contemplative quiet as the last color drained from the western sky.

Wyatt stood behind the porch swing, idly twirling a champagne flute, lost in the music. He knew this piece well. He and Rose had heard it at the Philharmonic, one rare spring night when neither of them was required on stage. Shakespeare's poem set to music: *My lady sweet, arise...*

"Nice piece. Who's that?" Dodge asked him from the swing, a companionable arm around Augusta.

"Schubert," Wyatt swallowed his irritation. "The Ständchen."

His reverie broken, he eyed the quartet. He would study them at more leisure over the next few days. They were to stay in the guest cottage which, refitted with more luxurious appointments, would house the Roosevelts in August. The blond man with flushed cheekbones and blue eyes that blazed like gas jets was the bassist, a Polish immigrant rumored to have been some sort of nobleman in his own country. The first violinist, a young American barely out of the Peabody Conservatory, had big brown eyes and a mop of dark curls. The other two he didn't remember.

The second violinist wasn't the equal of the Peabody graduate, every note correct but lacking the relaxed flow that gave the other man's playing an ineffable, melancholy grace. A bearded, taciturn fellow with curly chestnut hair, little rectangular spectacles, a strong Italian accent when he spoke at all. Perhaps the Peabody man's influence would rub off after a while.

The aroma of herbed oysters in cream wafted from the kitchen. Germain emerged from the dining room, bent and spoke in Augusta's ear. She rose in a cascade of aquamarine silk.

"I hope we shall be livelier at dinner." she gestured towards Germain's retreating back. "Lila, dear, would you like Germain to call Dr. Webb?"

Dr. Webb, pleading a recent bout of fever, had been excused for a pre-dinner nap. Mrs. Webb's hands fluttered briefly. "Oh, no—no, thank you, dear. I think it's best just to let him sleep— will it be all right if he joins us when he wakes?"

On the mahogany dining table, bare wood with reed mats in the informal style of Vermont summer, crystal winked, silver sparkled, and mounds of pale roses perfumed the air. The caretaker's trout in its buttery almondine coat took pride of place amid terrapin soup, duck, saddle of mutton and the early strawberries blanketed in cream.

After dinner, the men left the women to sip demitasse in the great room and returned to the porch. Dr. Webb had still not appeared. Oil-lamps cast haloes of light into the warm darkness.

"Electric's all very well, but you still want a bit of atmosphere after dinner," Warren Dodge was telling Wyatt. "What do you make of our company?" He joined Wyatt on the porch swing, his cigar tracing an inclusive circle around them.

"Webb surprised me—with all he's accomplished, getting that railroad across the Adirondacks and so forth, I was expecting a fellow with more—drive? Energy?"

"Webb's changed since I first knew him. As if that railroad took it all out of him. My wife wonders if he's well. There've been rumors at the Union Club about a nervous condition. Starting about the time he was blackballed—"

"A man with his pedigree? What happened?"

"No one knows. There doesn't have to be a stated reason, and there wasn't. Still, the President thinks the world of him. He stayed at Shelburne last year."

"Will the quartet be here for the President's visit?" Wyatt rose and stepped towards the screen door, inhaling the scent of peonies on the night breeze.

"Yes. No room for overnight, but Mrs. Dodge has an afternoon reception in mind, along the lines of the one Fisk gave him back in '01—you remember."

Wyatt turned to Dodge with a sardonic smile. "I was a bit preoccupied that day."

"Yes. Well. It'll be a much smaller group, naturally—it's

supposed to be a getaway, but you know TR—" he shrugged, "if there are hands to be shaken—"

"There'll be a list," Wyatt's eyebrows rather than his tone made it a question. "And someone at the dock who'll recognize everyone who's been invited—"

"A list, yes, but checking people at the door?"

Wyatt felt his color rise. "If we had checked a bandaged hand, McKinley would be alive. You wouldn't have me here if you didn't think it mattered."

"Sure I would." Dodge's voice lowered. "You got Milly Van Dorn and Lizzie Fisk off my back for the span of a whole dinner. I was afraid Lizzie would start in on me again about Amy's schooling."

"I didn't say a thing," Wyatt protested, resuming his seat.

"Exactly. You gave those two just what they wanted: an audience. And divided your time pretty equally, I might add. Try the Armagnac." Dodge handed him a snifter from the low burlwood table in front of them.

"Observant." Wyatt swirled the brandy, let the pungent vapors bloom in his nostrils.

"Bored, rather. Mrs. Webb and Fisk were on a great tear about golf. Lord preserve me from ever having enough idle time for that. I gave up trying to follow. Wonder what happened to Webb—seems odd, disappearing for the whole length of dinner—"

"What's Van Dorn's story?" Wyatt's subject sat in a striped chaise longue, manfully feigning interest in Fisk's account of a revolutionary method for marble cutting.

"Oh, Gerald. Good fellow. Works for Morgan. Doesn't have to now, of course, but they go back a long way. He's Union Club, naturally."

"There's money, then?"

"Pots of it. Finger in a lot of pies."

"What about the wife?" Wyatt jerked his head towards the great room. "They happy?"

"Hard to tell. He thinks she hung the moon, but…" Dodge shrugged.

"…but she flirts a lot. Pretty woman like that, young as she is—"

In the great room, Milly Van Dorn, bright-eyed, was nodding at something Mrs. Fisk was saying, a tiny liqueur glass perched between her fingers. "Now that she's got the money behind her, some confidence in herself—gives a woman a certain glow."

"Which she turns on a fellow like the beam of a lighthouse."

Dodge chuckled. "Seems to me it's been aimed pretty steadily since you got here. How was the boat-ride?"

Wyatt turned his head away and puffed on his cigar. "No complaints. Nice day, good-looking woman. Not my type, though," he felt compelled to add. "Van Dorn's escaped from Fisk—looks as if he's going out for a stroll. I'll join him for a bit."

He finds himself back in the Temple of Music, the organist softly playing Schumann's "Träumerei", the dense, sweaty line of people in their dark Sunday suits crawling forward, each pausing long enough for a friendly word, a quick hand-clasp from the President, moving reluctantly on. Milburn, chairman of the Exhibition, thin-lipped and running to fat, having insisted on pre-empting Foster's usual protective place at the President's left hand. Chief agent Foster behind him, Wyatt to Foster's left, a nominal employee of Pinkerton's but trusted by the Secret Service as one of their own.

The little Italian at the front of the line again, all smiles and eagerness, grasping both of the President's arms and pumping them vigorously, holding on too long. Wyatt's heart begins to pound, he thinks of the assassin Bresci and the other anarchists, but this time—this time he only watches the Italian's hands, sees nothing up the sleeves, does not step forward to pull him out of line, lets him pass on instead. And this time his gaze shifts in time to the man behind, pale, skinny, poorly dressed, spots the dark cylinder beneath the handkerchief in his hand, edges quietly

around Foster and Milburn and out from behind the tall Negro to
grab Czoglosz by the wrist, thrust the arm up in the air. The crack
of the bullet echoing harmlessly in the cavernous darkness of the
Temple ceiling...

Wyatt woke heartsick and sweating, wondering if the dream
would ever let him go. He lay still while his pulse slowed,
drifting in and out of a doze, listening to the Sunday morning stirrings of the birds. His room had a door out to the verandah. Around five o'clock he stepped quietly out to breathe
the cool, green-scented air. Barn-swallows made great arcs on
the lawn, twittering and scolding, swooping back and forth to
their tiny clay-pot nests under the eaves. He followed a narrow path that ran through a thick clump of young popples and
alders and along the edge of the south bluff. The unbroken
expanse of ink-blue water lapped the shore, glittering in the
morning light.

A few yards beyond him, where the path gave way to lawn,
Milly Van Dorn stood alone looking west, away from the sun's
slow climb above the Green Mountains. He stopped before
she could hear him. How different this face, thinking itself
unobserved, from the one she presented to the world: the
rosebud mouth drooping at the corners, the merry blue eyes
of yesterday abrim now with tears. She shivered in a morning
gown of thin muslin. He watched her wrap her arms around
each other and drop her head, letting the tears fall freely.

He felt a catch in his throat. The urge came to him to go
to her, put something warm around her shoulders. But the
only gentlemanly thing to do was to withdraw. To admit to
witnessing her tears would be a mortal breach of manners.
Once safely out of hearing range, he walked down the lawn to
the east garden and made a wide circuit around the Camp, back
out towards the northern dock and the guest house, across the
little causeway to linger on the wooded neck of the island where
the birds roosted.

He heard a door slam at the guest cottage: the household was setting about its business. He came back across the causeway, along the west shore beyond the tennis court, crossed the shale beach at the end of the great west lawn and climbed back to the south headland. A wooden flagpole, painted white, crowned the highest point of the cliff, some fifty feet west of where Milly Van Dorn had been standing. This was his favorite spot on the island. He strode to the flagpole and grasped it, half-consciously gauging the distance to the green fields of the Vermont mainland. His returning glance swept to where the cliff fell away, a steep fifteen feet or so, to shale and scattered boulders below.

His eye stopped on something he had not seen an hour before, when he had watched Milly Van Dorn on the cliff's edge: something large, bobbing just below the surface of the water five feet from the shore.

Large, and clothed.

CHAPTER 4

He ran back down the slope to the lawn and shingled beach from which he had just climbed. Without taking off his shoes, he waded around the brow of the cliff to where a narrow strip of sand and flat pebbles widened into a patch of graveled beach. From there, the lake bottom fell off steeply; he was in a foot of water while no more than a foot from shore. In front of him, wavelets lapped gently around the body of Gerald Van Dorn, curled shrimplike and face down in three feet of clear, sun-dappled water. The edges of a maroon satin dressing gown eddied just below the surface, a tassel of its loosened belt bobbing on the little waves. From the back of the neck, a thread of blood twisted in the water like an eddy of smoke from a cigar.

Wyatt waded out to the body and pulled at the left shoulder to turn it over, his shoes slipping on the bright green water moss that covered the rocks. The sightless eyes were glazed and partly open, like a sleepwalker's. He caught at the back of the neck with one hand and felt around the throat with the other. No pulse. The corpse bobbed gently as if trying to turn itself face down again. Strands of weed on the edges of the drooping mustache. Was it the heat of his own fingers he felt, or was there a trace of warmth at the throat?

He began dragging Van Dorn from the water by the armpits. Once he had the body hauled up on the beach, he straddled the legs. He racked his brain for the procedures of artificial respiration, remembered. Pinched the nose with the head tilted back. Breathed into the mouth, his own breath coming faster and faster, his face growing hot. Flapped the arms up and down like the handles of a bellows to blow the lungs clear. Pressed the chest, then the abdomen with both hands. This produced a rush of air, as if he'd stepped on a swimming-bladder, then a trickle of water from the mouth, lightly foamed. He turned the body over with difficulty, tried the arm movements again.

It was useless. He had known it would be, and his heart sank. Another death on his watch… A dribble of watery blood ran from the back of Van Dorn's head onto the shale. After twenty minutes Wyatt stood up, his face burning, and pulled a handkerchief from his pocket. Mechanically, he checked the watch that came out with it: six-fifteen. He mopped his brow and the back of his neck.

His mind raced to his talk with Van Dorn, after last night's dinner. The night air cool on the lawn, the sky a bride's train of stars. They'd talked of planets and constellations. Van Dorn would order a telescope from Abercrombie's as a thank-you gift for the Dodges. Tongue loosened by good wine and brandy, he'd spoken of his first wife Malvina, their son who was six when she died, whom he'd neglected afterwards, his long years of solitude. "A sort of gray fog, don't you know." Then he'd seen Milly on stage. "Gilbert and Sullivan—always liked them. The lovely thing was, she didn't laugh at me…"

The end of their conversation came back to Wyatt now with poignant clarity.

"I've been thinking it's about time to throw it all over, you know," Van Dorn had said. "Buy Milly a tiara and take her on the Grand Tour, mingle with the crowned heads and the opera divas, that sort of thing. Before I get too old. Come home, start a little family again—if the stars line up right." A fleeting expression had shadowed his pink, good-natured face.

Wyatt wondered how many nights he would lie awake, wishing he'd found out what it was…

"You're up early."

Warren Dodge caught Wyatt's upward, startled look. He stood grinning at the top of the cliff, early sun gleaming on his white trousers. "What's that you've got—good God, what the hell—don't move! I'm coming down—" He turned back towards the path that ran between the shrub thicket and the edge of the cliff. He reappeared on the shale, racing down a steep path which Wyatt had not yet discovered. Four lithe steps brought him to Wyatt's side.

"I saw him from the cliff," Wyatt's breath was ragged, his voice a monotone. "I went back down by the beach and waded out."

"Was he—like this?"

Wyatt shook his head. "I was trying artificial respiration."

"What was he—has he drowned? What was he doing out in his night-clothes?" Dodge bent to pick up a wet, satin-clad arm, stood, let it drop again.

"Damned if I know."

"You're sure he's—"

"Try it with me once more," Wyatt said, knowing it was useless.

When they stopped, Dodge sat down on a driftwood log, red-faced and breathing heavily.

"How are we going to tell Milly?" He ran a wet hand across his face and through the thin strands of his hair. Wyatt's mind flashed a picture of Mrs. Van Dorn on the cliff, little over an hour before, crying and looking towards—what? How long had Gerald's body been in the water?

He nodded at the body. "Did you hear him get up?"

Dodge shook his head slowly. "No. There were the usual creaks in the night, but there's the big room between us and the guest rooms."

"Anyone else out?"

"Germain was in the kitchen a few minutes ago—" Dodge stood abruptly. "Dear God, Wyatt, the President! What are we going to do?"

"Best cancel it. We'll have to let them know, and Wilkie will want to call it off. I would, if I were him."

"But we can't—Gussie was—it's an accident. It had to be."

"It's up to the coroner to decide that." Wyatt stared west towards the South Hero peninsula.

"The coroner? You can't be serious, man—they'll have the police in here. A man in my position—"

Wyatt cut him off. "Warren, the man's dead. We don't know how or why. You can't sweep a thing like this under the rug. No matter how expensive a rug."

Dodge walked a few paces away from him and rubbed the bridge of his nose between his finger and thumb.

"But, look here, the guests. The Fisks and the Webbs. You're proposing to subject them to an investigation, drag them into—"

"What makes you sure it was an accident?" Wyatt turned back towards Dodge.

"Well, what else could it be, for God's sake?"

For answer, Wyatt pointed to the blood, congealing now in a thin crescent behind the left ear. Dodge knelt and touched the red stain, his fingers coming away sticky with it. He knelt at the water's edge to wash it off. He scanned the water as if expecting to find the answer to Wyatt's question, rose and waded a few steps, bent and picked up something from the lake bed which he pulled out and shook off.

"His field-glasses." Water and fronds of weed dripped off the strap of a set of leather-encased binoculars. "He fell off the edge. If you weren't careful, if you strayed off the path for a better view of the lake, where it peaks there, at the very edge—"

"It's not out of the question." Wyatt scanned the cliff, calculating angles and trajectories. "But that wouldn't have got him far enough out to drown. Unless he pulled himself up and crawled farther out."

The sarcasm had its intended effect. Dodge folded his arms and stared at him.

"I won't have the police all over this island."

"They'll be here sooner or later," Wyatt said. "Easier sooner, I'd say."

"But if it's—foul play, you've already disturbed the scene, haven't you?"

"For God's sake, Warren, I had to see whether the man was still alive." Wyatt looked back at his friend for a long moment. "But you've got a point. We're in the best position of anyone to figure out what happened. The trail's still warm, if there is one. Presumably no one's left since last night."

"Wyatt, I want TR here. It means the world to me and Gussie. We'll never have this chance again." Dodge's eyes were steel-gray, his lips a tight line. "It's what we hired you for." He rolled his wet shirt-sleeves down and bent to retrieve his dropped cufflinks, ignoring the stricken look his words produced on Wyatt's face.

Wyatt found his voice. "You'll have to give me a free hand. Nothing and no one off limits. Give me the week and I might be able to—"

"Two days. We can't keep people here past that. It's unendurable to think so. And there's this to deal with." Dodge pointed towards Van Dorn's corpse.

"Three days."

"Tuesday night." Dodge spoke in the tone he used for final offers.

"I think you'd best tell Mrs. Van Dorn," Wyatt said. "Bring her down and let her see it for herself."

"I'll have a word with Augusta first. I'll get her to wake her up and come with her."

Wyatt bit back the information that he had already seen Mrs. Van Dorn that morning. "Help me pull him farther out of the water. And show me that path you came down."

They came back up the cliff path and along the east side of the Camp. A merganser drake, black crest bristling, perched on the roof of the generator-house, his neck feathers bronze in the early light. The sleeping areas were quiet, but as they approached the steps up to the kitchen door they could smell coffee brewing and sweet rolls baking. Germain was overseeing the table setting for breakfast.

"You gents fall out of a boat, or what?" He surveyed their water-stained clothes. "The ladies are up," he added to Wyatt. "There's talk of getting you men to row them over to South Hero for church, so they wanted breakfast early."

"Nobody mentioned anything about that last night." Dodge's voice betrayed nothing out of the ordinary. "Where are they?"

They sat in chairs on the east verandah, in thin, high-necked frocks, wrapped in shawls against the slight chill in the morning air. Fisk and Dr. Webb were strolling around the perennial beds, arguing companionably. Wyatt noted that Milly Van Dorn seemed to have recovered her spirits completely. She was pink-cheeked and bright-eyed, clasping Mrs. Fisk's hand and chattering rapidly. The women stopped and turned as Wyatt and Dodge entered from the great room.

Augusta Dodge rose. "There you are, Warren. I was about to ask Germain to go and—"

"You didn't get Gerald out fishing, did you?" Mrs. Van Dorn asked with mock disapproval. "He was gone when I woke up—"

Dodge took in a sharp breath, let it go. "Mrs. Van Dorn, may I speak to you?"

She rose, a puzzled expression in her blue eyes, questioning looks on the faces of the others at Dodge's formal tone on such an airy morning. Dodge opened the door to the dining room for her and stepped in, followed by Wyatt. Dodge laid a hand on her arm while Wyatt pulled out a chair for her.

"What's wrong? What has happened?" The words tangled in her throat.

"Milly, it's Gerald. We found him—Wyatt found him. He's dead. He was in the water, he's been—"

"No, no," she frowned. "That can't be. Gerald doesn't swim, so what would he be doing in—" She stared at him as though he had said something in a foreign language. Wyatt went back to the verandah and beckoned Mrs. Fisk to follow him. She walked in, saw the blood drained from her friend's face, turned to Dodge.

"Mr. Van Dorn is dead," Wyatt said. "We found him in the lake this morning, an hour ago."

"Oh, my dear!" Mrs. Fisk dropped to her knees by Milly's chair and put her arms around her. Mrs. Van Dorn's chest began to heave. She seemed to gulp several times as if trying to get enough air, half-rose, gave a strangled little cry, and slumped back into Mrs. Fisk's arms.

"Gussie!" Dodge threw open the verandah door.

Fisk and Webb came running up from the garden. Fisk, longer-legged, landed on the verandah and followed Augusta Dodge into the dining room. He took in the distress on his wife's face, Mrs. Van Dorn's limp body heavy in her arms. Dr. Webb's face appeared in the doorway behind him.

"Van Dorn is dead," Warren Dodge said. "Wyatt found his body in the lake. He appears to have drowned."

Nelson Fisk stared at him for a moment, blanched, put a hand over his mouth, and all but ran back out to the garden, past an astonished Dr. Webb.

CHAPTER 5

We'll have to get the county sheriff in at once." Nelson Fisk spoke earnestly and urgently, his elbow on the burled walnut mantel. Above him on the fireplace, a mountain-goat wore the detached look of one who shared his opinion but tactfully chose not to voice it.

"Good heavens, Fisk," Dr. Webb half-rose from the banquette, "you're assuming this was foul play?"

"You heard Mrs. Van Dorn—Gerald wasn't a man who'd go splashing around the lake in his nightclothes. And he seemed perfectly healthy last night."

"But with his weight, surely a heart attack, or apoplexy—" Dodge began.

"—isn't likely to have landed him five feet out in the lake with a gash on the back of his head, is it?" Fisk said.

Webb rose and paced the floor. "If he fell from the cliff—"

"—he'd have landed on the shingle, not in the water," Wyatt said. He watched the men's faces set into uneasy silence as the implications sank in. The room seemed to chill and darken; perhaps it was just a cloud passing over the sun.

"With all due respect, Dodge," Dr. Webb ventured at length, "if it was foul play, aren't all of us potential suspects?"

"Doctor, I've known Wyatt here for a long time." Dodge's fingers dug into the back of a brocade chesterfield. "He's handled a number of difficult matters for me. Of course this must be investigated. I think he's the man for the job, not the local police. In any event, this island straddles the town line between Grand Isle and South Hero. They've never resolved jurisdiction. Politically speaking, it's a no-man's land."

"How do we know Mr. Wyatt's not a suspect himself?" Fisk asked.

"You don't," Wyatt said from the other side of the fireplace. "I'm not sure I'd take this course if I were in your position."

"I brought Wyatt here to make sure the President would be safe. He makes his living on security. Why would he have wanted to harm Van Dorn?"

"Why would any of us, Warren?" Dr. Webb said, reasonably.

"Someone did, or may have." Wyatt looked down at Webb, who froze and blinked back at him as if braced for an accusation. "Doctor, would you be able to determine the cause of death?"

Webb let out a breath. "It's been twenty years since I practiced...I might be able to tell whether he drowned. I've never lost the habit of carrying the bag. Dosed the children when they were sick, and so forth. But, my dear man, a post-mortem? You've got a town health officer, young French-Canadian fellow, what was his name, surely he'd be the person to—?" Webb scanned the faces above him, looking for reinforcement. His gaze settled on Dodge.

"Dr. Caron, yes," Dodge said impatiently. "He's somewhere in Quebec. Gone for a week, he told me, visiting the in-laws."

"Are you still qualified to issue a death certificate?" Wyatt asked Webb.

"Certainly, but that's altogether different. You need a town official's permission to remove a body—"

"Look, Dodge," Fisk perched on the arm of the sofa, "under the circumstances, wouldn't it be better just to scrap the President's visit? His people will have to know of this, in any case."

Dodge's mouth set stubbornly. "If it was an accident, I don't see why he should change his plans."

"And if it wasn't?"

"We're in a better position to find out than the police." Dodge took up Fisk's stance at the edge of the fireplace. "You said so yourself, Wyatt. Look, of course I'll tell the President's people. Whether he decides to come or not, we still need to know what happened here. Let's find out what we're dealing with if we can."

"But how are we to do this?" Dr. Webb looked around as if seeking an exit.

"I'll have Germain set you up in the ice house."

"If there was a crime, the scene's been disrupted," Fisk pointed out.

"It was off the south cliff." Dodge caught Wyatt's warning look an instant too late. "There wouldn't have been any traces to go on, since he was in the water. And we had to make sure he wasn't still alive. Wyatt tried bringing him round—"

One of the maids entered. "What is it, Bridie," Dodge snapped.

"Sur, forgive the disturbance, but Mrs. Dodge asks would you please come out to the dinin' porch." She bobbed her head and withdrew.

Dodge rose and crossed the room to the porch. Augusta grasped the back of a slatted chair, her knuckles white.

"You're not going to let them bring the police here, are you?" she said without preliminary. "After all our hard work and the time we've spent—"

"It would be much the wisest thing, Gussie." His voice was soft.

"You're already too late, don't you think? Between you and Wyatt, you've already interfered with the scene of the crime, if it was one, removed evidence—"

"Which argues for not making it any worse," Dodge put an arm around his wife's shoulder. "But you do have a point. How is Milly?"

"Dr. Webb happened to have some morphia, thank goodness. She's sleeping in our room. She didn't want to go back to theirs. Elizabeth and Lila are with her. Who would have wanted to hurt Gerald? Such an amiable man." Her eyes filled and her mouth twisted.

"We don't know that anyone did," Dodge kneaded the back of her neck absently. "It may have been an accident. What on earth was wrong with Fisk? When we told him Van Dorn had drowned, he ran out as if he were about to vomit."

"Elizabeth told me after. When he was about Jeremy's age, he was out on the lake in a sailboat with two friends. A storm came up and the boat capsized. They clung on for two hours and very nearly drowned before a fishing boat got to them. It took him a long time to venture off dry land after that, and when he heard about Gerald it brought it all back. Rather viscerally, I'm afraid."

Dodge swung his gaze around the room. "Where's Amy?"

"I sent her down to the cottage with Germain. To her little laboratory, as she calls it, in the cellar. I told her to stay there or go and play with her birds' nests until we called for her. She wasn't pleased."

"And Jeremy?"

Augusta's hand fluttered to her breast. "I haven't seen him all morning. How could he have avoided hearing all the commotion?"

"At his age I slept like the dead," Dodge said, immediately regretting his choice of words. He left the dining porch and went to the door of Jeremy's bedroom. There was no answer to his knock. He went in and found both small beds in the room empty, hobnail bedspreads neatly knifed under the pillows. The maid was coming down the corridor with a pile of clean sheets.

"Bridie, have you seen Mr. Jeremy this morning?"

"I'm not long up from cleanin' the cottage, sur," she peered at him over the pile, "but I've not seen him meself. I'll ask Bernadette and the cook."

"You didn't make his bed?"

"No, sur, sure an' I haven't been in his room today at all."

Neither had anyone else in the household. Dodge summoned Amy to search the island for her brother. She came back alone, plopping heavily down on the banquette next to Dr. Webb.

"One of the skiffs is gone," she announced. "The old boat that came with the island. The one I named after the merganser. I painted it red around the gunwales. I bet Jeremy took it."

"Might have gone off to paint somewhere." Germain stood in the door of the kitchen, where he was supervising lunch preparations. Picnic plans for an excursion to nearby Abenaki Island had, of course, been abandoned.

Augusta turned towards him. "Did he bring any painting things with him?"

Germain hesitated. "Mrs. Van Dorn might have lent him hers. He was hang—uh, he was watching her the other day, when she was painting the elm avenue."

"She wouldn't have lent them today. She was planning to do a group sketch of us on the picnic—a little impression, I believe. Mrs. Webb was telling her about the French painters doing quick sketches in oils, and she thought she'd try it." Augusta turned back to her husband. "Milly does have some artistic talent, my dear, you should see her—oh, what am I saying?" She opened her arms, momentarily flustered. "Why would Jeremy have gone off in this way, when he knew he was to be at the picnic?"

"Why do boys his age do anything?" Dodge shrugged.

"Maybe he went off to meet a girl," Amy offered from the banquette.

"Amy!"

Wyatt came in from the verandah. "How is Mrs. Van Dorn?"

"Jeremy's gone." Amy sat up straight and glared at Wyatt. "He took one of the boats. He didn't sleep in his bed last night. I think he's got a girl-friend."

"Really, Amy!" It was Dodge's turn to chastise his daughter.

Augusta took a deep breath. "Milly's still asleep. Mrs. Webb is with her. Germain thinks Jeremy may have gone off to paint, with Mrs. Van Dorn's supplies."

"Then he'd have come back before the picnic, wouldn't he?" Wyatt asked, "Since she was going to paint the outing-party?"

Augusta plumped a cushion on the chesterfield. "He should have been back long since."

Lizzie Fisk bustled into the room from the bedroom corridor. "Augusta, dear, can you ask the maid to get a tisane for Milly? She's awake, and quite agitated—"

Mrs. Van Dorn appeared in the mouth of the corridor, Lila Webb hovering behind her. She leaned on the doorframe, her face pale, her eyes puffy.

"Someone will have to get word to Will." Milly began to cry again. "Now he's an orphan." The men stared at her and gave one another guilty looks. Until now, no one had thought of Willem Van Dorn, Gerald's only child and Jeremy's roommate at Yale.

Augusta went to her and laid a hand on her shoulder. "Perhaps that's what Jeremy went to do."

Germain shook his head. "Beg your pardon, Miz Dodge, there's no reason to think Jeremy knows Mr. Van Dorn is dead. He might've taken the boat out earlier than that. Nobody saw him this morning, am I right?"

Dodge's voice was uncharacteristically gentle. "Even if he did know, Milly, I'm sure Jeremy would have left that up to you."

Milly gave a mirthless little laugh. "I don't see why. Will was closer to Jeremy than he was to me," she blurted, her eyes filling again. "He never liked me."

"Now, Milly—" Augusta patted her shoulder again.

"No, it's true," Milly went on, her voice rising. "He wouldn't even come to the wedding. Gerald let him get away with it, I thought it wasn't right, but Gerald said he'd been so attached to his mother, so I didn't insist, I didn't want to be the wicked stepmother from the fairy tale—"

"He seemed to have got over it the last time we saw all of you." Dodge's polite tone had an edge of impatience. "I recall his being quite attentive. Well, I suppose it's possible Jeremy's off painting and lost track of time, or heard about Mr. Van Dorn and went off to send Will a telegram. In either case he'll be back before nightfall."

Germain addressed himself to Augusta. "I've laid out a little lunch on the dining-porch. In case anyone needs anything."

Milly Van Dorn closed her eyes and waved him off. "I don't want any lunch."

"Neither do I," said the other women in unison.

The men, Wyatt noted with grim amusement, felt no such constraints and headed for the dining-porch. The memory of trying to blow life back into Van Dorn's corpse was too fresh for him, and he only picked at a salad, his mind drifting away from their talk. Who was the last to see Gerald Van Dorn alive? His wife, most likely, if the drowning was an accident. If drowning it was. Water was a useful medium for disposing of bodies. If it wasn't an accident, who had reason to want him dead? Wyatt's work had taught him not to make assumptions, which made what they were about to do all the more questionable. Where was Jeremy? Why had Mrs. Van Dorn been crying on the cliff at daybreak? How had her husband's body come to be in the water below, less than an hour after Wyatt saw her standing on that cliff?

With a reluctant Dr. Webb dispatched, over Fisk's continued protests, to gain Milly's permission for the post-mortem, Wyatt walked the shale beach below the southern cliff with his head bowed, examining the rocks and the cliff face. If Van Dorn had been knocked on the head, the weapon could have been almost anything— a rock, a log, an oar, a length of pipe. The slight tear in the scalp at the back of the head suggested something fairly heavy, with an edge to it, or at least a protuberance. There wasn't much on this beach that would have qualified. No large rocks within sight that would have made a reliable weapon. And in any event, he concluded after an hour's fruitless perusal, any rational killer would have taken such a weapon with him and dropped it out in the deep lake, along with anything else he wanted to get rid of.

He walked slowly back up the path to the shrub-thicket, scanning once more for footprints. He had done this when he and Dodge took the path back up to the Camp after finding the body, but the only prints he had clearly identified matched the soles of the shoes Dodge had been wearing. Now there were those same prints leading uphill, along with his own, but that was all. Wyatt had found one of Van Dorn's bedroom slippers in the shallows, floating free of the body. He was carrying it now, a soggy tartan moccasin with a light herringbone pattern on the sole. There were no prints to match it on the cliff path in front of the thicket. Though bare and still slightly soft in a few spots from the previous night's rain, the path was mostly grassy.

Perhaps Van Dorn had encountered someone on the west beach. It had a sizeable patch of sand and fine gravel, and the water was shallow for a good twelve to fifteen feet out. He could have waded out easily—to accept an offered conveyance for bird-watching, perhaps? But there were only blurred traces of the many different feet that had walked on the small strand on the previous day—no fresh slipper-prints, or shoe-prints, either.

On the elm-lined path that led from the Camp's north end to the dock at the island's neck, there were vague impressions of recent activity—a partial arc of a sole-rim in two or three spots. But no full prints, nothing to identify a specific shoe or its wearer, and even these petered out before the path made its three-way split: to the right, to the wooden dock where several skiffs and small pulling-boats were tied up; to the left, across a bed of larger rocks, to a long, partially built stone jetty that would soon accommodate larger pleasure-boats such as Dr. Webb's steam yacht.

Straight ahead, the path ran up a small rise into dense scrub on the northern headland, where gulls and cormorants nested and another, narrower path teetered around the edge of a rocky promontory. A headland jutted out over the water, high enough for a careless slip to result in a fatal fall. Wyatt had had trouble bringing the boat to the cliff's edge during his surveys. Snaggle-toothed rocks just below the water's surface made navigation treacherous. No one who had an alternative would try to get onto the island from here. Its sole virtue for that purpose lay in the prospect of concealment from any likely observer.

Rocks poked up through the path, forcing Wyatt to slant-step his way along the edge of the line of stunted firs and scrub-oaks to avoid erasing the evidence he was after. There were few spots flat or soft enough for a footprint to register. He found a few partial prints, one of which he could make out as a lady's boot, almost certainly Amy's, the other indecipherable. Frustration rose in him with the day's growing heat. No weapon, no useful prints. If there had been a murder, the killer had left no trail.

CHAPTER 6

D r. Webb returned to the reassembled group, his manner nervous but alert, transformed from gentleman on holiday to brisk man of medicine.

"She'll allow the post-mortem. I took the liberty of asking Germain to write something up for her to sign, just so we're all square on it. And I'll want two witnesses. She wanted to see it again—the body—she said, but of course I forbade that absolutely. It was bad enough her having to look at it at all. She's still on the edge of hysteria. I gave her a little more of the tincture."

"Let's you and I volunteer, if it has to be done," Fisk said to Wyatt.

"Are you sure?" Wyatt had heard the story of Fisk's youthful mishap from Warren Dodge.

"Quite." Fisk's tone was curt. Dodge did not demur. As the owner of the island, with the most to lose from an unhappy outcome—murder meant scandal, and scandal meant the end of his hopes to host the President—he could wish for nothing but a determination of accidental death. Wyatt and Fisk followed Dr. Webb through the kitchen and down the cellar stairs. They crossed the back lawn to the ice house, a small hip-roofed cube of brick which sat near the shore behind the kitchen.

The interior was dark and low-ceilinged, the space windowless, no more than eight feet by eight. Thick pallets of straw, loosely secured by baling wire, surrounded the great ice-blocks, which rose to the roofline opposite the low door but were only waist-high near it. Germain had hung two oil-lamps on hooks from a beam in the ceiling. The aureoles of light barely penetrated the gloom once the door was closed. They had laid Van Dorn's body on a tarpaulin over two of the ice-blocks. Rigor mortis was not yet fully advanced, and the face wore an enigmatic half-smile, like pictures of the Buddha Wyatt had seen. He dragged a loose block of straw beneath him for a seat.

The chiaroscuro of the scene, the intent faces of Webb and Fisk surveying the body, reminded Wyatt of Rembrandt's "Anatomy Lesson." He shivered in his still-damp shirt, wishing for a jacket. Dr. Webb arrayed his instruments and set Wyatt to taking notes in a buckram-bound journal. Fisk helped him remove the dressing-gown and the nightshirt, which he cut away where necessary.

"Before we go too far," Webb nodded towards Wyatt, "tell me what you did when you pulled him out of the water."

Wyatt recounted his efforts to resuscitate Van Dorn, including the attempt at artificial respiration.

"When you summoned me to look at the body," Webb said, "I took a temperature reading, after the others had dispersed, using a, uh, rectal thermometer. That was about eight-thirty. I also took a reading of the lake temperature. Based on the usual rules of thumb—which in my opinion are questionable, but they are all we have—I would say Van Dorn had been dead for no more than a couple of hours. You were right in noting that there was some residual warmth when you found him in the water."

"So, about four-thirty or five, you think?" Wyatt opened his pen and capped it.

"A little earlier, if anything."

"What do you think is the earliest possible time of death?" Fisk's deferential tone suggested a lawyer questioning his expert witness.

"Probably not before four." Webb turned back to Wyatt. "Now, this is a most important point. When you first began to manipulate his limbs, to start his breathing and such, did anything come out of his mouth?"

"Some air. And a little water."

"What did it look like?" Webb's spectacles glinted in the dim light. Over his shoulder, Fisk's white, narrow face loomed ghostly above his dark beard.

"Just—water, I think. Lake water, I suppose, greenish or brownish perhaps. Maybe a little saliva, a couple of bubbles. Not much. A few tablespoonfuls, I'd say."

"Not foam? Not a plume of foam, fine bubbles like shaving-soap lather, when you compressed his chest?" The doctor frowned. His finger traced the jugular notch at the base of Van Dorn's throat.

"No. Should there have been?"

"Do make a note of that. It may be important. If his lungs were saturated, you'd have seen the foam, and that is the one definitive sign of a drowning. Though I'd also expect the body to have sunk in that case. You see," Webb pressed both hands down on Van Dorn's chest with no perceptible result, "no sign of it now either."

"If the lungs were waterlogged, that foam would be there, and there would be little doubt of the diagnosis," Webb went on. "If they are not, it doesn't necessarily mean the victim hasn't drowned. There are cases in which the larynx—the voice-box, that is—closes off in a spasm and prevents the air from getting to the lungs, just as effectively as if the water had got in." His hands mimed a lid slamming shut.

For that matter, Wyatt mused, drowning could occur after a head injury that rendered the victim unconscious. So this dubious effort might not tell them much in the end. Other physical signs might be more important. Where did that trail of blood in the water come from? Dr. Webb's voice reached him. He bent to take notes. *Minimal evidence of alveolar saturation given absence of significant foamy exudate—presence of artifacts indicating a minor degree of freshwater infiltration.* Drowning, perhaps—but not by much.

Wyatt looked up. "Doctor, when I found him, there was blood—a thin trail of blood floating in the water."

"Not uncommon in drowning cases, as I recall. Especially if we're dealing with the type of laryngospasm I mentioned. Haemorrhage in the region of the temporal bone, probably. Pressure on the inner ear."

"How produced?"

"In the struggle to get air, or rather not to breathe in water." Webb had assumed a tone of professional detachment. "The pressures build up in the cranial cavity to such a degree as to rupture the small vessels—"

"Which would suggest he was conscious when he hit the water?" Fisk asked.

Webb hesitated. "Well, yes, it would. Before we go any further, though, let's be sure we've noted what the externals told us. I'm sorry to say, Wyatt, that you may have complicated the picture in pulling him out as you did. There are a number of abrasions on the back and legs I'm pretty certain can be attributed to postmortem trauma—"

"From the body bumping off the lake bottom as I pulled him in."

"Yes. You did the right thing, of course, not knowing for certain that he was dead. I'd have done the same," Webb added. An image floated unbidden before Wyatt's eyes of Dr. Webb, once compared by Amy to a field-mouse with spectacles, struggling with Gerald's inert white bulk. Very like a whale. He suppressed a smile. Shakespeare was good for appropriate quotes at inappropriate moments…

"Nothing significant on the ventral surface," Webb was saying. "A large contusion on the left shin, which could have come from tripping on a sapling-stump while out walking, any number of things."

"Right on the front?" Wyatt's pen hovered above the lined paper.

"Not quite. About six inches up from the tarsus on the lateral surface of the tibialis anterior." He pointed out the spot.

"Got it." Wyatt's pen-nib rasped across the paper. About where you'd hit, he thought, if you pitched—or were pushed—backwards out of a boat.

The front of the body yielded nothing more of note. Fisk and Wyatt helped Dr. Webb turn it face down, the way Wyatt had found him. Some pooling of the blood, postmortem, from the couple of hours the body had lain on its winding-sheet of sailor's canvas in the ice house.

"Otherwise unremarkable," Dr. Webb concluded. He looked up. "It certainly gives all the appearance of a drowning, though there should be—should have been—more froth from the lungs."

"What about the back of the head? Seems to me that's where the stream of blood was coming from." Van Dorn's pale hair, a mix of blond and white, was darker for being wet, but Wyatt was sure the darkness at the nape was more than that. He wanted to lean in and part the fine hair around the occipital crest, but he held back, waiting to see what Dr. Webb would do.

"Well, I didn't see anything of note, but—" Dr. Webb's fingers went to the area as if guided by Wyatt's eyes. They ridged through the hair, stopping as a little puddle of red came up and stained them.

"Dear me, it looks as if he's had a knock on the head at that. There's a haematoma—some swelling here, and the blood, of course, consistent with hitting his head on a rock, perhaps—"

"Or being hit by something?" Fisk's white face swam forward from the gloom.

"Well, my dear fellow, that would put a different color on it altogether."

"Is there any way to tell which it was?" Wyatt half-rose from his bale of straw.

Webb sighed and polished his glasses. "It's a question of probabilities, as I see it. I've always been for Occam's razor—the simplest explanation compatible with the facts. There were the field-glasses, after all, and we know he was a birding man. The likeliest explanation is that he fell off the headland, knocked his head on something in the water, something that rendered him unconscious, with drowning secondary to that. But let's have a look at the internals and see what that tells us."

They turned the body on its back once more. For a long moment Dr. Webb's scalpel paused a foot above Van Dorn's almost hairless torso. Then, in a raptor's swoop, it dropped and carved a great Y along the body. Red lines bloomed along the incision.

"You wouldn't normally see this," Webb said, "but it's typical in a recent death involving water, and it can be another indicator of drowning. Infiltration of the tissues. Keeps the blood more or less liquefied."

"But how did he get five feet out in the lake?" Fisk's tone was almost exasperated. "In his nightclothes, no sign of a boat anywhere, or a struggle, and no place of any height on the island you could fall from where you'd land right into the water. To hit the water from that south headland, you'd have had to take a running jump at it, and even then you might not get more than a couple of feet out."

There was such a spot, Wyatt knew: the narrow trail around the rocky bird sanctuary on the north end. He hadn't found Van Dorn's footprints there, but with the soft slippers he'd worn and the state of the path, that might not mean much. If you were careless or half-asleep or didn't know your way, and the light was poor, it was just possible—

Dr. Webb was laying open the digestive tract. Wyatt gave thanks for the ice-bed, which kept the resulting effluvia barely within tolerable limits.

Webb fingered Van Dorn's entrails like a Roman augur. "When did we finish dinner last night?"

Fisk pondered. "About ten-thirty, I'd say. Is this telling you anything?"

"Van Dorn ate heartily, as I recall. The stomach is empty, and there's very little fluid in the small intestine. But stool formation's well under way, and fortunately for our working conditions here, there wasn't the typical perimortem catharsis—I mean, it's still there. Which suggests he died at a minimum five hours after finishing dinner, though the average for this stage of digestion would be more like eight hours. Particularly since it was a heavy meal, as I recall, with a good deal of fat and a relatively slight amount of vegetable matter. Was he at all dyspeptic, do you know?"

"I didn't know him well enough—" Fisk and Wyatt said simultaneously.

"Nor did I. Assuming he had a pretty average digestive tract, I'd say on that basis it's unlikely he died before, say, four or five a.m. That's a crude estimate, of course."

Webb continued with a dissection of the heart. "No evidence of an infarct, though as I recall you might not see it this early. But I'm not seeing any thrombi—clots, I mean," he added for Wyatt's benefit.

"Apoplexy a possibility?" Fisk put in from his station behind Webb.

"Not out of the question. But I'll be frank with you. I feel I'm at my limit here. A cranial dissection is a matter for an expert— not to mention the degree of mutilation involved." Webb pulled folds of skin back together as if buttoning a coat.

"How extensive is that head injury?" Wyatt asked. "A glancing blow or a heavy one?"

"Not sure. Somewhere in between, I'd say."

The north cliff dropped sheer into five or six feet of water. A heavy man could have lost his balance, fallen, hit his head on one of the submerged rocks, drowned—but could he have floated all the way to the other end of the island in not much over an hour? How did the lake currents run? If it had happened at dawn or just before, surely Wyatt himself would have spotted the body drifting southward, when he made his circuit to avoid confronting Milly Van Dorn in her strange grief. But nothing was adding up quite right. Death by drowning, secondary to a head injury that left the victim unconscious in several feet of water. Occurring no later than an hour or so after daybreak. He waited to see what Dr. Webb would conclude.

Webb scrubbed at his hands with a dishcloth. "Well, I'm damned if I can tell you exactly what happened here. He died by immersion, of course, evidently after a blow to the back of the head. But how he got there I'm not entirely sure. Could certainly have been an accident."

Fisk went over to the door and cracked it open, letting in a welcome burst of fresh air and sunlight. "And what if it wasn't? Damned funny business altogether. A fellow like Van Dorn, who liked a warm bed as much as the next man, far as I could see—traipsing about in his dressing-gown at all hours of the night, ending up in the lake?"

"Never saw him so much as wade any time he was near water," Webb said. An image came to Wyatt of Gerald Van Dorn crossing the causeway in the wake of a young girl in a short white dress. Cormorants' eggs. He was a birding man. *What an exciting find, my dear. I should very much like to see them...do take me in the morning, won't you? Will they hatch soon, do you think?* And they had found binoculars...

"Dr. Webb, you said there was damage in the inner ear?"

"Well, I assumed that was where the blood was coming from. But I couldn't really say without dissecting the head, and—"

"But if he did, it would be from struggling not to inhale water?"

"Well, yes, I—oh, I see what you're saying. That would have meant he was conscious when he entered the water."

Fisk pounced. "But there could still have been a fall, or a blow to the head, just not one that knocked him out?"

"Yes," Webb said. "I was afraid of this. All so vague and complicated. You know, I think I had better take a look after all. I'd hoped to avoid the, er, mutilation, but—I'll check the larynx while I'm at it, though a spasm might pass off post-mortem. We should be able to hide most of it when we, er, when the body is dressed for burial." The scalpel sliced a neat hairline around the back of the ear. Wyatt and Fisk looked away.

"Well," Webb said some time later, "I suppose laryngospasm is a possibility..."

Wyatt looked up from reviewing his notes. "What about the inner-ear damage you'd expect to see with that?"

"Oh—ah, well, I didn't see anything definitive on that. It doesn't always happen, of course." The doctor waved a dismissive arm.

Fisk folded his arms. "So you can't say whether he died naturally or not."

"There's nothing natural about a death by drowning, in my opinion. But, no. And I doubt anybody could. Given which, it seems to me, accidental death is the simplest and most reasonable conclusion to draw. And the likeliest, for that matter."

But was it the likeliest… Milly Van Dorn's tears, Jeremy's disappearance—Wyatt's instincts were leading him elsewhere.

"What about drugs?" he asked suddenly.

Webb looked up, startled. "What do you mean? What sort of drugs?"

"Could he have been taking a sleeping-draught of some sort, or some medicine that would affect his balance, or his alertness?"

Webb let out a breath and frowned. "It's possible, I suppose."

"He didn't look to me like a man who was going to need a sleeping draught," Fisk observed. "Between the wine and brandy and an ample supper—"

"They can test for that sort of thing, can't—"

Webb cut Wyatt off. "It's not specific for opiates. There are alkaloids that develop in the body after death that sometimes mimic the chemistry—you couldn't prove—"

"I wasn't thinking only of opiates, Doctor. Can you rule out poisoning?"

"There's no evidence of gastrointestinal inflammation as you'd see with arsenic. Which is the one other tasteless substance capable of killing a man in relatively small quantities—that's why I went right to opiates. Of course we can have his blood analyzed. If you think it necessary." Webb's tone suggested that a professional would not.

Wyatt gave Fisk a look of inquiry. Fisk nodded and turned again to Webb.

"You can't say for sure this wasn't murder. I think we owe it to the family to leave the possibility open. In fact, to proceed on the assumption that there was foul play."

"I hardly see what service that does to the family," Webb protested. "And as for the Dodges—"

"Forgive me, Seward, but if your wife died in such circumstances, and the post-mortem came out this way, what would you want done?"

Webb flushed and started to say something but thought better of it. He looked at Wyatt's face, closed and neutral. "I suppose you agree with him?"

Wyatt nodded slowly. "The musicians." He stood and snapped the notebook shut. "Are they still here?"

"Far as I know, no one has left," Fisk said, "except Jeremy Dodge."

"Seems to me we should find out if anyone can shed more light on this."

Dr. Webb was blinking rapidly behind his glasses. "Well, my dear fellow, so much for discretion if you do that. If it were just us, I mean, but—the quartet, they'll go back to the mainland—to the City—with who knows what stories, and—"

"Perhaps we should see how Mrs. Van Dorn is doing, and defer this question for a bit," Wyatt said. "I'm sure Mr. Van Dorn's son will be interested in the outcome of your investigations as well."

"Lord, yes, Will—someone's going to have to tell him," Webb said. "We don't even know where he is, do we?"

CHAPTER 7

Leaving Webb to tidy up the results of his work, Fisk and Wyatt emerged from the ice-house, blinking in the strong sunlight. Fisk pointed towards two figures on the dock, tying up a small sailboat.

"What's this?"

Wyatt followed him towards the dock. He recognized Jeremy's red-blond hair, damp at the neck and flopping into his eyes as he bent to secure the boat's line to a cleat. The other young man looked to be around Jeremy's age, his hair a lighter blond and wavy, almost curly, parted in the middle and tamed with brilliantine. He was a half-foot shorter, and broader in the shoulders than his companion, classically handsome, with a long, sculpted nose and full lips. The face evoked something familiar. Michelangelo's David, Wyatt thought.

Jeremy straightened up. "Oh, hullo, Wyatt. Mr. Fisk. This is Will Van Dorn, my roommate—"

"Where's the boat?" Fisk barked.

"What? We came over in this—Will rented it from a fellow in Keeler's Bay. Oh, you mean, how did I get over there?" Jeremy beamed and threw open his arms, an uncharacteristically expansive gesture. "I swam."

"All that way?"

"Yes, I've been working up to it, and last week I decided—I knew Will was coming in on the early train this morning, so—" he looked from Wyatt's set face to Fisk's. "What's the matter?"

"Will, may I speak to you for a moment?" Fisk took the boy's arm and led him up the incline, past the boathouse to the avenue of elms. Will looked back over his shoulder at his friend, puzzled.

"You didn't take the skiff?" Wyatt asked Jeremy.

"What skiff?"

Wyatt looked out across the water and cleared his throat before turning back.

"Gerald Van Dorn is dead."

"He's what? When? What happened? He was fine last night—Will—" he started towards his friend's retreating back, but Wyatt's hand on his arm stopped him.

"We pulled him out of the lake this morning. When did you set out on your swim?"

"Just around first light. What would that have been—about quarter to four? From the west beach. What time did you find him?"

"Did anyone see you? Did you see anyone?"

"Everyone was still asleep, far as I knew. I made the bed so Bridie wouldn't have to—" The news was sinking in and Jeremy's face went white. "What happened to Will's—"

"We don't know. He drowned, apparently, but that's about all we can tell. How or why—?" Wyatt shrugged and shook his head.

"Wyatt," Jeremy's voice was choked, " I can't tell you how awful this is. Will was coming to apologize to his father. He told me when he picked me up. They'd had a fight, he felt terrible, but he was going to make it up to him—make everything all right between them—and now—" He sat down heavily on the dock and rubbed his face with his hands.

"What had they fought about?"

Instead of replying, Jeremy clasped Wyatt's arm. "What about Milly? Is she all right?" His anxious gaze turned towards the Camp. Wyatt's memory flashed to the dock the day before, when Jeremy had betrayed his feelings for the dead man's wife.

"Mrs. Van Dorn is resting, last I knew. Where did you get your clothes?"

"Oh—that. Will and I had planned this. I left a set with the fellow at the rental place in Keeler's last time I was over there. I didn't want to say anything to Ma. She'd have discouraged me. But it was something I wanted to do—to test myself, you know? It's three miles across here to Keeler's Bay. And I could always have pulled out at Kibbie Point if I'd got tired. And after I was in the bay, it was light enough, there were fishing boats around, I could have yelled for help if I was in trouble. In any event, I made it in—oh, about three and a half hours, I think."

"If you're going to pull stunts like that—" Wyatt wondered at his own testiness— "you might at least have thought to have a boat alongside. What if you'd cramped up? The water's not that warm yet. We'd have had two drownings this morning." On another day he would have applauded Jeremy's initiative, a useful outlet for all that adolescent energy. Jeremy stared at him, his face hurt and puzzled.

"I'd better go and see about Will." He rose and started up the elm avenue. Wyatt sat down on the edge of the dock, struggling with a sudden access of guilt. He'd told Milly Van Dorn he'd welcome her friendship. That term covered a lot of ground. Maybe he'd been too quick to dismiss the idea of rivalry with Jeremy for her attention. After a few minutes he followed the elm path to the house.

Dodge came down the verandah steps to meet him, squinting in the sunlight. "One of the musicians is missing."

"Which one?"

"Fellow with the red beard. Violin, wasn't it? He was gone when the others woke up. Which wasn't until after seven, they told Germain."

"The Italian?"

"Is that what he was? Didn't hear him talk." Dodge looked over Wyatt's shoulder towards the ice-house. "You done down there?"

"Jeremy swam to the shore. Says he didn't take the skiff."

"Swam? It's three miles or more—"

"A test he set for himself. He did well."

"You think this fiddler took the boat, then?" Dodge stared westward as if expecting to spot the missing craft.

"Good place to start. Fisk talk to you yet?"

"He and Lizzie took Will to see Mrs. Van Dorn. What'd you find out?"

"Webb was inclined to say drowning subsequent to a fall," Wyatt noted the momentary flash of relief that crossed Dodge's face. "It's the simplest explanation, in the absence of other evidence—"

"It was an accident, then."

"He hit his head somewhere. It's equally possible that someone hit it for him." Wyatt watched Dodge's face cloud over. "I'm sorry. The doctor admits he can't rule out foul play."

Dodge's lips tightened and he glared at him. "You mean you and Fisk got him to admit he can't. You were right. We never should have had this done here. Should have got the body into the hands of professionals—"

"I don't doubt Dr. Webb's professional knowledge, or his powers of observation. Seems to me he's kept up pretty well after all this time. But objectivity is another thing."

"Meaning what?"

"That he was no more anxious than you to conclude that a murder happened on your property."

"You think it did. You and Fisk. Who did it, then?"

"A man turns up dead, another goes missing—seems to me the musician's the one to start with." Wyatt began walking back down towards the dock, Dodge following. "Are the lake currents always northerly?"

"Usually. You get some strange stuff early in the season— sloshes around a lot in the spring and fall, I've noticed. You thinking he drifted from somewhere else?"

"I suppose it's possible," Wyatt knelt on the dock and looked north, letting his hand trail in the water. "How fast are the currents?"

"Fast in the spring," Dodge said. "Slows down from there."

"What do we know about this violinist?"

"Not much. Can't remember what he looks like, tell you the truth."

"Let's talk to the rest of the quartet." Wyatt rose and wiped his hand on his trousers.

Dodge had the three musicians summoned to the west porch, where they perched uneasily on the wicker chairs their audience had occupied the night before. Wyatt sat on the edge of the burlwood table, where he could face all three of them at once. Dodge stood, grasping a chain of the porch swing.

The second violinist had been a new recruit. Their usual man, Czerny, had disappeared early the previous week without an explanation, so they had planned to beg off the engagement at the Webbs'. But this fellow Rossi, "the wop," as the lead violinist called him, had turned up three days later at the gate of Shelburne Farms. He had been sent by the absent Czerny, who had been summoned to the bedside of his mother, taken suddenly ill and feared to be dying.

The new man had brought an apology from Czerny for the abrupt departure and a request that he attend on the Webbs to see if, as they quoted him, "I can-a be of-a help to *la Signora.*" He auditioned with a few short pieces for Mrs. Webb and Perlstein, the first violinist, who pronounced his playing "a bit lacking in expression, but adequate," and was duly engaged. The evening concert on Heron Island was his first with the group.

"Bit of a surprise in a wop." Perlstein eased back in his chair, but shot up straight when the wicker gave a loud creak under him. "More normal for them to get carried away, hair flying, working up a lather and all that."

"Describe him for me, if you would," Wyatt said. "I didn't get much of a look at him when he was here."

"Let's see. About—what, a bit taller than me—five foot ten or eleven, I'd say. Curly hair, carroty red—curlier than mine, even—rather untidy. Doubt he'd ever heard of hair-oil. Heavy beard, longish—average build, I should think?" His companions nodded agreement. "Wore glasses. Couldn't see much of his mouth. Strong nose, wide nostrils—I noticed that. Skin— maybe you'd say reddish complexion, or bronze, cheekbones on the high side."

"Not bad," Wyatt smiled. "Where did he say he was from?"

"Genoa, wasn't it, Zab?"

"Carrara, I am thinking he said. He came on boat from Genoa. He spoke like revolutionary." The heavy Slavic accent of Zabielski, the cellist, required concentration. Dodge was leaning forward from the swing. "Malatesta he mentions. Some other Italian I do not remember. Bakunin, Emma Goldman also. His heroes of revolution. He is talking about friddom stolen from pipple even in great country of America. Government is selling workers out to kepitalists. Some such. It is all nonsense. I do not pay him too much mind." He gave a dismissive shrug.

Czoglosz had been a devotee of Emma Goldman, Wyatt remembered. After the President's death she was blamed by many for inflaming the assassin to his deed.

Perlstein's curls bobbed agreement. "His English was pretty poor. He'd only been in the country a few months. Had a relative in the old Five Points or some place he was bunking with. Grabbed his chance to get out of there—"

"What did he have to say about the guests, here on the island?"

"Hmm. Nothing very specific. Something about it being a playground, um…"

"Go on. What?"

"—uh, for fat old plutocrats and politicians. And, uh, their fancy ladies. Well, that wasn't the word he used, exactly."

Dodge's nostrils flared and Wyatt suppressed a smile. "How did he meet your regular man?"

"Czerny? A while back, when he was playing at—what was it?— some workers' benefit in a union hall somewhere, Czerny came up and talked to him." Perlstein rose and paced around the half-circle of chairs, jiggling the chain on the other side of the porch swing from Dodge. " They kept in touch. Then after Czerny went back to the City, to see about his mother, he ran across Rossi and told him we might be able to use him up here. Well, naturally he jumped at the chance."

They had slept in the guest cottage and hadn't noticed the violinist's departure, were not even awakened by the hubbub attending the discovery of Gerald's body.

"There's four beds in the cottage." Perlstein swept back a handful of black curls with a habitual, elfin gesture. "Zabielski and Mercado shared one room. Soon as we arrived, Rossi—if that was his name—said he slept light and asked me if I snored. I had to admit I do, so he insisted on taking a mattress down to the cellar. There's that bulkhead door on the outside? That's how we got him down for the night after he got so plastered—so you see how he could have come and gone without waking the rest of us."

None of the three, despite nocturnal visits to the lavatory, had looked into the cellar on the way in or out of their rooms.

"Germain made sure we got a decent allotment of wine." Perlstein looked sheepish. "He's a capital fellow, for a colored man, isn't he? So we slept pretty sound."

"Rossi was drinking a lot?"

"He seemed to be putting away his share. That's when he got started on all that talk of imperialism and what have you. We figured it was the drink talking. Zab here—" he waved a hand towards Zabielski—"tried telling him talk like that could get him thrown out of the country—"

"Ah—you mean the Immigration Act," Wyatt said. The new law, a misguided and inadequate response to McKinley's assassination, prohibited avowed anarchists from entering the United States. "Did he have any particular villains in mind?"

"Well, he went on a bit about poor old King Umberto getting what was coming to his class. Didn't think much of America and the Spanish war. Seemed to have it in for McKinley and Roosevelt in particular. Czoglosz was a hero of justice, he said—or something like that, wasn't it, Zab?"

The bassist nodded gravely, blue eyes blazing into Wyatt's face. "But Roosevelt, he said, Roosevelt was brains behind it all."

"I wonder at him being so candid, hardly knowing you."

"I'd told him right off I was a German Jew." Perlstein glanced at Dodge as if expecting signs of disapproval. "Well, I mean, I was born here, but my parents weren't long off the boat, and he probably figured Zab and Mercado here for sympathizers—"

"I am from San Juan," Mercado put in from the wicker ottoman where he was sitting, placing the accent Wyatt had been trying to identify. Many Porto Ricans were unhappy about America's continued occupation of the island after their supposed liberation from the Spaniards. He didn't blame them.

"And you, Mr. Zab—Zabielski?"

"From country, not far from Cracow. My parents were once—what you say—nobles, small aristocrats? But poor now. I ship for America when I am eighteen."

"I got the wind up a bit when he started talking about Roosevelt," Perlstein said.

"Why?" Wyatt leaned forward from the edge of the table.

"Oh, you know—TR was stopping with the Fisks two years ago, when he got the word about Mr. McKinley, and the Fisks are here, and maybe he thought TR would be coming back to see them again, and wanted to get an in—to get at him, maybe—"

"Mmm…but then, why leave so abruptly?"

"He woke up and figured he said too much?" Perlstein raised his eyebrows and shrugged. "I wondered, when they told us about poor Mr. Van Dorn—"

"Whether Rossi had killed him, and taken the boat to get away?" Dodge broke in.

"He's a banker at Morgan's, isn't he?" Perlstein's chair creaked as he shifted. "So maybe a friend of Morgan's, too? That would make him a capitalist oppressor, to this fellow. Maybe he'd figure him for a consolation prize, if he'd blown his cover on getting to the President with his careless talk."

Mercado leaned forward, opening his long-fingered hands for emphasis. "But the anarchists—don't they try to make a—what is it the French call it—a *beau geste*, a grand gesture?" He slapped his hands together. "Something very public, and noisy, you know, a bomb, or a shooting at the Opera—"

Anarchists, in Wyatt's experience, could be pretty clumsy about their *beaux gestes*. "Any idea where the fellow might have gone?"

Perlstein frowned. "Back into some rat-hole on the Lower East Side, I'd guess."

"Shave off beard," added Zabielski, gloomily. "We would never reconn—what is word—recognize him again."

"But what about your usual fellow—Czerny? The one whose mother was sick. He knew him, didn't he?"

"Good place to start," Perlstein said. "Czerny's from Buda-Pest. That lot all bunks in together down there, south of Delancey Street."

"But you have seen no sign of Rossi?" the cellist frowned at Wyatt.

Dodge sat down heavily beside Wyatt on the burlwood table. "There aren't many places to hide on a ten-acre island."

"Well, now what are we going to do?" the first violinist stared west through the porch-screen. "Mrs. Webb's soirée is a week from Thursday—"

"—And he has taken your boat!" Zabielski, the cellist, waxed indignant on Dodge's behalf.

"That's the least of it." Dodge rose and looked at Wyatt, who nodded. "Thanks for your help, gentlemen."

CHAPTER 8

Wyatt followed Dodge up the slope to the flagpole and the spot where he had first seen Van Dorn's body.

"They knew the President was coming. All of them, including this damned anarchist." Dodge's tone was a mixture of surprise and fury.

"How could he have known? Almost two months before he's due to visit? And there's no reason to think this is even connected."

"Someone opened their fat mouth. We'd talked to the Webbs some time ago, about having the quartet here for the visit. I'd asked them not to mention the reason, but who knows? One of the staff overheard, or Lila let something slip, and Czerny mentioned it when he was recruiting the fellow to replace him. So he could have been infiltrating the place. Making an early reconnaissance."

"He didn't do much of a job of it, then. You think he killed Van Dorn?" Wyatt peered over the edge of the headland, trying without success to envision a fall from this spot that would have landed Van Dorn in water deep enough to drown.

Dodge stared down the southern expanse of the lake as if expecting to see the anarchist materialize in the stolen boat. "It's possible. His English was poor—he might have got mixed up and thought Roosevelt was coming here this time. Might even have thought Gerald was the President. He looked a bit like him."

"With his glasses on, I suppose. About the same build, when TR's not watching his weight. But Van Dorn was taller and a lot older. It seems pretty far-fetched."

"Maybe he was just sizing the place up," Dodge conceded.

Wyatt crossed his arms and turned back to face Dodge. "But in that case, why would he have left? Especially by sneaking off in a stolen boat? What good would that have done him?"

"Got the wind up, maybe. Out early, saw us with Van Dorn's body, figured he might be blamed, or didn't want the authorities asking him questions."

Wyatt remembered the sound of a door slamming on the guest cottage. It was just possible...

"Lost his nerve," Dodge went on. "Or maybe he was just a stalking-horse for some group that wants to finish what Czoglosz started. I suppose you don't want to rule out anything at this stage. But if someone's after the President, there are easier places to get at him than here."

"Once he's here, though, it would be harder for him to get out of range. This fellow goes back to his revolutionary cell, or whatever they call themselves, fills them in on the place, where to make a landing, and so forth. Two months from now they sail by, dressed like respectable citizens on a Sunday outing, get close enough to toss a bomb, and—" Wyatt gestured southwards to a sailboat, bobbing against the dark blue of the lake like a starched handkerchief in a suit-pocket.

"Well, if you think that could happen—" Dodge began reluctantly.

"—we need to tell the President's people, and let them—"

Dodge held up a hand and his voice turned metallic. "No. Let's understand one thing. Your job is to clear this up in time to get the President here. As we've planned. I don't want you talking to them now. They'll call it off on general principles. Figure out what happened. Find this fellow. You've got a few weeks. We don't know that he, or anyone, had anything to do with Van Dorn's death. And I'm damned if I'll let this chance go by on some speculation—"

Wyatt's tone hardened in its turn. "Don't forget, we've also got a nest of Italian anarchists not fifty miles from here. That paper I found with the strawberries, remember? Now that we know

Galleani's with them, they may be a serious threat."

"But this Rossi fellow was from New York. That's how he got the lead to the Webbs, running across the other man—Czerny, was it?"

"You're right. We have to track him down." Wyatt started back towards the Camp. "We'll find Czerny and see what he knows about him. And find out what happened to the boat. Meanwhile, we have a corpse in need of disposal, and we still don't know how it got that way, or whether this fellow was in on it."

"I suppose we need to keep going with these—interrogations, then."

"Have you room for young Van Dorn?"

"We can move Milly into Jeremy's room, and put him and Will into theirs—uh, hers," Dodge spotted Germain on the verandah and waved him over. "Come here a moment, will you?"

Milly Van Dorn had borrowed a black dress from Augusta Dodge. It was notably too large for her in the bosom and unsuitable in cut for mourning, but the women had agreed it was important to make an effort. She sat in one of the striped armchairs in the great room, languid and tragic-looking in the lengthening shadows of the afternoon, surrounded by solicitous cups of tea and chicken broth. She was made for merriment, Wyatt thought; her pleasing, open looks required cheeks made rosy by laughter. Now the blue eyes were dulled, the cheeks pale, the life drained out of her. The other ladies had found oddments of black to attach to their clothing.

"Where's Will?" Dodge asked his wife in an undertone. "How did he take it?"

"Jeremy's with him. He's in rather a bad way, I'd say. He'd come to apologize, you see, and—" Augusta turned a palm upward.

"I tried to tell him it was all right." Milly Van Dorn's tears welled up again. "Gerald couldn't hold a grudge if you paid him. He said it was perfectly natural—"

Wyatt perched across from her on the arm of the chesterfield. "What had they quarreled about?" he asked gently.

"We were—I mean, Gerald—was going to sell the Blauwberg estate—the place on the Hudson, you know, and Will said he mustn't, it was his mother's, she'd have wanted him to have it—"

"Who had she left it to?"

"Well, she died suddenly, you see, without a will, so that meant everything went to Gerald. It's a gloomy old pile as far as I'm concerned, dark and damp, but of course Will spent all his summers there, as a little boy—" she was taking ragged, shuddering breaths between phrases, "—it did have nice grounds, and I said to him, 'Gerald, dear, don't you think you should just let Will have it if it means so much to him,' and he said, I remember his exact words, 'Milly, my dear, that's sweet and generous of you, but it's not good for any of us to dwell in the past, he must think about his future—'"

Her tears spilled over and she reached for a wet, balled-up handkerchief. Mrs. Fisk handed her a clean lace-edged triangle, giving Wyatt the kind of look one might visit upon a mongrel who crossed a silk carpet after a roll in the mud. Milly sank back into the chair, her bosom heaving, her face flushed, spent for the moment. Wyatt cast his eyes down, then up at Dodge, who took the cue.

"In the circumstances, we think it best if we all stay here for the next couple of days. Mr. Wyatt has agreed to help us look into the situation and see what light we can shed on Mr. Van Dorn's death."

The group sat in an awkward silence. Mrs. Van Dorn looked up at Wyatt with an expression he could not quite place. Entreaty, perhaps, but what she might wish to entreat from him he could not imagine. The screen door to the porch clattered to, admitting a set-faced, red-eyed Will Van Dorn, back from a sojourn on the western beach with Jeremy.

"What's wrong with having the police look into it? That's their job, isn't it? What does any of us know about murder, anyway—?" Will stopped, registering the shocked looks on the faces ranged around the great fireplace.

Jeremy reddened and dropped his head. "No one's saying it was murder, Will. Not yet, at any rate." Wyatt studied Will Van Dorn's face. He, too, had blushed and looked confused.

"I'm sorry." Will drew a hand over his swollen eyes. "You're right, no one did. Why would anyone want to hurt Father?"

Wyatt wondered if he was the only one who saw the look flicker from Will's face to Jeremy's and back—another look which he could not quite interpret.

Dodge went to Will and put a hand on his shoulder. " Here's the trouble with the police, Will. Around here they don't amount to much. You have a village constable of sorts in South Hero, and a couple of county sheriffs, who don't have experience with much worse than a spot of sheep-stealing. Or at most a husband brained with the wife's frying-pan. I don't doubt they'd jump at the chance to investigate it. But I suspect all that would come out of it would be our ruined reputation. We'll have to report it, of course, eventually. Dr. Webb will be in touch with the county medical examiner, such as he is. But, frankly, I think we're at least as well equipped to investigate this as they are."

"But what if it was murder, and one of you did it?" Will's hand swept the room. "I'm sorry to even—it's just that—you've already ruined it, doing the postmortem—"

The indignation in his face died away and his eyes, an uncommonly beautiful blue like his father's, fixed on Dodge and brimmed over. He pulled a handkerchief from his pocket, turned away from Dodge and blew his nose, muttering "Excuse me."

"We didn't know you were coming, Will. We thought it would be the best thing. Of course we'd have waited and talked to you about it if we'd—"

Fisk walked over and put an arm around Will. "Mr. Wyatt and I were there as witnesses. We've got it all written down. You can look it over, when you're up to it. I admit I had my doubts, but Dr. Webb knew what he was doing, I assure you."

His long arm reached out and pulled over a wooden side chair. "Sit down. Take a breath."

Will slumped in the chair and looked up at the two men on either side of him.

"Of course. You did what you thought was best. I—appreciate it." He took in a deep breath and sat up. "But I hope you'll understand—" he looked over at Milly, who had been still and silent as he spoke, "for our family's sake, I'm going to ask the City police to look over the evidence. Whatever it is. Commissioner Murphy's a friend of Father's—"

From across the room, Augusta gave Dodge a panicked look. Will caught it and held up a hand.

"Please. I understand you don't want a scandal. But they'll be discreet, you know, and anyway, this anarchist fellow, the violinist, Jeremy said—if it was murder, it would have been him, wouldn't it? Won't he have gone back to New York, most likely? They can help find him."

Dubious looks made the rounds of the room. Wyatt broke the awkward silence.

"It makes sense. They won't have the scene to work with, of course, but there's been more than one witness for everything we've done since finding the body. And I know they're capable of discretion. I've done a little work with them."

Will gave him a grateful look. "The awful thing is—well, one more awful thing—Father hated anarchists. He was scared to death of them. I always told him it was ridiculous. He'd never even met one. But—"

Milly Van Dorn broke in. "It's true. Mr. Morgan gets death threats from them all the time. He sleeps on his yacht when he's in New York, they can't get at him there—"

"Did Mr. Van Dorn ever receive such threats?"

"Well, no, not that he ever told me of, but Will's right—he was frightened just the same."

Germain crossed the room to Dodge and whispered something in his ear.

"Mr. Germain reminds me the ladies haven't eaten in some time. He's having the staff prepare something simple and nourishing."

"Germain's a capital head in a crisis." Dr. Webb, on the banquette next to the fireplace, beamed gratitude.

Mrs. Fisk touched Augusta on the shoulder. "I'll go and fetch Amy, shall I?"

Germain's idea of simple and nourishing ran to a beef consommé with vegetable juliennes and chicken breasts in a *velouté* sauce with baby spinach from the garden, accompanied by a venerable Pomerol and followed by a warm fruit compote. Wyatt took him aside in the kitchen after the meal and complimented him on his choices.

Germain shrugged but allowed himself a small smile. "Where I come from, we figure a good meal's gonna to improve any situation."

"Even Mrs. Van Dorn seemed to be digging into it," Wyatt said. "Walk out with me for a few minutes, will you?"

CHAPTER 9

Germain followed Wyatt across the lawn to the west beach. There was a light breeze, the sun sinking through a corona of clouds, turning the lake surface into a mosaic of beaten gold and pale violet.

"Mardi Gras colors." Germain gazed meditatively over the water.

"You have an artist's eye," Wyatt said. "Most people would have said pink and blue. But if you really look…what did you think of those musician fellows?"

"Mrs. Webb has a good ear for talent. They're solid, mostly. I play a little fiddle myself, time to time. Second guy was a bit—what do I want to say, mechanical?"

Wyatt skipped a pebble across the water, watched the colors break up like a kaleidoscope pattern. "You talk to him much?"

"He didn't have much to say. To me, anyway. I've noticed that sometimes these foreign fellows—well, they don't quite know what to say around a colored man."

"Where did he come from? Did he say?"

"North of Italy somewhere. Zab—the cellist—talked to him some. Said he came over eight or nine months ago, steerage on the *Perugia* out of Genoa. Hooked up with some folks on the lower East Side, worked as a day-laborer. Played the violin for the working folks at Cooper Union. I guess that's where this Czerny fellow met him last week—the violinist he replaced in the Webb's quartet."

"Wonder why he'd come all the way up here on the off chance of an engagement with the Webbs." Wyatt watched a fishing boat shoot through the dying light towards Keeler's Bay.

"*Sais pas,*" Germain shrugged. "I suppose this other fiddler must have told him the Webbs were pretty well off—and minus one violinist, stands to reason they'd want a replacement. Maybe he figured it was worth the chance, 'specially if this Czerny was suggesting it."

"We need to get hold of Czerny."

"Should be able to find out where he is from the others, I'd guess. Want me to ask?"

Wyatt paused. A blue heron—was it the same one he'd seen days before?—swooped from the sky to land under the south headland. It stood in the shallows, needle-thin, one leg upraised. He touched Germain on the arm and pointed to the bird. They stared at it in silence for a few moments while the sun sizzled out in the lake. A few last, plaintive bird calls echoed in the cooling air.

"Did you hear anything this morning? When you got up?"

"Seems like I heard somebody get up in the middle of the night," Germain frowned, remembering. "Could have been close to dawn, though, I don't know. I sleep pretty sound as a rule, but I thought I heard a door open and close, and feet in the hallway, bare or slippers maybe. Then I went back to sleep."

"What time did you get up?"

"Oh, a little before six, I guess. I went out for a while. Thought I heard a door slam on the guest cottage. So I went over there looking for the new guy. I got thinking I'd passed out too much wine to those fellows. They were out on the beach around midnight and the fellow was holding forth, you know, ranting on about something. Then he passed out, more or less, and I guess they got him on his feet and helped him down to the cellar. Probably never took off his clothes. So I went over in the morning. I thought I should see if he was all right."

"And was he?"

"He wasn't there. His good clothes were there, on the bed—the monkey suit, you know? Except for the shoes. I went looking for him then, on the island, but no sign of him. Saw you walking around. You didn't look like you were in the mood for company. Haven't had too many early risers here, so far."

"There were three of us out that morning, at least."

Germain ticked names off on his fingers. "You, and Mr.

Dodge, and somebody from the cottage. And then me, and Mr. Van Dorn, whenever he got there. Assuming he hadn't been there from sometime during the night. That's five."

Wyatt wondered whether Germain might have seen Milly Van Dorn returning from her solitary grieving on the headland.

"Any sign of anyone else?"

"Not that I saw. Doesn't mean there wasn't. What do you think happened?"

"I wish I knew." Wyatt wasn't ready to speculate with anyone he hadn't ruled out as a suspect. Without speaking, they started slowly back towards the Camp. When they were halfway up the elm avenue, Dodge opened the door of the north porch and came down the steps to hand Wyatt a demitasse of coffee. Germain discreetly withdrew down the east lawn towards the kitchen.

"Pumping my staff for clues?"

"I'll want to talk to everybody. You never know who saw or heard something. Did you find Amy? How is she taking all this?"

"She liked Van Dorn." Dodge watched the last light sink into the lake. "They were going to go and look for eggs across the causeway. After breakfast."

"Mind if I talk to her?"

"Talk to anybody you need to. Just clear the thing up soon."

"Do you want her mother there?"

"Not if you want Amy to tell you anything useful. She's taken to clamming up when Augusta comes near. Must be the age." Dodge sat down on the porch step and gestured for Wyatt to join him.

"I need to head for New York," Wyatt stretched his legs out in front of him, "and see if I can track down your violinists."

"See what Webb knows first. Or Lila. She's the one who got the group together to start with."

"How well did the Webbs know the Van Dorns?"

"Whatever Milly may have told you, they weren't all that close. Webb and Van Dorn doing business together over the last few years, mostly. A few dinner invitations back and forth, Mrs. V. calling on Mrs. Webb, that sort of thing. In the same circle, more or less, but not what Gussie would call intimate."

Wyatt sipped his coffee, which had gone lukewarm. "You said Van Dorn was in your club?"

"That's right. He was a Union man. I also belong to the Met, same as Webb. Gerald and I knew each other from the club. He introduced Milly to Augusta at the opera, and Gussie invited them up last summer, shortly after the Camp was finished. Surprised me a little. Milly's never seemed like Augusta's type."

"How so?"

"Oh, you know, that girlish and flighty thing. And she suspected her of fortune-hunting."

Perhaps also a little too young and pretty for prolonged association, Wyatt considered, aware as he was of Dodge's eye for a good-looking woman.

"Seemed fond enough of the old man, I must say. Decent fellow, Van Dorn. I'm sorry he's dead. However it came about." Dodge stared gloomily at his feet.

Wyatt had a fleeting moment of wonder about the nature of Dodge's regret.

Dodge started from his reverie. "Think this paper you found in the strawberries has something to do with it?"

Wyatt bent and pulled a handful of chickweed from the perennial border. "That paper came from Barre. Our violinist met Czerny in New York. So, my guess would be a different crew altogether. No doubt the paper's circulating that far south already. Naturally they'd read it."

"So that's the place to start looking for him."

"New York's a big place to hide. I'd best talk with everybody here first and see if anything comes out."

Dodge shot his index finger at him. "Don't forget you're on a deadline."

"So much for pretending I'm a guest," Wyatt shot back.

CHAPTER 10

Nelson Fisk seemed to feel Van Dorn's death more keenly than anyone, almost re-living his own near-drowning on Lake Champlain as Wyatt questioned him.

"There's no reason to think he suffered," Wyatt spoke quickly, anxious to relieve the man's distress. "You heard Dr. Webb—he seems to have been unconscious by the time he hit the water."

"Dear God, I hope so." Fisk searched Wyatt's face for reassurance. "I wouldn't wish that feeling on my worst enemy."

The Fisks had met the Van Dorns only once before, at a house-warming gathering for the Dodges' new camp. He was grateful to Gerald Van Dorn, who had been instrumental in financing Webb's new Grand Isle railroad, which made it easier and more profitable for him to ship marble from the Fisk Quarry. Though he had friends among New York's wealthy and powerful, he and Elizabeth stuck to a quiet life in Vermont.

"Governor," Wyatt used the title conferred in Vermont by courtesy on those who had held the office of Lieutenant Governor, "you know why I was here."

"Yes, of course."

"Your association with the President goes back farther than anyone else's here. What do you think of his coming to visit, in light of what's happened?"

"As to that," Fisk smiled, "I'd say charging up San Juan Hill with the fellow counts as much as any length of acquaintance—"

Wyatt ignored the compliment. "What if this had happened at your home?"

"Well—as you can imagine, I'd have been as devastated as Dodge is." Fisk spoke with no trace of irony. "And naturally that dreadful afternoon two years ago is etched in my brain—"

he paused for an awkward moment, "Just as it is in yours. Mr. McKinley was my friend, and poor Ida—such a lovely woman. So frail. And they adored each other. He'd been at my home four years before, for the Fish and Game banquet, just like—" Fisk looked away in his turn and swallowed before turning back.

"But, see here, Wyatt, the only question that matters now is whether this puts the President at risk. If Van Dorn died accidentally, it doesn't. If he was killed, and the killer's motives were personal, it still doesn't. If he was killed by someone with political—or ideological—allegiances, then that person blundered terribly. Meaning one of two things: the crew that's behind him will try getting to the President elsewhere, or if their judgment is sufficiently poor, they'll try something when he's here, assuming they can find out when he's to be here. But forewarned is forearmed, as they say, and I've no doubt that you and his people can devise appropriate precautions."

"You put things very clearly, sir. I'm obliged to you."

"I've put them a little coldly, too, I'm afraid. When I think of him, going that way, and that poor girl—" Fisk shook his head. "Elizabeth and I were commenting, just the other night, on how devoted he was to her. What a dreadful business for her."

Seward and Lila Webb sat opposite Wyatt on white wicker chairs that glimmered in the evening half-dark of the southern verandah. Kindly Mrs. Webb had encouraged the men to violate protocol and smoke after-dinner cigars in her presence.

"It's all been so very upsetting, hasn't it? And I'm sure you gentlemen can use something to calm your nerves," she said with an anxious glance at her husband. The ivory bodice of her gown glimmered like a dove's breast in the twilight.

"I didn't know Van Dorn all that well, until a few years ago—the railroad business." Webb waved a hand westward from his rocking-chair. "After that, our wives called on each other, of course—" he looked towards Lila, who nodded. "And then Watson, my oldest boy, got to be friends with Will. I'd known of

Van Dorn through Morgan, naturally. We're rather an insular little tribe, and I believe he and I were at college around the same time—"

Wyatt rocked gently in his chair, blowing smoke windward.

"Columbia, wasn't it?" In the west, a last faint tinge of red was fading from the sky. "I live near the new campus, up at Morningside Heights. Nice buildings. Same firm that did the Union Club?—"

"The Metropolitan, you mean," Webb snapped, a flicker of something—pain, anger?—crossing his face at the mention of the Union.

"Of course. The Metropolitan. But the campus would have been farther downtown, when you were there."

Webb nodded.

"You did practice for a while, after medical school? Ever miss it?" Wyatt had been wondering about the medical bag, never far from Webb's side. He wondered about the doctor's absence from dinner the night before Van Dorn's death, his moods which seemed to alternate between anxiety and dreamlike insouciance, the faint but noticeable tremor in the man's hands, Lila's protective, hovering air. And something in the eyes, even now in the dim light, something he couldn't put his finger on.

"Well, now and then," the doctor's voice pulled him back. "I liked the idea I was doing something helpful. I was thinking, when I was doing the, uh, you know, on Van Dorn—I might have gone on and qualified as a surgeon. I help out the vets when the mares are foaling, even do a little sewing-up when needed. Surprising how it all comes back to me. As if memory lived in the hands. But, to be honest, it was the puzzle of medicine that intrigued me," Webb said. "Like detective work in some ways, I suppose."

"Fortunate for Mrs. Van Dorn you had the morphia with you." Wyatt's tone was casual. The Webbs looked at each other, startled. Perhaps even a flash of alarm, quickly suppressed.

"What? Uh—oh, yes. It was, wasn't it. I think it helped her over, uh, the initial shock."

Wyatt let the silence hang between them. Inwardly he did a slow count to ten.

"Standard element in a medical bag these days," Webb said at last, blinking rapidly. "Very helpful in emergencies. You find someone injured, that sort of thing."

"How long's it last?"

"What d'you mean?"

"Does it go bad in there after a while? Have to be replaced?"

"Well—eventually, I suppose. Most medicines do. Why do you ask?"

Wyatt smiled. "Just curious. Did you know Van Dorn at Columbia?"

"Oh, I might've crossed his path there once or twice, but we were a couple of years apart. Can't say I really knew him there at all." Webb shrugged dismissively. Again, there was a flicker of something Wyatt couldn't identify.

"Do you know of any enemies he had? Anyone with a grudge against him, or something to gain from his death?"

The Webbs looked dubiously at each other. The doctor gave a one-shouldered shrug and Lila slowly shook her head. "Hard to imagine," Webb said after a silence. "He always seemed such an amiable fellow."

"When did you meet the new violinist?"

Dr. Webb started at the abrupt change of gears. "The—uh—who? Oh, the replacement for Czerny, you mean. I didn't take much notice, really."

Lila leaned forward. "We hosted a musicale at the Shelburne house last week, a larger group than our little quartet that time. More like a chamber orchestra, flutes and harps and a pianist. Mr. Czerny had gone missing a day or two before. Very surprising! He seemed such a sober and reliable young man. I told the concertmaster to find somebody to fill out the quartet for our visit here. And then this Rossi, or whatever his name is, had evidently made his way to Vermont—"

"—and turned up on cue, so to speak," Webb added.

"The concertmaster gave him a quick audition, and told me he was all right. I confess I wasn't impressed by his playing, but there was hardly time to quibble since we'd promised to bring them here in a few days. I must say it did seem providential," Lila added, "his appearing like that."

"Did you make inquiries? About his background?"

Lila shook her head ruefully. "Vermont's too small a place for dishonest doings—or so we've always thought. And then we heard about poor Mr. Czerny's mother, and how he had sent him, and seemed to know him quite well—and there were the other three to keep an eye on him."

"But look here, Wyatt," Dr. Webb interposed, "we don't have firm evidence that poor old Van Dorn's death was anything but an accident. And for the Dodges' sake that's how I'll report it to the Town, to get the certificate allowing us to move the body. I don't think it right to subject our hosts to scandal and gossip on such limited evidence."

Wyatt traced a path of red light with a shrug of the arm that held the cigar. "But Van Dorn didn't strike me as the sort of fellow given to early-morning wanderings in his dressing-gown. Much less ending up in the lake." He rose and paced a few steps to the corner of the verandah, his white shirt gleaming in the twilight.

"What about the birding business?" Webb looked up, his expression hopeful.

"Seems to me he'd have dressed first," Wyatt turned back to face him. "And why didn't anyone hear him getting up and going out?"

Webb shook his head. "All the cases I remember from medical school were so cut-and-dried. But I practiced long enough to know real life isn't like that."

"I'm afraid it isn't," Wyatt threw his cigar towards the vegetable garden, watching it arc a shower of red sparks.

"The Van Dorns have stayed with us on a number of

occasions," Lila remarked. "As I recall, Milly was neither a light sleeper nor an early riser."

Wyatt took that in but did not contradict her. "Thank you for your help." He nodded to Webb and made a slight bow in Lila's direction. "If you will excuse me, Mrs. Webb? I should chat with Miss Dodge before it grows too late." He made a mental note to check the toxicology tests on Van Dorn's tissues as soon as they were done.

Amy was sitting in a Morris chair on the balcony with a large book in her lap, her sharp features almost angelic, to Wyatt's eye, in the soft light of an oil lamp. She was in long-sleeved white muslin, to which she had added a dark blue sash in an attempt at sympathy with the mourning Van Dorns. Absorbed in the book, she didn't hear him coming up the stairs until he almost stood over her. She started and blushed, snapping the book shut.

"You scared me. I didn't hear you come up."

"I'm sorry," Wyatt perched on the balcony rail. "May I ask what you were reading? It must have been something quite fascinating."

"It's *Hamlet*. Mother thinks I'm too young, but—"

"I won't tell," Wyatt smiled. "Do you know, I once played Laertes in Washington?"

"Did you really? He seems a bit—well, stuck-up, you know, and you don't—I'm just at the part where he's giving Ophelia a lecture about how she shouldn't let Hamlet—you know, and she gives it right back to him."

"*...do not, as some ungracious pastors do, show me the steep and thorny way to heaven; Whiles, like a puff'd and reckless libertine, himself the primrose path of dalliance treads,*" Wyatt smiled at her, reminiscent.

"You know her part too!" Amy's eyes widened.

"Sometimes you learn other people's parts as well or better than your own, just from hearing them often enough."

"Oh, dear, I wouldn't! I don't know how people can learn all those lines. I'd be terrified of getting it wrong."

"It's not as hard as you'd think. If you do it often enough, it's like riding a bicycle."

"Ah! I can do that. But I don't think I should like to be Ophelia. She goes crazy and dies, doesn't she?"

Wyatt looked away for a moment. "Yes," he bit his lip and sat down on the ottoman beside her. "Yes, she does. That's a beautiful book. May I look at it?"

She handed over the book gingerly. The binding was gold-stamped olive green leather, faced with marbled paper in pale blues and blood-reds.

"It's really Jeremy's," Amy leaned over him and turned the pages to the front flyleaf. "Mother gave it to him for his birthday. She teases him sometimes. Says he's a Melancholy Dane."

"He's a pretty good tennis player for a Melancholy Dane," Wyatt said lightly. "And a good swimmer too, apparently."

"Oh, I don't think he really did that," Amy tossed her head. "It's much too far. I think he took the skiff and met Will that way."

"Why would he lie about a thing like that?"

She looked at Wyatt as if he were a cretin. "Boys lie all the time. Isn't that what Laertes says? 'You can't trust any of us'?"

"My goodness. Such a cynic, at so early an age."

"Well, it's true. Father tells Mother he's going out to his club, but I think he's going off on rondy-vooz with younger women," she nodded with finality.

It was Wyatt's turn to flush, having accompanied Dodge on one or two such excursions. "What monsters you think us males to be."

"Oh, it's perfectly natural. What men and women do together. The only odd part is if you don't want to—except to avoid more children, of course."

"You astonish me."

"Well, I wouldn't want to, if he was ugly, or old, or mean, I guess—well, even old would be all right, as long as he was handsome. You can be old and still be handsome—" she glanced quickly up at him, then lowered her eyes again, reddening.

"Did you think Mr. Van Dorn handsome?"

She looked full at him, startled. "Oh, no. I mean, he wasn't ugly, he had a nice friendly face, like a walrus, but—"

"Well, Mrs. Van Dorn must have thought he was handsome."

"Oh, really," Amy snapped the book shut with asperity. "She married him for his money. Everybody knows that. That's what you do, then you take a young lover. It's in all the books, the ones my mother reads. She and Mrs. Van Dorn trade them back and forth—"

"The young lovers?" Wyatt's eyebrow shot up.

Amy broke into a giggle. "No, silly, the books. I've been reading them. Mrs. Van Dorn has been leaving them out on the porch. Mother hides hers in the drawer of her nightstand."

Wyatt cleared his throat and composed his features. "So, you and Mr. Van Dorn were going birding yesterday morning?"

"He said he'd come and look at the cormorants' nest, the one I was talking to Mrs. Fisk about—she said she might come too, if it wasn't too early. But when I got up, no one was up, and if I tried to wake up those two, I'd have wakened Mrs. Van Dorn and Mr. Fisk too, and that would have been rude, so I just went out by myself."

"What time was that, about?"

"Let's see—the clock was striking the half-hour when I went out. So that would have been five-thirty."

"And you went right over to the causeway?"

Amy nodded.

"Did you see anyone?"

Amy rose and stared at her reflection in the dark window. "I saw you, going past the tennis courts. And Germain coming out of the guest cottage."

"Germain? Are you sure? Where was he going?"

Amy pointed above the bookcase to a map of the island, engraved with old-fashioned lettering. "Towards the beach, past the tennis courts, just like you." Her finger traced the route. "He looked as if he was following you."

"And this was five-thirty, you think?"

"I know. Just after."

"Mr. Germain must be devoted to his job, to be up and doing so early."

"Germain would do anything for Papa."

"And what about you? Where did you go after that?"

"I went to look for the cormorant's nest. I didn't get too close, though—the mother bird was in it. So I went out to the edge of the cliff with my field glasses and tried to see if there was anything to look at on Abenaki Island. But the birds were just dots."

"That cliff's pretty steep." Wyatt traced it on the map.

"Yes, it drops right off. It's higher and steeper than the south headland. And there's not much of a path—it goes right along the edge. I went there once after it rained and I nearly fell off. Please don't tell Mamma."

"Did Mr. Van Dorn know where the nest was?"

"I told him. But I'm not sure he'd have found it without my help."

"Do you think he might have got up early to look?"

Amy frowned. "I suppose he might have. But, then, he'd had such a lot to eat and drink, I can't imagine him getting up by himself at that hour. That's why I decided to go without him. Oh, I don't mean he was drunk," she answered Wyatt's look, "but he was so sleepy by the time he went to bed—"

"I thought you were in bed by then."

"I was up here in the loft, with Cook and the girls. We were playing rum poker and watching everybody down below. See, if you're here," she sat at a small table in the corner to illustrate, "you can see down there but they can't see up. Don't tell Mamma that either, or we'll all get in trouble. I was watching Mr. Van Dorn and he could hardly keep his eyes open."

"Then whatever would possess him to be out at the crack of

dawn in his dressing-gown?" Wyatt folded his arms and leaned back on the balcony rail.

"What do you think? He had to go to the lavatory, of course, and he heard a noise outside, and went to see what it was."

"Sounds reasonable."

"Maybe he thought it was me, up early to find the eggs. But it wasn't, of course. It was the killer!"

"The killer! You think somebody killed him?"

"Don't you?"

"I've no idea." Wyatt's tone was as casual as he could make it. "Who do you think could have wanted to kill him?"

"Mrs. Van Dorn's young lover," Amy said. "Or maybe Mrs. Van Dorn herself. So they could get his money and run away together."

"Does she have a lover?"

"She must have, don't you think?"

"Well, who could it be?"

"Jeremy." Amy folded her arms. "He's been mooning about after her ever since she got here. And he went to visit them a lot when he was at college."

"He's Will's roommate. Wouldn't that be natural enough?"

"He was *painting* her," Amy nodded as if this settled the matter.

"Artists aren't in love with every woman they paint, surely."

"Jeremy is. Three years ago, there was this girl in Newport, he was smitten with her, absolutely smitten. And he got her to sit for him. But she was nineteen, and engaged, and she broke his heart. Jeremy likes older women."

"But when we couldn't find Jeremy this morning, you thought he'd gone off to meet a girl."

"Well, he might have. To try and make Mrs. Van Dorn jealous."

"You don't like your brother very much, do you, Amy?"

"He's certainly never paid much attention to me. And he's so moody—look at him sideways and he sinks into gloom for days. Unstable, I call it."

"Are he and Will much alike?"

Amy's eyes darted briefly away and she turned pink again. She went to the balcony and leaned over the rail, keeping her face out of Wyatt's line of sight.

"Not a bit. Will's all right. He's a man of action. Did you know he's on the varsity eights at Yale? And he did Algernon with the Dramat, you know, in *Earnest*. The play, I mean. He told me once he wanted to climb the Himalayas. He asked me if I wanted to come with him, but I said it would be too cold. Why couldn't I have had him for a brother, instead of Jeremy?"

"Did he like Mrs. Van Dorn?"

"He thought she was a fortune-hunter at first. But they get along all right now."

"Mrs. Van Dorn says Will never liked her."

"Oh, that's nonsense. She just said that to get more sympathy."

"What about Jeremy?"

"Well, I think he's her young lover, but of course a woman like her would have more than one string to her bow. She flirts with anything in trousers. And the thing is, men love it. You've no idea how ridiculous it looks."

"You're not crazy about Mrs. Van Dorn either, are you?"

"I don't dislike her. She's pleasant enough. I just think she's vapid and shallow. Mother does too, only don't tell her I said so."

"Heaven forbid," Wyatt held up his hand. "So why are they friends, then?"

"I haven't any idea, except—well, you know how men's wives are supposed to be friends with one another. I think it's stupid. If I didn't feel a sympathy with someone, you wouldn't catch me pretending to be friends with her. It's hypocritical."

"So, how did the killer get Mr. Van Dorn into the water, in his dressing gown?"

"You used to be a Pinkerton man," Amy plopped herself back down and opened the book to a picture of the Prince confronting his mother in her chamber. "It's your job to figure that out."

CHAPTER 11

Germain was in the cellar after Tuesday's breakfast, packing wine bottles into a straw-lined crate. Wyatt watched the quick, efficient movements for a moment before announcing his presence. Germain straightened quickly and turned to him.

"I talked to Amy last night, about what she saw when she went out that morning. She saw you and thought you were following me."

"Well, I wondered what you were up to, being out that early."

"What else haven't you told me?"

Germain's eyes flicked away, and he seemed to shrink under Wyatt's stare.

"Care to revise your answer to that question about whether you saw anyone else?"

The dark eyes flashed anger for a moment, then he took in a deep breath and let it out. "You mean Mrs. Van Dorn. But you must have seen her too."

"When did you see her?" Wyatt's tone was sharper than he had intended.

"When I first went out. All right, it was a little before five. She was running up the slope to the cliff on the south side, up by the flagpole there—" Germain stopped and ran his fingers through his short, nappy hair.

"Go on." Wyatt sat on the edge of the crate. "What then?"

"*Alors*, she drops to her knees, almost at the edge, and she—she bends over, you know, and her sides start heaving, and she's vomiting, from the looks of it."

"Are you sure?"

"I didn't get close enough to see, but you know, I can't think what else it would have been. Nothing else looks like that."

"So you didn't see her look out to the water before she started—"

"Throwing up? *Non.* She kinda came scurrying off the verandah and went straight for the headland."

"Why did you decide to keep that from me?"

Germain put down the bottle he was holding and stared at Wyatt. "You know what happens where I come from, they catch a Negro spyin' on a white woman?"

"You weren't spying. You just happened to see her when she came out. And besides, what harm could come to you? There's no one here who would have—"

A bronze flush spread over Germain's finely molded features and he spoke through clenched teeth. "God's sake, man, they're killin' us and no one raises a hand to stop 'em." He reached into a back pocket and pulled out a newspaper. "Not just in the South either. All it takes is one white gal's say-so, and—"

He handed the paper to Wyatt, the *Burlington Daily Free Press* from the day before the grocery delivery, folded around a headline: 'Negro Brute Lynched in Delaware.' A man named George White, burned at the stake by a mob that claimed he had confessed to the rape of a minister's daughter. The death was described in voluptuous detail.

Wyatt's gorge rose. "It sounds like the *Free Press* approves."

"How north is far enough north?" Germain's lips twisted bitterly.

"I'm sorry." Wyatt realized that he didn't know Milly Van Dorn well enough to dismiss Germain's anxiety out of hand. The thought was like a punch in the stomach.

"Dodge was the first white man I ever met that color didn't matter to."

Wyatt swallowed. "About this—throwing up you saw. I take your point, and this goes no further for now. But I need to know what she was doing out there. Wouldn't a lady be more likely to, uh, deal with something like that in the lavatory?"

"Not if she didn't want to wake anybody," Germain resumed

pulling bottles off shelves and placing them in the straw with uncharacteristically nervous movements. "Hard not to make noise."

"But, still, running away from the house like that—"

"*Oui*, as if she was trying to hide it."

"Why would she want to—oh!" Wyatt saw the light at last.

Germain laughed. "I'm trying to be a gentleman here. But if you ask me, I'd say the lady's found herself in an interesting condition."

"Wouldn't she be happy about that? Producing an heir to the Van Dorn fortune?"

"Don't know that she wasn't. Hard to feel happy when you're throwing up, I guess. Anyways, I thought I'd best go off and check the boat-lines for a spell."

"I saw her a little while after you did, not far from there. And if your theory is right, I wouldn't say she's any too happy at the prospect."

Germain paused with a bottle in his hand. "Ruin her figure for the Season, for one thing."

"Maybe that's all there was to it," Wyatt shrugged. "Will she see the Dodges when they're back in New York?"

"I'd guess so. Miz Dodge anyway. Her house is only a couple of blocks away. Want me to keep an eye on things?"

Wyatt hesitated, unsure how much trust he was ready to place in the man. *Germain would do anything for Papa...*but this could only help. "People talk in front of you as if you weren't there. Seems to me that might be handy in a situation like this."

Germain nodded, acknowledged the frankness. "It's made for some interesting discoveries over the years."

"Discoveries you've kept to yourself?"

"Mostly. Helps me keep my job. There's got to be somebody knows something about what that man was doing out there in his dressing-gown before the crack of dawn."

"You might get farther than me in some cases," Wyatt said, "if only by listening carefully."

Germain stopped and looked hard at Wyatt. "Boss off the hook here?"

"No one's off the hook yet. Not even you and me. But you have to play the probabilities. I'll talk to him if you like."

"I'll let you know if I need that. Don't bother yet."

"Thanks." Wyatt extended his hand and Germain took it. Wyatt started back up the cellar stairs, stopped and turned back. "Something else I've wanted to ask you for a while. Not that it's any of my business. What made you decide to leave New Orleans?"

"You mean, besides Dodge?"

"People don't often just pick up and leave a place they've lived all their lives."

"Colored people do it all the time nowadays. 'Specially when your native state would just as soon see you dead, and if they can't find an excuse to do that, they strip you of your citizenship. Most of the Southern states have, now," Germain went on, answering Wyatt's puzzled look. "Louisiana did it in '98. Disfranchisement's the fancy name for it."

"Can they do that? What about the federal government?"

"Raised no objections that I know of. Maybe I should button-hole the President about it if he gets here. Seein' he's gone so far as to have Mr. Booker T. to the house for dinner. And him a *Negro*." Germain smiled sardonically and returned to his bottles.

No one else had been awake or seen anything unusual on the morning of Van Dorn's death. Bridie was obliged to report, with stammers and blushes, that she had found the Fisks dead asleep in each other's arms when she went in to see if they wanted tea. Cook vouched for her and Bernadette, as they did for her.

He released the party the next evening as promised. They would all head to New York for Van Dorn's funeral and interment. Afterwards, Wyatt would begin the hunt for the fugitive violinist with a visit to Czerny, the man he'd replaced. The musicians had directed him to Orchard Street, in the Lower East Side.

Elfreida conveyed Gerald Van Dorn's body on its catafalque of ice to Burlington. Fisk engaged a local undertaker to embalm the remains and coffin them in appropriate splendor for their train journey to New York and the funeral, which was to be at the Episcopal Church of St. Thomas on Fifth Avenue, next door to the Webb mansion and two blocks north of the Union Club where Gerald had been a fixture.

The loss of Gerald seemed to have muted any disharmony between Mrs. Van Dorn and her stepson. Will fetched wraps and brought cups of tea with the care of one handling a delicate invalid. Presumably, neither would ever want for money. Milly was wealthy, attractive, and still young. Wyatt guessed she wouldn't remain a widow much beyond the minimum term dictated by propriety. Her frame of mind had improved considerably in the days since the discovery of Gerald's death, and she seemed to recover a degree of her former glow in the penitent solicitude of Will and the island's other guests. Germain reported a lively conversation between her and Mrs. Dodge on the merits of henrietta silk for summer over conventional crape, permissible trimmings and jewelry, and whether six months was too early, "since we are, after all, in the twentieth century now," to make the change to the dove-grays and mauves of second mourning.

Wyatt examined the cellar of the cottage, where the violinist had slept. To the right at the foot of the inside stairs was Amy's tiny laboratory, a jumble of leaves, eggs, old nests, and rock samples spread out on boards. The larger room, to the left, was an auxiliary pantry for jars of preserves and vegetables. Here the musician had set up his mattress on a pair of wooden pallets. All that was left of the man's stay were the tail-suit he had worn for the evening's entertainment, and the starched collar detached from the shirt. It was still crisp but there were brownish stains around the inside surface, as if it had been worn frequently and never quite come clean. A rumpled white bow-tie and embroidered waistcoat, carelessly flung on the floor, as if he had undressed—and re-dressed—in haste. The violin was gone along with whatever other possessions he had brought.

The outfit was borrowed, no doubt. The man could have sold it, but it wouldn't have been worth the encumbrance on his way. A pair of good black shoes, on the other hand, would have been worth taking. Wyatt pulled up the mattress and saw something white that had been wedged under it: a folded newspaper. The second issue of *Cronaca Sovversiva*, dating from two weeks earlier.

CHAPTER 12

Wyatt leaned back in a red brocade chair, contemplating the marble splendor of the new Union Club dining room. The look was Georgian neoclassical, with triangular pediments above the doors and Ionic capitals on fluted columns. Blood-red velvet drapes and the exquisite marquetry of the floor, in walnut, maple and cherry, barely warmed the marmoreal chill.

"What do you think of the new place?" Dodge sat at ease in a silk suit across an expanse of snowy linen and winking crystal.

"You'd have to say impressive." Wyatt reached for his water glass.

"It's all right, I suppose. Hidebound a crew as we are, we're all having trouble adjusting to the new digs. You're thirty blocks farther from the Street, and the mid-day traffic is a nightmare. Granted, the old place was poky by today's standards. But still—oh, there's Fairbanks." Dodge swallowed the last of a Macon that had paired well with the creamy coquilles St.-Jacques of the first course. "And Potter. They were at school with Van Dorn." He waved them over and made introductions, signaling the under-steward for another bottle of wine.

"Join us, won't you, fellows? They just got this in. Good summer wine."

Fairbanks pulled up a chair next to Wyatt. A cadaverous sort in a morning-suit with a cold gray-blue eye, he had made his fortune in industrial scales and, like Dodge, summered in Vermont.

"Damn shame about poor old Van Dorn." Fairbanks adopted a funereal tone, sipped the wine with a practiced air. "They did an impressive job with the reception, I must say."

"Delmonico's," said Potter dreamily. Even draped in the sable dignity of his Appellate Court robes, he resembled the popular conception of St. Nicholas. "Too bad Van Dorn wasn't there to enjoy it. Did you try that turbot?"

"Mr. Dodge says you gentlemen had known Mr. Van Dorn for a long time."

Potter cracked open a crusty roll and slathered it with butter. He swirled the wine in his glass and took a deep sniff. "Lord, yes. A *bon vivant* even in his youth. Capital good fun. Not a bad wine, this. Have you tried it with oysters?"

"College days!" Fairbanks allowed Dodge to refill his glass. "Gerald was on the football team, you know. Did rather well as a defender for a couple of years."

Dodge and Wyatt looked at each other in surprise.

"You wouldn't know it to look at him now, of course," Potter said, "I mean—recently, that is. He was out of it after the tendon problem, wasn't that it, Henry? Quite the Sigma Chi man after that. Not the same as being on the team, of course."

"Funny you should mention that," Wyatt said offhandedly. "Dr. Webb mentioned he'd been a Sigma Chi man too."

Fairbanks and Potter exchanged looks. "How is old Webb these days?" Potter asked after a silence.

"Same as ever," Dodge said with a shrug.

"Why'd you ask?" Wyatt's tone was as casual as he could manage.

"Oh, no reason, no reason." Potter poured himself more wine. "Only that… rumor has it he hasn't been well of late."

"Really?" Wyatt shot a warning glance at Dodge, who had been about to speak. "What do people think is wrong with him?"

Fairbanks interposed. "Frankly, one hears he's become more or less of an invalid."

"That covers a lot of ground," Dodge said.

"Nervous condition of some sort. What I hear, he's holed up in that place of his in Vermont for months at a time."

"It's a nice place, from what Mr. Dodge tells me," Wyatt said blandly.

"Seems to require an awful lot of medicine, whatever it is," Potter added.

"What kind of medicine?" Wyatt met Dodge's eyes across the table.

"Well, to be truthful—the word is he's become a dope-fiend," Potter said. "That's what got him blackballed here, is what I heard."

"Who'd blackball someone like Dr. Webb?" Wyatt sipped the claret that was now accompanying a roast pheasant.

"Oh, it's practically a sport in these parts," Fairbanks said. "It's not as if you need an excuse—"

"D'you remember?" Potter nudged his companion, "At the Opera Ball, the week after? The fellow was madder than a wet hen, absolutely seething."

"I heard it was Van Dorn that did him in," Fairbanks said. "Hail-fellow-well-met for the most part, but a real stickler for standards. Only the officers know for sure, of course."

Dodge dabbed his mouth with a snowy napkin. "If I'd known about that, I'd never have asked them to the island at the same time."

Wyatt made a mental note to telephone the Vermont medical examiner for the toxicology results. Gossip though it might be, Potter's assertion was enough to heighten his suspicion about Webb's involvement in Van Dorn's death. He adopted a puzzled air.

"I was under the impression they were friends."

Fairbanks fixed on Wyatt the pitying glance of an Ivy Leaguer obeying the dictates of noblesse oblige in the presence of the provincially educated.

"My dear fellow, friendship has nothing to do with it. The system relies on anonymity."

That one may smile, and smile, and be a villain. Rather a nasty trait in a friend…

"You think Van Dorn might have blackballed Dr. Webb? We'd only just met, but he struck me as the type who wouldn't have an enemy in the world."

"Were there any Jews in the party?" Potter's question caught Wyatt off guard.

"Jews?"

"Knowing Van Dorn's feelings about the race, I shouldn't be surprised if he was afraid of being done in by one of 'em, or he'd got one of 'em riled up enough…"

"Remember what a fuss he made when the rumor got round about somebody proposing Bergdorf?" Potter allowed Dodge to refill his glass. "No good telling him the Knickerbocker Club was all over Jews—'those are German Jews,' he said."

"Well, admittedly, you've got to be careful. Look at the Rothschilds—one of 'em's a member of Parliament now. There were quite a few Jews at Columbia, though. One or two of them were good enough fellows. I was by way of being friends with that Goldberg chap—what was his first name? I was about to say Christian name, but that don't work—" Fairbanks relished his own joke, his laugh like grating metal. "Elijah?"

Dodge shifted around in his seat and scanned the room.

Wyatt tried without success to catch his eye. "Uh—so there aren't any Jews here?"

"Oh, there might be one or two, under cover, so to speak," Potter said. "But I don't think the club would knowingly admit a practicing Hebrew, do you, Dodge?"

"I don't suppose so." Dodge signaled for the waiter to bring coffee. "But you might not always know."

"A lot of them try to assimilate," Fairbanks said. "Look at the Belmonts."

"Oh, no need to worry about that," Potter gestured towards a neatly dressed man in gray, supervising the carving of a roast. "Cartwright there would smoke them out before they were formally proposed. That man would have been an asset to the Pinkertons."

"The chief steward," Dodge told Wyatt.

"So he'd pass the word to the members, and someone would blackball the man?" Wyatt nodded in Cartwright's direction.

""He'd usually just have a quiet word with the fellow who was going to propose him, and that would be the end of it," Potter said. "Fellows were usually grateful to be spared the embarrassment. 'Just say there are no vacancies in the membership at present,' and they'd have the sense not to push it."

Fairbanks drew a mother-of-pearl cigarette case from his pocket. "Most of your anarchists are Jews, aren't they? No country of their own, so they go about wrecking other people's."

"Be fair, Henry," Potter said, "that's only the lower orders. There's a whole contingent of respectable Israelites in town—been here longer than we have, in some cases."

"Wouldn't have made any difference to old Gerald," Fairbanks said. "He always said he could smell a Jew a mile off."

"He was terrified of anarchists—do you remember? When McKinley was shot. He was sitting in one of the wing chairs in front of the library fireplace. The old library." Potter allowed himself a nostalgic sigh. "He puts down his paper, shakes his head—'If we don't stop letting these hordes in from the Balkans, they'll do us all in eventually,' he said. No good telling him that Czoglosz fellow was American as you or me."

Wyatt looked at Dodge, who was signing for the bill.

"I'd best be getting back to work. A pleasure to meet you, gentlemen." Wyatt rose and held out his hand.

Dodge looked up at him from the bill. "I'll hear from you in a day or two." It wasn't a question.

CHAPTER 13

Wyatt emerged from the Union's south entrance into blinding afternoon sunlight. He walked east past St. Patrick's Cathedral to Third Avenue, loping up the steps two at a time to the El station, already missing the cool air and tennis games of Vermont. The car rattled its way downtown, the buildings growing smaller, grimier, more cramped-looking. The old steam-powered cars had run for the last time while he was in Vermont, all replaced now with electrics. People living along the El tracks would no longer have to put up with the cinders and fumes, though it must still be a purgatory of noise. Most didn't have a choice, he supposed.

He descended to Grand Street and Bowery, began making his way slowly east through the crush of vendors' stalls lining and clogging the streets in every direction. Strawberries, soup greens, muslins, flour, soap, kosher meat, cheap delftware, brooms, tatty lace curtains, overalls, bread—everything a household could need was here on the street. Smells of fallen produce rotting underfoot, unwashed bodies, soapy water from laundries, coffee beans roasting, stale back-alley privies. A thundery rumble of beer-barrels rolling down the cellar steps of a tavern. And people, thousands of them, elbowing each other aside on the street: grimy boys in caps and gallused trousers, women with round shopping-baskets and sweat stains under the arms of their blouses, wisps of hair clinging to damp necks, haggling with the vendors in shrill voices. The vendors bellowing their wares. Men lifting sacks of flour into buildings, leading balky cart-horses through the crowd, smoking on balconies, boaters and derbies at jaunty angles. A high-pitched babble in a hundred languages, life lived at a high, desperate pitch, the sidewalks awning-shaded but impassable. The sun beat down on the center of the street where he walked, a slip of paper in his hand.

He threaded his way down Grand Street between a row of fruit stalls and a gang of ragged street-urchins throwing stones at an alley-cat. Bleeding on the head and haunches, the creature limped under a cart and cowered in its shadow. A heavy-jawed boy of about ten, in britches that were too small for him, tried to dive under the cart and grab the cat. Rage rose in Wyatt like a flood-tide. He hauled the boy up by his suspenders, straightened him and slammed him against the cart.

"Get the hell outa here and don't come back," he snarled, shoving the boy away so that he barely kept his feet. The bully stared at Wyatt's blazing eyes for a moment, like a rabbit mesmerized by a stoat. When Wyatt raised a hand as if to strike, he snatched up his fallen cap and took to his heels, the other children following. Wyatt reached beneath the wooden cartwheel, speaking to the cat in soothing whispers, but it slunk away into the dark, out of reach under the line of carts. He couldn't bear to see animals hurt. He'd been made to drown a litter of barn-kittens on the farm once, one of his uncle's attempts to toughen him up. He had wept in secret for days after, vowed to leave the farm when he grew up and never come back. Unlike most of his childhood vows, he had kept that one.

He continued down Grand Street and turned south onto Orchard, stopping passers-by to ask if they knew where Karel Czerny lived. Most didn't seem to understand him. The other members of the quartet had told him the violinist lived in a tenement on Orchard Street between Grand and Canal. The two short blocks appeared to contain thousands of apartments, none of them seemingly inhabited by anyone who spoke English.

The facades of the buildings were red brick for the most part, with eyebrow moulding over the windows, and entrance stoops painted in rich reds, deep greens and yellows. A first glance suggested modest comfort and elegance within. Wyatt paused to watch a landlord's agent in galluses and shirtsleeves, derby pushed back and forehead beaded with sweat, negotiating at the bottom of a wrought-iron stoop with a prospective tenant. The supplicant was an exhausted-looking Irish *paterfamilias* with wife and four children, newly liberated from the congestion and squalor of steerage. They would find little better than shipboard conditions in the cramped, windowless back rooms of a tiny apartment upstairs—an apartment they would not be allowed to see until the rent money was turned over and it was too late.

On the last block he was stopped by an angel-faced newsboy hawking his last few papers in a beat-up Panama several sizes too big for him. The boy's shrewd blue eyes took in Wyatt's summer wool suit, his careful threading through a crowd of scarved women and men in waistcoats. The smell of boiled cabbage sat on the block like a canopy.

"Whatcha lookin' for, mister?"

"Do you know where I could find Karel Czerny?"

"I might," the boy wiped his nose on his sleeve. "Who's lookin' for him?"

Wyatt retrieved a new quarter from his jacket pocket. He flipped it in the air and the boy's free hand reached up, lightning quick, and caught it.

"You need a fiddler?"

"I might. Is he any good?"

"He's the best, mister. He's even played with the Me-tro-pol-itan Opera."

"Is that a fact? That's a long way uptown."

"He's played at the Vanderbilts' too." The boy spoke as if they were next-door neighbors.

"What's your name?"

"Mike. It's really Milosz, but Mike sounds more American, don't it? What's yours?"

"Dade Wyatt." He offered the boy his hand. Startled, Mike took it. " How old are you, Mike?"

"Eleven. Well, in a coupla months."

"How d'you happen to know Mr. Czerny?"

"He's my uncle. We live in the same apartment, him and Aunt Magda and my momma and me. And the baby. She's my cousin."

"And your grandmother?"

"No," the boy looked puzzled. "Nonny died three years ago. When I was a little kid. Come on—it's in here. Upstairs."

The tenement Mike took him to was a narrow five-story building with ornate cornicework and tiny wrought-iron balconies. He led Wyatt up green metal stairs, splotched with rust, through a heavy front door into a narrow, stifling hallway. In the Stygian gloom Wyatt could just make out a pressed-tin roof and a floor tiled with small white hexagons. The building smelled of cooking fat and lye soap and disinfectant.

"It's the fourth floor." Mike's thick-soled shoes clattered up the bare wooden stairs. Wyatt followed him in near darkness up to the left-hand door at the top of the stairs, a flimsy-looking affair painted green.

"Wait here a minute." Mike pushed open the door and disappeared. As the door closed slowly behind the boy, Wyatt could hear a woman's voice, high and angry, berating the boy in a language that he presumed must be Hungarian. A few moments later the door reopened to reveal Mike and a small woman in a dark cotton dress and apron, wisps flying out from the bun which held her hair tightly away from her face. Mike said something to her in which he heard "Wyatt", and then to him, "This is my aunt. She don't speak English. She wants to know who you're from and what you want."

Wyatt removed his boater with his left hand and held it at his belt. "May I come in?" he asked. Mike relayed the request. The woman looked him up and down and replied.

"She says you can come in but you have to leave your shoes outside. She just washed the floor and I caught hell for getting footprints all over it." Mike's face split in a grin full of mischief. "See, I can say stuff like that and she don't understand."

Wyatt followed them into the kitchen. An archway on the right led to a bedroom with no window, barely big enough for a double bed. Beyond the kitchen was the parlor, which held a lumpy sofa-cum-daybed and overlooked an interior courtyard. The room was clean and looked freshly wallpapered. Dusty sunlight angled in through its open window. In the tiny kitchen, a few pots hung neatly on the wall over a sink full of soapy water and washing, opposite a small stove. Between them sat a battered wood table and three mismatched chairs. The place smelled of laundry soap and furniture polish. In a corner near the parlor window, an infant chuckled and cooed in a wooden cradle.

Mrs. Czerny took a chair and gestured for Wyatt to sit.

"She was doing the wash too." Mike pointed to a metal washboard propped at the foot of the sink.

"I'm sorry to have interrupted. I was hoping to find Mr. Czerny at home." Wyatt explained who he was, adding that he wanted to ask him a few questions about his work at the Webbs'.

The woman's face clouded when she heard the name, before Mike had even finished translating. She began speaking rapidly.

"She don't have anything to say about no Webbs. They let Uncle Karel go, with no warning, no explaining or nothin', just a note." Mike looked up at his aunt, who nodded for emphasis.

"Let him go? What about his mother? The other musicians said he had to come home—she was dying—"

"She doesn't know what you're talking about," Mike said. "Like I told you, Nonna died three years ago." The baby started to whimper and Mrs. Czerny rose to lift it from its crib.

"What is your husband doing now?"

"Trying to find work before we all starve," came the reply. The baby's whimper turned into a howl. The young woman rocked it and patted its back. "There's an audition at the Metropolitan today, but there are so many people, the chances aren't so good."

"Does she still have the note?"

Mrs. Czerny rose impatiently and dumped the baby in Mike's arms. In the parlor she pulled at the handle of a drawer on a rickety little table, which jerked stiffly open, rattling the table-legs. She extracted a piece of elegant cream stationery and handed it to Wyatt. It bore Lila Vanderbilt Webb's monogram—or at any rate the same initials—but the writing did not look like a female hand, nor did it resemble Dr. Webb's inchoate medical scribble. It merely stated that, while Mr. Czerny's services had been satisfactory, they were no longer required, and that his earliest departure would be appreciated. The signature was unintelligible.

"There seems to be a misunderstanding here," Wyatt said. "May I take this? I may be able to help."

Mike's aunt looked skeptical when he relayed the request, but shrugged and nodded assent.

"Do you know where I might find Mr. Rossi? Your husband's friend, who substituted for him?" Mike relayed the question, and the woman looked baffled, shaking her head.

Wyatt described the substitute violinist. "This man, uh, also claimed to be some sort of anarchist," he added. As Mike translated, Mrs. Czerny first looked startled, apparently at the anarchist reference, then her face went blank.

"She has no idea who I'm talking about, does she."

Mike shook his head.

"And you've never heard of someone by that name, or seen anyone with your uncle who looks like that." Another shake of the head. He'd been afraid of this since meeting Mike in the street.

Wyatt promised Mrs. Czerny, via Mike, that she would hear from him again within the week and gave them his address. He asked Mike to walk him downstairs, extracting a dollar bill from his money-clip as they left the apartment and handing it to him. The boy frowned.

"What's this for?"

"Your information's been very helpful. I appreciate it." Mike's face split in a sunny grin. He ran back upstairs, calling to his aunt as he went.

Wyatt threaded his way back through the jumble of carts and stalls towards the Canal Street El station. He thought of walking towards Elm Street to see how the subway construction was coming along, but decided to skip the racket and dust. The great excavation was finally under way, after all the fights and competing schemes and Tammany bribery. He still doubted that the line would ever be complete; meanwhile, the construction was disrupting traffic from City Hall to Grand Central, tearing up the old cobblestones to create a moat around Union Square, scarring the old Dutch streets of lower Manhattan. He couldn't imagine himself riding on an underground train. It was a claustrophobic's nightmare, the idea of being trapped under the city in a narrow, dark tunnel, perhaps immured alive by an explosion. Despite the sun and the warmth of the day, he shivered to think of it.

He took the Els to Columbus and 103rd and walked the remaining half-mile to his apartment on 107th, just west of Broadway. He and Rose had moved to the fourth floor of the brownstone building nine years before, while Columbia was building its new Morningside Heights campus, before the influx of professors and students had driven up demand and rents. The dozen flats in the building were managed by Mrs. Baird, Wyatt's landlady, a formidable Scots dowager of unimpeachable antiquity and inflexible routines.

After his wife's death, the flat had felt too big for a man living alone, and too full of memories. When he told Mrs. Baird he was thinking of moving, she had folded her arms across her black bombazine dress and eyed him shrewdly.

"It's only my own opinion, Mister Wyatt, but it doesnae do to have too many changes at the one time. Ye might give yourself a wee bit longer to think it over."

He had stayed. There would have been a lot worse places to grieve. The living room window caught the southern light and a glimpse of the Hudson. Morningside Park was just to the northeast, Riverside just at the end of the street. Off the apartment's narrow hallway ran the living-room, a bedroom on each side, the larger of which he used as an office and library, the modern luxury of a tiny indoor bathroom, and at the end, a sizeable kitchen, little used now.

He raised the living room blinds, which had grown dusty in his absence, opening the windows at the top to let in fresh air. He picked up the pile of letters he'd left on the hall table and sat in the window seat with the window cracked open, reading his mail in the sunshine. The usual advertising circulars, an announcement of the forthcoming season at the Metropolitan Opera—the fabled Caruso was to make his American debut at last.

The small living room was papered in cream with yellow and orange sprigs of flowers. He'd thought it too light, but Rose had pointed out how much smaller the room would look in the dark green and gold pattern he favored. Rose had loved light and air…his eyes rose to the photograph in its gilded baroque frame. Her angel's face with its long, patrician nose smiled down on him like Dante's Beatrice, her gold hair crowned with a chaplet of roses. Ophelia, his favorite of her roles.

A letter from the Metropolitan Club informed him that he had been proposed for membership by Mr. Warren Dodge and Dr. Seward Webb, and inquired as to whether he wished his name to be placed before the Membership Committee. He felt flattered at first, then surprised. He was occasionally un-comfortable with his position on the fringes of Society, and he couldn't help feeling gratified by this tender of acceptance into its ranks. But Dodge had not mentioned the matter to him, nor had he expressed any interest in joining a club. Why now?

CHAPTER 14

Wyatt was barely awake and had just lit the gas stove to boil a kettle for his morning coffee when he was startled by a peremptory three raps on his front door. Who had got past Mrs. Baird? He opened the door to a stranger, a short, wiry fellow of perhaps sixty, wearing a derby and a black wool suit that looked much too hot for the weather. A polite tip of his hat revealed a head of close-cropped hair, more white than gray. Too well dressed for a workman, though that was the first impression.

"James Macalester." He spoke in a thick Scots accent, thrusting out a red, bony hand. "Would you be Mister Wyatt?"

"I would." Wyatt cautiously took the hand. "To what do I owe—"

"I should've said Inspector Macalester, of the Central Detective Bureau. May I have a word?"

Wyatt waved him in. Macalester left his hat on a peg by the door and strode down the corridor of the flat to the kitchen, looking into the rooms to right and left.

"You've the place to yourself, do you?" He nodded immediately as if Wyatt had answered. "Ah, I've interrupted your coffee-making."

Wyatt spooned the fragrant grounds from a paper sack into a pot. "Can I offer you some?"

"No, thanks. Kind of you to ask. I'm a tea-drinkin' man myself. You'll be wonderin' how I got past the outside door. I'm an old friend of the good Mrs. Baird, and she sent me on up, seein' it was by way of a professional visit."

Wyatt tried to place the accent. Lowlands, certainly, very different from his landlady's crisp Highland diction, which was much more intelligible to the untrained ear. Glasgow? The guttural consonants and the varying pitch of the voice suggested it. "What can I do for you, Inspector?"

"All right if I sit down?" Macalester plopped himself in a kitchen chair. "I'm looking into the death of Mr. Gerald Van Dorn. That would appear to give us a good deal in common."

"How did you—"

"Our Commissioner was a friend of the deceased. The younger Van Dorn had a wee word with him after the funeral. There seems to be some question as to the exact cause of Mister Van Dorn's untimely demise." Macalester's pale blue eyes bored into Wyatt's.

Wyatt groaned inwardly. Will had given notice of his intent, but this was precisely what Dodge had feared and hoped to avoid. He got up and poured himself a mug of coffee, stalling for time as he tried to think of ways to deflect the man's queries.

"So the Commissioner's asked you to investigate?"

"He said that Doctor Webb had resumed his former profession long enough to conduct a post-mortem. There being nobody in the capacity of coroner available, I was told."

Wyatt nodded.

"I called on the good doctor and asked to have a wee look at his report to the town health officer in Vermont," Macalester went on. "He said it wasn't in final form as yet. But I'd a look at the notes—your notes, I gather—and I didn't think there was anythin' particularly conclusive."

"Autopsy findings in a drowning are often inconclusive."

Macalester's pale eyebrows rose and his gaze turned cold gray.

"Oh, I've no doubt there was a drownin' involved. Or perhaps I should more properly say an immersion. You find a fella floating on his face in three feet of water, that rather suggests itself. But the interestin' question is how he got there."

"Lots of ways," Wyatt said easily. "A fall, maybe."

"Maybe so. But the young fella's under the impression it's suspicious. Naturally enough, I suppose, in the circumstances.

I paid a wee visit to the widow as well. I don't think Mrs. Van Dorn thinks it was an accident, though she tried hard enough to make me think she did."

"Why would she want to do that?"

"Mister Wyatt, you're an intelligent man, by all accounts. And surely you know that the great ambition of young ladies from Mrs. Van Dorn's former station in life—Miss Dawkins as she was then—is to marry a rich old fella with a bad cough?"

"I know nothing of her former station in life. Are you suggesting—"

"Och, I'm not sayin' she had anythin' to do with it, necessarily. Not directly, at any rate." Macalester raised a hand to forestall Wyatt's protest. "But we know that Mister Van Dorn's death leaves her well situated, does it not? And in her position, I might also wish to convince myself it was an accident. Easier on the conscience that way."

Wyatt sipped his coffee and eyed Macalester coldly. "So what do you think happened?"

"Well, now, I wasn't there," Macalester parried, "An' you bein' the fella that found the body, I think that question's better directed to you."

"How did you find out about me?"

"The widow said you were the only one that knew anythin' about it."

"I know what I found in the water. That didn't help me much."

"Mrs. Van Dorn spoke of you in what I should describe as admiring terms. Clear head in an emergency, that kinda thing. The lady seemed to think there was very little ye didn't know, Mister Wyatt."

"Well, she's wrong."

"What were you doing on that island?" the Scotsman asked abruptly.

"I was a guest." Wyatt stood and refilled his coffee mug. "I've known the Dodges a long time."

"If ye don't mind my sayin' so, ye don't seem to move in the same circles as the Dodges as a rule." Macalester's gaze swept around the room and he nodded as if the question was resolved. For a few moments the mechanical tick of a mantel-clock was the only sound in the room.

"I was an invited guest. A friend."

"Oh, friend, I've no doubt. But I don't think friendship's incompatible with employment, is it?"

"Why don't you just say whatever you've got to say, Inspector?" Wyatt tossed the dregs of his coffee into the sink.

"A retired Pinkerton man might be of great use to a fella like Mr. Dodge, I should think." Macalester rose and leaned against the stove. "Suppose you just tell me what it was Mr. Dodge had you looking into—or who."

"Even if I were," Wyatt kept his tone even, "you'd hardly expect me to breach a client's confidentiality, would you?"

"Are you a lawyer or a doctor, Mister Wyatt?" the Scotsman barked back. He reminded Wyatt of a white-haired terrier.

"No, but—"

"You've no privilege, then." The eyes were leaden, the arms folded.

Wyatt sighed. The man wasn't going to go away. "May I see your credentials?"

Macalester removed a leather wallet from his breast pocket and handed it to him. It contained a badge with the unmistakable open laurel wreath of the New York police, and an identity card. Wyatt scrutinized them, then folded the wallet and tossed it back.

"Look, Inspector, what's your jurisdiction here? This death occurred in Vermont."

"And escaped the attention of the local constabulary, if I'm not mistaken. You were all happy enough to give it out as an accidental drowning. Avoid the bad publicity and so forth. But we've a request from the son and heir to look into it. And near as I can tell, just about everybody that was on that island is a legal resident of the city of New York. Including the victim."

"The good doctor saw fit to certify the death as accidental," Macalester went on. "But I think our brethren in Vermont could be persuaded to view it differently—if an official inquiry came in from the home district of the deceased, like. At least one of the island's visitors may be a fugitive from justice. And that person may be here in the City. The Commissioner thinks that's enough to go on for now. But not to worry, I've no intentions of turning this into fodder for the Police Gazette. The Detective Bureau is capable of discretion."

"Why are you interested in this? Surely you have more pressing matters—"

"*Any man's death diminishes me.*" Macalester declaimed. "You're a college man, Mr. Wyatt, so you'll know the origin of that. It's not as though we're lookin' for extra work. Lord knows we're busy enough with murder and mayhem on a nightly basis in the seedier sections. But sometimes we're guilty of excessive zeal goin' after criminals of the poorer class, while we turn a blind eye to the depredations of our wealthier citizens."

"You think one of the party killed Van Dorn?"

"Or had him killed, maybe. I don't know that. But if you're honest, Mister Wyatt, I've no doubt you'll agree with me that it's a distinct possibility. Furthermore," Macalester resumed his chair, "we've a string of unsolved crimes in the City. Crimes against the wealthy for the most part, which we think may be the work of our substantial and growing anarchist contingent. From what Doctor Webb described, there seemed to be such a person among the musicians. A man that disappeared after Van Dorn's death."

"That would suggest him as the culprit, wouldn't it? If there was one."

"It might, though it doesn't mean he was. Now. What were you doin' on that island?"

Wyatt sat down again. "There are things that can't be in your record."

"I'm listenin'." Macalester sat bolt upright with his hands on his knees.

"Mr. Dodge is expecting an important visitor there."

"An' he engaged you to make sure there wouldn't be any spanners in the works for this—ah—important visit."

"Something like that."

"What kinda things was he worried about?"

"Safety. Security. I was doing some background checks on the guests—"

"Governor Fisk and Doctor Webb needed to have their backgrounds checked?" Macalester cocked an eyebrow and grinned.

"Well, not them so much—"

"I think you were on the lookout for more than guests, myself." Wyatt found Macalester's complacent nod infuriating. "Word has it Mister Dodge is considerin' standin' for Congress. On the Republican ticket, naturally. An' perhaps he'd like to talk things over, quiet-like, with somebody who could give him a leg-up there—"

Wyatt masked his surprise with a shrug.

"Somebody important enough to need security protection. That sounds like the good Mister Roosevelt to me."

"I haven't heard about Dodge standing for anything."

"Surely it would be a lot of trouble to go to, just to have the man over for a friendly social visit," Macalester said. "An' bloody inconvenient—if you'll pardon the expression—to have a dead body about the place."

"Accidents happen."

"Och, come on, Mister Wyatt. What in God's name was a man like Van Dorn doin' out in the water in his semmit at six o'clock in the mornin'?"

"Damned if I know."

"Damned if you don't." Macalester stood and stared down at his quarry. "Maybe it wouldnae be so inconvenient at that, if it could be passed off as an accident."

"What the hell does that mean?"

"Just how far would you be willin' to go for your employer, Mr. Wyatt?"

Wyatt sat back and met Macalester's gaze. "Suppose you tell me."

"Suppose Gerald Van Dorn had found out somethin' that would keep Warren Dodge from his Congressional seat, and ruin him in society into the bargain?"

"Such as?"

"Ye're not tellin' me ye don't know?"

"Know what?" Wyatt exploded in exasperation. "I'm no good at guessing-games."

"That his wife is a Jewess—"

Wyatt's eyes widened. "Augusta?"

"Och, aye. It's given out she's a connection of the Havemeyers. But I've done a wee bit homework, and I traced it back. She's actually a cousin of the Wertheimers. On the mother's side."

"The Asher Wertheimers?!"

"Mrs. Dodge," Macalester said, "is as Jewish as Father Abraham."

Wyatt shook his head as if to clear it. "And you think Van Dorn knew this and wanted to—what? Blackmail Dodge, or—" Wyatt remembered something Dodge had said. *Gussie invited them up...Surprised me a little... Milly's never seemed like Augusta's type.* Had Gerald told Augusta what he knew, and made Milly's acceptance into Augusta's social world the price of his silence?

"Black*ball*, I should think, would've been nearer the mark," Macalester was saying. "The chap never made a great secret of his aversion to the Israelites. Though he seems to've been a nice enough fella otherwise, from what I've been told. Like yon Merchant of Venice, I suppose."

"So, how would Van Dorn have found this out? And how would Dodge have learned that he knew?"

Macalester smiled like a teacher with a promising pupil. "You've got right to the heart of the matter, Mister Wyatt. As to

113

that, I can't be sure. But it seems Van Dorn made quite a hobby of genealogy. He'd traced himself back to the *Mayflower*, I'm told, on his maternal grandmother's side. Though I'm damned if I understand why it makes such a bloody big difference to you Americans which boat your lot came over on."

It was Wyatt's turn to smile. "We don't have clans. A man with a clan name knows where he stands in your part of the world, doesn't he?"

"That's true enough in the Highlands. Those of us from the workin' part of Scotland are a race o' mongrels. Which is to say sturdy and intelligent. Now, returning to the subject at hand, I'm not sure just how Van Dorn came by his information—"

"How did you come by it?"

"Triangulation, I call it." Macalester paced the small kitchen and stood in a sunbeam from the window. It highlighted the crags of his cheeks and his pursed, reddish mouth. "Who'd have a motive to murder our Mister Van Dorn, I asked myself. What mischief might he have done to a member of the party on Heron Island? Or be thinkin' of doin'? So I sent a young fella from the force out to the clubs. He's a plainclothesman, from a background you wouldn't normally associate with police work. He can go into a place like that, no bother. And he came back with the story of Doctor Webb being blackballed from the Union Club."

"Dr. Webb?" Wyatt felt his earlier misgivings confirmed about having Webb handle the postmortem.

"Aye, and not so long ago either. The assailant hasn't been identified, nor the exact reason, though it needn't take much, I'm told. About that same time, a couple of years ago now, the good doctor also saw fit to buy shares in the journalistic enterprise of the infamous Colonel Mann."

"*Town Topics?* That gossip-rag?"

"Rag it may be, but it has demolished more than one pillar of society in this town. To prevent which, a number of them have been persuaded to make sizeable investments, so-called, to keep their dirty linen off his front page."

"Blackmail payments."

"In all but name. Webb's so-called investment is one of the highest we know of."

"The police keep track of such things?"

"Where we suspect illegal activities may be involved. Now, with over thirteen million to his and his wife's name, Webb can afford to throw a paltry fourteen thousand at this so-called colonel to prevent minor embarrassments if he so chooses. But I'm inclined to think the chappie wouldn't have demanded, and got, so large an amount for anything short of—"

"Something that would ruin Webb completely." Wyatt's heart sank. The morphia in the medical bag, the nervousness, the withdrawal from company—and the eyes, that was what had eluded him until now, the pupils constricted even in the dusk of the verandah on Heron Island. It all confirmed the gossip in the Union Club dining room. Dr. Webb was a morphine addict. Or, as the Pharisees of the age would put it, a dope-fiend. Had Gerald Van Dorn known? And acted on what he knew?

"Have you any idea what that might have been, Mr. Wyatt?" Macalester's voice startled him from his reverie.

"I hardly know the man." The doctor was a beloved figure in Vermont and in the Adirondack towns that had benefited from his railroad-building. Wyatt liked him. He wasn't prepared to throw Webb to the wolves just yet. He needed time to investigate on his own, to check the toxicology results. He didn't want to believe Webb would kill.

"That doesn't answer the question."

He had to keep Macalester from reading his thoughts.

"To answer it, then—I have no idea what it might have been. As you noted earlier, we don't move in the same circles."

Macalester raised a furry eyebrow, but he let it go. "Well, then, we're going to have to find out."

"You think Van Dorn knew whatever Colonel Mann had found out about Webb, and tried to blackmail him with it?"

"Blackmail I doubt. He didn't seem short of money. But blackballing is another matter, and perhaps the good doctor found out who did him in at the Union Club."

"So, assuming Webb thought—or maybe even knew—that Van Dorn had done such a thing, why would they socialize? Much less agree to spend a week on an island together? And for that matter, if your theory about Augusta Dodge is correct, surely the last place Van Dorn would want to be is her private island?"

"It seems unlikely, right enough. But we've got two families on that island with secrets that the late Mr. Van Dorn may have come to know. And perhaps was inclined to act upon, in the interests of preserving the social order."

"Social embarrassments, possibly, but secrets worth killing over?"

"Och, there's no telling what the upper crust will do to further their aims in life. Look how much Morgan spent building the Metropolitan Club out of spite at the blackballing of his friend King."

"That's hardly murder."

"Other than on the bank-book." Macalester shook his head in wonder. "I don't think Webb's the likeliest at that, though he's certainly a possibility. He seems happy enough at the Metropolitan, which has rather put the poor old Union in the shade, and as they say, livin' well's the best revenge. I think it's more likely somebody who felt more immediately endangered by Mister Van Dorn."

Wyatt's mind drifted back to the smiling, rotund figure, marveling at the beauty of the Milky Way, reminiscing about his pursuit of Milly as a stage-door Johnny…even with the evidence mounting, he was having difficulty reconciling that benign image with a character capable of petty grudges and vicious anti-Semitism.

"It must seem strange." The Scotsman seemed to read his thoughts. "But as you may know, there's a lot of interest among the gentry at present in the notion of improvin' the race. The purity of bloodlines, an' all that sort of thing. Not to mention the common perception that all Jews are anarchists. Look at what's happened to poor wee Mrs. Goldman since Mr. McKinley was killed."

Wyatt, who had once heard poor wee Mrs. Goldman give a fiery and highly specific denunciation of the captains of industry, thought the lady quite capable of taking care of herself, and said so.

"My only point being," said Macalester with mild irritation, "that it isn't likely to do an aspiring politician much good to be associated in the public mind with a despised race, and one which, fairly or not, is viewed by many as a threat to the body politic."

"But the German Jews have been fixtures in New York society for generations. The Harmonie Club is the height of gentility, and some of the founders of the Knickerbocker—"

"But Gentiles don't marry them, Mister Wyatt. Exceptin' the former Mrs. Vanderbilt, who I think married Belmont to spite her former spouse."

"Why would Augusta Dodge conceal that, assuming it's true?"

"You know the answer to that one," Macalester said. "Our Mrs. Dodge is an ambitious woman—for herself, and for her husband. Else why the fuss about havin' Mister Roosevelt to the island? They'd met him at Fisk's, and at Shelburne Farms, surely."

"And why would Van Dorn accept an invitation like that, if he intended to do his hosts such a bad turn?"

"Maybe he didn't," Macalester said. "He'd have known the week was a dress rehearsal for the President's visit. And who can resist a chance to hobnob wi' the great? Maybe he took Dodge discreetly aside the evening before, and told him what he knew. Suggested out of mere neighborly kindness that Mister Dodge reconsider his interest in standin' for Congress. Given the unfortunate circumstances of his wife's birth." Macalester adopted his version of upper-crust New York speech, "'Which are bound to come to light, my dear fellow; these things always do.'"

"A lot of maybes. Van Dorn backing another horse, you think?"

Macalester looked pleased. "I hadn't considered it from that angle. That would be well worth looking into." Wyatt silently cursed himself.

"But, look," Wyatt said, "if Van Dorn knew this, chances are there were others who did too. As you said, it's hard to keep things like that a secret. Dodge would have to keep knocking people off, like Macbeth—"

"And your man Dodge, you'd think, is realist enough to know that that wouldn't work in the end. Well, maybe so, maybe so. Though I must say it took a lot of digging on my part to come up wi' the information. An effort like that would hardly be worth the time of anybody but a dedicated genealogist and racial purist, or a homicide detective. Maybe Van Dorn was the only one who'd found it out, and Dodge might have thought he could keep it quiet otherwise. But, grantin' your point, we're still left with the question: what happened to Van Dorn?"

"Why are you so unwilling to believe it was an accident?"

"I could ask you the same question, Mister Wyatt. Why would you be slumming south of Delancey Street, if not to find out something about this case?"

"Dodge isn't my only client." Wyatt rose and opened a pantry-cupboard. The prospects for breakfast were unpromising: two tins of soup and a jar of bread-and-butter pickles sent from the farm in Ohio at Christmas.

Macalester came over and closed the pantry door. "Avoidin' the question won't help." He walked back down the hall to the study, Wyatt following in his wake.

"If you think I was on this case, as you put it, you mustn't think I had anything to do with Van Dorn's death."

"I haven't ruled that out entirely, but I'll admit the probabilities weigh against it. Now, suppose you tell me what you were doin' yesterday among the Levantines of the Lower East Side." Macalester settled himself in the wooden swivel chair with a proprietary air.

"You were following me?"

"I had you followed. But the fella lost track of you around Grand Street."

Wyatt looked down at the floor and cleared his throat. "I was visiting a lady friend." He looked down sheepishly into Macalester's bright gaze. The Scotsman threw back his head and guffawed. He wiped tears of merriment from his eyes.

"Well, I have to give you credit, Mister Wyatt. What won't you plead to in the interest of your client's privacy? But my goodness, in the middle of the workin' day? Next you'll be tellin' me you prefer your meat kosher."

Wyatt shrugged and bit his lip. "I do, actually."

"It's the wrong side of Broadway for that sort of thing," Macalester said. "Unless the Vice Squad is even more derelict in its duties than I've been led to believe. But here's what I'm goin' to do: I'm goin' to enlist you."

Wyatt turned towards his bookshelf and pulled down a volume. "I'm employed at present. By Warren Dodge."

"I'll keep that in mind, and discount your information accordingly. What did you find out south of Delancey, by the way?"

There was no harm in telling the man. He might even be able to help. "The violinist—the fellow who seems to have left with the boat—his whole story was a lie." Wyatt sketched the circumstances of Czerny's replacement.

"He said he was from New York?"

Wyatt nodded. "That part may be true. He knew who Czerny was, and where he lived, and who the quartet was engaged with. And he seems to have had access to the Webbs' household, probably the Fifth Avenue house but it could even have been Shelburne—he'd got hold of some stationery—"

"An enterprisin' fellow, from the sounds of him. Quite the planner, eh? So the Webbs' servants might know something about him." Macalester rose and began scanning Wyatt's bookshelves, hands comfortably clasped behind him.

"Worth a try, I suppose. But I don't see how you can do that discreetly."

Macalester turned from the shelf that held Wyatt's Shakespeares. "We don't suggest he had anythin' to do with a murder. I'll just send a bluecoat or two down to visit the servants' hall at Number Six-Eighty and tell them we're looking for a fella matching his description. Wanted for questioning on an immigration violation, or some missing silver somewhere, or some such. Routine inquiries. I'm savin' you for the good stuff."

"For what? Snitching on my boss? You can forget it."

"I've taken enough cheek for one day. I want you to talk to the widow. I think you might have been headin' her way in any event."

"Only for a spot of fortune-hunting," Wyatt said with a sardonic smile.

"Ah, then perhaps I was right in suspectin' you, but wrong about your motive. She didn't seem your type, I must say."

Wyatt felt himself flush and gritted his teeth. "And what would that be?"

"She's a looker, right enough, though I'm not sure she'll age well. But she seemed a wee bit flighty for someone like you."

"If I'm after profundity, I can get it out of books." Wyatt waved an arm towards his perilously laden bookcases. "Tailing me and getting my landlady to spy on me doesn't mean you know me."

"A good-lookin' fella like you could have his pick of the ladies, at least for an interlude. But in nearly five years you've not formed a new attachment, am I right?"

"A gentleman never tells." Wyatt's smile grew, if possible, colder.

"All right. Enough of this bobbin' an' weavin'. We've both got other things to do today. So here's what I expect: that you win the lady's confidence and find out how things stood between her and Mr. Van Dorn, and who else might have been in the picture. Waitin' in the wings, to use a term of your former art. Meanwhile the boys and I will look into the anarchist angle."

"And what if I refuse?"

"My alternative is to run you in as at least an accessory and let a couple of the boys at the headquarters—"

"Rough me up until I talk?"

"See if they can induce a more cooperative frame of mind. Now, unless I'm much mistaken, it won't cause you much heartache to get some truth out of Mrs. V."

"And how do you suggest I do this?"

Macalester shrugged. "How'd you planned to do it? A sympathetic friend, a potential suitor—I'm sure you've it thought out already. Besides, she knows Dodge has you looking into the business, so she'd be expectin' to be asked a few questions, now that the first shock is past."

Wyatt reached for Macalester's hat and handed it to him. "As you say, we're both busy men, so if you'll excuse me—"

"I expect to hear back from you by week's end. And when you're done with that, I've some questions for you to ask Mrs. Dodge."

"Forget it." Wyatt refilled his coffee cup and left Macalester to find his own way out.

CHAPTER 15

In his best black suit and almost-new derby, Wyatt stood on the marble steps of a brownstone in the upper east Fifties, its bay windows twinkling in the afternoon sun. He heard a deep-throated bell chime in answer to his push of a button, one of the new electric ones. A plump young maid in a black-ribboned cap opened the door and stared at him frankly, with a tiny smile of appraisal.

"Good afternoon, miss—my name is Dade Wyatt." he handed over a black-edged visiting card. "Would Mrs. Van Dorn be at home? I am sorry to be calling so soon after—but the matter is of some importance."

The maid squinted at the card and cocked an eye at him, answering in an Irish lilt. "I don't know, sur, Mr. Van Dorn has gone out—I mean Mr. Will," she added hastily in response to Wyatt's startled look. "If you'd care to wait in the hall a moment, I'll see if the Missus is at home."

Wyatt entered a large square hallway paved in harlequinade tiles, like a chessboard turned at an angle. A white marble staircase widened gracefully at the bottom, set off by a carved mahogany balustrade. Through the open door of a heavily furnished parlor, he glimpsed a Connemara marble fireplace, its opening hidden for the summer behind a needlepoint screen, huge ferns and aspidistras in brass pots, a Persian rug in shades of cream and turquoise. On the far wall, a bird-tree in a glass case, dozens of bright-feathered creatures arranged artfully, as if alive, along its branches, the larger ones on the bottom. His flesh crept at the thought of the slaughter that had put them there.

The maid returned. "The missus says, will you wait for her, please, in the library, and she'll be down to collect you in a few minutes. She says there's sherry and cigars and you're to make yourself at home till she comes."

"Very kind." Wyatt bowed and gave the girl a smile that melted the aches out of her back. He followed her into a room to the right of the foyer, a walnut-paneled library in the best and most conventional of taste: calf-bound volumes with gleaming gold titles, comfortable-looking leather armchairs, and a great dark blue and red Turkey carpet over the oak parquet floor. He had been in a hundred such libraries in the City. Dimly lit by electric sconces, it smelled of lemon furniture polish, faint traces of cognac, whisky, and masculine conversation, and lilies: a great Chinese bowl of them stood on a round table in the center of the room. How did lilies become funeral flowers, he wondered. Thick jacquard drapes were drawn across the windows, as befitted a house of mourning, and bows of crape drooped from the valances.

He was examining a set of Dickens novels when the door opened behind him. Her step was light and swift; he turned and she clasped him by both hands.

"Dear Mr. Wyatt, how kind of you to come and see me!"

She was in a stylishly cut black silk dress, slim-fronted in the new fashion, with a high neck, and lace on the bodice in defiance of strict mourning custom. An overskirt of crape, and no jewelry except for her diamond wedding band, but the carved jet combs that held up her hair were of uncommonly fine workmanship. She had her roses-and-cream color back, and a trace of the old merriment in the blue eyes. A robust, healthy woman, Wyatt thought with appreciation.

"How do you do, Mrs. Van Dorn, now that the—"

"Oh, the funeral was such a trial." She shook her head and sat down in an armchair, gestured for him to do the same. " It went on forever—hundreds and hundreds of people, and poor Gerald, so High Episcopal as he was, we knew he would want the full treatment, but, really, it was all so very tiring, I've done nothing but sleep for the last few days."

"It was most impressive. I'm sure Mr. Van Dorn would have been pleased."

"Oh, you were there?" her voice held surprise and a hint of reproach. "I didn't see you. Did you come to the reception?"

"For a little while, but there were so many people, and—"

"Of course—how thoughtful you are. You didn't want to trouble me to have to be nice when I wasn't feeling a bit like being nice. But, really, I'd never have trouble being pleasant to you." She rang a small silver bell on a side table, summoning the maid.

"Mary, would you bring us a pot of tea and a few of those scones?"

"Darjeeling, mum?"

"Oh, no, bring some Lapsang Souchong."

Wyatt groaned inwardly. He detested tea.

"Gentlemen prefer the stronger varieties—no, please, Mr. Wyatt, it's no trouble, I was just about to have some when you called, and it's been so quiet these last few days—and this is such a nice room for tea, don't you think? Mary, will you open the drapes? I can't bear all this gloom, I need to see a little daylight. I rarely came in here when—when Gerald was alive, oh, it sounds so strange to say that! It was his *sanctum sanctorum*, he always said, when he wasn't at the Club or the office this is where you'd find him, though he'd never have tolerated the lilies, but then—" Sunlight flooded in on the tears pooling in her eyes.

"I'm sorry, Mrs. Van Dorn. I should have waited—"

"Oh, no, please! I truly am glad to see you. I—I suppose I'm not the sort of person who's cut out for solitude, one's supposed to withdraw from the world for a year, and I shall, of course, poor Gerald deserves no less, only it's…" her hands fluttered like little wings and she clasped them together to still them.

"I hope you won't think it presumptuous of me to ask, but— have you not had friends to visit? People who can bring solace in your loss—the ladies of your circle?"

"There have been some. I should not complain. But they are so very morbid! They come all in black with long faces and murmurings about tragic loss, and they're mostly the old hens too, who are downright tiresome—I have seen one or two old friends from younger days, which is a great relief—"

"And Jeremy Dodge has called, I suppose? To see Mr. Van Dorn?"

She seemed to hesitate for a moment. "Yes, of course. To see—Will."

The maid re-entered with a silver tea tray, which she set at Mrs. Van Dorn's elbow.

"Shall I pour, mum?"

"No, thank you, Mary. The scones look very nice." She bestowed a wintry smile on the girl, who bobbed a half-curtsy and left.

Wyatt took a deep breath and began. "Perhaps you took a little comfort in seeing how many friends and admirers your husband had. I don't know when I've seen a church so full, at a funeral."

"That's true, I suppose. Though I would have said many were acquaintances, and colleagues, you know, from the Bank and his clubs and so on—"

"Clubs? I'd heard your husband was a Union man, all the way."

Before Wyatt could demur, Mrs. Van Dorn poured two cups of tarry tea and handed one to him. "Oh, certainly, but there were others, you know, philanthropic concerns, City commissions, and so forth."

"Was your husband interested in politics? I thought I recognized the Republican Chairman there—Senator Hanna? That's quite an honor."

"Oh, they had been talking. Gerald told me—he said Mr. Hanna wanted him to stand for Congress. I think it was all in his mind, myself, I mean, really, can you see Gerald out making stump speeches?—" She broke off and put her knuckles over her mouth. "You know," she went on after a deep, shuddering breath, "—I can't quite believe he's gone. I wake up in the night and think, well, he's staying at the Club again, and then

I remember..." she turned her head and gazed at the bowl of lilies, biting her full lower lip. She was particularly fetching in profile, Wyatt thought, like a cameo. He wondered if she might actually have loved the man. Perhaps in some fashion she did.

"I guess your husband didn't strike me as the politician type. It is rather a rough-and-tumble world, isn't it? Especially in New York."

"Oh, indeed, but I suppose if he'd decided to do it, with Mr. Hanna and his friends backing him—well, it has been a Republican seat, until recently at any rate, but then, since dear Mr. Roosevelt went to the White House—I'm sure they'd like to have it back."

"I wonder who'll be nominated now." Wyatt squeezed a wedge of lemon into the tea. He wondered how long he could pretend to sip at it before she noticed it was still full.

"Oh, I'm sure there will be plenty of candidates. There always are, aren't there? Not that I pay any attention, but I can't see that Dr. Wilson fellow staying in for long."

It occurred to Wyatt that she paid more attention to politics than he would have given her credit for. "Mr. Dodge seems interested in politics too. Do you suppose it was part of what made them friends?"

"Oh, who knows what you men talk about in those stuffy old clubs of yours." Her tone had a trace of the old flirtatiousness. "Though he did seem curious—I remember, we were strolling on the south beach one day last week—was it only last week? He wanted to show me some fossils he'd found in the cliff-face, and he asked me if Gerald had ever thought of running for public office. 'Why are you asking me?' I said. 'We don't talk about such things.' And he said—" she blushed and looked away for a moment, "'You're right at that, Milly my dear—who'd want to waste a conversation with a pretty woman talking about politics? Even if he is married to her?'"

Wyatt cleared his throat. "Mr. Dodge is naturally distressed at what happened. I suppose he feels somewhat responsible, in a way. Mr. Van Dorn was his guest, and so he asked me to—to see if I could shed any more light on what happened, find out what might have led him to be out in the water at that time."

"Oh—naturally, poor Warren, and Gussie, how upsetting for them to have such a thing happen there, at their little retreat from the world—I feel so badly about that!" She spoke as if the death had been a social transgression on her husband's part, a drunken insult or a broken vase.

"Well, I think their first concern is doing right by Mr. Van Dorn—and you—and satisfying all of our concerns about how and why it happened."

"Why—it was an accident, wasn't it? He drowned. Wasn't that what Dr. Webb found out?" She poured herself more tea and stirred sugar vigorously into it.

"Had Mr. Van Dorn done anything like that before? Got up so early, and gone outdoors in his nightclothes?"

"He might well have, for all I know. I sleep late and soundly as a rule—Gerald was usually up and dressed and at breakfast by the time I got up, or so his valet and the maids would tell me—you couldn't have proved it by me, certainly."

Wyatt took a bite of scone. He sipped at the tea. With the lemon it was barely tolerable. He leaned back in the chair, affecting an air of thoughtful relaxation.

"The thing I've wondered about, though, is what got him up so very early that day, and out without dressing."

"Birds. Gerald was a fanatic about them. When we were in the country, that is. Something woke him up, I suppose—a bird-call he wasn't familiar with, or one he'd heard but hadn't seen. So he just grabbed his field-glasses and went off looking for it. It wouldn't have been the first time."

Wyatt rose and walked over to the window. "Hmm—that's certainly possible. But how do you think he might have ended up in the water?" he kept his tone conversational. "He wasn't a swimmer, you said—"

"No, and so if he got there, he wouldn't have been able to get himself out, I'm afraid. Especially with the dressing-gown weighing him down. I think he must have fallen in from somewhere."

"But he wouldn't have landed in the water, would he, if he'd fallen in from the headland there, where we found him?"

"There are cliffs, though, aren't there? Augusta said so. On the other side of the island—where Amy was going to take him to see the birds' nests. He must have gone out there, and lost his footing, and then floated round to the other end…"

Silence hung between them for a moment.

"Mrs. Van Dorn," Wyatt began awkwardly, "There's something I must confess to you—"

She half-rose and he saw color rise into her face, her expression an odd mix of curiosity, hunger, and astonishment. She put a hand to her throat.

"Mr. Wyatt!" She raised the hand to restrain him. "Please— do not say anything—it would be so improper now—I was sure I sensed something, that day, when you rowed me to the mainland, I am never wrong about such things, but of course you were a perfect gentleman, and now—surely you must see that I am not in a position at present—" the tone strove for indignant but stalled at cautionary.

Wyatt bit his lip and turned scarlet. This was the last thing he had expected. Or at any event, almost the last.

"Forgive me," he broke in, "I am not making myself understood—I—ah—saw you on the headland that morning." There; it was out. "I didn't mean to spy, I assure you, but I was up early myself, out for a walk, and—"

The blue eyes went cold. "And you think you saw me? When was this?"

"Oh, a little after five, I'd say—I should perhaps have made my presence known, but, to speak frankly—I felt I had stumbled on you in a moment of, ah, intentional solitude, so—I withdrew."

"I came out to get a little fresh air. I was not feeling well. I think it must have been the oysters—I didn't want to disturb anyone. Gerald was already up, of course."

"Did you see him?"

"Of course not," she snapped. "Don't you think I'd have told you all then, if I had? Really, Mr. Wyatt, you should have let me know you were there."

"Mr. Germain mentioned that he'd seen you as well. He did say you—uh—didn't look well at the time."

"One has no privacy at all in such a place!" She went to the window-sill and stared out into the street. "I was only trying to spare the others from my little indignities. And, naturally, I was too embarrassed to mention it afterwards, especially since I hadn't seen or heard anything out of the ordinary. So much for my good intentions," she laughed lightly. "But, really, Mr. Wyatt, are you sure you weren't spying on me? I hardly know whether to be alarmed or flattered at the thought."

"I often rise early in the summer," Wyatt said, "and I'm something of a wild-life fancier myself. I'd seen a heron the day before, fishing under the cliff, and I thought I'd go and have a look for it. I make it a practice never to spy on ladies— or, at least, I haven't since I stopped acting. It was called for at times, in some of the roles I played." He could give her that much, to soften the misunderstanding.

"You were an actor! I knew there was something fascinating about you—Augusta never told me that. Tell me—did you ever play Romeo? I think you must have."

"Once or twice in my early days," Wyatt said. "He wasn't my favorite. Overly impulsive."

She knitted her brows, appraising. "No, I think you'd be more the Hamlet sort. Or Mark Antony? I often thought I should love to play Cleopatra!"

"Age cannot wither her, nor custom stale her infinite variety." Wyatt had played Enobarbus too, and loved his famous speech. She positively sparkled at the gallantry.

It was only his sense of duty that forced Wyatt to cloak the sunny moment with a dark cloud. "Mrs. Van Dorn, can you think of any-one who might have had a reason to wish your husband dead?"

The blue eyes again assumed china-doll blankness. She shook her head. "What a terrible question. No, I really can't imagine. Gerald was a sweet, kind man. I'm sure he never hurt anybody in his life."

"I'm sorry. It is a terrible question. But even people who never hurt anybody are sometimes murdered for reasons that make sense only to the killer." Wyatt stood and put his teacup on the table, turned around to look Mrs. Van Dorn full in the eyes. "If they stand between him and something he desires, for example—"

He detected a momentary flush, but she recovered. The room was stuffy, the scent of lilies heavy on the still air. She broke the oppressive silence at last.

"Perhaps after all there is some—some business rivalry I'm not aware of. You might make inquiries at Morgan's. Those big corporations—I'm given to understand they're rife with jealousies and petty power struggles. But of course I'd know nothing about that. Gerald didn't trouble me with his business affairs." She rose quickly and took a step over to him, extending her hand. "It was so kind of you to come to see me, Mr. Wyatt—"

Her eyes rolled back. Before he could catch her, she dropped onto his feet in a dead faint, in a crinkly pool of crape.

"Damned corset!—she can't breathe—" Wyatt hissed through clenched teeth. Pinioned by her weight, he stretched over and barely reached the bell for the maid. He was trying to extricate his feet from the fabric of her dress when the library door opened.

"Jaysus, Mary and Joseph!" the maid rushed across the room. "What's happened to the Missus?"

"She's been taken ill. Help me get her up. Do you have any smelling-salts?"

They carried Mrs. Van Dorn over to a divan under the window. Her face was stark white with a green tinge, her skin moist and cold. Her eyelids began to flutter and she gasped for air.

Wyatt bent to listen. "You need to loosen her stays. She's not getting enough air."

The maid looked horrified.

"Do it, for God's sake!" Wyatt hissed.

"I can't, sur, I'm not a lady's-maid, and Julia's gone out—"

"If you don't, I will," Wyatt snapped. "She can't wait."

"Oh, Mother of God." the girl bent to loosen the sash of Mrs. Van Dorn's dress. "You'd best go for Doctor Tinmuth. He has his surgery in his house—two blocks down the Avenue and three doors round to the left. You fetch him and I'll—"

Wyatt was out the door before she finished. In ten minutes he returned with the doctor, an angular old soldier in an old-fashioned frock coat. They mounted the marble steps and rang the bell.

"Have you attended the family long, doctor?"

"I had known the late Mr. Van Dorn for twenty years." The doctor's tone was icy, as if he thought Wyatt presumptuous in asking. "Mrs. Van Dorn for some time less, naturally. I had not thought the home would be open to callers so soon." He knitted his prodigious brows.

"I had been asked to consult with Mrs. Van Dorn on a few matters relating to her husband's death."

"By the lady herself?"

"Ah—no. By her host on the island. Where—"

"Where Mr. Van Dorn met his untimely end. I see." The doctor passed into the checkerboard lobby. "You may leave now. I will have matters in hand."

"Of course." Wyatt let himself out and the door slammed heavily behind him.

Surely Tinmuth would detect Mrs. Van Dorn's pregnancy, perhaps even knew of it already. A swollen abdomen would be apparent to him when he examined her, concealed though it had been from Wyatt under layers of crape and silk and the stays. How far along was she? And, he wondered seriously for the first time, was Gerald Van Dorn the father of his wife's child?

CHAPTER 16

Germain answered the Dodges' telephone and allowed that he could use a cold beer on such a hot day, if Wyatt could wait until late afternoon. Wyatt stationed himself by the trolley stand at the West 59th Street entrance to Central Park until Germain arrived, wearing a light brown suit, a buff waistcoat with a gold watch-chain, and a dark brown derby. The downtown horse-trolley pulled up and they stepped aboard.

"You been investigatin' much since I saw you?"

"I saw Mrs. Van Dorn today."

"She wasn't too prostrate with grief to receive you?" Germain gave the conductor a handful of small coins.

"I'd say she was glad enough to receive me—until I started asking her unpleasant questions." Wyatt related the fainting episode.

"So she's still *enceinte*."

"Why wouldn't she be?"

"Shock like that can bring on a miscarriage sometimes," Germain shrugged. "And ladies in her class don't have to go through with the thing if they don't want to."

The air in the trolley-car was hot and still, even with the windows open. The wool of Wyatt's suit prickled and sweat ran down his back like a column of ants.

"You think she'd—?"

"I don't know. Might depend on what the will said."

"What would that have to do with—oh, you mean, how another heir might change things." They swung off the trolley at Hudson and Christopher and walked a few blocks east.

"Depends on how it divides things up." Germain took off the derby and mopped at his brow with a handkerchief. Wyatt peeled his jacket off and pinched his damp shirt away from his back.

132

"In any event, another child won't be a good development from Will's point of view."

"No matter whose it was. But it would be worse if the kid wasn't Van Dorn's. You think Will might have doubts on that score?"

Wyatt considered for a few steps. "Could he do anything about it if it wasn't?"

"Probably not, 'less he had some clear-cut evidence Mrs. V. was steppin' out on his father."

"I imagine she'd have been careful about that."

Germain swung open the scarred door of Haggerty's saloon. "Duck your head—the door's low. And watch the step down."

The ceiling was low, too, and dark-beamed. A battered oak bar made a tight horseshoe in the middle of the narrow room, which smelled of sawdust, stale beer and cheap cigars. At tables in the far reaches of the room, groups of lean men in shirt-sleeves, derbies pushed back from sweating foreheads, played cards and argued over racing prospects and aldermanic candidates. Some of them were Negroes, far darker than Germain.

"This is what we call a black-and-tan place." Germain pulled out a chair for Wyatt and signaled the bartender with two up-raised fingers. "Porter all right for you?"

Wyatt nodded. "So, why do you think this child mightn't be Van Dorn's?"

"Wistful look on the man's face when he looked at her, for one thing."

"Hmm. You are observant."

"As if he kept hoping she'd give him something he wasn't getting," Germain said. "I've seen that look before, on old men with young things like her."

"But surely, once they were married—"

"Ladies manage to feel poorly a lot when it suits them. It needn't have been that, even. Maybe he just had, you know, difficulties."

"Any candidates you can think of for cuckoo in the nest?"

"Hard to say. The Dodges saw a lot of them this past season, but of course I didn't get out with them. When she came to the house, though, she talked on a lot about some up-and-coming opera singer. Tenor, baritone, I can't remember. At first I thought she was just hankering back to her career as a singer, but later I got the impression it wasn't so much his voice she admired."

"She mention any names?"

"Something Italian." Germain drained an inch from his porter. "Not that that narrows it down in the opera world. She hosted a reception for him, back in January or so, when he made his debut at the Met. Miz Dodge went. She might remember."

"Any other men in her life that you know of?"

"Not 'less you count Will and Jeremy, when they were home from school," Germain laughed. "But no candidates for paramour that I know of. Which doesn't mean there aren't any."

"Seems to me she's pretty friendly to most anything in britches."

"Give yourself some credit, brother—she only goes after the good-looking ones." Germain grinned at Wyatt over his glass. "Oh, she flirts a lot. But not so's it'll stick, generally."

"What about her and Dodge? He seemed pretty taken with her himself."

"You've know the man as long as I have, maybe longer," Germain said. "And maybe better in some respects, *non*?"

Wyatt shrugged.

"And we both know he ain't no choirboy. But as long as I've known him, he's been pretty careful. Miz Dodge would draw some lines, seems to me, and that would have to include anybody they socialized with."

Wyatt wondered which of them Germain was trying to convince.

"So what's your theory?" Germain drained his glass.

"I don't have one. But it sure seemed to me that Mrs. Van Dorn wants to think—or wants us to think—the death was an accident. When you saw her that morning—when she was—"

"I took it for an insult to our cuisine at first." Germain sipped at the creamy foam on his second beer. "But if someone's going to get sick on your cooking, it'll usually happen later that evening, small hours at the latest. And did you notice the way she held her hand over her belly? It's like they know, even before they know."

"I bow to your experience in such matters." Wyatt raised his glass. "But then, passing out like that—"

"Smitten by your attentions, no doubt. No, you're right. That's another sign. How they can ever have a healthy child, strapped into those corsets like that, long past the time—"

"Must be hard to have to hide away for months, especially a sociable woman like Milly Van Dorn."

"She doesn't have a choice now," Germain said. "Two birds with one stone, at least, assuming she keeps the child. Gets a chunk of the mourning period out of the way."

"I thought of that too. Like serving concurrent sentences. You know, I was surprised—she told me Van Dorn was thinking about running for Congress."

"Is that a fact."

"I wouldn't have taken him for the political type. I wonder what Mr. Dodge would have thought about that."

Germain raised one shoulder. "Ask him."

"We've talked about a lot of things over the years, but not politics—except about TR visiting, of course. Wonder why he's still so set on him coming, after all this."

"Be a big deal for anybody, having the President come to visit," Germain said. "'Specially for the Mrs. And of course his daddy was a Congressman for a while."

"Wonder if he's ever thought about getting into politics himself," Wyatt mused, as if to himself.

"Why not if he did? He'd be as good as the next fellow."

Wyatt glanced at him quickly and looked away. "Tough situation. A man who might run against you in the caucus turns up dead on your property where the President's due for a visit—wouldn't seem to do you any good."

"That's why he wants you to find out what happened, isn't it?" Germain's voice had an edge.

"Because he might seem to have a motive?" Wyatt looked straight at him.

"Come on! He didn't even know for sure if Van Dorn was going to run."

"What I'm wondering," Wyatt said, swallowing the last of his beer with a quick tilt, "is what Van Dorn knew about him."

"Just where in the hell are you going with this?" Germain's lips tightened and his nostrils flared. "You forgettin' who it is you work for?"

"I work for myself," Wyatt said. "Warren Dodge hires me from time to time to look out for his interests—"

"Doesn't sound to me like you're clear on what that involves." Germain almost hissed the words.

"Look, we don't know what happened to Van Dorn. Not one of us on that island—not one—is in the clear as yet. But if we're not careful, the matter's going to be out of our hands. Frankly, I'm not worried that Dodge had anything to do with it—but I'm not necessarily calling the shots on this investigation, or won't be for much longer anyway."

Germain looked at him, puzzled. "Didn't know there was an investigation."

"Neither did I, until a New York detective turned up at my door."

"A cop?"

"A plainclothesman. Seemed to think I was in on it. Not sure he still doesn't."

Germain tipped his hat back and swallowed the last of his porter, signaling for another round. Wyatt filled him in on Macalester's visit.

"So, the way I see it," Wyatt concluded, "I can try and figure out what happened, or this fellow and his bluecoats will be all over the island. And that will be the end of Roosevelt's visit, not to mention the Dodges' standing in polite society, which likes to keep itself aloof from scandals."

"He have jurisdiction?"

"Technically, no. But Will asked the Commissioner to look into things. And I can't see the county sheriff in Vermont declining to cooperate on a murder investigation, if it came to that. They may resent the big-city boys, but deep down they think they're gods, is my impression."

"So what're we gonna do?" Germain nodded thanks to the waiter. Foam ran down the sides of the two porter glasses and made rings on the scarred table.

"We?"

"You wouldn't have come to me if you didn't want some help."

"No, I suppose not."

"To the extent we're both suspects, like you say, it would boil down to the same motive, wouldn't it?"

"Loyalty?"

"It's what we've got in common." Germain leaned over the table to keep the beer from dripping on his trousers. "So, have you ruled out anybody so far?"

"The Fisks, Cook, the maids. Seems to me Jeremy's out. Will Van Dorn watched him climb out of the water in Keeler's Bay. To make it by then, he'd have had to leave before Van Dorn's likely to have drowned."

"Unless he took the boat and ditched it out of sight somewhere."

"I'd have to think our dago violinist took the boat." Wyatt wiped foam off his mustache with the back of his hand. "It's missing, he's missing—how else would he have got back to the mainland?"

"Maybe he's the one that swam. Or somebody picked him up. And Jeremy killed Van Dorn and then took the boat."

"Doesn't seem likely Jeremy would come back so soon, unless he's a lot more cold-blooded than he looks," Wyatt said. "And what's his motive?"

"In love with the widow-lady? He spent enough time following her around when she had her paints and easels and all. Like Mary's little lamb."

"Lambs don't kill people," Wyatt said. "Wouldn't make sense unless he and the lady had an understanding. Does that seem likely to you?"

"No," Germain admitted. "She was nice enough to him, but she never gave him the full treatment she gave you."

Wyatt cocked an eyebrow.

"You know what I mean." Germain's voice went falsetto. "'Oh, please, Mr. Wyatt, row me over to the mainland, you've got such nice big strong arms—and won't you tell me all about yourself on the way?'"

Wyatt laughed. "You should have gone into acting. But you're right—she has to make conquests. It's what she does to keep the boredom at bay. I'm not sure I could stand being rich."

"And female." Germain took a meditative sip of his porter. "You can move around a lot more easily in that world if you're a man. 'Sides, a lady like that would want to stay in practice. You never know—the man's twenty-five years older than her—when you might be looking for a new husband. Or a little bit of fun on the side."

"I wonder—"

"If she could have done it herself? Get him to the edge of a cliff out there and give him a good hard push? I thought about that. But he was a big heavy man—what if the push hadn't been enough to send him over? Or he managed to stay afloat? And then, when I saw her—you know, bein' sick and all—she was crossing from the house to the headland. Seems like if she'd pushed him, she wouldn't have gone back into the house and then out again, or not soon after anyway."

"I don't see her as the black widow type." Wyatt traced a finger around the wet ring in front of him. "And when I saw her, she just looked miserable, not like someone who'd just murdered her husband."

"Miserable about what, though? She seemed in fine spirits the night before."

"They call it an unhappy condition, don't they?" Wyatt said. "If it was Van Dorn's, she was looking at six or seven months shut away from Society—she'd miss most of the next Season. She told me she was hoping the Dodges could help Gerald get on the board of the Opera."

"Which would've given her more of an excuse to invite handsome tenors over to tea. And if it wasn't Van Dorn's—"

"Maybe she was facing the bill for the fun she'd already had on the side."

"Wouldn't show up for a while," Germain said. "Babies all look alike to most people. Or they see what they want to in their faces—'oh, look, he's got his daddy's nose,' that sort of thing. It'd be later on, toddler stage, you might start to notice. 'less the fella was a different color, of course." His face split in a crooked grin.

Wyatt gave him a sharp look, then smiled. "Maybe we need a closer look at Mrs. Van Dorn's social calendar for this past spring."

"You suppose the father might have—what? Rowed over to the island in the night, lured Van Dorn out in the morning and done him in, then rowed away again?"

"Maybe hid out on one of the neighboring islands. Cormorant or Abenaki," Wyatt said. "Complicated explanation, I admit. On the other hand, the Italian anarchist is a strong possibility, if I can ever find him. So, let's see: we've got Dodge with a motive, Jeremy possibly, you and me, maybe Webb—"

"The doc? Where would he come into it?"

"The boss's friends at the Union Club seem to think he may have been blackballed because someone thought he had a—uh, morphine problem."

Germain stroked his chin thoughtfully. "Well, I'd been wondering about that. Would explain a lot. Not showing up to dinner, that kinda distant look in his eyes—I knew a few hop-fiends in the old days in Lou'siana. And he'd come by the stuff pretty easy, being a medico. So you think Van Dorn might have known about that and done him in with the membership committee?"

"I don't know. But if Webb believed Van Dorn was the one, that might give him a motive."

"I can't see it. If they got a regular supply, hop-heads have a hard time getting up enough energy to get up in the morning, much less kill anybody."

Wyatt told Germain about Webb's "investment" in Colonel Mann's gossip magazine. "So it may have been on its way from blackball to blackmail. That might raise the stakes to murder."

"Any morphine in Van Dorn's blood?"

"The test isn't back yet. I thought about that. I asked Webb about drugs at the autopsy, and he startled like a guilty thing upon a fearful summons—"

"Like Hamlet's ghost," Germain laughed. "You still got a lot of that theater blood in you, brother."

"Said something about all the natural chemicals that could mimic opiates in the blood. I hadn't even mentioned opiates."

"Hmm. If the test comes out positive—"

"That would certainly argue for Webb as our man. If it's negative, it doesn't mean he isn't, but I'd say it lowers the likelihood considerably."

"You haven't mentioned any of the ladies."

"Other than Mrs. Van Dorn herself, it's hard to see how one of them would have pulled it off."

"Get him out to the edge of that cliff, on the north side where the birds are—he loses his footing, and—" Germain pushed his glass to the edge of the table, caught it neatly as it fell.

"Which would argue for bird-watching as the lure for getting him out. Mrs. Fisk—or Amy."

Germain roared. "The kid! Why not the cook, or the maids, while you're at it? Or the string quartet?"

"Other than the anarchist," Wyatt said, "And his is thin

enough, I can't see a motive for any of the others. None of them knew Van Dorn before, unless they're better liars than I think. We've got enough suspects without them. I propose to concentrate on the likelier ones."

"When's this cop gonna be after you again?"

"I expect he'll be knocking on my door in a day or two, looking for a progress report. So will Dodge, for that matter. He's not a patient man, as we both know."

"What're you gonna tell him?"

"I'm not sure yet." Wyatt downed the last of his porter. "I guess I'll head home and think about it."

"I got a better idea," Germain leaned across the table towards Wyatt. "Little parlor place I know of, just south of here. Over towards Wooster Street. Some ladies you might enjoy meeting. Another black-and-tan place, you might say. Lady I know from New Orleans runs it. You game?"

"It's getting late."

"Don't mind my saying so, but you look like a man in need of female company."

Wyatt laughed. "Where'd you get that idea?"

"Been watching you on the island. A little melancholy, in around the eyes. Come on—she does a nice supper, too."

"Isn't Mr. Dodge expecting you back?"

"It's my night off." Germain rose and signaled to the barkeep, ducking to keep his head from hitting the beams. "It's just off Broadway. Her name's Mrs. Beaudoin."

"From your neck of the woods?"

"Long time back. She came up here in '78, to get away from the yellowjack fever. Most of the girls that came with her have moved on. Got married to rich fellas, most of 'em, but she goes back south every now and then. Brought up some new ones a few months ago. Couple of 'em are quadroons, like me."

Wyatt couldn't think of a compelling reason to go home.

CHAPTER 17

M rs. Beaudoin greeted them in her lace-curtained parlor with the dignity of a Knickerbocker dowager. The green carpet bore a design of pink floribunda roses spilling from white urns, and the tufted couches were a soft mauve velvet. Wyatt bowed as he was introduced; to his surprise, she took his hand and gave it a dignified shake.

"It's always a pleasure to meet a friend of Mistuh Germain's." She made the surname into a soft "Jahmun."

"It is that, ma'am," Wyatt smiled into her eyes.

"Oh, you've brought us a charmer, haven't you? Well, now, there's a young lady here I think you'll enjoy getting to know, Mr. Wyatt. *Et bien sûr, votre jeune fille vous attendra comme d'habitude*, Alexis. You'll want some supper, in the Rose Room?"

She led them up a Persian-carpeted staircase and opened a door halfway down the corridor. The serving-maid who had followed her up on noiseless feet placed a silver ice bucket in a stand and presented a bottle of Laurent-Perrier to Germain for his inspection. He raised an eyebrow.

"Well, I guess we're going whole hog tonight. Worthy of the company, though, am I right?" He gestured to the girl to open it, which she did without so much as a pop, pouring it gently into the four flutes that sat expectant on the snowy linen tablecloth. The bubbles rose in straight lines like miniature gold beads.

Germain raised a glass and Wyatt followed suit just as the door opened on two young women in shoulder-grazing evening gowns. The taller was an almond-eyed, olive-skinned sylph with her hair in a ballerina's knot. She wore a black velvet ribbon around a long neck that rose from a swath of celadon green silk. Germain rose and took her hand, kissing it.

"Laura," he murmured. "*Enchanté de te voir encore, cherie.*"

"*Et moi la même,*" she replied gravely. "*Qui est ton copain?*"

"I am forgetting my manners." Germain gestured to Wyatt, who had risen and bowed. "*Mesdames, permettez-moi vous presenter mon ami Monsieur Wyatt.*"

The shorter and livelier girl, who had joyful brown eyes and an ungovernable mass of black curly hair, gave her hand to Wyatt.

"Miss Bella Duvalier," Germain said, "and Miss Laura D'Arbanville."

"*Enchanté de vous faire la connaissance,*" Wyatt managed, bowing again. Bella was in ivory satin, with pink rosebuds and tiny green leaves hiding in the tulle that swathed a healthy young bosom, her flawless skin like a sepia portrait come to life.

"Oh, Mr. Wyatt, you don't have to speak French on our account!" she laughed. "Alexis here jus' likes it because it reminds him of home—*n'est-ce pas,* Alexis?"

"*Comme tu dis, chère,*" he smiled.

The servant returned with a platter of oysters in a cream sauce with bacon and spinach. Mrs. Beaudoin's chef was certainly up to Germain's standards. The oysters gave way to a *consommé brunoise* and *suprêmes de volailles farcies*, the latter accompanied by an excellent claret. Germain had his arm around Laura in a fashion that seemed at once proprietary and protective, as if she were something both precious and fragile. Though Laura was the lovelier of the two by any standard, Wyatt found the vivacious Bella as diverting as Germain had predicted. She kept up a stream of cheery talk about their encounter with Fifth Avenue matrons at the Metropolitan Museum, who had taken her for an art student when she and Laura engaged them in a discussion about Barbizon landscapes. She had been to the Winter Garden recently for a performance of *The Country Wife.*

"The hero—'e pretends 'e is a, you know—*un castrat?*"

"A eunuch?" Wyatt suggested.

"*Oui,* only 'e is just pretending—"

"You ever do that one?" Germain asked Wyatt.

"Oh, you are an actor!" Bella cried, delighted.

"Not any more," Wyatt smiled, "but I did play him once, a long time ago."

"But only to pretend, *hein*?" She lifted an inviting eyebrow.

"You'd best check that out for yourself." Germain rose and helped Laura up from her cushioned chair. "If you'll excuse us—" he turned to a door on his right, and let Laura precede him into the adjoining room.

"So, Monsieur Wy-att who is so qui-et," Bella leaned into him, tickling him around the middle, "we mus' find out whether you are a—"

"Oh, I'm not." Laughing, he raised her by the hand from her chair. "At least, I don't think so. It's been a little while."

She grabbed the edge of his waistcoat and drew him to her. Her kiss tasted of the candied violets that had ended the meal. Sweet and fragrant, like late spring.

"How long have you been here?"

"Almost a year now. Laura has been here for some time. She and Monsieur Germain, I think..." her eyebrows arched and she smiled, nodding in the direction they had gone. "I like it so very much in New York. Everyone who comes here is so gentil. And I do mostly as I please, and Madame Beaudoin is so good—"

A wise woman who knows how to make the most of an investment, Wyatt thought before the girl's fingers began to explore the back of his neck. But thinking was overrated...he reached for the doorknob to the other room.

"And what does it please you to do now?"

The door gave onto a large bathroom with a huge clawfoot tub, filled with steaming, lilac-scented water. Through an arch beyond he could see a canopied bed with a lacy counterpane, the sheets already drawn back.

"Madame insists," Bella gestured apologetically towards the bath.

144

"Oh, I don't mind," Wyatt said, "as long as you join me."

Her face lit up. "Whatever you like, *chèr*."

"Let's make it whatever we both like."

She began loosening a row of tiny covered buttons along the back of her dress, her arms twisting in frustration.

"Please—let me help." Wyatt reached for her back. The pool of creamy satin dropped around her like petals falling from a rose. Beneath, she wore tulle petticoats and a pink satin corset, lightly boned; she didn't need much to keep her exquisite shape. She reached for his tie.

"Turnabout is fair play, *non*?"

It was an eternity of delicious frustration, but he had learned patience. He waited for her all through the sudsy, splashing laughter of the bath, the drying off in thick white towels, the carrying-off to the bed, perfumed with lavender, the exploration, the touches, the tastes. The need that had surged up in him fought with the urge to be gentle and slow, to savor the moment and stay in it, to learn and enjoy every smooth curve and undulation of that perfect sepia skin. At last the release, breaking open something within him, his own tears taking him by surprise.

"I'm sorry," he said. "It just…"

She put a hand over his mouth. "Please—say nothing. I am flattered." He let his breathing slow, felt himself go quiet. Propped on one arm, he wound her curls around his fingers, traced the lines of her exquisite body with his gaze, a sleepy half-smile on his face.

"If I could make you feel as I just felt…" he said after a while, "I'd be worth something in this world."

She looked steadily at him for a moment, then began to laugh in great lusty peals, infectious as a yawn or a sneeze.

"Oh, I am so sorry, but—you are so serious!" she gasped between trills of laughter. She strained up and kissed him on the end of his nose. He stared back at her for a moment, fell to her side and laughed as long and loud as he could remember since he'd been a farm-boy at his first circus. He took her in the crook of his arm and smoothed the curly hair back from her forehead.

He realized suddenly that he couldn't remember a single time when he and Rose had laughed like that. He had loved her with an intensity that anticipated its own loss, never felt a moment of comfort and ease and sheer joy like this in all their years together. *A man that loved not wisely but too well*…but it was she who had burned too brightly, consumed herself in her own flame, and he had had to turn away from it at last to save himself. And here, of all places, in a courtesan's bed, he began to forgive himself for that. Bella's laugh was an embrace of life. How long he had shunned that embrace…

"You are quiet again. *Tu penses trop, je crois.*" Bella's brow furrowed.

He smiled and kissed her. "No, I'm just thinking of how nice it is to be with you."

She smiled, gave a sigh like a sleepy child, and fell asleep in his arms. *I should go*, he thought, *but it would be a shame to disturb her*, and then he joined her in dreams.

He woke at first light with a sensation of something unattended to. The girl lay on her stomach, rosy sleep on her face, breath coming slow and even. He slid from the bed and retrieved his scattered clothes from the bathroom floor. Passing through the small supper room, he saw that the door through which Laura and Germain had left the night before was still closed. He put his ear to the door but could hear nothing. He tiptoed out into the corridor and stole down the carpeted stairs.

He would settle up with Germain later. And he would come back, with or without him. Today, he had to find out what had happened to the Italian musician. Macalester would be back soon to call him to account, and Dodge was waiting none too patiently for the resolution that would salvage the President's visit.

He reached the end of the block of old-fashioned painted brick houses and began to round the corner, missing the figure which stepped out from the shadows of a narrow alleyway. He felt something grab his arm, and an urgent tug at the sleeve of his jacket. Instinctively he whirled and seized the intruder by the lapels. The man let out a strangled cry.

"Mr. Wyatt!"

Who knew him here? The man before him was a stranger, small and slight, neatly dressed, with high cheekbones and dark, slicked-back hair. His accent was Slavic.

"Please—I must talk with you. I am Karel Czerny."

Astonished, Wyatt let go. "What are you doing here? How did you find me?"

"You had left address. And I send Milosz to your house and he puts on disguise and follows you and colored fellow on trolley to bar. Then to house on Wooster Street. He comes back and gets me, says looks like place you will be for some time—" Wyatt felt the back of his neck grow warm, "—and I come here and wait for you to come out."

"Why the cloak-and-dagger? Why didn't you just come to my house yourself, if you wanted to talk to me?"

"I was afraid you might have police waiting there for me— that it might be a trap."

"A trap? Why on earth—"

"Shh! Not a good place to talk. Please, follow me. A place for coffee— where the night warehouse-men go—"

Czerny led Wyatt southeast down Wooster Street to Canal and beyond. He had been hired as a violinist in the Metropolitan Opera orchestra the previous day, he announced proudly; the audition had been a success. He led the way to a cramped little café near the new Mulberry Bend Park which had replaced some of the worst slums of the old Five Points. He made only a feeble protest when Wyatt ordered and paid for two bacon-and-egg breakfasts. They settled onto a pair of rickety chairs around a tiny table.

"Now I must explain—"

"Eat first." Wyatt said, sipping gratefully on the strong coffee.

The man looked as if he hadn't had a decent meal in some time, and he fell on the food with abandon. He mopped up the last scrap of egg yolk with the thick toast that had been provided.

"This man you are looking for," Czerny began cautiously. "You told Milosz he is—an anarchist? A revolutionary?"

"He talked like one, the other fellows said. Ranting against capitalists and such."

"What did he look like?"

"Five foot ten or eleven, curly hair, auburn or chestnut I'd say. Full beard, medium build—well set-up fellow," Wyatt remembered. "Name was Rossi, claimed to be from Carrara. Said he'd met you playing at some workers' benefit at Cooper Union."

"But I never met this man, or even heard of him till now. All I knew was that I had been—what is the phrase—let go. Fired, don't you say?" Czerny frowned. "But he is Italian? Not Slav, like me?"

"That's what he said. Look, when you got this note from Mrs. Webb, or whoever really sent it—did you talk to Stefan or the other members of the quartet? Or contact them later?"

"My pride was hurt. I could not bear to go to my colleagues in such a state of disgrace. I thought perhaps they had said something bad about me to the Webbs. By the time I decided I must talk to them, they had left Shelburne Farms and gone to the island."

"That's too bad," Wyatt said. "Someone could certainly have had a word with the Webbs, and this fellow might have been exposed in time—"

Czerny still looked troubled. "It is so strange—this man seems to have known much about me, to follow me as he did and—take my position away from me. I am wondering—" he fell silent.

He's wondering if the man had found something out about him, Wyatt thought. *Something that could bring down the police on him—*

"Mr. Czerny—are you telling me that you are an anarchist also? And you came to find me because you were worried this Rossi fellow might have ratted you out?"

Fear leapt into Czerny's eyes, but he swallowed and nodded, then spoke quickly.

"You must understand, Mr. Wyatt—we are not violent. We study, we publish newspaper, some of us give speeches and lectures. This man you describe—he is no one we know of. Italians have their groups and we have ours. But I think also he is not of our beliefs. It is sacred thing with us, to keep silent about our activities. The man you talk of breaks his oath most terribly, if he was indeed of the brotherhood. We are not supposed to get so drunk to not be in command of our speaking. Even then, I have seen comrades who are drinking a great deal and still hold their tongues. No, I think your man was setting up a—how do you call it? Red fish of some kind."

"A red herring," Wyatt ventured.

"Exactly so."

"Mr. Czerny, I would be glad to speak to the Webbs to clear up this matter, if you wish to return to your former situation."

"Thank you." The young man's voice was grave. "I would desire to—clear the air, I think you say, between me and the Webbs, and perhaps to have a letter of good character. But now that I have secured this new position, it is better for me, you see, for I will not have to leave my home and my daughter who is so small."

"I am glad to know it." Wyatt realized with some relief that if Czerny did not come back to the Webbs, there would be no reason for him—or this brotherhood of his—to find out that Roosevelt was coming to the island. In that respect, at least, the substitute violinist had done Dodge a favor.

"But my comrades and I must continue to speak out, to write—there is so much injustice, even here in America—"

"Do you call for violence?" Wyatt's eyes were cold. "If you do, I count you no different from the criminals who practice it."

Czerny bridled and stared directly back at him. "If you knew how people have to live, you would understand," he said quietly.

"After seeing the results of your propaganda up close, Mr. Czerny, I can't think of anything that justifies it." The look of stricken surprise on McKinley's kindly face flashed before Wyatt's eyes. "But you'll have no cause to worry from me in this instance. You seem an honest man."

Czerny inclined his head.

"But I'd watch myself if I were you. There are laws now—they can throw you out of the country for that kind of thing. And I dare say you wouldn't want to have to go back to—"

Czerny had risen and was holding up his hand. "Mr. Wyatt—please. I must make you understand. I beg you to come with me."

They walked east several blocks and turned onto a narrow street. The stink of garbage assaulted Wyatt's nostrils from an alley where washing, barely stirring in the stagnant air, stretched overhead on pulleys between the back walls of five-storey tenements. Piles of rubbish everywhere, a starved-looking pup with a patch over one eye nosing through potato peelings, old soup bones, cabbage leaves. Boys kicking a battered ball, gap-toothed old men in combinations and galluses, smoking pipes on stoops.

Climbing the front stoop of a derelict-looking building, they almost collided with three men descending the steps. Young, muscular, and ill-clothed, they stared at Wyatt in hostile surprise and began berating Czerny, whom they evidently knew well, in some Slavic tongue.

The largest of them, a black-bearded fellow, shoved Wyatt in the chest and knocked him backwards down the stairs, barely able to keep his footing and grabbing a wobbly railing for support. The man followed Wyatt down and seized a lapel of his jacket, swinging him onto the sidewalk and grazing Wyatt's cheek with a roundhouse punch whose momentum threw him off balance and sent the assailant, with the help of a push from Wyatt, crashing to the pavement.

Wyatt spun round as the other two men broke off from yelling at Czerny and rushed towards him. He tried lowering his head and charging between them, but other men started running out of the alleyway and off the neighboring stoops, piling onto him. Wyatt's hat rolled away and his jacket was half pulled off before Czerny put an abrupt stop to the melée by standing on the top step and yelling something at the top of his lungs. It sounded like "Nem haziur! Derek ember!"

Whatever it was, it had an immediate effect. The crowd parted and backed away. Wyatt leaned on the shaky railing, getting his breath back. Czerny rounded on the three who had started the fight and berated them in his turn, the neighbor men listening intently. The men who had started the fight gave Wyatt looks of mingled embarrassment and annoyance. One of them retrieved Wyatt's hat and the other awkwardly brushed dust off his jacket before helping him back into it. The third offered a grubby-looking handkerchief which Wyatt waved away. The crowd began to disperse.

Czerny took Wyatt's elbow. "Let's go up, Mr. Wyatt. I am sorry."

"What the hell was that all about?"

"They thought you were the landlord. Your nice clothes, you see."

Czerny led Wyatt up the steps into a dank hallway and up a narrow staircase, climbing floor after floor to the top. Worn wooden treads, gray plank floors in the hallways, great holes and cracks in the walls, curls of peeling paint. He heard scratchings and scrabblings behind the walls, caught something gray slinking off out of the corner of his eye. Smells of stale tobacco and cooking grease, and foul privies at the turns on the stairs. The place was a firetrap. No wonder those men had it in for the landlord.

They reached the top and Czerny knocked on a door. It was opened by a barefoot, underfed girl in a shift that had once been white, barest buds of breasts swelling above the low scoop of the neckline. A seductive smile vanished when she recognized Czerny.

"What are you doing here?" A flash of green-gray eyes.

"I want him to see Tomàs."

151

"He's asleep. Where's—" Czerny raised a hand to stop her. She stepped back to let them enter a small, dark room with a stove and sink. The place smelled of sickness and something else, some yeasty funk that he couldn't quite place. Curtains, tattered and faded, covered the opening of the room beyond and another room on the right. A fluttering wheeze came from the room ahead, a horrible sound like scissors ripping silk.

She held back the curtain, dashing a straggle of dirty-blonde curls from her face. The room she admitted them to was not much more than two strides across and three long. Pale brown wallpaper on one wall, darkened by grease-stains. A narrow, curtainless window propped open with a stick, the air it admitted little fresher than what the room already held. Hanging on a nail near the window were a small jacket and shirt, frayed at cuffs and collar. A wooden crucifix on the wall, the corpus dangling by one nailed hand. A swaybacked chair by the side of a narrow iron cot on which lay a small boy, surely not more than six or seven, gasping for air, his thin shoulders heaving with the effort.

Czerny and Wyatt crowded into the room, all but filling it.

"The fever's come back," the girl said. The child's wasted, elfin face and pointed chin were pale, but the red spots in his cheeks glowed like brands. There were no sheets, only a scrap of blanket on the ticking of the thin mattress under the boy. No pillow but a shirt or undergarment of some kind folded under his head. A shawl covered him to the chest. His scrawny neck and shoulders were bare. As they watched he began to shiver convulsively.

"Consumption," Czerny gestured towards the boy. The girl pulled the shawl up around the child's throat. The shuddering wheeze filled the room.

"I know what I'm looking at," Wyatt snapped. "Why isn't he in a hospital?"

"What will they do for him there? Put him in a charity ward and leave him to die? There are no spas in the mountains for him with verandahs and nurses. At least here his sister can look in on him while his mother is at the sewing contractor's."

"And the father?"

"Gone to look for work in the mines in Pennsylvania. He worked in Paterson, but they fired him last year after the strike. They have no word from him for a while. Another child is expected soon."

Wyatt grabbed the jacket and shirt from the wall and bundled them into a wedge. He lifted the child's head gently and tucked the bundle under it.

"He needs elevation," he told the startled Czerny, who was staring at him. "The lungs fill up. Like drowning. This helps a little."

There was a knock on the outer door. The girl stepped lightly out of the room to answer it. Wyatt heard a man's voice, jocular and teasing, then hers, murmuring. The rattle of curtain-rings opening and closing again. The squeak of bedsprings. He realized now what the smell was that he'd noticed on the way in.

"Do you know how much she gets for that?" Czerny's eyes were blazing now. "Enough to buy a meat pie and a head of cabbage. With perhaps a little left over that she will save to buy a blanket or a pillow for him. But more profitable than anything else she can do. Their mother's wages pay the rent."

"How old is she?"

"Thirteen. A little younger, I am sure, than your perfumed ladies of last evening. She has some regulars now, so she does not need to go out on the streets so much."

Wyatt ignored the reference. "What's her connection to your—your brotherhood?"

"We found her walking the street one night. One of the brothers brought her in. She comes in the evenings and cooks for them sometimes. We pay her when we can, or give her some of the food to bring home."

More sound came from the adjoining room now, low moans and little shrieks and gasps and the regular screech of the bedsprings, in weird counterpoint to the shuddering wheezes and occasional brassy coughs of the dying child.

"And you let her keep doing this?"

"It is not for me or anyone to say. Except her mother, and what choice does she have? She has to earn a living like anyone else, and there is the new child on the way." Czerny's tone held no hint of irony. "There are two or three others like her in this building, dozens up and down the street. Some younger than she."

"Who owns this rat-trap?"

Czerny shrugged. "Some syndicate. Some corporation. If we knew, we would make them pay for what they do—you see how my friends acted, thinking you might be the owner! An agent rents the flats, collects the rents and evicts those who have not the money. He does this for many landlords. But he has nothing to do with repairs, he says. Nor does he seem to know who does."

"Look, let me at least get him some—" Wyatt reached for his money-clip. It was gone. So were his silver-gilt pocket-watch and chain. Rose's last gift to him, her picture on the inside of its cover. *I would not have given it for a wilderness of monkeys.* His apartment key was still in his vest-pocket.

"Those goons down there—!"

"They anticipated your charitable impulse, Mr. Wyatt. She and the boy will get some of the money, I am sure."

"The watch was a gift. I wouldn't have given that up."

"You must be happy to know how many will benefit from it," Czerny gave him a bleak smile. "When it has been sold. The brotherhood will see to it."

"I'm not one of your rich capitalists," Wyatt said through clenched teeth, "any more than you are. I work for them just like you."

"No one's ever given me a gold watch, Mr. Wyatt."

"If we weren't here with this child, I would knock you down."

"Then I will be wise to stay with him while you make your way home." Czerny fished in his pocket and brought out a handful of coins. "Misha—the dark haired one—said to give you this. So you could get back across town. I am sorry. But it could have been much worse."

Wyatt contained himself with an effort, decided to salvage

something from the situation. "You have my address. If you or any of those fellows get any wind of this bearded musician, you'll let me know?"

"Certainly. But it seems most unlikely, does it not?"

The child had fallen back into uneasy sleep. Wyatt stared down at him for a moment. The noise in the other room had given way to the scrape of belt-buckle and slither of clothes being picked up off the floor, murmurs of pleasantries. He pushed through the curtain, strode down the hall and found the front stairway.

It was late morning now, the weather sultry, threatening thunder, but the outdoor air was sweet after the hellish fetor of the tenement. He headed south on Park Row and west to City Hall. The land records of the Manhattan Borough Clerk's office could at least tell him the name of the hated landlord, the man who should be held accountable for the condition of the tenement in which the boy lay gasping out his life.

"Title search, please." He gave the address to a clerk in gold-rimmed spectacles. She nodded and went to a tall oak cabinet with brass pulls and label-frames, opened a drawer and flipped through the cards. She handed a card to him, went to open the gate that would admit him to the vaults where the land records lay in their great red leather books.

"Thanks, but it won't be necessary." Wyatt stared back down at the typescript on the card. *243 Catherine Street. Title transferred in 1895 to Dutch Masters Partnership. Principals Peter Bahrens, Herndrick TerHorst and—*

Gerald Van Dorn.

He handed back the card. "Heard of this outfit?"

"The Dutch Masters?" The clerk looked up from the card and smiled. "Only because they own half the slums in lower Manhattan."

CHAPTER 18

The El rattled north past a brown-and-gray ribbon of tenements. Wyatt sat staring ahead, his eyes unfocused. He tried to rid his mind of the face of the dying child, stop the wheezing sound in his ears of the lungs gasping for air, block the memories of Rose's last months that came back to haunt him again. The ache of loss renewed, of anger and helplessness. Odd how one could know that the city held thousands like Tomás, dying, all but abandoned in a crowded, indifferent world, and not feel the outrage and grief till forced to stare one of them in the face.

Work, as so often before, was his anodyne. He turned over in his mind the connections that eluded him. Could Czerny and his group really not know that Van Dorn had owned some of the worst slums in New York? It seemed unlikely. But foreign anarchists weren't the sort of people who visited City Hall to do title searches. They would surely be challenged if they tried in any case. And one thing was certain: Czerny had not been on Heron Island when Van Dorn died. Wyatt was sure now that he knew nothing of the man who replaced him.

Germain's account of the odd musician squared with what he had learned from the other players: the fellow was either an anarchist whose tongue was dangerously loosened by drink, or someone who wanted to be thought of as such. To cover what? An identity as a hired killer? That argued against his having been a stalking-horse for someone who knew of Roosevelt's intended visit. Such a person would surely have made himself as inconspicuous as possible. But it might be the strategy to adopt if you wanted to cover up a more private motive—of someone who wanted to kill Gerald Van Dorn for his own reasons, or on behalf of someone else with his own reasons. Or hers...

A loose-talking anarchist might be a handy fall-back in case a coroner's verdict came in as death by misadventure rather than accident. Since Dr. Webb's results were inconclusive, inclining more to accident, the man—if he was a killer—might have saved himself the trouble and complication of an elaborate charade. And it was this thought that convinced Wyatt—even more, he realized, than he had been convinced before—that someone killed Van Dorn, or had him killed, for a private and compelling reason. The Dodges had a motive, if Macalester was to be believed. Germain was not above suspicion, though Wyatt had little to base it on beyond the man's loyalty to an ambitious employer and a sense that Germain made his own rules. Webb himself might have had reasons for wanting Van Dorn dead. Mrs. Van Dorn stood to gain a good deal.

What about Jeremy and his infatuation with her? Could he afford to believe Jeremy's story about the early-morning swim to South Hero? Will Van Dorn had vouched for him, but people often engaged close friends to vouch for them. Heaven forbid, was even Amy a possibility? A pretty cool customer, if so—but there were men who abused children. Could Gerald, for all his seeming innocuousness, have made some overtures to her, or even molested her? It seemed fantastic.

His mind drifted to Will Van Dorn. Milly had said something about his coming to make up a quarrel. Something about an estate on the Hudson, or in the Adirondacks? Amy thought Will a "straight shooter", and Wyatt, despite his brief speculations on Amy's own motives, was inclined to take that on trust. The girl struck him as both guileless and a good judge of character. And presumably there were those who could vouch for Will's presence on the train up from the City the night before, or at least who would remember his alighting in South Hero.

But that didn't mean Will couldn't have been involved in his father's death. People of his station in life were accustomed to hiring others to do their dirty work. But what would be his motive? Was anger over the prospective loss of a beloved estate enough to make a son kill his father? Will had been open about the quarrel, and seemingly tortured with remorse when he learned of his father's death. And it had been he who insisted on calling in the New York police.

He needed to learn the contents of Van Dorn's will. Macalester would have thought of that already, might even have seen it by now. On the walk up the short street to his apartment, he remembered that Macalester was expecting a report on his visit to Mrs. Van Dorn, after which he had threatened to send him off to question Augusta Dodge. He still had a couple of days, though. Macalester had given him the week.

But the Scotsman was waiting for him at his landlady's. He came out of Mrs. Baird's door as Wyatt plodded up the front steps and into the hallway.

"Well! Don't you look like somethin' the cat dragged in. Visitin' the lady friend in the Lower East Side again?" Macalester's tone was insufferably cheerful.

"I had a rough morning."

"And most of the day, it seems. Care to elaborate?"

"No," Wyatt fished for his apartment key and started up the stairs. "Aren't you a little early?"

Macalester followed in his wake. "I'm afraid I've to inform you that a complaint has been lodged against you." Wyatt turned back and saw a hard twinkle in the policeman's eye.

"What kind of complaint?"

"By the good Doctor Tinmuth, on behalf of the bereaved widow. Something to the effect of you weaselin' your way into her house and making an improper advance."

Wyatt squeezed his eyes shut and rubbed the bruise on his cheek. "Oh, for God's sake." They reached his landing and he let himself in. Macalester walked into Wyatt's study and sat on the desk-chair.

"Now, despite your smart remarks about fortune-hunting, I don't think I was mistaken in assuming that you'd behave like a gentleman. So, suppose you tell me your side of things."

"Did he get this from her, or what?"

"I doubt the lady came right out with that. And of course the young fella would have heard about it too—Will, I mean—and no doubt had something to say about it. But the medical man says he found her in a state of shock, muttering something about 'don't let Mr. Wyatt—' and then the maid told him about how she came on the two of you, and you were goin' on about loosenin' her stays—"

"She swooned at my feet." Wyatt collapsed into an armchair. "*On* my feet, actually. She's far enough along that the damn corsets were constricting her breathing. She wasn't getting enough air—"

Macalester leaned forward. "Far enough along? She's in a delicate condition?"

"From everything I've heard and seen, yes."

"Well, now. That certainly puts an interestin' twist on the situation. What led you to this conclusion?"

Wyatt relayed Germain's story of the morning at the lake.

"So she's maybe three or four months along by now, would you think?"

"Who knows. Somewhere in there."

"She hasn't mentioned this to you?"

"Can't imagine why she would. But no, nor to anyone else as far as I know." Wyatt folded a wet washcloth and laid it over his eyes. "What does the will say?"

"You may well ask. I'll tell you, after you tell me what you found out about our friend the anarchist."

A grim laugh emerged from beneath the washcloth. "I was wondering when you'd get round to asking me about that, considering the damn trouble my inquiries got me into." Wyatt told Macalester the story of his visit to the tenement, omitting his activities immediately prior to the encounter with Czerny.

"Dear me, that all sounds most unpleasant." The Scotsman's voice held a note of genuine concern.

"Oddly enough, they don't strike me as a dangerous lot—if

I'd been who they thought I was, they'd have been entirely justified in beating me up, " Wyatt added, with a stab of pain at the memory of the stolen watch.

"But you say this Czerny himself is an anarchist?"

"In the debating-society sense. He's a violinist, first and foremost. I think he'll lose his taste for politics when he settles in at the Met. He's got a young family to feed, and now he has a decent job to do it with."

"But surely he might've been in league with the fella who replaced him—"

"He was pretty upset over the replacement," Wyatt said. "Hard to fake that."

"And he'd got the letter on Mrs. Webb's stationery, too," Macalester mused. "Though it could've been Czerny who forged that, I suppose."

"I don't speak their language, but when the wife heard what I'd come about, she let me know she was spitting mad at the Webbs. I suppose Czerny could have lied to her, but why give up good-paying work like that, especially if you're an anarchist yourself and could take advantage of the spying opportunity as well as any substitute?"

"Right enough." Macalester rose and looked out the small window towards the park and the river. "I paid a wee visit to Mr. Van Dorn's solicitor."

"He talk to you?"

"After a gentle reminder that I could subpoena the will if necessary. Quite the toff, our Mr. Pendergast. Silver-haired, silver-tongued—and silver-spooned at birth, if I'm not mistaken. If I were inclined to dandyism, I'd do well to meet his tailor."

"Who gets what?"

Macalester turned back from the window. "Patience, laddie, I'm coming to it. Our learned counsel is the estate's executor. The missus gets the town house and its contents, and then half of everything that's left—"

"Regardless of the number of children involved?"

"Aye, and that's what makes your news about her condition so interesting. Seems the son and heir will now be splitting his half of the fortune with a half-brother or sister, whose share will be held in trust by the aforementioned Mr. Pendergast."

Wyatt tossed aside the washcloth and reached for a crumpled towel. "What happens to Blauwberg? The country retreat?"

"Ah! Now that's an interestin' thing as well. Seems Mr. Van had had a wee chat with Pendergast last week and told him to prepare a deed of gift."

"For who?"

"Will, of course. He'd thought it over after their quarrel. He'd decided that if the place meant that much to the laddie, with the memories of his mother and all, he'd just make it over to him. Which would've taken it out of the estate altogether. However, he didn't live long enough to sign the deed."

"So now it's part of the residual estate? How much is it worth?"

"It'll depend on how it's valued. Mr. Pendergast says the old Hudson places aren't as fashionable as they once were, compared to Newport or the Berkshires, like. But he thinks it would run to about a third of the residual value, or a wee bit more."

"So if it was just Will and Mrs. Van Dorn, Will could keep Blauwberg—"

"Assuming she agreed, which I dare say she would. Whereas," Macalester returned and sat in Wyatt's desk-chair, "if there's a new heir to be reckoned into it, it'll have to be liquidated."

"Or held jointly by Will and the new heir."

"Pendergast wouldn't hear of that. It would be—what did he say? A breach of his fiduciary duty, when he could invest funds in railways and steel and such for a good return. He thought he was speakin' hypothetically, of course, since neither of us had an inkling about Mrs. V's condition."

"Did Will know about his father's change of heart?"

"It would seem not. By all accounts, including yours, he was distraught when he heard of his father's death, seein' as he hadn't had the chance to apologize for the quarrel. For that matter, Pendergast seems to think that neither Will nor Mrs. V. knew what was in Van Dorn's will."

Wyatt pounced. "But he's not sure about that. What if Van Dorn had told his wife of his plans to settle Blauwberg on Will?"

"And hadn't told Will? Oh, I see what you're thinkin'. A motive for gettin' rid of him before he signed it—keep her share of the estate bigger, and the baby's as well. But from what you've told me, it wouldn't have been necessary to murder him—she could've sweet-talked the old fella out of it if she'd wanted to."

"So where does this leave us, as far as family motives go?"

"Not much further along," Macalester said gloomily. "Will would've been better off if his father had lived to deed Blauwberg over to him."

Wyatt was thoughtful. "But he thought his father was going to sell it. That gives him a motive."

"Then why advertise the fact the minute he arrives on the island?" Macalester was enjoying the chess-game aspect of the conversation.

"True. And the irony is that Blauwberg will probably have to go anyway, to split the estate among the three heirs. As for Mrs. Van Dorn, her motive would arise if she knew of her husband's plans, but we've no indication she did." Wyatt sighed and rubbed his forehead. "It comes down to who knew what and when, which we don't know. Now, will you excuse me? I'd like to take a nap."

"You young folk have no stamina."

"I've had a long day already."

"You've told me that, but I'm not quite done with you yet. Some fresh air will do you good. Walk me back to HQ and we'll have a chat and some grub along the way—my treat. You've a lean and hungry look."

Wyatt sighed. He seemed to spend most of his time with this police inspector in a state of resignation.

After indulging in corned-beef sandwiches, chilled lager and further speculations on the impact of Van Dorn's will, they left the saloon and followed Broadway south towards police headquarters on Mulberry Street, at the northern edge of the old Five Points. Macalester flipped a dime at a ragged newsboy in exchange for a copy of *Puck*, whose golden namesake grinned and winked from his pedestal on a massive red building across Houston Street. The cover featured Roosevelt, in Rough Rider garb, charging up a hill where snarling plutocrats awaited him with kettles of boiling oil.

"Heaven knows what they'll do for material when he's retired." Macalester shook his head. Across Mulberry Street from *Puck*, Wyatt noticed a small greengrocer's shop displaying colorful pyramids of fruit.

"Strawberries," he held up a finger. "I'll be right back." He crossed the street and exchanged a handful of coins for a balsawood box spilling over with dark red berries.

"These'll be the last of the season." He proffered the box to Macalester, who took one and devoured it, stalk and all.

"Mister Wyatt, were you in any position to ascertain Mr. Van Dorn's capacities in—ahem—the romantic arena?"

"Why on earth would you think I would be?"

"You're a man of the world, are you not? Gentlemen are known to take their pleasures, in the company of other gentlemen, in discreet parlors about the City—"

"I never went drabbing with him, if that's what you're getting at," Wyatt snapped.

"Drabbing. An interestin' choice of word. Might Mister Dodge have done so?"

"What *are* you getting at, Inspector?"

"What I'm wonderin' about, is whether Mister Van Dorn could even have brought about his wife's condition." Macalester stopped with one foot on the Police Department steps. "Whether he was—entirely functional, in that respect. Gentlemen of his age and physical condition, as I understand, don't always find themselves able to—"

Wyatt remembered Germain's speculations on the same topic. It occurred to him it was hardly fair to suspect a woman like Milly Van Dorn of gross infidelities simply because she was an accomplished flirt; in the world of the wealthy, such behavior was social currency and acceptable pastime. Which led him, no help for it, to picture little Tomás and his sister in their foul tenement, where life was lived in deadly earnest.

"So you're thinking that once he learned of the pregnancy, he might have known the child wasn't his. But his death renders that moot, doesn't it?"

"Precisely my point."

"And in that case, even if his death were accidental, or caused by someone else, it would cloud the widow in suspicion? Possibly the son as well, if Van Dorn hadn't got round to telling him he wasn't going to sell Blauwberg after all."

"But Will's well out of it," Macalester reminded him. "He was on the train up to Vermont that night."

Two young women in flashy pink and blue satins sashayed down the sidewalk between Wyatt and Macalester, leering invitation and leaving a cloud of sickly-sweet musk in their wake.

"Evenin', ladies." Macalester tipped his hat as they passed, as if they had been the Misses Vanderbilt. He turned back to Wyatt.

"We've the punched train-ticket, and the conductor saw him come out of his sleeping compartment as they pulled in to South Hero. That would've been about half-past six, quarter to seven in the morning. Helped him off the train with his bags, too. He'd got on in New York and hadn't come out of his sleeper compartment since then. It was one of thae fancy ones with the wee lavatory in it."

Wyatt stared after the streetwalkers, pulled his gaze back to Macalester. "What about the violinist? We still haven't figured out who he was or what he was doing there."

"Come on up to my lair for a minute, then I'll let you go."

Macalester pulled open the door and let Wyatt precede him. "Him disappearin' along with the boat, and Van Dorn's death the same morning—you can't help but put the two together. And you say Czerny and his crew of anarchists knew nothing of him?"

"Nothing whatever. They're Slavs, for one thing, and they don't mix with the Italian lot, or so he claims. They're more talk than action, was my impression. Perhaps a little property damage from time to time to draw attention to their cause. Czerny was appalled by the man's indiscretion."

"We should see about the Italians, I suppose," Macalester unlocked his office door and gestured Wyatt to a wooden side chair. "Though there's not so many of them about now, in the City, since the Paterson business last year. They've been lyin' low. But I've a fella I can send down—"

Wyatt picked up a plump strawberry from the box and bit into it. The red sweetness burst open a memory. He sat the box on the edge of Macalester's desk.

"Inspector—there's no reason to assume the violinist was from New York. All that stuff about meeting Czerny at Cooper Union was lies—he could have been from anywhere."

"Why bother mentionin' Cooper Union, then?"

"Maybe that was just another diversion." Wyatt told him about the anarchist newspaper Germain had found in the strawberries, the same paper he'd found among the things the violinist left in the cellar of the guest cottage. " You could be from anywhere and have heard of Cooper Union. Maybe this fellow's a—what would you call him? A Galleanist."

"Now that's an interestin' thought, right enough! He might even have been a local, then. What's this place in Vermont with the nest of anarchists and socialists you were telling me about?"

"Barre. They're granite-workers for the most part. That's where the paper's being published."

Macalester reached over and grabbed a handful of strawberries. "These are nothin' to the Lanarkshire berries, mind, but they're not bad. Here's what we'll do. I'll go ahead an' send our fella out into the Italian neighborhoods here, and you have another wee jaunt back to Vermont."

"I don't speak Italian."

"Your fella spoke English, didn't he? And it's not as though they've been in America for years and haven't picked up the language."

"Granted, but my point is that they're not likely to open up to a total stranger. In fact, if they're anything like what I saw of the New York crowd—"

"You're an actor, aren't you?" Macalester turned from the window and eyed Wyatt.

"That only takes you so far. Inspector, it seems I need to remind you that I don't work for you."

"Mister Wyatt, it seems I need to remind you that you and your employer and his family are still under suspicion in a murder investigation. Now if you'd rather, I can call in the Grand Isle County Sheriff. I'm sure he'd be only too happy to look into a wee bit of skulduggery among the summering gentry. And while he's at it, ask the local M.E. to have a closer look at the death certificate, considering it was signed by a fella that's been out of practice for twenty years."

Wyatt let out an exasperated sigh. "Just how long are you going to trade on this?"

"As long as it takes. Besides, now that you've thought of it, you'd go off and do this yourself if I hadn't suggested it."

"I'd want to check it out, yes. But I wouldn't go in there unprepared."

"Well, now we're talkin' some sense. This paper you found was in a shipment from Burlington?"

"Burlington Grocery, yes. They're on the lakefront."

"You might start there and see if ye can find the fella that put the paper in the strawberry crate. It bein' a new one, I don't suppose it's the kinda thing they'd just have had lyin' about to use for liners."

"The *Free Press* would've been more typical at that. It almost seemed deliberate. As if someone were trying to send a message."

"Maybe so," Macalester murmured through a mouthful of strawberry. "Suppose you see if you can find the fella and ask him to be a wee bit more direct about whatever he was tryin' to say."

"They probably use a lot of day-laborers there."

"All the easier for you to get taken on. Do an honest day's work for a change."

Wyatt removed the basket from Macalester's desk. "Bad idea to insult a fellow when you're eating his strawberries."

"I bought you dinner, as I recall."

"After dragging me off on police business that you're not paying me for. Not that I didn't appreciate the dinner."

"I should think the Dodges' undying gratitude for solvin' this wee mystery before Mister Roosevelt's visit would be recompense enough."

Wyatt laughed. "That depends on what I find out in Vermont, doesn't it?"

"Ah, speaking of which—" Macalester braced his arms on the desk and leaned forward towards Wyatt, "since you'll be visiting the Dodges before you head up to Vermont, it wouldn't be a bad opportunity to see what Dodge knows about that black-balling business of Webb's. And look a wee bit further into the question of Mrs. Dodge's ancestry."

Wyatt rose, folded his arms and shook his head. "You can do your own damned dirty work. I'll go to Vermont, but I'm not going to spy on the Dodges for you." He heard the chill in his own voice. "Get your detectives to work them over if you have to. Warren Dodge is my employer and my friend. I've trespassed on that relationship quite enough already."

Macalester shrugged. "That's up to you, then. But I've got a job to do."

CHAPTER 19

Amy came in from the walled garden of the Dodges' brownstone through the back parlor's French doors, letting in a warm, rose-scented breeze. "Mother, when are we going back to the Camp?"

Augusta was embroidering a handkerchief stretched on a small hoop. "With indecent haste, if your father has his way. Really, with poor Mrs. Van Dorn in the state she's in, and no family of her own to turn to—"

"She's got Will. He's family."

Augusta looked up. Her maid had dressed Amy's hair not two hours since, and already it was as tangled as the tresses of Medusa. "It's not the same, dear. A mother, a sister, a cousin, even—it would make all the difference at a time like this."

Amy plopped heavily down on the sofa next to her mother. "Oh, really! Mrs. Van Dorn isn't poor at all, she's a rich young widow, and she won't be alone for very long. Her young man will turn up after a decent interval—"

"What young man? Good heavens, child, where do you come by these sordid notions?"

"Oh, stop being such a hypocrite, Mother. You've been thinking the same thing right along. There's no good pretending you haven't."

"And who might this young man be, do you think?" Augusta laid down the embroidery hoop and favored her youngest with an indulgent smile.

"Well, I thought it was Jeremy, but now I'm not sure because he was swimming that morning. Will saw him do the last hundred yards. But I still think she had a secret lover. Maybe an opera singer, or somebody from the orchestra.

She spent a lot of time at the Opera last season. She was a singer herself—she must miss it, don't you think? So much more exciting and romantic than living with a stuffy old banker. Even though he was a nice one," she added as an afterthought.

"Please, dear, don't put your feet on the settee—you never know about married couples. A difference in age and interests doesn't mean there isn't deep attachment. And you can't always have excitement and romance."

"Mother, why don't you ever talk about your parents?"

The abrupt transition startled even Augusta, who was used to them. "What an odd question. You know about them—they died before I married your father."

"So if Chip and Jeremy and I weren't born yet, they weren't really our grandparents, were they? I mean, how can you be related to someone who was dead by the time you were born? I'd say that only makes them ancestors. So it wouldn't matter whether they were rich, or respectable, or what religion they were or anything, would it?"

"I think you could stand a little fresh air, child. Go and ask Hepzibah to go for a walk in the Park with you."

"She's helping Mr. Germain with the flowers." Amy picked up her mother's embroidery hoop and peered at it, trying to make out the emerging pattern. "Elsie Wertheimer asked me to tea for next Thursday. Can I go?"

"I think we'll be on our way back to Vermont by then," Augusta stretched a languid arm along the back of the sofa. "Another time, perhaps."

"She thinks we're distant relatives," Amy said. "I didn't know we had any Jews in the family."

"I can't imagine why she would say such a thing."

"Some Jews are very nice, I think. Hepzibah is, for one."

"Lots of people are very nice." Augusta picked up the embroidery hoop and rose. "That doesn't necessarily mean we're in society with them." She shooed Amy from the small parlor.

"Go and find Hepzibah. I'll go and see what plans your father's been making."

A maid entered with a visiting-card on a salver. "A Mr. Wyatt is here, madam."

Augusta received Wyatt in a pumpkin-gold morning dress that set off her lush, Junoesque looks. "Warren is at his office. I believe he was planning to return for lunch. Are we 'in the clear,' as they say, Mr. Wyatt?"

"There's no reason so far to cancel the President's visit." Wyatt perched uneasily on the edge of the fragile-looking side-chair she indicated. It occurred to him that what it cost would have funded a year's treatment for the consumptive boy.

"Then it was an accident! I thought as much all along." She sank into the sofa-cushions. "How fortunate that I had left all the orders in place—we shall have to rush a bit, but we should be able to get everything together in time—"

"Well, as to whether it was an accident, we still can't say. The New York police are still concerned that Mr. Roosevelt could be in danger. They've asked me to follow up on one or two other matters in Vermont, which might lead to a suspect in Mr. Van Dorn's death. And once those are resolved, I will have to talk it all over with the President's security men—"

"What on earth do the New York police have to do with this?" Mrs. Dodge half-rose, hand to her throat, her face flushing. "I thought you had kept the police out of it—"

"Will Van Dorn asked them to look into his father's death, as he told us he would. One of their senior detectives is making a private inquiry on behalf of the Commissioner, who was a friend of Van Dorn's. He assures me that if we cooperate he has no intention of making anything public—merely wants to satisfy the Commissioner's concerns."

"I see. So we are all still under suspicion, I take it. How disagreeable. As for the President's security men—must you talk to them? If this visit to Vermont satisfies the police that he would be in no danger?"

"Mrs. Dodge, politicians like to know as much as possible about any situation they're venturing into. I don't think the President would take kindly to less than a full disclosure of the recent—uh, circumstances if he learned of them after the fact. And the situation is still unresolved. But, being the kind of man he is, I also don't think he'll allow it to deter him from his visit."

"I am glad to hear you say so. You must do as you think best, though—you always have. That is why Warren reposes such confidence in you." She rang for a servant.

Wyatt stood up but made no move to leave. "He did not honor me with his confidence in regard to his political interests."

"Political interests? Oh—you have heard about the House seat. Really, one can't keep anything private in this town. But, then, I forget—" she laughed lightly, "you are a security man. The truth is, Warren won't make a final decision until he learns whether Mr. Roosevelt will back him, or another candidate."

"A sensible approach on his part," Wyatt said. "And it is none of my affair, after all. Though I do understand more clearly now the importance of the visit. The island would provide the privacy for a confidential discussion of that kind."

"You don't think—" she began. "I had not considered how the—ah, incident on the island might look from that perspective."

"You mean—a cloud on Mr. Dodge's reputation?" Wyatt took a breath and plunged on. " I suppose such an event must provoke a certain amount of loose gossip."

"What kind of gossip?" she said sharply.

"Oh, people see conspiracies everywhere—what people have to hide, who knew what about whom, and so forth, what people might not wish to have known—"

"Whatever are you talking about?"

Wyatt saw her color deepening, her breath coming faster.

He leaned an elbow on the mantel. "Oh, some old story about the Union Club and its policies—who gets in, who gets black-balled—I doubt there's anything in it. I expect Mr. Dodge will know, and clear it up instantly."

"You mean, Gerald Van Dorn might have known something detrimental— about someone on the island, and this person killed him to keep it quiet?"

"Well," Wyatt said, "that, or he'd already spilled the beans, and someone wanted to get back at him."

She stared at him for a moment before the door opened and a maid came in. One of the two who had been on the island, Wyatt remembered.

"Bridie, we will be returning to the island late next week." Mrs. Dodge kept her tone casual. "Please have Mr. Germain come to me to make the arrangements."

"Very good, mum." The maid withdrew.

"Mr. Wyatt," Mrs. Dodge resettled herself on the sofa with much rustling of silk, "if you have heard something—derogatory—that might lead you to draw conclusions about the motives or my family or guests, you should disclose the matter at once."

Wyatt swallowed and took a few steps towards the window. "Since you insist," he began, "I will venture to raise a matter which in no way reflects dishonorably on your family, but— the Inspector is under the impression that your own ancestry might constitute a barrier to your husband's advancement, if it were widely known."

"The Inspector—?" White-faced, she rose and went to the fireplace, clutching the white marble of the mantel as if to meld into the stone. "Who told you this?"

"Inspector Macalester, a detective who works in the Manhattan Borough."

"I have never heard of him."

"No reason you would have," Wyatt said, conciliatory. "He seems to stand well with the Police Commissioner. I'm not sure how he came by his information, and I certainly have no idea whether there is any truth to it—nor would I make any judgment if it were true. I do know that he has kept it close."

A vein pulsed in Augusta's temple. "I have been a good wife to Warren! I have supported him in every aspect of his life to which I have been admitted—which is not all of it, I assure you I know that well—and it is too bad, too bad!— that someone should seek to ruin his plans—to ruin us in society—by playing on—" she paced back and forth in front of the fireplace, wringing her hands as she spoke.

"—on bigotry against a race that to my mind has contributed much to the advancement of civilization," Wyatt said mildly.

Augusta took a deep breath to calm herself. "My grandmother came from a branch of the Wertheimers. She married a Goldberg. My mother converted to Christianity on her marriage to my father—and was shunned by her family for the rest of her life. Which was a short one. She died giving birth to a stillborn child—my sister, that would have been—when I was four. My father followed her to the grave within a year. I was adopted by his sister and her husband."

"I am sorry." Wyatt lowered his eyes. "The prejudice works both ways, then."

"My mother's family saw her abandoning the faith of the ages. Those who despise the Jewish race, on the other hand, do not do so for religious reasons."

"I believe it is envy in many cases," Wyatt said. "You have my sympathy in this, Mrs. Dodge. And my utmost respect. But what must be known is this: did Gerald Van Dorn know of your family history?"

She stopped dead and again put a hand to her throat. "Oh, dear God, they think I—they think we—? Please tell me this is all some horrible dream." She dropped into a yellow chintz armchair. Wyatt stood silent, his arms folded, looking at her. Agitated, she rose again and looked him full in the face.

"Yes. He did know. I'm not sure how he found out, but he came to visit one day when Warren was out—he'd just become engaged to that woman. She was staying with an elderly aunt of Gerald's—none of us had called on her as yet, we were trying to avoid it—we all thought she was an *arriviste*, after him for his money. He was telling me how happy he was, and then he started talking about how he hoped 'dear little Milly,' that was what he called her, 'would be welcomed by his friends and their ladies, if only for his sake.'" She stopped and wrung her hands.

"Was that all?" Wyatt asked gently.

"I said nothing at first. He kept smiling, but his eyes had a—a chill to them. 'After all,' he said, 'it's amazing how many people in the City manage to rise above circumstances of poverty, or inferior breeding,' —he stressed that—'as long as their friends are willing to overlook such things.' And he looked straight at me, and he didn't smile. I knew what he meant, of course. And he knew that I knew. So I called on her the next day—what else could I do? And that's how our so-called friendship began."

"Do you think he might have brought this up again with Mr. Dodge, to warn him not to run for Congress?"

Augusta shook her head in terror and raised a hand to ward off the question.

"Warren does not know. At least, I have no reason to believe he does—did. Do you suppose Gerald told him?" Too late, she covered her mouth with her knuckles as the implications sank in. "No. No, he would certainly have spoken to me." She shuddered, and clutched at Wyatt's folded arms. He let them loosen and she seized his hands.

"Please, Mr. Wyatt, please—Warren must not know."

"Must not know what?" Warren Dodge stood in the open doorway, the jacket of his summer suit folded neatly over his arm. "Gussie, what in God's name is the matter?"

His wife gave a little cry and pushed past him out of the room. He stared after her, then turned to Wyatt.

"I take it you weren't discussing a birthday party." His pale eyes fixed on Wyatt's, cold and unblinking.

"No."

"I'm waiting."

"You heard the lady." Wyatt stared back at him. "You'd best go talk to her. Warren—it's not a matter for blame."

"I'll be the judge of that." Dodge flung his jacket over the back of the yellow chair. "Wait here."

"I'll be in the library, if it's all the same to you," Wyatt said to Dodge's retreating back.

The leathery, masculine atmosphere of the library was calming. He poured himself a finger of whisky from a cut crystal decanter.

Germain entered, soft-soled. "What's all the fuss about?"

Wyatt shrugged. "Seems the Dodges have something to talk over."

"We going back to the island?"

"I don't know yet."

"You got this thing figured out?"

"No. If anything, it's getting murkier. I need to go back up to Vermont."

"Shouldn't have taken you out and muddled your head the other night."

"On the contrary," Wyatt smiled, "that's been the bright spot in my week so far." He looked at his shoes, then at Germain. "You did me a kindness. I need to settle up with you."

"Your turn next time, if you're game for another visit."

"Fair enough. Good thing I have no other expensive habits. Germain—you said people talk in front of you as if you're not there. I want to put Dodge in the clear as much as you do. So help me out. What did he and Van Dorn talk about when they were alone?"

Germain gave a soft chuckle. "Perpetuities and consols. How long the Mexican silver mines would last. Whether Cannon would do anything in the House for currency reform. If I'd had to listen for any length of time, I'd've been asleep on my feet, I swear to God."

"Any gossip? Who's doing what to whom? Who knows what about who's hiding what?"

"A little of that," Germain conceded. "Old stuff, mainly. Recirculated from the club, near as I could tell. Stock tips—that was Van Dorn. My impression—he seemed to be trying to ingratiate himself with our man."

"They talk politics at all?"

Germain furrowed his brow, thinking back. "A little bit. Who was gonna stand on the Republican ticket for the House seat here, whether TR cared, that sorta thing. Real general, though, as if each was trying to find out what the other was up to without tipping his hand."

"Friendly?"

"Yeah, seemed that way. My read is, Van Dorn wanted the boss's help getting a seat on the Met board. 'Cause the wife was after him about it. Did you know she used to be a singer herself? He said she sang like a lark."

"I'd heard that," Wyatt said. "Maybe Van Dorn didn't tell him, after all."

"Tell him what?"

"What Mrs. Dodge is telling him right now, I expect."

The library door opened. Warren Dodge stood back to let his wife precede him. Both were grave-faced, but calm. Augusta clasped her hands. Dodge took her left hand in his and tucked it under his arm.

"Mrs. Dodge has told me what you learned from that police inspector."

Germain took a step towards the door, but Dodge raised a hand.

"You can hear this, Germain. Lord knows I've no secrets from you by now. Wyatt, do I understand that this is not widely known?"

"A talk with Inspector Macalester might set your mind at rest on that score. I understand the inquiry was discreet. I think family matters can remain confidential."

"And may we also hope that we will no longer be under suspicion in connection with Van Dorn's death?"

"You really didn't know? About—" Wyatt looked from Warren to Augusta. Both gazed at him steadily.

"I had wondered." Dodge's eyes darted to Augusta's face. "There was some gossip. But it wasn't a concern to me. By God, I don't count anyone's worth by his ancestry. It's what he can deliver that matters—what kind of fellow he is. You men should know that by now. Why should I apply a different standard to my wife?"

"Ancestry?" Germain's brow furrowed.

"I'm a Jew, Alexis." Mrs. Dodge took a deep, shuddering breath. "My grandmother was a Wertheimer, my mother a Goldberg. The police somehow found this out and thought we might have killed Mr. Van Dorn, or had him killed, to prevent its coming out and ruining us in society."

"Van Dorn knew about this?" Germain's hand reached for Augusta's shoulder, but Wyatt saw him check the comforting impulse.

"Macalester thought he might have," Wyatt said. "And then when we had that lunch at the Union—"

"Fairbanks and Potter—that's right. Going on about what a Jew-baiter Gerald had been," Dodge told Augusta. "Well, I can see where that wouldn't have helped. I still don't understand why Mrs. Dodge didn't give me more credit than she has. But, there, it's all out now, and that's the end of it as far as I'm concerned. I mean—it's out between us. But it needn't come out generally, am I right?"

"No reason I can think of," Wyatt said.

Augusta Dodge swallowed and looked at her husband. "I wish to say, before these colleagues of yours, Warren—I feel you have been most understanding about all this. I should have reposed more faith in you than I have shown. Please forgive me." And then Wyatt saw something he had never expected to see in his lifetime: the cool gray eyes welled up and spilled over with tears. Dodge put his arm around her shoulder.

"This is where we tiptoe out and leave the lovebirds to themselves," Germain said to Wyatt. Augusta sniffed loudly, picked up a cushion from the yellow chair and threw it at him.

"Not quite." Dodge handed Augusta his handkerchief and gave her a quick squeeze. He turned to Wyatt. "Germain, ask Cook to put aside some lunch for me. Wyatt, you and I have a few things to catch up on."

The others took the hint and withdrew. Dodge shut the door firmly behind them and turned back to Wyatt, grim-faced and furious.

"Let me understand something here. I've been paying you to find out who—if anyone—killed Van Dorn so we can clear things with the President and his people. And some New York policeman I've never laid eyes on, who wants to pin it on me for some reason—has you running around digging up dirt about my wife's ancestry?"

"The dirt was dug when I met him. The Commissioner assigned him after Will Van Dorn talked to him."

"Will!—damn him, there was no need for that."

"Be fair. Wouldn't you have done the same if it was your father?"

"Maybe," Dodge admitted grudgingly. "So what have you found out that *is* of any use? Anything?"

Wyatt bridled but let it go. He told Dodge about Czerny and the missing musician's fabrications, the speculation that after all the missing musician might have come from Barre. He turned from the whisky decanter to search his employer's face.

"May I ask if you plan on standing for Congress?"

"I don't know yet. I have been thinking about it. I'm not sure I'm cut out for it. People have been after me to do it, no doubt because Father was in Congress and they assume I'd want to follow in his footsteps. I was planning to talk it over with the President, see what he thinks of the idea." He gave Wyatt a small smile. "I should have asked you about it at that. I do value your counsel."

"Politics isn't my territory. Did you know Gerald Van Dorn was interested?"

Dodge's impatient hand sliced the air. "Heaven's sake, Wyatt, I was fond of Gerald—truly I was—but can you see that old water buffalo mounting a serious campaign for Congress? The man's idea of violent exercise was walking a block and a half to the Vanderbilts' instead of taking a carriage."

"Hanna was flattering him, then?"

"Prior to picking his pocket on behalf of whoever he does want to stand. Which may end up being me. So what next? What about this business with Webb and morphine Germain was telling me about? There was something to Fairbanks's gossip after all?"

"The toxicology tests came back. They're negative for morphine, no other drugs or poisons either. That makes Webb less likely, though it doesn't rule him out. I may drop in at Shelburne Farms when I'm back up that way, see what I can learn."

"This policeman's got you off hunting terrorists in Vermont now?" Dodge leaned forward in his leather wing-chair and glared at Wyatt over his tumbler.

"Unfortunately, it was my idea." Wyatt tossed down the last of his whisky. "It occurred to me that the violinist needn't have been from New York at all, and I made the mistake of saying so to Macalester. There's that nest of anarchists in Barre where the new paper's being published. Italians, too. He could as easily be one of them."

Dodge put down his drink and gave a snort of exasperation. "How long will this take?"

"A couple of weeks."

Dodge rose and ran a finger along a shelf of books. "I had a letter from Wilkie, wanting to know how things stand. He says the President has another invitation for August if he can't come to the island. He didn't say, but I think it's Sheldon."

"The alderman?"

"I'd heard he might be after the House seat. And the man's

such a toady, he's bought a summer place out on the North Shore. He's put in a cricket pitch because he heard TR's taken it up. We're running out of time, Wyatt."

"I know that. But it seems now the anarchist is just as likely to have been from Barre as from New York. And if I don't go along with Macalester, he's likely to contact Roosevelt's people and put the kibosh on the visit altogether."

"Why would they listen to him?"

"They'd have to, if it's a question of the President's safety. Besides, Roosevelt knows him from New York days."

"Suppose you find this Rossi fellow—"

"I telephone Macalester. He comes up on the next train with a couple of New York detectives, and they make a quiet arrest."

Dodge pulled a leather-bound tome from the shelf and opened it. "What gives them jurisdiction?"

"He's an immigrant, not a citizen. Any number of things they can nab him on and hold him for a while. Once they've got him, he's out of the way for purposes of the President's visit."

"Who else is still a suspect?"

"Pretty much all of us, as far as Macalester's concerned. Though I hope he'll listen to reason—it's obvious Mrs. Dodge's ancestry was news to you."

"Yes, it was. I don't mind telling you it was a shock. And, by God, I would kill anyone who tried to drag her down because of it. Or me. You can tell your policeman that if you want." Dodge put the book back on the shelf.

"He's still wondering about Webb—that blackballing business."

Dodge waved a hand. "That part I can clear up. I'll have a word with Cartwright at the Club. All he has to tell me is whether Van Dorn was involved in voting out Webb—it shouldn't matter now that the poor fellow's dead. If he wasn't involved, I presume that would take Webb out of the running."

"It's still possible Van Dorn tried some kind of blackmail on Webb, as he did on Mrs. Dodge. But their friendship seems to be genuine, from what I've seen. I'm inclined to look elsewhere for now."

Dodge held the door ajar and glowered at Wyatt.

"I suppose I've got to keep paying you for all this cloak-and-dagger business."

"Actually, I—"

"It's fine. Just get me what I need. Sooner rather than later." Dodge walked out and shut the door behind him.

CHAPTER 20

Wyatt stepped off the night train into the cool, dim cavern of the Burlington station, welcome shelter from the July sun, already fierce and unblinking. Grateful for the rowing calluses that would allow his hands to pass for a working man's, he had packed a small, shabby valise with coarse shirts and overalls and cheap cloth caps picked up from vendors' carts on Hester Street. He wore an old suit and derby he'd been on the point of retiring, something a laboring man might wear to search for work but would discard in favor of overalls once he was hired.

He walked south along blue-stoned sidewalks towards the King Street docks, where ferries, barges and pleasure-steamers tied up. Aromas of coffee, nutmeg, pepper and cinnamon eddied on the warm air from Berry and Hall's spice mill on College Street. Even at this early hour the air was full of the crash and bang of unloading cargo, of wheel-rattles and the shouts of draymen, the whine and shriek of saws from Shepard & Morse's great lumber yard. The *Vermont III* lay at anchor, loading passengers, its gleaming bulk rocking gently on the tide. He passed the new Lake Champlain Yacht Club, a great double-roofed bungalow nestled among sheds and wooden jetties, where Dr. Webb held the honorific of Commodore.

South of the steamer wharf, the waterfront was lined with mountains of coal and raw lumber. Beyond them to the southeast rose the square red bulk of the Queen City Cotton Company's mill. Great ugly swags of electrical and telegraph lines stretched above Wyatt's head between insulators on three-barred poles. The Burlington Grocery Company sat at the confluence of two rail lines at the east end of the King Street wharf. The merged line ran between the main warehouse and a number of annexes, an ice house, and a building that housed the tents and awnings the company frequently supplied along with provisions to summer residents like Dodge.

He had decided to borrow Macalester's accent and pass himself off as a Glaswegian. Italians and Lowland Scots shared an interest in labor politics, which might give him some basis for camaraderie. Being taken on at Burlington Grocery proved easy enough, though he was startled by the parting comment from the rat-faced man in the front office who had hired him.

"One more thing. You're not one of those labor agitators, are you? Those socialists? We've had a few of those and, believe you me, they're not tolerated for long hereabouts."

Wyatt managed to look shocked. "I'm no socialist, sir. Just an ordinary workin' chap lookin' to earn an honest livin'."

The man eyed him with what he no doubt thought was shrewdness and waved him out. "Fair enough." He began filling an old briar pipe from a glass jar.

Wyatt changed into overalls in the small washroom and found Spencer, the foreman, directing half a dozen men unloading a barge that had come up the lake from the Champlain Canal. They were hoisting crates of bananas, pineapples and other tropical fruits on dollies and stacking them on steel shelves that ran down the middle of the warehouse. Spencer was tall and lean, the muscles in his arms like knots in thick rope. His eyes had an alert gleam. He paused in his directions to look Wyatt over and nodded.

"Crew's short. Your timing's good. Give Calcagni over there a hand with those banana crates. Eddie!" he called. "This is Baird. New man. He'll help you with the bananas."

"Name's Jimmy Baird." Wyatt offered his hand.

"Eddie Calcagni." The man was short, swarthy and powerfully muscled, his black hair cropped close to his head, his eyes large, deep brown, intelligent. Early thirties, Wyatt guessed. No accent, or not an Italian one at any rate.

"Where ya from?"

"Sco'land," Wyatt said. "Glasgow. Where I come from, 'ca' canny' means be careful."

Calcagni's expression didn't change. "Good advice. We've got some cousins that settled there. Ice cream business. Here, grab this." He picked up a banana crate as if it were full of feathers and tossed it over. Startled, Wyatt managed to catch it and hoist it onto a shelf. Calcagni nodded, grinned and reached for another crate.

The work day would be the standard ten hours, with a half day on Saturday. They broke for dinner at noon, signaled by a shrill whistle that ran up and down the length of the waterfront. The crew included three Italians, two French-Canadians and a Finn. The foreman Spencer was a Yankee from New Hampshire.

Calcagni stopped Wyatt on the way out of the warehouse. "You got a place to stay?"

"I thought I'd find a cheap hotel for a coupla days, then see if I could find a boardin' house, like."

"Save you a step," Calcagni said. "I'm bunking in at Mrs. Fecteau's in the North End. On Pine Street near Pearl. Twenty-minute walk from here, or you can take the trolley. One of her lodgers just moved out and she asked me to look out for somebody."

Wyatt narrowed his eyes. "What's the tariff?"

Calcagni laughed. "Spoken like a true Scot. Now an Italian, first thing he'd ask is how's the food. Ten bucks a week'll get you three squares and a flop. She gives dinner pails, too."

Guido, a native Italian from the crew, caught up to them. "You talkin' about Mrs. F's? A good place. She take good care of you."

"I'd take it most kindly if you'd introduce me." Wyatt stopped and assumed a worried look. "It's no' a temperance place, is it?" This produced guffaws from his companions.

"She don't allow no liquor in the house," Guido said. "But that don't stop a man from drinking. Long as you don't come in a-roaring drunk, she don't care."

"Sounds all right."

"Keeps it Canuck clean too," Calcagni added. "You gotta take your boots off outside."

"Does she darn socks?" More laughs from the crew.

"Never asked. She'd probably charge you extra for that."

Wyatt's room at Mrs. Fecteau's was tiny and Spartan, as clean as Calcagni had promised. The food, starchy and plentiful, recalled the meals of his farm childhood. He fell into walking back and forth to the warehouse with Calcagni, savoring the golden summer evenings and the mingled scents of spices and lakewater off Battery Park after long days among the blood-and-vegetable reek of the warehouse. He found himself relishing the well-earned exhaustion and the deep, untroubled sleeps it brought, its contrast with the anxiety-tinged lethargies bred of indolence he'd encountered in the drawing-rooms off Fifth Avenue.

Calcagni introduced him to the regulars at a waterfront saloon, a tiny old brick building with a cracked stoop more or less open to the docks and a battered wooden bar with a tarnished brass foot-rail. Wyatt's adopted accent was becoming second nature to him, even as his sense of urgency was rising. Dodge needed to hear from him soon, but he'd let the week go by until he felt trusted by his co-workers. On Saturday, he and Calcagni hoisted mugs of beer at the tavern to celebrate the end of the work week.

"I thought all you Tallys in Vermont worked at the stone-cuttin'."

Calcagni toasted thanks to Wyatt for his third beer. "Thought all you Scots did too. Most of us do. That's where I'm from—Barre. But I had a big fight with the old man and decided I'd go off on my own for a bit, do something different. See how I liked it."

"I havenae seen my own faither in—oh, what'll it be—six years." Wyatt was making it up as he went along.

"Back in the old country, huh?"

Wyatt nodded.

"He wanted me to marry this girl from Viggiù." Calcagni wiped foam off his mouth with the back of his hand. "They brought her over to set her up with a husband. Well, you could see right off why she had to leave to find one. Butt-ugly, an' walleyed! I shouldn't talk about a lady that way, I guess. It's not like looks are the only thing. But I couldn't see makin' her sleep with a sack over her head every night."

"We've a song in Scotland," Wyatt said. "Gi'e me a lass wi' a lump o' land...'"

"It woulda had to be Manhattan Island. Maybe not even then." Calcagni shook his head and stared out at the lake, where white sails sparkled on the deep blue water. "Look at that," he pointed towards a long, sleek sailboat just outside the breakwater. "Wouldn't it be something to go for a ride in one of those?"

Wyatt remembered cool spray on his face, the rush of the prow through the water, Dodge's complaints about boats as holes in the water into which you sunk money. He pulled himself back with an effort.

"Yer faither's in the stone trade, is he?"

"Cutter. One of the best," Calcagni admitted. "He wanted me to do that too. It pays well enough, and the hours are better than here. I did it for ten years. But the damn noise and dust—well, the dirty secret is they're dyin' off over there. Cutter's consumption. The crystals get in your lungs and tear 'em up. Takes twenty, thirty years off your life. My father's got it, but he won't admit it."

"Is it an infection, like?"

"Granite dust. From the compressed-air tools they use, and the bosses being too stingy to put in filtering equipment."

"Can they not strike?" Wyatt made it sound as if this were the logical step to take.

"They've struck for wages and hours. They strike all the time. But there's things the bosses will never give on, short of somebody putting a gun to their heads."

Wyatt grinned. "It's been done, I'm told."

A worried look clouded the sunny cheer of Calcagni's face. He put a hand on Wyatt's forearm. "You sound like an anarchist. Better not let Spencer hear you talking like that."

"He's not here, is he?" Wyatt looked around with mock anxiety. The bar was crowded with dock workers, big brawny men talking animatedly with their hands in French and Italian and nasal Yankee. "'Besides, I thought you Tallys were the anarchist lot. You an' the Jews, eh no?"

"There are some Scots too—" Calcagni checked himself. "What I've heard."

"Och, you're better off here," Wyatt jerked his thumb in the direction of the warehouse, steering things back to safer ground for the moment. "Couldn't be doin' with all that noise and dust mornin' till night. Still," he said, his tone wistful, "thae wages sound hard to beat. Maybe I should take myself down there an' try it out."

Calcagni shook his head. "Money's nothing if you don't have your health. But you can't convince the men of that. It's all they know, a lot of them. Can't see themselves doing anything else."

"The office-man asked me if I was a socialist. What are thae fellas so worried about?" Wyatt kept his voice low but his tone casual.

"It was Homestead that started it, I guess. When Carnegie's partner almost got killed by an anarchist. Wonder he didn't— the fella put five bullets in him."

"Ah, but that was a long time ago." Wyatt took a pull at his beer, trying to make it look like a long swallow.

Calcagni assumed a pedagogical tone. "Sure, but then there was the McKinley business. Every rich businessman in the country figures there's some bomb-thrower out to get him now."

"Not in Burlington, surely."

"Well, not so much here as Barre. They almost got the police chief a couple of years back."

"Bomb-throwers?"

"*Anarchisti*, is what they call themselves."

"Did they not get the jail, or hung?"

"A couple of them are in jail. They couldn't make it stick on the others."

"So they'll've been lyin' low since then."

"Well, it looked that way. But things have gotten stirred up again." Calcagni's voice lowered to a confidential whisper. Wyatt leaned towards him to catch the words. "Somebody in Barre's started putting out this Italian newspaper—" The barman placed another mug in front of Calcagni. He picked it up and drank off the foam.

"One of the loaders brought some copies of it into the plant, couple of weeks ago. Well, Spencer caught him with them. When he found out what they were about, he gave him the boot. That's why they needed a new man on the crew, when you came."

"I didn't know Spencer could speak Italian."

"He doesn't. But it wasn't hard to figure out what the thing was about. All you had to do was look at the title."

Wyatt supplied the appropriate look of inquiry.

"*Cronaca Sovversiva*," Calcagni said. "Even a moron could figure out what they're getting at with that."

"An' he gave the fella the heave-ho for havin' a newspaper?" Wyatt's tone was indignant, but he kept his voice low.

"They figure if you get one shop on the waterfront cranked up, the whole town'll be on strike, or worse. The cotton mill especially. Look what happened in Paterson last year. A lot of people got hurt."

"Oh, aye, the silk workers."

"Galleani was lucky to get out of that one. They had a hundred cops or more on his tail."

"Who's Gally Annie?"

"Don't tell me you haven't heard of him. If there's such a thing as an anarchist leader, he's it."

"Like yon Mrs. Goldman?"

"The Italian version."

Wyatt drained his beer. Calcagni caught the barman's eye and pointed at Wyatt's empty mug for a refill, forestalling a demurral.

"Where'd the fella escape to?"

"Nobody knows for sure. But the betting is, with this new paper and all, he's landed in Barre. That's what my kid brother tells me, anyways."

"Right enough? Is he not feart he'll get caught?"

"Hell, we don't know for sure that it's true. Carlo Abate's the editor—so the masthead says, anyways. But there sure are a lot of quotes from Galleani."

"You've seen this paper yourself, then?"

"I rescued a couple of copies off the rubbish heap. Spencer threw them there for burning. Pretty rabble-rousing stuff. If you didn't know better, you'd think they were all set to blow up the world. Just for fun I lined some fruit crates with 'em that were headed for some rich guy's place out on the lake. Give him a scare, if he knew any Italian."

So here was the mysterious terrorist who'd lined Dodge's strawberry crates with the *Cronaca*. Wyatt stared out across the water.

"Not likely the fella would ever see it. He'd not be unpackin' the groceries himself, surely." He was on the verge of asking too many questions, but decided he could risk one more. Abate's had been one of the names on a list of "known subversives" in the area, given to him by the Montpelier police when Roosevelt came the previous summer. He'd tracked the man down before the speech and had a look at him. Abate had come and listened to the speech but had done nothing out of the ordinary.

"This Batty fella, he's a union man, like?"

Calcagni laughed. "Anything but. The union fellas are social-ists, mostly. Abate's a sculptor, good one too. Works by him-self. Came over about ten years ago. Lost his wife and three of his kids in a fever. Does statues and fancy stuff for tombstones, runs a drawing school for the stonecutters' kids. Now, that guy's an anarchist from way back."

"There can't be much worth chuckin' bombs at hereabouts."

"Abate's not a bomb-thrower. I doubt if any of 'em are. Lots of talk and plotting and secret meetings and such. But so far, except for the police chief business, it's been just—propaganda. That's what they call it. Doesn't mean they wouldn't get around to bombs, I suppose, if the chance came along. Or guns at least."

"But yon Gally Annie fella, he sounds a bit more—serious, is he not?"

Calcagni shrugged. "Far as I know, he's never actually killed anybody."

Wyatt decided it was time to change the subject. "There's somethin' I've been meanin' to ask you. I miss that good Tally ice cream you used to get in Glasgow. Is there anywhere in Burlington—"

Calcagni gulped the last of his beer. "I got just the place for you. On the corner of Pearl and Battery…"

They were unloading bananas again on the following Monday, a sultry day threatening thunder. Wyatt had hefted a crate on his shoulder and was following Guido towards the shelves when he saw something that looked like a spotted brown and yellow necktie slide out of Guido's banana crate and down his back. For a second or two that seemed like half an hour he stood paralyzed, his eyes fixed on the slow, sinuous glide of the thing while his heart began to hammer in his chest. He dropped the crate behind him, whirled round and scanned the ground for the machete he'd been using earlier to separate banana bunches.

"Don't move!" His voice was a hoarse scream. Guido froze in mid-turn. The necktie fell to the floor and began forming itself into an S. It was about four feet long. Wyatt ducked down and seized the machete, swung it up and brought it down three inches from Guido's ankle, cutting off the snake's head with one blow. For several long seconds, the body continued to writhe, the only sound the dry rustle of its scales on the floor. The startled Guido, realizing what had happened, tossed the banana crate away and ran off halfway down the warehouse. The crate crashed and splintered, scattering its yellow-green contents on the floor.

Their end of the warehouse had gone totally silent. Still wearing the gauntlets he used for loading and unloading, feeling cold sweat trickle down his back as his heart continued to pound, Wyatt waited till the convulsions had stopped before picking up the horrible small head. The snake's speckled eyes stared malevolence at him around the deep pit in its forehead. It had a yellow chin. *Barba amarilla*. Fer-de-lance, the deadliest snake in Latin America. They could reach eight or nine feet. This one had been young, and slow. They were nocturnal as a rule.

Spencer strode forward. "What the hell—" With an effort, Wyatt pulled himself back into character.

"A bloody great snake o' some kind. I don't know if it was poisonous or not. But it was crawlin' down Guido's back an' I didn't think I should wait about to find out."

The men gathered round and stared at the thing in Wyatt's hand in horrified fascination. Spencer nodded at the severed head. "This, ah, happened once before. A long time ago. They're quite poisonous, and quite aggressive, I've been told. You find them in Costa Rica, where the fruit came from. It's rare for them to make it all this way alive. Baird, you spared us a good worker. We're obliged to you."

Guido had tiptoed back towards the fallen crate and was staring transfixed at the snake's velvety brown and yellow scales. He looked up at Wyatt as if waking from a dream. "*Grazie*," he said fervently.

"Nae bother," Wyatt shrugged. Calcagni translated for Guido, though exactly how Wyatt wasn't sure. "Best bury this or burn it, I suppose." They scooped the coiled remains of the snake into a bucket. Wyatt tossed the head in after it. For the rest of the day they poked through the crates with long sticks before unloading them.

Thunder was rumbling in the distance when Wyatt and Calcagni headed out of the warehouse.

"When you went for that snake," Calcagni said over a porter at the waterfront saloon, "you sounded different. More like an American. And how did you know it was poisonous?"

"I didn't," Wyatt said, using the old politician's trick of answering only the last question. "But it stands to reason if it was in a crate o' bananas, doesn't it? Tropical, like. Good chance of it, anyway."

"Say it again."

"Say what again?"

"What you yelled to Guido."

"Don't move!" Wyatt tried to blend accents. "What're you, some kinda detective?"

"I could ask you the same thing," Calcagni said. "And another thing. You knew what that thing was. You were all white and sweaty and your teeth were clenched. Now, how does a guy from Glasgow know a pit viper when he sees one?"

"I'd seen one at the Bronx Zoo. An' I don't know anybody that wouldn't be feart o' a snake as big as that one."

"Let's go." Calcagni picked up his jacket and dropped a handful of coins on the bar. "We'll be late for supper." They walked north into Battery Park, their feet crunching on the gravel of the walkway that ran around the edge of its lush green lawn.

"See, the thing is, if you were really a Scotsman, you'd've pecked me out for suggesting you weren't. But you avoided the question instead."

"I don't know what you're on about." Wyatt stared up at the sky, watching the thunderclouds roll in. "If you don't think I'm a Scotsman, would ye mind tellin' me what ye think I am?"

"You seemed awful interested in what's going on in Barre. That got me thinking you might be a labor guy, or more likely a fink of some kind."

Wyatt's mind raced. Calcagni was his link to the Italian subversives in Barre, where he might find the man who had killed Gerald Van Dorn and fled. Who might be biding his time to come back and attack the President. If he let the insult go, it was as good as admitting the truth of it. If he fought with Calcagni, it could be the end of their association.

He drew a breath. Straight-faced and in his best imitation of a Scot doing a Southern accent, he said, "When you call me that, smile." He hoped Calcagni had read *The Virginian* along with the rest of mankind, or at least heard of the famous line. He turned away and began walking east across the grass towards the boarding house. "C'mon, it's goin' to storm in a minute."

Calcagni caught up with him. "Nice try. But I know what I heard and I say you're a fink."

Wyatt spun on his heel and unbuttoned the sleeves of his shirt. The blood rushed to his face. He knew the anger welling up in him was as much a reaction to the close call with the snake and the frustrations of his search as to Calcagni's taunt, but it would serve. Feelings were an actor's raw material.

"A fink! I know well what a fink is. An' I'll not take that off anybody." He pushed the sleeves up to his elbows and assumed a boxing stance. Calcagni hesitated for a moment, then did the same. Wyatt landed a snappy, taut punch on Calcagni's jaw. Calcagni came back with a left hook that caught Wyatt under the right eye. A small crowd of workmen gathered in a circle around them, calling out jibes and encouragement. There was a flurry of ineffectual shots, a few wide swings, blows that landed on the chest and shoulders. Wyatt felt the blood pounding in his temples and his shirt soaking with sweat. Calcagni tried an uppercut that missed its mark. Wyatt felt the rush of air past his right ear. He landed a solid one on the right side of Calcagni's nose, producing a gush of blood. Calcagni reeled, staggered back and held up his hands.

"All right," he said. "Enough. You've made your point." He pulled out a large, grubby handkerchief, tried to contain the stream of blood that was making its way down the front of his overalls. The men around them dispersed, laughing and murmuring.

"Sit down," Wyatt said, pulling out his own handkerchief. He mopped his face with it and walked over to the fountain in the middle of the green. He dipped the handkerchief in the bowl of the fountain, wrung it out and dabbed it around the right eye, a mouse swelling where Calcagni's punch had landed. It felt cool and soothing. He dipped it in the fountain again and brought it back to Calcagni, who took it and blotted more blood from his nose.

"I've not broken it, have I?" Wyatt tried not to sound worried.

Calcagni took the bridge of his nose between his finger and thumb and wiggled it gently, his eyes tearing up with the pain. He shook his head. He perched on the edge of the park's great cannon, his back to the afternoon sun, his face in shadow.

"Whatever you are, you've got a better left hook than I do. But I caught you fair and square." He rose and walked over to the fountain, soaking Wyatt's handkerchief in the basin and watching the blood turn pink and disappear. He reapplied it gingerly to his nose. "Maybe you're not a fink. I like to think I'm not a big enough fool to've drunk beer with a man that can't be trusted. And what you did for Guido—you could have run away. That was decent. But you're no Scot either, are you? What are you up to?"

Wyatt gave up. The reverse was true, after all; he'd drunk beer with Calcagni and he trusted him. "A man was killed. I'm trying to find out who did it and why."

"You are a detective, then. I was right."

"More like a private security agent. I work for the fellow who owns the place where it happened."

"Why hasn't he just brought in the cops?"

"We weren't sure it was a murder at first. It looked like an accident. But then, the morning we found Van Dorn's body—the man that drowned—we also found this one fellow had stolen a boat and left sometime during the night. An Italian named Rossi…" Wyatt sketched the rest of the story. "The night before Van Dorn died, this Rossi got drunk with the others and spouted a lot of anarchist bunk."

"A boat? You were on an island?" Calcagni held out his hand, palm up. The first fat drops of rain were falling. The air sharpened with the smell of ozone. Wyatt nodded.

A fork of lightning streaked the sky to the west. Calcagni's eyes widened over the wet handkerchief.

"The Dodge place, isn't it? The place that got the strawberries—"

"—with the copy of the *Cronaca* lining the crate."

"So that's why you're here. But that was just a joke. It didn't have anything to do with anybody dying." Calcagni dabbed his nose again, the blood now making only small berry-stains on the wet linen.

"Dodge's steward found it and gave it to me. And then we found another copy under the fellow's bed, after he'd gone. Let's get under that tree." The rain was falling in earnest now, rattling on the gravel path. Wyatt led the way to a clump of maples on the park's lawn. They squatted under a tree in the center.

"Here's what doesn't make sense," Calcagni said. "What would be the point of Rossi killing this Van Horn—Dorn fellow? Especially after getting plastered and spilling his guts about being an anarchist."

"I don't know. Some kind of initiation—a test, maybe. Depending on what group the fellow belonged to. Van Dorn worked for J.P. Morgan, pretty high up, personal friends. They've been after Morgan off and on for years." Rain was percolating its way through the maple leaves and onto their heads.

"Well, if that's what he came for, and had blabbed when he was drunk, maybe he figured his b est bet was just to do it and disappear." Calcagni dabbed rain off his forehead with the splotched handkerchief. " You figure he's in Barre?"

"He could be in New York. He said he'd come from there. But if he is, I don't know where to start to find him. And having that newspaper, and being Italian—well, I figured it would make sense to look in Barre."

"Why're you so anxious to find this guy? Van Dorn's family out for revenge?"

"Not so you'd notice. They seem to want to think it's an accident. The instinct to avoid scandal runs pretty deep in people of their class." Even as he said it, Wyatt realized this was unfair. Will Van Dorn had been the first to suggest that his father's death was murder, and he had pushed for bringing in the police from the beginning.

"Mr. Dodge wants it cleared up," Wyatt went on. "He doesn't like the idea of somebody doing murder on his property and getting away with it. But he's as anxious to avoid scandal as anybody, so he didn't want the police in on it." He told Calcagni the rest of it, omitting any references to Roosevelt or his hoped-for visit.

The rain had eased off to an intermittent patter. "Another thing," Calcagni rose and tested the air with an upraised palm, "Your man Rossi doesn't sound to have been the brightest candle on the Christmas tree. How'd he get this fella out of bed in the middle of the night, or the early morning?"

Wyatt rose to join him and they walked across the wet grass towards the boardinghouse. "Bird call, maybe. Van Dorn was a big birding man. Look here, are you going to rat me out at the warehouse? Because if you are, I'll be leaving right now."

"I should. You planning to go to Barre? That's where I should rat you out. See what kind of shape the Galleani crowd leaves you in once they catch up with you."

"I've got nothing against the anarchists. It's supposed to be a free country, you can say whatever you like. All I'm after is the man who killed Van Dorn."

Calcagni stopped abruptly at the edge of the Pearl Street sidewalk. A few stray raindrops fell as the last of the stormclouds passed overhead, and he dashed them from his face with one hand. Wyatt halted and met Calcagni's stern, neutral gaze.

"I won't rat you out here," Calcagni said. " And I probably won't in Barre either. It doesn't sound like you're after anyone I know. But I'm not going to help you. You go to Barre, you're on your own. I've got enough problems with people back there, I don't need to add to them. I will tell you this. I don't recommend the Scotchman act. You did good with it here, till the snake business. And I'm pretty sure I'm the only one who caught on then. But the anarchists—they'll sniff out a fink at a hundred yards. I was you, I'd give up the whole thing for a bad job and go home."

"I can't do that," Wyatt said. "It's my work. It's what I do."

Calcagni shrugged. "Pays a lot better than warehousing, I expect. But I'd take my chances with the poisonous snakes before I'd go stirring up that hornets' nest in Barre. Think about it."

CHAPTER 21

Wyatt pulled out Dodge's letter from his pillowcase, picked up from General Delivery three days ago. The President's men were pressing him for answers. Dodge, not a patient man at the best of times, wanted an answer from Wyatt by return mail. He'd had nothing to tell him then. Now he had a little more, but not much.

There was no point in staying on at the warehouse. He'd learned what he came for, though it didn't help much. And he'd learned that Luigi Galleani was probably in Barre, a man who kept box-scores of assassinations as if they were baseball statistics, a hunted man who might be willing to risk everything on one throw of the dice. Who by now probably knew of Roosevelt's frequent visits to Vermont. Who might be a threat to Roosevelt irrespective of the violinist and his role in Van Dorn's death.

He had told Calcagni enough to get himself shot if the anarchists learned who he really was and what he was up to. Especially if Rossi was in their midst. Would Calcagni keep quiet? On the whole, Wyatt thought so. But he couldn't help wondering what he'd do if the situation were reversed, if a man who'd won his trust on false pretenses went off on a hunting expedition among his lifelong friends and relatives.

To ask the Barre police about Galleani, if they weren't aware of his presence, might bring down consequences on the anarchists that would destroy any chance of learning if Rossi were among them. It could even result in Galleani's arrest. The man hadn't hurt anyone directly, so far as Wyatt knew; he had no wish to be responsible for that. Not the police, then. But he'd get nowhere trying to meet the anarchists head on. Some of them might know of him from last year's arrangements for Roosevelt's speech in Montpelier. He had been careful to keep his name from getting out, but there had been a reference in one of the local papers to "a man swearing people in as temporary Secret Service agents"—

John Macy. That was the reporter's name, from the *Barre Evening Telegram*. A smart-mouthed, cocky young fellow who had run him to earth at the Pavilion Hotel in Montpelier. He covered labor and social issues, knew all the local hotheads, and had given Wyatt numerous tips on people to look out for. He'd know about Galleani, if anyone outside the anarchist circle did. And maybe he'd have heard of Rossi too. He wondered how the man got his information. Some of the anarchists might actually trust him. You knew where he stood. He didn't "pussyfoot around," as Roosevelt might say—Roosevelt was the only person Wyatt had ever heard using that quaint expression—pretending to be a sympathizer. And he never gave the kind of specific details in his articles that could be used to hang a man.

He rose at daybreak and quickly packed his small, battered suitcase. He knocked gently on Calcagni's door. Sleepy-eyed in his nightshirt, Calcagni opened it, yawning and frowning like a newly wakened infant.

"You're up early."

Wyatt leaned on the doorjamb and spoke quietly. "I'm leaving. Will you tell Mrs. Fecteau, and Spencer?"

"What do you want me to tell them?"

"I've gone to Barre to try my hand at the stone trade."

Calcagni grinned. "Scots. Always after the money, right?"

"That's the idea." Wyatt picked up the suitcase again.

"What about your wages?"

"It's only the one day. Here's a note authorizing you to collect it for me."

Calcagni looked at the scribble dubiously. "Where do you want me to send it?"

"Buy a couple of rounds for the boys at the saloon."

"What's your real name?" Calcagni began rubbing his eyes, remembered too late his swollen nose and winced at the pain.

"You haven't decided about ratting me out in Barre."

Calcagni, fully awake now, looked him in the eye. "You're right, I haven't. Well, good luck to you then, Jimmy Baird or whatever your name is. It was fun while it lasted."

Wyatt offered him his hand and he took it. A few steps down the hall, he heard Calcagni's voice just above a whisper.

"But I do know what you look like."

Wyatt turned around. Calcagni sketched a wave and shut his door.

Alighting from the train in Montpelier, Wyatt walked across State Street to the Pavilion Hotel, a confection of red brick and white pillared verandahs next to the Statehouse. In the bathroom he lathered his shaving brush and unfolded his razor, pausing a long moment to look at himself in the mirror.

Carefully, slowly, he shaved off his mustache. The face that now looked back at him was almost a stranger's. He hadn't been clean-shaven since his acting days, since before Rose had—he looked younger but worn out, melancholy as Hamlet, the long space above the upper lip pale against the summer-bronzed face. A few hours outdoors would fix that. He packed his kit away and headed to Barre Street to catch the electric trolley.

John Macy's rimless glasses winked on a nose that reminded Wyatt of the sharp end of a parsnip. He grinned up at his visitor from an overflowing desk in what passed for a City Room at the *Barre Evening Telegram*. Macy's window was open to the warm midday breeze, too light to clear out the smell of stale smoke and old ink. The room was a-tap with a dozen typewriters racing the early edition deadline.

"Sure, I remember you. The fellow who organized the goon squad when Roosevelt was here."

Wyatt opened his mouth to protest but Macy held up placating hands.

"Okay, they didn't beat up anybody—they just looked it. You look different. Get a haircut or something?"

"I'm older." Wyatt's air of weariness was unfeigned. He'd lain awake much of the night.

"I just filed my stories for the day. Take a load off your feet. What are you up to?" He waved to a chair whose legs looked as if they'd served for teething puppies.

"I'm looking for a violinist," Wyatt said carefully. "He filled in when one of Dr. Webb's quartet had to leave for a while. When the job was over, he headed off but didn't leave an address. Dr. Webb liked his work and wants him back for a chamber orchestra concert they're giving."

"Working for old Webb now? You go from protecting the President to filling in orchestras?"

"Pays well," Wyatt said. "Fellow's name is Rossi. Said something about being from Barre."

"Why are you coming to me?"

"I don't know where to start looking for the fellow. Thought I might get farther talking to you than blundering around in the granite sheds." Wyatt tilted the chair back and affected a relaxed air.

"Not a bad idea," Macy said. "There's sixty-eight of 'em in town. That'd take you a while. I know some of the Italians. The agitators, mostly. You think he's part of that crowd?" Macy's small eyes narrowed shrewdly.

"Could be for all I know. He was spouting some rubbish or other about capitalism one night, after he got drunk with the other musicians. Doesn't have to mean anything."

"This may be your lucky day. The Stonecutters' Union Band is giving a concert in the park this evening. There's a crowd of troublemakers if I ever saw them. The music's not bad, though. Somebody there might know this fellow."

"Or he may have come back to play with them," Wyatt said thoughtfully.

Macy frowned and raised an index finger. "Wait a minute. Why would he have just taken off? If Webb pays so well and liked his work, why wouldn't the fellow have hung around hoping to be kept on?"

Wyatt shrugged. "Maybe his proletarian conscience was bothering him."

"Fat chance," Macy smiled. "Where a lot of money is concerned, I've never yet known a man to stand on principle. How long you in town for?"

"Till I find him. Which I hope won't take more than a day or two."

"Don't suppose it would be worth more than that. When's Webb need him for?"

"Ah—a week from Sunday. A soirée sort of thing. At Shelburne Farms," Wyatt added unnecessarily.

Macy gave him another shrewd look. "Best get moving, then. Where are you staying?"

"Same place as last time, in Montpelier."

"Wouldn't it have been easier to stay here in town? You worried the anarchists might be after you from the last time?"

"Can't think why. Nobody got hurt, or even harassed much."

"What's the first name?"

"Whose? Oh, the fiddler. I don't know."

"Well, that really narrows it down. Didn't Webb have a record from paying the man? Account book or something of the sort?"

"Casual labor sort of thing. They paid him in cash, just put him down as G. Rossi."

"Great. Let's see, Giovanni. Guiseppe. Guido. Giacomo. Giulio. Garibaldi, even. Not ringing any bells." Macy dropped his feet from the desk and rocked forward, propelling himself out of the chair. "Meet you on the Town Green at six. Unless you think you'd better not be seen with me."

Wyatt avoided the trap. "Why would I care about that? I'm just looking for a fellow to offer him some decent-paying work."

If you're after something to do in the meantime, go look at the new cemetery. Abate did the entrance—it's pretty impressive."

"Carlo Abate?"

Macy grinned. "Yup, that one. The anarchist rabble-rouser. It's Hope Cemetery— up the road apiece. Be a long walk, but it's worth it."

A pair of severe, elegant gray columns with niches that held draped female figures flanked the entrance of Hope Cemetery, sloping down to walls of granite block on either side. Wyatt had never seen Carlo Abate's work until now, and the austere beauty of the design moved him. The eight years since the cemetery's opening had already afforded numerous opportunities to showcase the granite-carvers' art: exquisite angels, miniature Greek temples, statues of prosperous-looking burghers so realistic you could see the strain-marks around their waistcoat buttons, delicate sprays of roses, enormous mausoleums—larger, Wyatt thought wryly, than the average apartment in the Lower East Side, and no doubt several times more costly to build.

As he walked back down Maple Street into the center of Barre, he caught a tide of low-pitched sound coming towards him from Main Street: the clatter of hobnailed boots on cobblestones, hacking male coughs, arguments, banging of dinner-pails against tool-belts. The end of a workday in the granite sheds.

Three thousand men tramped north past stores, saloons and livery stables to the Italian district, past flat-roofed brick buildings that gave way to clapboard apartment houses. Men in billed caps and long aprons, covered from head to foot in white granite dust that glittered in the gold light of the summer afternoon, a race of statues come to life.

The lines of men spilled to the width of Main Street, avoiding trolley-rails slicing the cobblestones. The music of their native language rose and fell in mellifluous waves, cross-hatched with flat stutters of English. They hawked up spit the color of charcoal onto the stones. The wave of men crested, broke, flowed north.

An army of ghosts.

These, he realized, were the men Calcagni had spoken of—men who toiled unshielded from the white dust whose crystals, cutting into their lungs like tiny razors, would bring them an early, agonizing death from cutter's consumption. The artists who carved the beautiful colonnades, the angels, the great mausoleums, carving their own deaths into monuments for the rich. Granite was the fashion now, the reason Barre was a boomtown. The pale gray stone would last far longer than marble and support much larger structures, eternal homes for those who would defy the Biblical adage that you couldn't take it with you. He remembered a new book in his library, partially read. What was the phrase the author had used? Grimly humorous in this context: *conspicuous consumption.*

The concert on the Town Green vfrustrated his hopes. No one in the Stonecutter's Union Band, or in the audience, resembled what he remembered of Rossi. He cursed himself again for not taking a better look at the man when he'd had the chance. Too much to hope that it would have been so easy. The crowd enjoying music-hall favorites like "The Sidewalks of New York" and "The Band Played On" was mostly families, the men in boaters or derbies, solid, mature types in their thirties or beyond. Doing their best to be inconspicuous, members of the Barre constabulary sweated in dark blue gabardine, scanning the crowd for troublemakers.

Wyatt noticed a man with curly salt-and-pepper muttonchops, his hair receding from a pompadoured widow's peak, handshaking his way through the crowd, beaming beneficently on the children and patting their heads.

"Who's that? Seems like I've seen him before."

Macy laughed. "Don't tell me you've forgotten old Bill Barclay. Scotchman—from Aberdeen. The original Granite City. Been here thirty years maybe, but you wouldn't know it. Not content with owning half the granite sheds in town, he's supposed to be running for mayor next year. Sure looks it."

The band struck up the "Internationale" and the men in the crowd scrambled to their feet. They stood straight and solemn as if the band were playing the National Anthem. As the music moved from introduction to main theme, some began to sing—in Italian, in English, even in French. Barclay withdrew to the periphery of the crowd and looked on, an amused half-smile on his face. Wyatt found himself oddly moved by the fervor in the workmen's faces:

"*Su lottiam! —L'ideale/nostro alfine sarà/l'Internazionale/ futura Umanità!*"

As if they thought the song could change the world.

"Is this for the Socialists?" he whispered to Macy.

"All-purpose," Macy hissed back. "Socialists, anarchists, your downtrodden workers in general. They all play it and they all sing it, every chance they get."

"That can't be much fun for the likes of him," Wyatt nodded towards Barclay.

"Oh, it don't bother him a bit. Part of the reason he's done so well—he gets along with the union types better than any of the other owners. Man's crazy like a fox—he's all down to earth and straight shooter on the surface, but he knows exactly what he's doing. Divide and conquer."

The band dispersed from the gazebo, mingling with the crowd. Macy shook out his jacket and put it back on. "That man's got a better handle on who's doing what among the crazies than anybody in this town, themselves included. You should go talk to him. Maybe he knows something about this fiddler of yours."

"Not a bad idea." Wyatt shrugged on his own jacket. "But where do you find the young fellows? This is a family crowd. He'd have been in the band, if anything. Are there taverns, or meeting-halls, or—"

"There's a benefit dance at the Labor Hall tomorrow night, for some bunch of strikers down south. They'll all be there—Italians, Scots, anarchists, socialists, the lot. It's the place to be,

205

especially for the young, single fellows. Good-looking man like you might pick up a little action."

"I'm a bit old for that." Wyatt reflexively stroked his non-existent mustache.

"Long as you've got a little money and can show a girl a good time, they won't care," Macy grinned. "Good place to spot the troublemakers too. There's usually a spot of fisticuffs as the evening wears on."

Barclay surprised Wyatt the next morning by emerging from his office shortly after his visitor was announced. Wyatt had given his name as Baird, stating his business as "seeking advice on behalf of my employer, a fellow industrialist, concerning labor relations." Thankfully, Barclay's secretary hadn't insisted on a visiting-card. But once behind the closed door of Barclay's office, in a low-roofed annex away from the scream of diamond saws and the surf-pound of air-tools, he re-introduced himself and mentioned that he'd been in Barre the year before.

Barclay's caterpillar eyebrows waggled. He stared at Wyatt for a long ten seconds. "Wyatt. Hmmm. Ah, yes! The fella that deputized some of our men when the President came. No wonder you didn't lead off with your right name."

"You have a good memory, sir. As for the name, best if we keep it that way." Wyatt took in a large, bare room, furnished with only a solid desk, a couple of cabinets in the same dark wood, and a pair of leather guest chairs. A row of tall, grimy windows like those in the rest of the finishing plant.

"A good memory's a handy thing when you're running a business of this size." Barclay's Aberdonian burr was undiminished by long residence in America. "Dodge. Paper man. Dab hand at mairgers an' acquisitions, is 'e not? Like his father before him."

"So I'm told." Wyatt took the chair Barclay's hand waved him to, and Barclay took the slat-backed wooden swivel chair behind the desk. "I'm more involved in other angles of his business."

The furry eyebrows arched upwards. "Not strikebreakin', surely. Ye don't look the type at all. By the bye, did you not have a big mustache," Barclay accented the second syllable, "when you were last here?"

Wyatt smiled. "You do have a prodigious memory. Not strikebreaking. I confess I got myself in today on somewhat false pretenses—"

Barclay's laugh boomed around the walls. "You're after a job, is it?"

Wyatt grinned back at him. "No, sir. Not at all. I didn't want to say to your, uh, staff, but—Mr. Dodge has asked me to investigate a suspicious death that took place at his holiday home here in Vermont."

"And what would you hope to find out about such a thing here?" Barclay leaned across his desk, inviting a confidence. Absurdly, Wyatt found himself bending towards him and lowering his voice.

"The prime suspect is an Italian with anarchist leanings."

One furry eyebrow shot up. "Is he now? Well, this'd be a good place to start at that. Say more."

Wyatt kept the story as short as he could, but Barclay seemed unhurried and all attention, nodding thoughtfully, resting his cleft chin on his palm.

"Rossi, you say. There's maybe half a dozen Rossi families in town." Barclay pushed an electric bell on the wall behind his desk. The secretary who had admitted Wyatt stood in the open doorway, a bespectacled, thirtyish woman in a striped shirtwaist and a slim gray skirt.

"Miss Buzzi, you're looking well this morning. Would you fetch the City Directory, please?" The woman glided out without a word and returned with the large green buckram volume, which she laid on Barclay's desk. She stood with her hands clasped in front of her, awaiting further instructions.

"That'll do for now, thanks—unless," he turned to Wyatt, "you'd like a cup of tea?" Wyatt waved a hand in demurral and

Miss Buzzi glided out again, as if on rubber wheels.

"Excellent woman. Secret weapon with the unions, too—she's the shop steward's niece. Now, let's see. Rossi. Here 'tis. No, was wrong, seven of them. Forgot Aldo, the old fellow on Blackwell Street. But right about the main thing—none of them has a young fella that fits your description, with or without a beard." Barclay closed the book with a loud whack. "Either he's not from here, or he's brand new in town, or he gave you a false name. And, yes, before you ask—" he held up a forestalling hand, "—know them all personally. And their families. Photographic memory's a curse at times, but it comes in handy for the most part. Now, once more on the description?"

Wyatt sketched Rossi from memory, the red-gold beard, the copper hair, the little glasses, the halting but impassioned English his colleagues had reported. Barclay shook his head.

"Not ringing any bells under any name. Still, you never know—there's a lot of new people in town these days, what with the works expanding as they are. Hired twenty new fellows just last week. And, of course, he'll look different if he's shaved the beard."

Wyatt took the now tattered copy of *Cronaca Sovversiva* from his jacket pocket, unfolded it and handed it over the desk to Barclay.

"Would you know anything about this?"

Barclay took a pair of pince-nez from a drawer and perched them on his nose. He scanned the front page, turned to the inside and peered at the masthead box.

"Had heard this was out and about." Wyatt found Barclay's avoidance of the first-person pronoun both distracting and intriguing.

"Hadn't seen it yet," Barclay was saying. "Abate's a fine sculptor, a wee bit crazy as who wouldn't be after losing a wife and three weans as he did. Thought he was all talk, but this'd make you wonder. Just started, eh?"

"You read Italian, sir?"

"Speak it too. Have for years. Stands to reason, if you're going to get anywhere with these lads. They don't know it, though. Part of the secret. They go off and huddle during negotiations, think themselves safe, not realizing every word's noted and understood." Barclay sat back in his chair with a proud grin.

"There's a rumor abroad that Luigi Galleani's taken up residence here. Would you know anything about that?"

The furry eyebrows arched again. "Would make sense, now that you mention it. This," the back of the big hand slapped the newspaper, "coming out and all. You're thinking this Rossi fellow might've come here on the coattails of Galleani, or be looking for him to offer his services as a thug or an assassin for the cause?"

"If I were Galleani, I wouldn't hire him. Van Dorn's death was bungled."

"How bungled?" Barclay poured a glass of water from a steel pitcher and offered it to Wyatt.

"There was no good reason for it. Van Dorn's not one of your prominent robber barons, like Morgan or Frick. No symbolic value."

"Practice? Guilt by association?" Barclay's eyebrows contracted. "Don't suppose the fellow looked like somebody famous, did he—case of mistaken identity? What'd this Van Dorn fella look like?"

Wyatt described him. Barclay mused. "Sounds a wee bit like President Roosevelt." Wyatt shrugged noncommittally. "The former object of your professional attentions. Had he any reason to think our Colonel Rough Rider might be visiting Mr. Dodge?" Wyatt's shake of the head came a fraction of a second too late. Barclay's pale blue eyes took on a shrewd glint.

"Webb and Dodge are friends. Webb was of the party, you said, and the violinist fella came from Webb's. The good doctor's entertained TR on several occasions. What's more likely than that Dodge might ask His Nibs in for a cup of tea, and a few days' stay at his country estate? And why else does Dodge bring you in to oversee security?" His smile was an arrow that had found its mark. Wyatt sighed.

"This must be in strictest confidence—" Wyatt acknowledged Barclay's nod, "He has been asked. That's one reason Dodge is so anxious to clear all this up, and without the police. Otherwise, Roosevelt's men won't let him come."

"Dear, dear. It certainly doesn't look good when you're expecting a visit from the Chief Exec and one of your guests turns up dead, does it? Especially if it might be the work of some foreign terrorist still on the loose. Well, now. Can't help you right off, but who knows—the fella may turn up here looking for a job, in which case let us know how to find you." Barclay took a long gulp of ice-water.

"Now, as to Galleani. If he's here he's obviously in cahoots with Abate. Who's a good man, very talented, but a bit wildeyed on politics, as this confirms." Barclay ran his finger down to Abate's name on the masthead. "Hadn't thought there was any more to it than talk, but Galleani's wanted for inciting violence. You'd best tread warily."

Wyatt nodded. "Where do I find Abate?"

"Studio's over on—where was it—Blackwell Street. North end of town. But you can't just pop in, can you, and say, 'Hello, there, you wouldn't happen to be harboring a would-be Presidential assassin, would you?'"

"Will he be at the charity dance tonight?" Wyatt rose and took up his boater.

"Ah! Don't doubt it. They're family occasions as well as courting opportunities. They all go. If Galleani's really about, he'll be there too. Now, you've the obvious problem of being a stranger in town. Good thing you got rid of the mustache. Sheer luck to have remembered your face—not many who'll be able to do that. Macy sent you here? You can go with him. They won't talk to you, but they won't throw you out either. You'll be able to have a good look round for your man."

Wyatt extended his hand. "You've been most helpful, sir. I know Mr. Dodge will be very grateful."

Barclay took the hand and pumped it vigorously. "Wouldn't mind meeting Dodge some day. Lot to talk about. Like the sounds of that island of his. Wouldn't mind a wee place like that—family's growing fast. Eight of 'em now, six boys."

Wyatt wondered how Amy would react to a horde of wild boys in her bird sanctuary. "I'll let him know. I'm sure he'd enjoy it."

He went to let himself out and found the door unlatched. The dark vestibule with the secretary's immaculate desk was empty, but he thought he'd heard the faint rustle of a skirt just before he came through the door. Or perhaps it was only the hiss of an air-powered bumper from the finishing shop, polishing a tombstone to a gray satin glow.

Fresh from the ministrations of the Pavilion Hotel's barber, the shabby suit of his travels cleaned and pressed, Wyatt met Macy under an electric arc light at the corner of Granite and Main Streets.

"You clean up good." The reporter tucked a small notebook and pencil into his jacket pocket. "Planning to mix a little pleasure with the business?"

"That the labor-hall?" Wyatt pointed towards a large, new-looking brick building. They joined a crowd waiting their turn to pay at the door. A granite medallion, a muscular arm holding a hammer above the letters S.L.P., crowned the granite door frame.

"Socialist Labor Party," Macy said. "Built by the Socialists, but the anarchists chipped in. For all their speechifying and fights, it's all one big though not necessarily happy family. I'll show you the ones I know."

The dance band was having trouble making itself heard over the cacophony of voices in the hall, whose bare walls ricocheted sound.

"Ask a few ladies to dance," Macy yelled into Wyatt's ear. "It'll make your looking around more natural. Meet me at the bar in a half hour and I'll point you out the subversives."

Wyatt circled the room, adopting the casual stance from earlier days of a young buck on the lookout for a pretty young thing to dance with. Knots of young men stood drinking beer in the corners, working up the courage to approach the unattached girls who huddled in knots of their own, drinking lemonade. He'd be more likely to find Rossi in such a group than among the couples, he reasoned. Revolutionary fervor didn't make for settled attachments, indeed often substituted for them.

Half an hour later he'd come up dry, though a number of dark-eyed maidens with fashionably pompadoured hair had tried to catch his eye from behind bright cardboard fans imprinted with the name of a local undertaker. Macy handed him a schooner of beer.

"No luck, eh? Well, the night's young. Over there, in the corner, near the stage. See the thin-faced fellow with the goatee?"

"With the kids?" Wyatt noted the protective arm around the shoulders of a boy and girl of perhaps eight or ten. The man was deep in conversation with two others, one a tall, horse-faced man with a thin beard that did not quite conceal a long scar on his cheek.

"That's Abate. And the tall fellow next to him? Galleani, I'll wager anything. We had a picture of him in the paper's morgue from the story on the Paterson riots last year. See if your man's floating around them anywhere, trying to get himself noticed."

Wyatt kept the pair in his peripheral vision as he drifted through the crowd. The band played a lively mix of operatic waltzes and music-hall ballads—there was the inevitable "Brindisi" from *La Traviata*. Occasionally he stopped long enough to squire a young woman onto the dance floor. Most of his partners, it seemed, were recent imports from Italy, including a plump, walleyed young woman who must be Calcagni's spurned fiancée. He waltzed with her twice from a sense of vicarious guilt, trying to ignore her hopeful look fading to disappointment as he withdrew. Fortunately the ladies spoke little English, and he was able to murmur "*no parliamo Italiano*" when they tried to keep him for a conversation. Let them take him for a newly arrived Scot.

The separate knots of young men and women thinned as the complement of couples grew, and some lucky bachelors were being allowed to walk their conquests home. The niceties of chaperonage which would have applied in more bourgeois surroundings were not evident in this working man's world.

No sign of Rossi or anyone like him. Wyatt was ready to give it up for a bad job; perhaps after all the man had disappeared into some Italian neighborhood in New York, in which case it would be up to Macalester's lot to track him down.

In the silence between dance numbers he heard a clatter at his feet. A woman's paper fan lay on the floor. He bent quickly to retrieve it, looked up into a pair of smoky eyes, a face like an Egyptian queen's, olive-skinned and full-lipped. The girl could not have been more than twenty, in a gown of blue sateen trimmed with machined lace, a gold locket around her long neck. He turned the handle for her to take the fan from him, smiled and bowed. Her long lashes closed as she nodded her thanks. The band struck up "La Donna é Mobile" and Wyatt, ready to salvage something from an otherwise fruitless evening, mimed his request for a dance. She nodded and allowed him to lead her onto the dance floor. Later he would remember that as he put his arm around her waist, she gave another slight nod of her head, to a woman who stood near the corner where Abate and Galleani still held court. It was Barclay's secretary, the silent and efficient Miss Buzzi. Then they were off in a dizzy whirl that left both of them laughing and pink-cheeked.

"You dance very good." Her English was heavily accented.

"You inspired me. May we have another?" Wyatt gestured towards the band, which was beginning a slow rendition of "Annie Laurie."

"Perhaps you would be so good to fetch me a lemonade?" She smiled and sat down on a cane-bottomed chair, unfolding her fan.

"It would be my pleasure, Miss—"

"D'Agostino."

"Dade—uh, James Baird, at your service. I will be back." Wyatt headed for a vestibule at the back of the hall, where a lemonade stand had been set up. Before he reached the booth, a skinny, gaunt-faced man stepped into his path.

"*Scusi*," Wyatt said politely. The man did not move, stared at him, lips twisting into a hostile snarl under a thin, droopy mustache. He barked something in Italian, of which Wyatt could not make out a word, but the intent was clear enough. The man thrust a trembling finger towards the dance-hall. His voice rose.

He thinks I've stolen his girl. Wyatt made conciliatory gestures, turned towards the back door, but the man was wound up like a clockwork toy and was not to be cut off in mid-rant. Where was Macy? He could help him out of this—

Two bulky men, granite-loaders by the looks of them, bracketed Wyatt and pinned his arms between them, half-steering, half-dragging him into an alley behind the hall. The lean-faced man followed, his harangue winding down and abruptly cut off by a fit of coughing, a horrible, hollow, sloshing percussion in the sudden, dark quiet outside.

Wyatt tried to throw off his silent captors but they held him firm, dragging him northwards down the side of the building that ran parallel with Main. He straightened up and landed a kick in the crotch of the man on his right, off center but hard enough to make him howl and loosen his grip. The distraction allowed Wyatt to twist out of the grasp of the second man, but before he could run the man seized him by the right arm and punched him hard in the gut, doubling him over. The man caught his jaw with an uppercut as he tried to straighten up, and he lost his balance. He fell back and smashed his head on the hard-packed ground, stunned into darkness. From some distant place he felt hands picking him up, a voice: "*Scusi—mi amico—un poco ubriaco...*"

He was dreaming, but it was as vivid a dream as he could ever recall. He was lying on a divan, his shirt and trousers unbuttoned, his feet bare. The smoky-eyed Egyptian was straddling him, her dark hair tumbled loose, in a satin corset that laced under creamy breasts, nipples hanging like ripe cherries just out of his reach. She was smiling down at him, stroking his chest, whispering something he couldn't understand, her legs pinning his arms, reaching between his legs...time seemed to eddy and drift. He felt himself swell in response to her touch, there was no help for it, he tried to free his hands...she took one of his hands and held the fingers to her breast. There were flashes of something like lightning, popping sounds, drifts of white smoke... he stirred, tried to raise his head, but the hand that came to caress his face held a sponge soaked in something sickly-sweet and sharp and chemical. For a panicked moment he fought for breath, and then he drifted away again.

CHAPTER 22

He woke to throbbing pain in his jaw and the back of his head, a sick sensation in his gut. By the dim light of an oil lamp he could see the rafters and beams of a steeply pitched roof. Twisting his head painfully, he saw that he was lying on a piece of wood flooring which partially covered the bare joists of an attic floor. Opposite him was a small round window. He raised himself on his elbow, and a man—he thought it must be the thug who'd sucker-punched him—rose from a chair and shouted something in Italian to the floor below. Wyatt struggled to a half-sitting position but the man waved a knobby cudgel at him. Awash in nausea and with the pain stabbing like blunt knives behind his eyes, he slumped back.

I'm getting careless in my old age. Who had brought him here? Italians, anarchists surely. He'd slipped up somewhere...Barclay. Or rather, Barclay's secretary. The door ajar, the rustle of skirts. She'd listened to the conversation, or part of it. *My secret weapon. The shop-steward's niece.* It worked both ways. He remembered the look his dance partner had given the woman in the corner, her slight nod of confirmation which he'd taken for approval. When would he learn?

Something lingered in his nostrils, a sickly-sweet smell, acrid at the edges. How long had he been unconscious? There had been dreams, more than one, vivid dreams, he couldn't remember now, but there had been the woman...chloroform, that was the smell. They'd used it on him, whoever they were, he had no idea how long he'd been out, he was drifting away again...he forced himself back. The room swam, stopped, came back into focus. Another wave of nausea broke over him and passed on.

"Who are you?"

The dark-faced man shrugged and leered at him with small, piggy eyes, waggling a matchstick in the corner of his mouth. A hatch was withdrawn. Light from below, a ladder placed, cautious footsteps climbing. The man stood above him, brandishing the club. Wyatt raised a forestalling hand. A head appeared above the opening, a thin, ascetic face with round glasses, a neat mustache and goatee, soft dark eyes, thick hair neatly slicked back. Abate, the sculptor. He boosted himself on powerful arms into a sitting position on the flooring, swung his legs and stood to make way for another man, the larger of the two who had abducted Wyatt from the dance.

The dark eyes scanned Wyatt's bruised face with concern. Abate snapped something in Italian to the man who had come up behind him. The reply was conciliatory, servile.

Abate nodded slowly. "I remember you. Last year, when Roosevelt came to Montpelier." The English was softened by its Italian inflections, graceful, deceptively soothing. "The man they brought in. You work for the White House."

"No." Wyatt shook his head, regretted it. His stomach heaved and the room swam out of focus again. "That was a one-time thing."

"Who are you working for now? What are you doing in Barre?"

Wyatt seized the offensive. "Why'd your goons kidnap me and whack me on the head? I've been drugged too. What in hell is going on here?"

"You would not have come of your own accord." Abate's eyes shifted to the big man, but his head didn't move.

"I wasn't offered that option," Wyatt said with asperity.

Abate smiled and shrugged. "You haven't answered my question."

"If you set your thugs on me, you must have some idea of your own about what I was doing here." Wyatt struggled to a sitting position and leaned his back against a brick chimney. Abate said something sharp to his companions, who shook their heads.

"As I predicted, the chloroform was not helpful. Not in that respect. What is reasonable to assume? You are again here to spy for a visit from Roosevelt. But nothing has been announced, no speech, no occasion. So, a private visit, somewhere near here. You would have done better to stay away. You have—what do they say? Tipped your hand. What is your name?"

"Baird."

Abate looked at his two companions, who shrugged.

"Baird. Hmph. You know who I am?"

"Haven't a clue."

Abate laughed. "Really, Mr. Baird—or whatever your real name is. You must think us very stupid. Perhaps there is another reason you are here. It would have to do with the newspaper?"

"I don't work for the newspapers." Wyatt said, deliberately misunderstanding. He winced as another stab of pain shot through his head.

"But your friend Macy does. You spent last evening together, at the band concert, and the dance tonight. Perhaps your employer wishes to know more about certain—subversive chronicles being published here?"

"Macy will be looking for me." Wyatt's head was clearing now. He struggled to his knees, but Abate's hand pushed him gently back.

"Not for a while, I think. If he was watching you, he would have seen you dancing with Miss D'Agostino—seen you slip out, seen her follow you after a discreet interval, assumed you had gone off together for—an interlude? Even a news-hound like Macy knows when his presence is superfluous." Abate gestured to the guard for the chair and sat down. Light and shadow from the oil lamp played across his long, thin face.

"But enough. Who is this man you are looking for? This Rossi?"

"A violinist." Wyatt's tone was exasperated. "He was in a chamber orchestra over Burlington way. He played well. The man who hired him wants him back. He was an Italian and I figured he could be from here."

They knew about his conversation with Barclay, but they wouldn't want to give the Buzzi woman away as their source. If he got away from here, or was allowed to leave, it would put her job at risk, possibly get her arrested...

But Abate surprised him. "That's not the way Miss Buzzi tells it."

Wyatt feigned ignorance or forgetfulness. "Who's Bootsie?"

"You are looking for someone named Rossi because you think he killed some cohort of Dr. Webb's. On an island in Champlain owned by a man named Dodge, or Warren. He spoke like an anarchist, so you think he is part of a plot to kill someone more important than this Van Dorn who died there."

Wyatt scrambled unsteadily to his feet. "Where is he?"

The guard started forward but Abate, rising from his chair to face Wyatt, gestured the man back.

"In your imagination," he said softly. "Or elsewhere, perhaps, but not here. This Rossi sounds like an excuse to go fishing for revolutionaries in Barre. The man who died—surely he could have drowned, or been killed by someone else there."

"Rossi disappeared on the morning the body was found."

"After getting drunk and running his mouth about what a big anarchist he was? Do you really think we would have any use for such a fool? Perhaps he realized how stupid he had been, knew that his foolish talk would make him a suspect, and slunk away to wherever he came from. Which I assure you was not here."

Circumstances notwithstanding, Wyatt was inclined to believe him. Rossi had nothing to offer these people. The murder of Van Dorn, if he had done it, was the kind of bungling indiscretion that could endanger them all. He would find no sanctuary in Barre.

But now there was a larger threat than Rossi, one Wyatt himself had unleashed by allowing his conversation with Barclay to be overheard. Luigi Galleani, the arch-anarchist, a wanted fugitive and the spokesman for every Italian-speaking terrorist and subversive in Europe and America, now knew that Theodore Roosevelt had plans to visit a Vermont island in August. Nothing easier than to look at the President's official schedule in the newspaper and see where the gaps were. And to find out which of the islands was owned by a man named Dodge, or Warren.

It was Wyatt's fault. He'd have to tell Dodge to call off the visit and take his lumps and there was an end of it. Dodge had no patience for ineptitude. Nor for excuses, even the reasonable one that Barclay had guessed Wyatt's real mission and had a confidential secretary who was an anarchist spy. He'd be finished in this line of work. What would he do? Perhaps he'd have to try acting again. But he'd been out of that world for too long...he thought of the Adirondack boat, the solitary cabin in the woods. Meanwhile there was the small matter of getting out of here alive...

Abate's voice brought him back to the dim attic, his face in a blur of tawny gold light against velvet black. He gestured for Wyatt to sit on the floor.

"So now that we have saved you the effort of looking for this man who is not here—if he exists at all—there is something you will need to do for us. You remember the man who called you out at the dance?"

"The fellow you used to trap me. The skinny one, with the cough."

Abate's face darkened. "Do you know why he is skinny and why he coughs? His lungs have been destroyed by granite dust. He is thirty-five. He is one of the most skilled carvers in—I dare say in the world. There is much I could learn from him as a sculptor. But he will die before the year is out, because the men who own the granite sheds—Barclay and the others—will not spend the money to install dust filters for the air-tools that make them so much money. Cutter's consumption, they call it—"

Wyatt felt rage churning his gut, felt it boil over and let it go. "Damn you! Don't lecture me about consumption! I lived with it night and day for five years—"

Abate stopped and his dark eyes searched Wyatt's face. His face softened momentarily. "Your wife?"

Wyatt nodded curtly. Empathy flashed between them for an instant. He forced his breathing to slow. The anger had flared up precisely because he did understand, he'd seen the men in their slow march along Main Street, heard that all-too-familiar coughing. And he saw the loss in Abate's eyes. He remembered what Calcagni had said: *Lost his wife and three of his kids in a fever...*

"Can you hear of this and wonder why we are anarchists? So now we come to the point. My—comrades—here and elsewhere mistrust Mr. Roosevelt and his intentions. I think perhaps he has some genuine care for the poor and the working-man, but to them he is another tool of the rich—"

Wyatt cut him off. "—so Galleani wants to add him to his list of successful assassinations."

Abate laughed. "You have seen our newspaper. But who is this Galleani you speak of?"

"The man who's pulling your strings. What's the point in games?" Wyatt rubbed the back of his head, which was throbbing painfully since his outburst. "He's holed up here. He's behind this Subversive Chronicle of yours. I saw him with you at the dance."

Anger flickered briefly on Abate's face, replaced by a bemused smile. "The last we heard, he had fled to Canada. America is not a safe place for such as he. But to the point. We must have a face-to-face talk with Mr. Roosevelt, either to convince my colleagues that he is a good man, or—"

"To give them a clean shot for popping him off, like McKinley? And you want me to help you with that? You must think I'm as crazy as you are."

The big man who'd brought Wyatt in balled his fists and took a step towards him, but Abate's hand held him back. The tiny window now held a faint gleam of daylight.

"We don't wish to kill anyone. All we want is to find out whether he stands for the working man or the rich. He comes to Vermont, he gives us that occasion, we talk with him, we go away."

"And what if you don't like what he has to say?"

"We will tell the world. That is what our paper is for. But here is an opportunity, Mr. Wyatt. If he gains our trust, we will tell them that too. He stands for election next year, as you know." Abate turned the chair around and straddled it.

"Galleani put you up to this, didn't he? Why doesn't he have the guts to come and talk to me himself?"

"He doesn't sp—" Abate caught himself. "I don't know what you're talking about."

Wyatt shrugged. "Have it your way. But you can't expect the President to agree to a meeting with a crew of terrorists— people who celebrate assassinations—"

"You are right— it will have to happen unannounced. He and his men will not choose to talk with us. So you will make the arrangements for his visit just as you had planned. You tell us the dates and the location, and we will do the rest."

"Not a chance," Wyatt snarled. There was no part of him that did not ache. "Unless we get the murderer, the visit's off anyway."

"Of course we will send you away with an escort—" Abate nodded towards the big man, "—who will stay near you to make sure you stick to the arrangement. A pair of shadows, if you will. They will telephone once a day to report on your progress. But I give you my word, Mr. —Baird, or whoever you really are—we want only to talk. No harm will come to anyone." Abate's dark eyes shone with fervor and sincerity.

"You can't guarantee that. No one can. Your thugs here can't follow me everywhere, you must realize that. All I'd need is a few minutes alone in someone's office and the whole thing's off."

"Then perhaps it is just as well that I allowed my—ah, colleague to persuade me of the need for these. I doubt anyone will think much of your story once they know how you really spent your time in Barre."

Abate turned to the man who had followed him up, who handed him a large brown envelope. He removed a sheaf of photographs and held them out to Wyatt.

There was his dream, in shades of sepia and white, the half-naked, smoky-eyed woman, stroking his bare chest, his fingers grazing her nipple, he lying beneath her with the dreamy, glazed look of a satisfied lover, his eyes half-closed…there were a dozen or more. The photographer was skilled, and he had had a field day.

"This is monstrous!" His cheeks burned and blood pounded in his ears.

Abate returned the photographs to the envelope. "Indeed, and she not even eighteen. A dozen witnesses from the dance will attest that you went off with her, that they saw you slip some sort of pill into her lemonade—and spending your employer's time and money in such a fashion. What will your Mr. Dodge, or Mr. Warren, think of your anarchist tales when the Secret Service shows him these?"

"He won't believe it."

"Surely the camera does not lie."

"Can you really be so unscrupulous—as to let a woman degrade herself—"

"I would never have thought of it myself," Abate shook his head. "But I must admit that it was a good idea. It is not only men who sacrifice themselves for our cause. The young lady is still a maiden, despite appearances—fortunately you were in no state to—" Abate cleared his throat and blushed "—my comrades would not have let things go so far. And if you cooperate with us, these need never see the light of day. You preserve her reputation as well as your own."

Wyatt's mind hobbled to catch up with what he'd seen and heard. He tried to follow the chain of consequences like moves in a chess game. Do what the man wanted, and put the President's life at risk. Out of the question. Pretend to go along, tell Macalester or Roosevelt's man Wilkie, get this crew arrested—but what then? Galleani disappears, Abate denies everything, produces the photos…at least the President would be safe…or stall for time, refuse to go along, think of a way to get out of here. If he could shake off the anarchists, they'd have trouble finding out Roosevelt's plans, and his security men would be on the alert…

"Do what you have to do." Wyatt sat down again, his back against the chimney, and spread his hands in resignation.

Abate frowned. "We have no wish to harm you. But you must see that this is your only option. I suppose we must leave you up here for a while to think about it." He signaled to the big man, who opened the trapdoor. The ladder sat braced against the side of the opening. The man with the cudgel handed down the chair, then the oil lamp to Abate as his head receded below the floor. Then he scrambled down the ladder one-handed, gripping his club firmly with the other hand. He pulled the door shut after him with an iron ring and Wyatt heard the rattle of two heavy bolts slamming to. He was alone in the dim, empty attic without so much as a pocket-knife. Nor, he realized, the ache in his bladder pounding for relief, with even the amenity of a jug of water or a chamber-pot.

The baking eternity of the day that followed became Wyatt's vision of Hell for years afterwards. His tongue cracked with thirst, the evil aftertaste of the chloroform still in his throat, his body slick with gritty sweat, he charted the sun's slow course above, baking the roof of his oven-prison. Peeling his clothes down to his underwear brought little relief. His mind swam with the stories he'd heard as a child of the Indians staking their enemies out in the desert heat, their faces and private parts smeared with honey. The stuff of nightmares.

The little window would be too small to crawl out of, even if he could get it open. A louvered triangle opposite the window let in a minuscule amount of outside air. Solid steel, bolted to the wall. The house was square, probably dropping off sheer at the gable end—sixteen or twenty feet, depending on how the ground sloped. The crowns of maples in summer fullness kept him from seeing what lay below, but from the direction of the sun's travel and the street-sounds, the ding-ding of a trolley car, he realized he must be on a side street north of Main—in the heart of the Italian district. Where the anarchists were surrounded by friends. Would Macy have taken his departure at face value, as Abate said, or would he come looking for him? For that matter, had Macy believed his story about an innocuous errand to find a musician for Webb? He fervently hoped not.

He crept over the surface of the attic, pawing among old newspapers stuffed into the floor-joists, looking for anything— a nail, a screw, a stray piece of flashing—a tool or weapon. All he found was an old tin of shellac, light and near-empty when he picked it up, the lid stuck firmly shut. Beyond that, nothing but the broken top of a kitchen match, the one the fellow with the cudgel had been chewing on while Abate conducted his interview. About half an inch of splintered wood dipped in blue sulfur. Well, shellac was flammable. If he got desperate, he could set the place on fire—

Which was not, he reflected, such a bad idea. One of the floor-joists was splintered where the pine had dried out. He pried at it carefully to extend the split, managed to release a foot and a half of it before it snapped off in his hands.

Long hours later, he heard noises below, footsteps on stairs, low-pitched male voices. He hid the can and the splintered stick under the lip of flooring in the space between joists. He wanted to call out, beg for water, tell them anything to relieve the torture of thirst and heat. He stayed quiet. No one came. Surely they should wonder whether he had passed out or suffered from heatstroke. Surely they would come and check on him...

The sun's rays were piercing the attic window now like red-hot spears. He heard footsteps below the hatch. He withdrew to the corner where he'd shed his clothes, lay still and half-closed his eyes to slits. The bolts shot back and the trapdoor slammed open. The head of the big man, the larger of his abductors, appeared like a rising moon. He was covered from head to foot in fine white dust: a granite worker by day. He scanned the floor, his eyes falling on Wyatt's seemingly moribund body in the corner. His face registered alarm. He called down to someone below, then climbed up and stood on the attic floor, not visibly armed, but with a bulge in his hip-pocket that could be a sap. Wyatt felt a rush of air from below, cooler than the attic's but still warm. Another set of feet on the ladder behind him, the club-wielding thug once again brandishing his weapon, also ghost-white with granite dust.

Wyatt calculated the odds. He'd have surprise on his side, but they were both larger than him, and there was the club, and probably another weapon in Number One's pocket. A steel-toed boot poked him in the ribs. He rolled away from it and made a croaking sound, opened his eyes weakly and closed them to half-slits again. The men traded glances. A rapid exchange ensued, evidently a debate on whether to send for Abate or a doctor or both. The large man seemed to favor the move; Number Two was skeptical.

Number Two descended the ladder and handed up an enameled pitcher and a basin of water. The big man took the basin and tossed its contents unceremoniously over Wyatt's head. The blissful shock of it tingled the length of his body. He sat up abruptly as if coming out of a stupor. The man handed him the pitcher, picking up the club again and watching with narrowed eyes as Wyatt began draining the pitcher in greedy, sloppy gulps. Abruptly, he snatched it away before Wyatt had drunk half of it. It splashed on the man's hands and forearms, turning the ghostly white to hairy brown.

"*Basta*," he snarled. He passed the pitcher and basin down to his companion, who shouted something up at him. "You talk now?"

"No. You should've asked me that before you gave me the water."

The man caught only the "no" and turned from him with a shrug. He withdrew below, slamming the bolts behind him. Wyatt wondered if, in spite of the odds, he should have tried to take them. He checked the pocket of his trousers, where he had secreted the match-head. Still dry. Wyatt wrapped his mouth around the wool of the trousers and sucked as much moisture out of the fabric as it would yield.

The sounds from below subsided and a door slammed. Wyatt sat in his singlet and shorts, watching the sun set over the maples from the little window, the varnish-can open at his booted feet, stuffed with the newspapers and shirt he had soaked in the shellac.

Quiet below, and darkness at last. A thin aura of light from the electric streetlights on Main, barely enough to make out the shapes of the trees. His damp trousers were bundled around the base of the can, to insulate it long enough for him to hold it.

He waited another hour, perhaps longer.

Time now.

He got as far back on the flooring as he could and took a running ju-jitsu kick at the window glass. It shook but didn't break.

Another kick, this time with the heel of the boot, and the glass shattered. He wrapped the trousers around his hand and cleared away the shards, giving him an opening perhaps fourteen inches in diameter. He struck the half-inch of match-head across the nails of his boot, willing himself to hold onto it as it flared. He had the splinter of floor-joist ready. Its tip caught, glowed, began to fade. He blew on it gently and it flared with a sickly yellow, wavering flame, good enough for his purpose.

He took the can, its bottom once again cushioned by his trousers, and steadied it at a tilt against the lip of the window with his left hand, bringing the flame to its rim. The shellac-soaked newspaper flared up, spread its heat to the rag of his shirt. The flame shot up into the night sky, catching the dark red eaves of the roofline as it went.

The next part would have to go fast. He only had one chance. Already he could feel heat searing his palms. He tossed the flaming can sideways and backwards onto the roof. He heard it roll, rattle, and stick—as he'd hardly dared hope—caught in the gutter by leaves and twigs, no doubt, and soon he saw the red flickers around the corner and at the peak of the roof above him. Blisters were rising on his hands. He'd deal with that later. Someone would see the flames, surely, someone would call in the fire company before the flames engulfed the roof and roasted him alive or forced him to kick out a hole and break his neck jumping from three floors up…

It couldn't have been more than ten or fifteen minutes, but they seemed to encompass the span of his life. As they might, if help didn't arrive soon. The roof on the south side, where the can had landed, was growing hot to the touch. He heard the crackle and hiss of flame spreading along the south eaves. Then, mercifully, the clang-clang of a fire engine's bell, coming closer, but still a distance away when something slammed against the side of the building. He stuck his head out of the shattered window.

Three floors below him, John Macy was maneuvering an extension ladder into place. Behind him was another man, his face in shadow.

"You'll need an axe," Wyatt croaked. "Window's too small to get out." The second man disappeared for a long two minutes while Macy stood poised on the lower rungs of the ladder, then returned to hand something up to Macy and hold the ladder steady as he climbed. Wyatt grabbed the axe from Macy while he was still three feet below, waved him back down and began bashing a hole around the window frame while Macy moved the ladder aside. The fire was licking its way into the attic space behind him now. The axe stuck, was released, splintered a ragged opening big enough for Wyatt to crawl backwards through the hole. He descended the ladder on shaking legs.

"Where'd you get this?" Wyatt began turning the ladder on its side. The man with Macy grabbed it out of his hands and Wyatt turned to stare into a face that was out of context at first, then came into focus.

"Calcagni?"

"Place belongs to a house-painter. Keeps all his tools in the barn round back." Calcagni jerked a thumb behind him. "What are you doing in your skivvies?"

"Let's get the hell out," Wyatt rasped. Calcagni nodded. Flames leaped and danced around the roof of the house. The fire-bell clanged, coming closer. Macy stood uncertain for a moment, and Calcagni grabbed him by the shoulder and steered him out behind the barn. The roof hissed and crackled behind them.

"They'll be coming up Main Street," Calcagni said. "We're on Fortney. We'll head down Pleasant and over to Maple. Can you run?" Wyatt nodded. The three took off through backyards, leaping low fences and gates. In one backyard, washing hung on a line. Calcagni tugged at a set of overalls without breaking stride, sending the clothespins snapping off into the air. He thrust the trousers into Wyatt's chest. "Soon's we find an alley, put these on and get decent. Anyone's coming after us, you'll stick out like a sore thumb otherwise. Don't worry, they're my cousin's. We'll get back over towards Main."

They came out on a long street lined with frame houses.

"Full of Italians," Macy muttered. "Keep going." The three ran on, panting and sweaty, Wyatt clutching the overalls which he'd bundled under his arm. His blistered hands stung. They'd be agony before long. They passed a house where a group of men craned their necks from the verandah, trying to figure out where the fire was. Spotting the runners, the men clattered down the porch steps and began to give chase, dropping pipes and cigarettes as they went.

"Dammitall," Macy panted. "Those fellows are anarchists. I heard they were hiding Galleani somewhere in here."

Calcagni looked back, jerking his arms in exhortation. "Just keep running!"

Wyatt ran easily despite his dehydrated state, but Macy, unaccustomed to exercise, was having trouble keeping up.

"We get separated—" Calcagni pointed south, "—head for the train depot. It's over there."

"Good idea." Macy let his pace slacken and took in long, wheezy breaths. "Catch the local back to Montpelier with Calcagni. I'll meet you there later. Better if we split—they'll get nothing out of me."

"I'm obliged," Wyatt bounced along the sidewalk. "I was beginning to worry. You spot the flames?"

"Calcagni came down from Burlington looking for you. Lucky he thought to come to me."

"I came after you this morning. Just had a feeling something bad was up." Calcagni's feet rang evenly on the pavement. "Macy told me he thought you'd gone off with a girl. I didn't buy it. When you didn't turn up by noon—"

"Skeptical sorts," Wyatt said between gasps. "Good thing."

"Figured they'd have you somewhere in this neighborhood. Saw the fire—you start it?" Calcagni's head twisted back. The flaming roof was three blocks behind them now.

"Only way I had of getting out. Wasn't my first choice for an exit."

"They'll lose the attic at least." Calcagni didn't slow down. "C'mon, the Central Vermont leaves in two minutes."

The pounding feet echoing their own were getting closer. They reached Maple Avenue. An empty horse-drawn coal-cart was clattering south on the paving stones, on its way to pick up a load from Conti's yard near the rail depot. Macy dashed across the street and lost himself in the darkness of an alley. Calcagni and Wyatt ran for the cart and jumped on. It was bouncing so badly the driver didn't notice. The two clung swaying to the slatted sides of the wagon as the driver shouted "Haw!" and the wagon hurtled left onto Main Street, easily out-distancing the knot of men who stopped running and stood shouting after them. Wyatt felt the skin flaying from his hands, but he held the stolen overalls tight under his arm.

"I was you," gasped Calcagni, "I'd hop that train to Montpelier, get yourself seen to at the Heaton." Swaying wildly off the corner of the wagon, he pulled a ticket from his coat pocket and handed it to Wyatt. "See where it's just pulling out—I'll go this way—"

"Pavilion," Wyatt gasped, dropping from the wagon and running towards the train. "Ask for Baird when you get there."

"Not a chance. I'm going back to Burlington. Don't need any trouble with this bunch—don't think they saw my face but you never know." Calcagni's voice faded away as he cut across the tracks and around to the other side of the train.

Wyatt found a tiny toilet on the train and stayed there long enough to pull on the overalls before handing his ticket to the conductor just as the train pulled into Montpelier. The clerk on duty at the Pavilion was a brisk young man with a high collar and a striped shirtwaist. His eyes goggled when Wyatt asked for his room key. Small wonder: the face that glared back from the beveled mirror behind the clerk was a deranged coalminer's, unrecognizable as his own.

Wyatt reached his room, near-dead of exhaustion. He had just enough energy to fill the sink, dunk his face in the washbasin and drink himself sick before soaking his ravaged hands in the cool water and wrapping damp towels around them. He collapsed on top of the hobnailed bedspread, still in the stolen overalls, and slept like a dead man.

The throb of his hands woke him early the next morning, as blistered as the surface of the moon. It could have been worse, but he'd have to have them seen to. Apart from the pain, there was the risk of infection if the blisters burst. He took a long bath, shaved gingerly around his bruised face and broken lips, left the upper lip with its returning stubble. His one change of clothes hung in the room's little mahogany wardrobe. He still had his wallet, having gone to Barre with only walking-around money. He had a massive breakfast delivered to his room. Bacon, fried eggs, hotcakes and syrup, home fries, toast and strong coffee—they had never tasted so good.

To a well-starched but kindly nurse at the Heaton Hospital up the hill, he passed off his hand injuries and bruises as "a bit of clumsiness with an oil-lamp." He wondered how Macy had fared after they'd parted company at the coal-wagon and hoped the young man hadn't been recognized. He had misled Macy about his purpose—though Macy had intuited as much—but he hadn't intended to compromise the reporter. Had Galleani been in the group that pursued them? He'd had an impression of someone tall and commanding, directing the others who gave chase.

By late afternoon, he had delivered the overalls to a postal clerk to send to Calcagni's address in Burlington and landed on the overnight train to New York. He'd find a way to thank him and Macy later. His hands were salved and bandaged, his one remaining suit of clothes pressed neatly, crisp against his blissfully clean body. He'd had enough of Barre anarchists to last several lifetimes…and yet he couldn't shake the vision of the ghostly army marching up Main Street, the artist-laborers killing themselves carving rich men's monuments. The dark well of loss in Carlo Abate's eyes that mirrored his own.

A new pit of anxiety opened in his gut as the euphoria of escape wore off. How to explain to Dodge that the President's visit was off? *Just make sure I get what I need*, Dodge had said. Precisely what Wyatt had failed to do. *Nothing to be done about it till I get there.* His head lolled against the scratchy red-and-blue plush of his parlor car seat and he fell asleep.

CHAPTER 23

As promised, a chaise and driver were waiting for Wyatt and Macalester when they stepped off the train in Oyster Bay two days later. Sagamore Hill, a Queen Anne confection with a huge verandah overlooking the Sound, dominated a hillside sloping down to the deep blue of Long Island Sound. Barefoot boys screeched and tore around after each other on the sunny lawns, and they could hear the pock-pock of a vigorous tennis game in progress somewhere to the side of the house.

John Wilkie, the President's silver-haired security chief, who could have doubled for a prosperous Wall Street man, greeted them on a side porch.

"Inspector. Mr. Wyatt. Good of you gents to come out. We've got a lot to talk over, what I hear."

"I'm not sure what you'll make of it when we're done," Wyatt said.

A younger man with a huge handlebar mustache and close-cropped blond hair emerged with a tray that held a metal coffee service, thick white mugs and a mountain of craggy scone-like pastries.

"Mrs. Halliburton's famous currant buns," Wilkie gestured an invitation. "The President's secret vice. Inspector Macalester, Mr. Wyatt, allow me to present my new colleague Walter Armbruster. Most recently of the Philippine Military Constabulary. Governor Taft was kind enough to bring him to our notice."

"That sounds like a good name for a security man," Macalester said. Armbruster pumped his hand heartily with a paw that looked as if it could crush bones.

Wyatt rose and extended a bandaged hand. "Glad to know

you." Armbruster glanced at the bandages, grinned and, to Wyatt's relief, gave his hand barely a squeeze.

Wilkie stirred sugar into his coffee. "What's been happening on Heron Island?"

Wyatt gave them the details, from his discovery of the body to the investigation to his encounters with Czerny and the Barre anarchists.

"Macalester was in touch with me, before you ran afoul of that lot in Barre." Wilkie nodded towards the Scotsman, who was splitting a bun and lathering it with whipped butter. "There was enough to be concerned with even then. There's plenty to suggest that this was a murder, by whom or for what reason we don't know. An anarchist who disappears, same time the body's found. I don't like coincidences. And now the cat's out of the bag, at least as far as the location and rough timing of the visit."

"I suggested to Mr. Dodge that he engage additional security guards." Wyatt gingerly buttered a bun. The cocaine salve the hospital had provided wasn't entirely effective. "Pinkertons, perhaps, or others you'd find acceptable."

He'd been more than a little surprised at Dodge's reaction to his news: after the expected initial eruption, he'd apologized for the outburst. "How would anyone have known that Barclay fellow employs an anarchist spy?" From there, he'd viewed it as a management problem with a number of potential solutions, and no hint of blaming Wyatt for the security breach.

"As to that," Wilkie said, "if we decided to do it, I've no doubt Armbruster here and a couple of our other fellows could handle the situation. An island, though—" he sipped his coffee thoughtfully, "—you're a sitting duck. It may be difficult to get onto it, but all it would take is one determined lunatic, managing to evade detection till it's too late. And here you may have a whole crew of them. You've had no luck tracking this Rossi fellow in New York, I take it?"

Macalester shook his head. "Sergeant Petrosino and his people have been on it for a fortnight—"

Wilkie straightened up in his chair. "The chap who found the Murder Stable?" Wyatt remembered the gruesome story, two years old now: sixty bodies in various states of mutilation, victims of the notorious Black Hand which had exported its crime organization from Sicily to the Lower East Side.

"That's the one. He has people that can go anywhere in Little Italy. But not a trace of this Rossi among the known subversives—and believe me, Petrosino's lot doesn't miss much. It's a right puzzle," Macalester concluded gloomily.

Armbruster hastily choked down a mouthful of bun. "What about Paterson?"

Macalester pounced like a terrier on a rat. "Good lad! First thing we thought of. Last known haunt of Galleani before he took it on a lam. He ran some anarchist rag there after Bresci—the fella that did in King Umberto. According to the Passaic County Sheriff, the others have been lying doggo since the silk strike. Our colleagues up the river are cooperatin', for a change. They'd like to get their hands on anybody connected to Galleani, so they were happy to have a good look for our man. No sign of him, though."

"I don't like the picture." Wilkie replaced his cup with a gesture of finality.

"Brigham's a good man, sir," Armbruster said. "Crack shot, and eyes like a cat. He wouldn't miss a trick if he's on duty. There'd be him and me and Fiorello, and Wyatt, of course—or would you be socializing?"

"I'd be working. The last go-round was by way of cover—to check out the island and some of the guests. That number's been reduced by two—the Van Dorns—and the President's known the Fisks and the Webbs a long time, so—"

"I still don't like it," Wilkie said, as though being urged into a chancy investment.

He was interrupted by a sweaty pink figure in tennis whites who bounded from the lawn onto the verandah, a racket swinging from his left hand.

"Currant buns!" the President whooped. The men clattered hastily to their feet. "Any lemonade?" He stopped abruptly and stared at Wyatt, the sun winking on the famous gold-rimmed glasses.

"You were in my unit, weren't you? On the Hill." Wyatt had forgotten the high-pitched voice, so at odds with the manly demeanor and reputation.

"Dade Wyatt, sir. A pleasure to see you again."

Roosevelt went to pump the bandaged hand and gave it a light two-handed clasp instead. He broke into the toothy grin that reminded cartoonists of piano keys. "Wyatt! Yes! Looking well—hurt your hands, did you?" His face clouded over. "But what did I hear—your wife—"

Wyatt looked down and nodded.

"Something else we have in common. I was very sorry to hear of it."

"Thank you, sir." Wyatt marveled at the mnemonic powers of career politicians. Roosevelt put an arm on Macalester's shoulder and shook his hand vigorously.

"Well! Good old Mac from Mulberry Street. How'd you get hooked up with this lot? D'you know, I thought of you last year, after we lost Big Bill—good friend of yours, wasn't he?" Macalester nodded, his deferential smile fading at the memory. The President's friend and bodyguard William Craig, a Glasgow native like Macalester, had been crushed beneath the wheels of a runaway trolleycar which destroyed their coach and very nearly killed Roosevelt himself.

"So you men are working out the arrangements for my little trip to good ol' Ver-mont? Hand me a bun, there."

Wilkie cleared his throat and passed the plate. "Frankly, sir, I'm going to advise against it. You heard about Mr. Van Dorn—"

"Oh, yes. Poor old Van Dorn. Drowning, wasn't it? Terrible thing. Poor Milly—lovely woman." He turned to Wyatt. "Have you seen her since?"

"Yes, sir. She's distraught, of course, but bearing up well enough, I'd say. The concern, I'm afraid—"

"—is that it may not have been an accident," Wilkie broke in. "There's a strong indication an anarchist may have been involved—"

"Anarchist, eh?" Roosevelt glowered.

"Yes, sir. And Wyatt here just had a run-in with a crowd of them in Barre. They've got wind of the plans for the visit—they don't know the dates, but they'll figure it out. They kidnapped him and tried to force him to arrange a— a confrontation."

"It's worse than that, sir, I'm afraid," Wyatt interposed. "From what I've learned, Luigi Galleani is among them, publishing a radical newspaper. Among other things, he seems to advocate assassinations."

Roosevelt's eyes opened wide behind the thick lenses. "Ah, him—the Big Chief, isn't he? Paterson silk strike. Wanted for starting a riot. Didn't kill anybody, as I recall."

"No, sir, but with respect, the middle of a riot isn't our preferred location for you," Wilkie said patiently.

A maid emerged with a pitcher of iced lemonade. Roosevelt grabbed one of the glasses and poured it to overflowing. "They tell me I shouldn't drink this stuff. Say it triggers asthma. Mind over matter, I say!" He downed it in two gulps and poured another glass. "Look here, Wilkie, I won't hear of not going. Edith and I have been looking forward to a few days without a lot of dashed reporters and importunate Cabinet secretaries tailing my every move. Edith in particular—an out-of-town trip with no speechifying, which she doesn't get very often, and I'm not about to disappoint her. You're on an island with a three-sixty view. You can see 'em coming and head 'em off, can't you? Can't live your whole life in fear. I've got every confidence in you men, every confidence."

A boy's exasperated voice hailed him from across the lawn. "Father! Where'd you go!"

He waved at them and began trotting back across the lawn.

"He forgot his racket." Armbruster picked it up and strode after him. "I guess we're going to Vermont."

"No help for it." Wilkie's nostrils flared and he shook his head.

"There are tennis courts on the island," Wyatt said. "Clay ones. Up to his standards, I'd say."

"Partners?" Wilkie replaced Roosevelt's glass on the tray.

"Dodge plays well. So does Jeremy, the younger son. Quiet fellow, but aggressive on the court—surprisingly so. Good friend of Will Van Dorn's. They've spent some time together since the father's death."

Armbruster was striding back across the lawn, his powerful arms swinging.

"They're both clean—as far as Yale's concerned, anyway. No radical societies, no overly bohemian activities. We have a lot of contacts in the local forces," Wilkie added, smiling in response to Wyatt's raised eyebrow.

"Fraternities and secret societies aren't considered subversive, I suppose."

"What I hear, they *are* the government." Wilkie shook his head. "Take your old boss there, Walt—Mr. Taft. Skull and Bones all the way, I've heard."

"He conceals the connection well." Armbruster caught Wyatt's smile as both pictured the amorphous bulk of the interim Governor of the Philippines. "So, what's next here?"

"You need to keep looking for Rossi," Wyatt nodded towards Macalester, "since he's still the likeliest suspect in Van Dorn's death. But I'm going to take a harder look at everyone else who was there, see if we can't get this cleared up before the visit."

"You're going back to Vermont, then?" Wilkie looked skeptical.

"After a few inquiries in the City. Young Dodge, for one, isn't off the list yet. I need to find that missing boat. And I'll have another look at the weak spots on the island, in case any of our friends from Barre decide to turn up at the wrong time."

Macalester raised a finger as if a thought had struck him. "Where will Secretary Hay be, while the President's in Vermont?"

Wilkie hesitated for an instant. "At his farm on Lake Sunapee."

"Can you reach him quickly, if necessary?—it just seems an appropriate precaution."

"Of course. We insisted on telegraph service there, after the President—Mr. McKinley—died. He didn't like it, but he saw the necessity of it. Now, Wyatt, you don't have that on the island—you'd have to go to South Hero or the mainland if you wanted that on your end."

"I'll talk to Mr. Dodge. You could lay an underwater line to relay to Western Union at South Hero. It wouldn't be too costly, and it would be a useful emergency measure in any event."

Armbruster's hand stole towards the plate of currant buns. "It would be easier if they'd just name a Vice-President."

Wilkie laughed. "Mr. Hay said he for one would rather be hanged—'spend your life bored stiff waiting to fill a dead man's shoes,' he said. Not that that was for attribution," he added quickly.

"He has a point," Wyatt smiled, "and the President's left us in a bit of a bind here. I wasn't expecting him to overrule you."

Wilkie frowned. "I certainly don't advise this trip, and I'll tell him so again if he gives me a chance. On the other hand, a fellow who's taken on rustlers and buffalo stampedes and Spanish cavalry—" he threw up his hands.

"—won't be put off by a ratty anarchist or two. Not from what I saw in Cuba."

Macalester laughed. "So he really was the hero he's reported?"

Wyatt hesitated. "Maniac is the word I would have used."

CHAPTER 24

As Wyatt approached the Van Dorns' brownstone, a fashionably dressed young man was coming hastily down the steps. His wavy chestnut hair was neatly parted, and his rubicund face wore a look of chagrin, an emotion to which Wyatt sensed it was ill used. He caught a whiff of pomade as the man brushed by him, slamming his hat on his head and muttering an apology in some foreign accent.

He rang the doorbell, wondering about his chances of being admitted after the last episode. The parlormaid, still wearing the crape-ribboned cap, scanned his face with fear and distaste.

"Missus Van Dorn is not at home." Her eyes darted down the street to the young man's retreating back and she began to shut the door in Wyatt's face. He put his hand on it to stop her.

"I came to see Mr. Van Dorn."

She looked confused for a moment. "Oh, you mean Mr. Will. You'll have to wait here in the vestibule. I can't let you in."

Wyatt handed over his card. "If Mr. Van Dorn is not at leisure, perhaps you would be good enough to ask him if he would meet me and Mr. Warren Dodge in an hour at the Union Club."

She closed the inner door. The vestibule sealed up like a narrow, stuffy box, the walls done in the old-fashioned faux-marbre technique achieved with paint and turkey feathers. A fragrant bouquet, wrapped in green tissue, drooped over the edges of a tiny table by the inner door. An unusual array: periwinkle, sweetbriar rose, ivy, balm of Gilead, amaranth, white daisies, lilies of the valley, others he couldn't identify. Wyatt racked his brain for their meanings. Something of sympathy, sweet memories, healing of grief, return of happiness. For Mrs. Van Dorn, from the young man he'd just passed? If so, a kindly, chaste, and eloquent selection. Or a more intimate message to be read between the lines—else why the discreet sprinkling of red rosebuds to remind the receiver that "you are young and beautiful"? He was about to reach for the black-edged card tucked among the flowers when the door reopened and the parlormaid informed him that "Mr. Van" would meet him and Mr. Dodge at the club.

Willem Van Dorn entered the great lounge of the Union Club as one accustomed to the place. Dressed in light gray summer wool, the mourning band conspicuous on his arm, he seemed to have filled out since his father's death. The mustache he had grown since Wyatt had last seen him made him look several years older and less like a Renaissance sculpture, still extraordinarily handsome but in a more earthbound way. Wyatt and Dodge rose to greet him. He strode towards them, glowering at Wyatt.

"Good morning, Will—uh, Willem." Dodge offered his hand. Will took it grudgingly, nodding towards Wyatt with a curt "Good morning" in reply to his greeting.

"Why did you wish to see me?"

"We're trying to get to the bottom of the business on the island." Dodge sat down and gestured for the others to join him. "Wyatt thought you might be able to shed some light on one or two questions that have been troubling us."

"Why would you think that? I wasn't there. And may I say, Mr. Wyatt, that you might have been aware that your presence at our home was unwelcome, after your last visit." He all but spat the last word.

"What did you hear about my last visit?"

"You know as well as I do—you made an improper advance on a woman in the depth of bereavement—I cannot imagine how a place like this would permit—I was told one had to be a gentleman to be admitted here—"

Dodge held up a restraining hand. "Will, that's not fair. Let Wyatt tell you his side of things, and you can judge—"

"But Doctor Tinmuth said—"

"Doctor Tinmuth is a fussy old woman, as anyone east of Central Park knows. And in your stepmother's state of mind, it's understandable that she might misinterpret—"

"He had no business calling on her in the first place."

"She could have refused to receive me," Wyatt pointed out.

"You represented it as an investigative matter." Will spoke through clenched teeth. "Though why you took such a responsibility on yourself, I cannot imagine—"

"I asked him to," Dodge said. "I wanted to clear up Gerald's—your father's death. Will, I know what you said at the time. But you didn't want the police all over this any more than I did, did you?"

"They are involved in any case—at my request initially." Van Dorn waved off a waiter hovering with a coffeepot. "I myself have been questioned twice by detectives from the Central Bureau. They demanded a detailed account of my movements, wanted to see my train ticket, for heaven's sake! As though one keeps such things. Fortunately, I'd left it in a pocket."

"I have also been questioned at length," Wyatt said. "In an investigation like this, everyone with a potential motive is a suspect, I'm afraid."

"You found my father's body. They were bound to question you."

Wyatt tried to keep his tone conciliatory. Grief took many forms; killing the messenger was one of its more traditional manifestations. "Exactly. And your testimony on the whereabouts of one of the many suspects is crucial to his alibi."

Will blinked. "You mean Jeremy? The idea's ridiculous. What possible reason could he have for wanting to harm my father?"

"That's not the point," Dodge said. "The police can't assume anyone with means and opportunity wouldn't have a motive—or vice-versa. We need information to rule people out."

"So they're sure it was murder, then."

"None of us wanted to think that. Webb still doesn't. But how would your father have ended up there otherwise?"

Will's face cleared and he shook his head. "I've been giving that a lot of thought. And the only thing I can think of is that he went birding and fell off a cliff somewhere. Admittedly, it's a stretch."

"As for Wyatt's call on your stepmother, I've known the man a long time and in many different circumstances, and I've not seen him behave as other than a gentleman."

"That doesn't prove anything," Wyatt smiled. "But—Mrs. Van Dorn mentioned when she saw me that she had not eaten for some time. The day was warm, the room rather close—the scent of the lilies was nearly overpowering. I've no doubt our conversation was distressing to her—and then my insistence to the maid, after Mrs. Van Dorn's faint—"

"—overstepped the bounds of propriety, to say the least," Will snapped.

"Granted, but I was concerned about your stepmother's distress. She was clearly not getting enough air—"

"You were going to—to undress her yourself, the maid said."

"I said that to shock her into doing something. She was giving me some damned—pardon me, some nonsense about being a parlormaid and not a lady's-maid—Will, I've seen men die for lack of air in a tight spot," Wyatt felt his own color rising, "and to let it happen for someone's notion of propriety—I'd rather be barred from every house on Fifth Avenue than allow that."

Will's eyes widened and his face recovered some of its boyish softness. "Well—I'll admit that puts rather a different color on the matter. It sounds as if I should be obliged to you for saving Mil—my stepmother's life. Or acting in the interests of her health, at any rate. Perhaps you're right about Tinmuth, Mr. Dodge. But you evidently said something to distress Mrs. Van Dorn," he turned back to Wyatt. "It was she who instructed the maids not to admit you."

"I feared there might have been some misunderstanding," Wyatt took the olive branch before it could be snatched back. "A misplaced gallantry on my part, perhaps. Or my insistence on so distressing a topic in such an early stage of her bereavement. I assure you my only motive was to assist Mr. Dodge in resolving the situation."

Will Van Dorn bowed acknowledgement.

"Will, Mrs. Dodge and I would like you to join us on the island for the President's visit." Dodge's tone was familial, even paternal. "I realize you are still in deep mourning, but the President inquired particularly after you and your stepmother. Perhaps if you were to visit just long enough to shake his hand—naturally we wouldn't expect Mrs. Van Dorn—you needn't stay for the soirée, though there would be no harm in it. A man has the obligation, which women are fortunately spared, to rejoin the world and tend to affairs in spite of bereavement."

Will hesitated and took a deep breath. "It would be rather soon. But since you offer so kindly, may I think it over and send you a note?"

Dodge rose. "Speaking of tending to affairs, I need to get the family off to Vermont. It's good to see you out again, Wi—Mr. Van Dorn. Tell me," he added, "do you think you will resume your studies this fall?"

"I'm not sure at present. I thought I might take a few months, see to the settlement of Father's estate, and so forth."

"You have a good man of business in Mr. Pendergast. It was your father who recommended him to me—for personal matters, that is. He's a fellow of the utmost integrity and competence."

"No doubt," said Will, "but I doubt anyone would have the family's interest so much at heart as a family member. Mrs. Van Dorn needs a great deal of support and counsel at present—naturally she is not conversant with worldly matters."

"As why should she be?" Dodge smiled. "Jeremy would be glad to have your company back at college—"

"And I his," Will said earnestly. "He has been a great comfort in all this. I will let you know soon what I decide to do."

Wyatt reflected that in Will's new circumstances, a college

education for anything other than sheer love of learning would be superfluous. He had relished his own time as a scholarship student at Ohio Wesleyan, its contrast with the life of a farmboy—the luxury of time for thought and contemplation, to explore science and philosophy and literature as if they were unmapped territories. Luxuries Will had enjoyed since babyhood.

Wyatt motioned Will back to his leather wing chair. "If I may trouble you with just a question or two—" Will shrugged assent.

"When you waited on the shore for Jeremy, as you'd arranged, when did he first come into view?"

Will rested his hand on his chin, eyes half-closed, remembering. "When he came around Kibbie Point, I think. I'd say he was a mile and a half out then, from where I was, which was just a short way east of the anchorage. The sailboat I rented had a set of binoculars—at first his head just looked like something bobbing in the water. I'd have said a seal, if I didn't know better, or a buoy, but then it kept moving—"

"And there was no sign of a boat anywhere?"

Will opened his eyes and looked at him sharply. "A boat? Well, there were a couple of small yachts moored in the bay, with their sails down—I suppose there must have been a fisherman or two out, but other than that, I didn't see—why do you ask? –Oh. You're wondering if he might have rowed part of the way, and got rid of the boat? No. I saw no other boats."

It occurred to Wyatt that no one had yet looked for the missing *Merganser* along the South Hero shore—a possibility Will had not mentioned directly, though it was a logical one. If the murderer had escaped in the missing skiff, he would hardly leave it to drift. But if he'd pulled it up onto a beach, hidden it in the woods—Wyatt himself, so far as he knew, was the only person who had made any investigation of the crime scene, if crime scene it was. He should have looked for that boat long before now.

Was Will trying to protect his friend? Did he perhaps know, or suspect, that Jeremy had a hand in Gerald Van Dorn's death—from which, so far as Jeremy knew, Will could only benefit?

"You and Jeremy are good friends, I believe?"

"Lord, yes, have been since Exeter days."

"And he stayed at your home frequently?"

"Not till the last couple of years. When we were still at school, before Yale, I mean, his parents wanted him at home for the holidays—"

"So he and your parents—I mean, your father and step-mother—had not met until fairly recently?"

"Oh, a couple of years now, I think it's been."

"What did Mrs. Van Dorn think of Jeremy?"

Will's brow furrowed and he shrugged. "She's fond of him; they have the common interest in art, you see, she thinks he's quite talented—"

"And how did he feel about her?"

Will's mouth tightened. "Well, he likes her very much. He thinks her beautiful. He's been working on a portrait of her, you know—"

"Indeed? How interesting."

"Look here, you don't really think Jeremy had anything to do with this, do you?" There was alarm in Will's tone. "I've seen no impropriety in their relations. And he confided in me. It would have been very difficult, I think, for him to have concealed anything of—of that kind, from me."

"I honestly have no opinion about anyone's involvement at this point," Wyatt nodded to the waiter, who refilled his coffee-cup from a silver pot. "It's still just possible it was all a bizarre accident. But there is one other piece of this we're wondering about—the fiddler from the quartet. Who'd been engaged by the Webbs to replace another violinist."

"I wasn't on the island till—after," Will said. "So I don't know anything about that, except what I heard later. Haven't the New York police caught up with him yet?"

"He disappeared overnight. That's where we thought the boat might have gone—the one that's missing. You're sure you didn't see any odd-looking boats on the water when you were waiting for Jeremy? Or any fellows around the train, or the harbor, fitting his description?" He sketched a few details of the violinist's appearance for Will's benefit.

"The train didn't get in till seven," Will said. "I made my way to Keeler's Bay, which took a half hour or so, and hadn't been out in the sailboat more than ten minutes when I saw Jeremy in the water. Wouldn't your fellow have got in earlier than that?"

"If he came towards that point on the shore at all. It's possible he went to the north, to the Grand Isle station, and took the train there. Or took the ferry to Plattsburgh and caught a train from there to who knows where."

"Sounds as if you'd have a lot of ground to cover, looking for that boat."

"There is something else I must ask you about—something Mrs. Van Dorn said on the morning of your father's death. An estate on the Hudson, I think—something you and your father had quarreled about, and you were perhaps coming to make amends—"

"Blauwberg? What did she say?" Will's expression didn't change, but Wyatt saw his grip tighten on the arm of his chair.

"That your father planned to sell the estate, and that you opposed his wish."

"Well, as to that," Will let out a breath, "my reaction was intemperate. It had many associations for me, as perhaps she told you—I spent a lot of time there as a child, when my mother was still living. It was hers, in fact, from her father. And afterwards, I realized I had spoken rashly—it's only a house, after all—" he waved a hand in dismissal. Wyatt watched his eyes, which were looking away towards the door.

"So you were planning to apologize to your father—" he took a gamble, "—even though he had been unmoved by your plea not to sell the estate?"

"I was out of line," Will gave Wyatt a sudden, sad smile, "and I should have known better—Father's an amiable old duffer, he responds much better to wheedling than to anger—he'd have come round in time, he often has in other matters—" he bit his lip and looked away.

Wyatt knew too well the remorse of words unspoken, the heart's ache to unsay words that had wounded when it was too late. "In any event, it does not matter now—he had not sold Blauwberg." He chose the verb tense carefully.

"No, he had not," Will looked up, clear-eyed again. "And I confess I'm glad enough of that, in the midst of—all the rest of it."

Wyatt cleared his throat. "Thank you for answering my questions. Perhaps I may ask a favor of you."

"What might that be?"

"To convey my respects to Mrs. Van Dorn, and my apology for the deep offense I gave her, which I hope she will come in time to view as having been entirely unintentional."

"I will be glad to do so," Will rose and offered his hand. "I am grateful for your explanation."

"My sympathies to you in your loss," Wyatt said with feeling.

CHAPTER 25

Alighting from the train at the South Hero station, Wyatt recalled something Will had said—about spotting Jeremy, that was it, coming around Kibbie Point, not passing it…perhaps it was simply a figure of speech. An exploration of the South Hero shoreline was long overdue. If a boat had been pulled up and hidden in the woods, it could have been disposed of long since. And the President was due in a few days.

The click-clack of the train's wheels from New York to Rensselaer had lulled him into a reverie. The tracks ran so close to the bank of the Hudson that the train might have been floating across the river's still, mirrored surface. Across the water in the golden evening light rose the vistas of tawny cliff, mountain and deep green forest that had inspired Church and Durand, paintings come to life. No wonder Will Van Dorn cherished his childhood home at Blauwberg, unfashionable though it might be. Wyatt hoped he'd be able to hold onto it when the estate was settled.

At Burlington, where he'd spent the previous evening, he had thought of contacting Calcagni, whom he'd never properly thanked for his rescue in Barre. But he didn't want to risk being recognized by his former co-workers at Burlington Grocery. It could wait a little longer, until all this business—he hoped— was safely over. Such trouble and expense so that two men could have a private chat about politics…

Will Van Dorn's train had left New York at eight-thirty the night before his father's death, crossing the new marble causeway from Burlington to South Hero about six-forty and arriving at seven. Such easy assumption of wealth that could justify a Pullman compartment with bath and sitting-room for an overnight trip—a compartment more spacious than the foul little room in the Lower East Side where the elfin-faced child lay coughing out his life...the image angered him, both for stabbing his heart unbidden and for the injustice of which it spoke.

From the train station to Keeler's Bay, it would have been a walk of less than two miles to the sailboat rental at the dock. Will had waited on shore until he'd spotted Jeremy, then sailed out to meet him, but Jeremy would not let him pick him up; he had insisted on swimming all the way to the shore. Again Wyatt wondered about Will's comment of seeing Jeremy "come around" Kibbie Point. Heron Island lay east and north of Keeler's Bay. If Jeremy had swum in a straight line—surely the shortest route— shouldn't he have been coming straight into the mouth of the bay, not around the Point?

If he found the *Merganser* anywhere near Kibbie Point, he would have to ask Jeremy Dodge some hard questions. He hadn't seen the boy do much swimming when they were on the island together. Was Jeremy capable of murder? Passionate and romantic he certainly could be. He might have attacked Gerald Van Dorn on an impulse, pushed him off a cliff where he was birding. But the meeting with Will was prearranged, and if Jeremy had planned to kill Van Dorn and use his swim as an alibi, he'd engaged in cold premeditation. It seemed at odds with the Jeremy Wyatt knew, depressive and passive, sparked alive from time to time with passionate impulse. Still, Wyatt couldn't rule it out. And even Jeremy's sister had speculated that he'd done it...though she was still only a child, really...

You could row from Heron Island to Kibbie Point in half an hour, forty minutes at the most—but it would take a good two hours to swim that distance. Taking the boat and ditching it would gain you over an hour, then—but Jeremy would have had to conceal it, get back in the water, and swim around to the bay where Will waited with the sailboat. And look his friend in the eye as if he'd had nothing on his mind but a vigorous swim.

Perhaps he had reasoned that he'd be doing Will a favor, saving Blauwberg from being sold and buying him independence, as well as clearing the way for Jeremy's own pursuit of Mrs. Van Dorn. With it all looking like enough of an accident to leave Will's conscience clear—if not Jeremy's.

Leaving his carpetbag at the ticket office, Wyatt changed into a pair of sturdy boots, recalling the rugged terrain along the lakeshore. He walked north to the Keeler's Bay boat launch, where he rented a pulling-boat for the day and chatted with the attendant, a gray-haired, lean man in green overalls.

"Young friend of mine was here a few weeks ago, about this time of day, picked up a sailboat," he ventured. "Light haired fellow, college man—"

"Oh, ayuh, Van Dawhn, wa'n't it? His father drowned over to the island there. Seemed like a nice young fella. Told me all about it when he brought the boat back. Pretty broken up, he was."

"D'you see him pick up his friend?" Wyatt kept his tone idle.

"The one that was swimmin' over to meet him? Nope. See, he was comin' in up to Kibbie Point, there—" he pointed east and slightly north—"couldn't see that fah from heah, don'tcha know. It don't look it but it's near on two miles out to th' point from here. He got him OK, didn't he? Young Dodge fella whose father bought the island from Phelps, wa'n't it?"

"Ayuh." Wyatt fell unconsciously into the local idiom. "Long way for a swim."

"Who knows what these rich young fellas'll get up to. Lotta excess energy they got to get rid of. You work on a fahm from th' time you're old enough to walk, that ain't gonna be a problem," the boat-man grinned.

"That's the truth," Wyatt said. "Did that myself, way back."

"Builds character." The attendant cast him off and waved him on his way.

Wyatt steered the boat around Kibbie Point and methodically began scanning the rocky shore to the south. The *Merganser* would likely have been pulled up into the woods, but not too far; the killer wouldn't have had time to waste. Along the shoreline, narrow margins of rocks edged thick woods. Already the day was growing hot. He'd check around every likely landing spot for a few hundred yards south of the point. Jeremy—if it had been he—would not have had time to ditch the boat at any great distance and still make the final swim to his rendezvous with Will Van Dorn.

The sun was high and blazing on the back of his neck by the time he gave up. He had searched a mile and a quarter of shoreline, almost to Paradise Bay, three times as far as anyone could reasonably have swum, or even walked back. He'd tramped into the woods for fifty yards north and south of each landing spot, gaining nothing for his pains but insect bites and the smell of sun-roasted balsam and pine in his nostrils. There were shelves and small cliffs jutting into the water that would have been impassable, or nearly so. No sign of discarded shoes or clothing, either. Could the boat simply have been set adrift, and fetched up farther down the lake? It would have been an imprudent move on Jeremy's part; Will might have spotted it as they sailed back around the point.

He was sweating and grimy. There were no houses in sight. He beached the boat, stripped off his clothes and eased himself into the water, relishing its cool, earthy-smelling silkiness on his burned arms and head. Then he thought of Gerald Van Dorn's corpse floating in colder water than this—and felt himself break out in gooseflesh.

He waded onto the shore and lay drying on a grassy outcropping backed by deep woods. In the far distance towards Mallett's Bay, white sails shimmered in the midday heat. His mind drifted to Miss Bella Duvalier, the womanly warmth and sweet lilac-and-bread smell of her nestled in the crook of his arm. He wondered if the doe-eyed Laura had felt so warm to Germain…

He pulled himself back. The absence of the skiff south of Kibbie Point didn't completely clear Jeremy, but it was hard now to imagine how he could have managed the killing and still made his scheduled appearance in the water at Keeler's Bay. Wyatt was glad of that. Finding the skiff hardly mattered now. The critical thing was keeping the President safe. The musician, if that was Rossi's true occupation, might be a blunderer as a criminal, but he'd been lucky. Some chance leak of information between rival groups of subversives must have led him to the Webbs and to the knowledge that Roosevelt was expected on Heron Island.

Wyatt came out of his thoughts and slipped into the water again. It was a shock now against his reddened skin. He struck out from the shore for a few yards, idly wondering what lay around the long point just to the south of the little strand where he had pulled up the boat. A biscuit-colored cliff about ten feet high, topped with shrubby evergreens, ran along the edge of the water for a hundred yards or so. He turned over and floated on his back, his eyes unfocused, in the direction of the shore.

A movement caught his eye—something white in the trees, just at the bend where the cliff began jutting out from the shoreline. A path opening between the shrubs to reveal a girl in a white apron and short-sleeved dress, a large brown dog loping behind her.

"Ethan!" the girl was shouting at him. "Get in here! Ma's lookin' for ya—boy, are you gonna be in trouble!" The dog bounded past her and straight into the water, heading straight for Wyatt, who straightened up hastily and began treading water.

"I'm not Ethan!" he yelled back.

The girl looked at him, then spotted the boat and the pile of clothes on the shore.

"Jeezum crow! I guess you're not! Hey, Barney, whatcha doin'? Come back here!"

The dog was churning through the water on a bee-line towards him.

"Go away, Barney!" Wyatt shouted. "Bad dog!"

The dog hesitated, not used to having its prey talk back to

it. Wyatt, his face flushing, paddled towards the shallows. The dog turned and splashed its way back to the shore.

"I'm sorry." He crouched in the water so that only his dripping shoulders, he hoped, were visible. "I didn't realize I was trespassing."

"Oh, you ain't." The girl gave him a gap-toothed smile. "Least, not on our land. It's over there, 'round the point. You see a young fella with dark hair 'n' a mustache sorta like yours?"

Wyatt shook his head.

"Don't worry, we go skinnydippin' here all the time. Nice day for it, ain't it? Fact, I was gonna go myself once I got Ethan back to Ma—" she stopped, blushing.

"Look, would you mind—um—" Wyatt began.

"Oh, yeah. Here, I'll just step over here for a few minutes 'n' you can get decent. C'mere, Barney!"

The dog bounded out of the water and shook himself off all over the girl. Wyatt kept low and crawled uneasily out of the water, gave himself a perfunctory wipe with his shirt, and dressed rapidly.

"Uh—I'm—decent now, thanks."

She turned around and came towards him, sticking out her hand.

"I'm Ellie Tarrant. We live round there, on Paradise Bay."

"Dade Wyatt. Pleased to meet you, Miss Tarrant."

She was sixteen or seventeen, big-boned, sunburned, wisps of light hair escaping from darker brown braids. Homely as an old boot, until there was that dazzling, gap-toothed smile, the eyes dancing with vitality.

"I've never been in Paradise Bay," Wyatt added.

"That your boat there?" She pointed towards it.

"I rented it up in Keeler's Bay."

"You fishin' or what?" She scanned the boat for equipment.

"No. I was looking for a lost boat. Didn't find it, though. We think it might've drifted away from my friend's place—" he gestured vaguely northward.

"Skiff? Kinda faded-lookin', red paint around the gunwales?" Wyatt looked at her in surprise. "Yes, it was. Have you seen it?"

"It's been sittin' on our beach since—oh, last week in June," she said. "We went out there one mornin' and there it was. Looks like they took Ethan's old bike, though. I thought it was a pretty good trade, but Ethan was hoppin' mad."

"How far is it around to—your place? Is it a farm?"

"Oh, ayuh, we got twenty cows—twelve milkers 'n' the rest bred heifers, an' the calves, a' course."

"Good sized operation," Wyatt said, respectful. "I grew up on a farm myself."

"Dairy, was it?"

"A little bit of everything. Grew some winter wheat, row crops—"

"You ain't from here. 'Course, I could tell from your accent."

"I didn't think I had an accent."

"Everybody's got an accent. You just don't notice it when it's yours."

He followed her back along the path in the woods, the dog wagging his wet, feathery tail behind them. A quarter mile later, the woods opened up at the edge of a pasture where Holsteins looked up from their ruminations to gaze at him with dull hostility. Crickets buzzed in the dry grass; swallows and bobolinks swooped and dived, protecting their nests. The farmhouse lay on a rise, white clapboards freshly painted and edged in bottle green, and a brown barn behind with a Gothic window in the loft above the double doors.

A youth with a mustache even more straggly than Wyatt's bore down on them.

"Where ya been, Ellie? Ma's callin' for ya."

"Lookin' for you," the girl replied smartly.

The boy's gaze focused on Wyatt, and his face darkened. "Who's this?"

Wyatt stepped forward and introduced himself, offering his hand. Ethan took it with an air of suspicion.

"I think I know what happened to your bike. Miss Tarrant tells me you found a boat on your property—"

"Is it yours?" the boy asked abruptly.

"No, but if it's the one I've been looking for, it belongs to my friends from the island out there—Heron," he added, realizing there were several islands within view. "I was rowing along the shore, to see if it had drifted out this way, and I saw your sister."

"That the place where the fella drowned?" Ethan grew animated.

"Yes, I'm afraid so."

"Didja know him?"

"Not very well." Wyatt decided not to feed ghoulish curiosity by telling the boy he had found the body.

"C'mon up to the house 'n' have dinner with us first. That boat ain't goin' anywhere," Ellie said. "Ma always cooks for an army."

"Oh, thank you, but I couldn't—"

"Sure ya could. Got fresh corn," she added seductively.

Mrs. Tarrant was probably Wyatt's age, but looked older in the way of overworked farm wives. She greeted Wyatt's arrival with maternal skepticism, but softened when he greeted her like a gentleman and referred to her daughter as Miss Tarrant. The kitchen table grew crowded with the arrival of her husband, a massive and silent man, shy as a bear, and two younger boys with the same wavy brown hair as Ethan and his sister.

"This'n' here's Tom, and that's Ira," Mrs. Tarrant said as they clattered onto the bench. Ellie ladled bowls of mashed potatoes and chicken stew from great black pots on the stove in the summer kitchen, while her mother drained boiling water from yellow-and-white ears of corn. The rich, steamy smell took Wyatt back to the farm kitchen of his childhood.

"We just picked 'em half an hour ago," Ira piped up at his elbow.

"I did mosta the shuckin'," his slightly older brother added.

"Ya did not," Ira said. A look from their mother silenced them.

Wyatt hadn't realized how hungry he was, and did full justice to Mrs. Tarrant's cooking. Over the meal he asked about the herd, and the hay crop, and the milking parlor, winning sporadic, smiling responses from Mr. Tarrant and curiosity about his own knowledge of such matters.

"I did a lot of chores on the farm myself when I was you boys' age," he told the attentive younger ones. "Grew up in Ohio. You know where that is?"

"Out west," Ethan said.

"Were you a cowboy?" Ira asked eagerly.

"No more than you. But I guess anybody who spends time with cows could be called a cowboy, couldn't he?"

"Nah," Tom said. "Cowboys ride horses 'n' rope steers an' stuff like that. It ain't bein' a cowboy when ya milk 'em." Ira looked crestfallen.

"It can be if you want," Ellie said, and he brightened.

There was a blackberry pie afterwards, the dark purple berries oozing from a celestially light, crisp crust, served with wedges of cheddar in the Vermont fashion.

Wyatt leaned back stupefied after a second helping. "Mrs. Tarrant, I don't know when I've eaten a better pie."

"Ira 'n' me picked the berries," Tom said. "But he ate mosta his before they even got in the basket."

Wyatt turned to Ethan. "If I may, I'd like to ask you about the skiff you found."

"It was Ellie here that found it," Ethan said. "Me, I just lost a bike."

"I'm sure they're connected. Did you see anyone when the boat appeared?"

Ellie shook her head slowly. "Nope. An' it wasn't there the night before, so it musta come in early that mornin', 'cause it wasn't much past eight when I found it."

Ethan frowned. "I thought you was out earlier than that."

"I wasn't either," the girl said, irritated.

"What day was that?"

"I can't remember the date—but it's when you was supposed to take that load of hay over to Tracy's for the horses," Ellie nodded towards Ethan.

"It was the day that fella was drowned," Ethan announced. "I thought about it afterwards. The day after I went to Tracy's with the hay—Sunday. 'Cause it was church that day."

"You're sure about that?" Wyatt's tone was sharper than he had intended.

"Oh, ayuh, 'cause we went to church after we found it, an' nobody knew about the drowned fella then, but the next Sunday, everybody at church was talkin' about it, an' sayin' it had happened the Sunday before. Was it his boat, the fella that drowned?" Ethan's tone was hopeful.

"Well, it belonged to the house, but he might have been using it. And it was that same day, you think—that morning—that the boat showed up on your beach?"

"Ayuh. An' same day the bike turned up missin'. I got that bike from one of the summer folk, for takin' him fishin', an' I'd fixed it up real good, an' I used it a lot—took real good care of it."

"So there's no chance you left it somewhere and forgot."

"Nope. I always kept it behind the barn, outa sight of the henhouse, 'cause them girls make such a fuss if anybody goes back there—"

"So you wouldn't have heard anybody go and take it?"

"Not even if I was in the barn, which I figure I might've been. 'Less he snuck in in the dark, but that don't seem likely."

"So whoever took the boat took the bike as well?" Mrs. Tarrant asked.

"You think this fella murdered that fella on the island?" Ethan asked suddenly.

Wyatt contemplated a denial, but the timing was too suggestive. "There may be a connection. But it's possible Mr. Van Dorn—that's the man who died—had an accident, and someone took the boat for another reason."

"That don't make sense," Mrs. Tarrant said. "Sounds like too much of a coincidence to me." Ellie looked at Wyatt, flushed and turned away.

Ira and Tom stared at him, wide-eyed. "You mean a fella got murdered over there?" Tom said in a half-whisper.

"Well, we don't know that for sure. Could I have a look at the boat?"

"Ethan'll go with ya." Mrs. Tarrant darted a look at her daughter, who scowled but began to clear the dishes.

The skiff was pulled up on a stony cove next to a small pulling-boat that belonged to the Tarrants. Getting to it involved a steep walk down to the southeast of the farmhouse, out of its line of sight. It was the missing boat, red paint on the gunwales and *Merganser* painted on the stern in gold letters—the only things on the boat that weren't faded. It was empty except for a pair of oars and a rusty bailing can. Wyatt knelt and scanned it carefully. No residues of blood on the oar handles or the ribs of the boat. Nothing at all.

"This is just how we found it," Ethan said, anticipating Wyatt's question. "It didn't have nothin' else in it."

"Was it beached, like this?"

"Ayuh. No way it coulda drifted in, if that's what you're thinkin'. Somebody pulled it up."

"Can you take me to where the bike was?"

They climbed the rise in a straight line from the shore to the barn, Wyatt noting again that they couldn't be seen from the house. But Ellie came out, wiping her hands, running down the hill to join them. They came along the far side of the barn. Ethan showed him the overhang of the barn roof under which he had kept the bike.

"Where would I go if I stole that bike and wanted to get out of here in a hurry?"

Ethan walked him towards a path that turned into a dirt farm road, and pointed west. "You'd just head that way, road takes a bend a quarter mile out, another quarter mile an' you'd come to the main road, after you cross the train tracks."

"How far would that be from the train station?"

"Oh, station's about a mile from there. Right in South Hero village. You thinkin' the fella hopped on the train with my bike?"

"Probably not with your bike," Wyatt shook his head. "I'd guess he ditched it somewhere. You got a tow-rope I can borrow? I'd like to take the boat back to the island. And tomorrow I want to come back and look for your bike."

"Aw, you don't hafta do that—it wasn't a real fancy one or nothin', you just hate to have somebody stealin' your stuff—"

"I need to find the fellow who took it. Mr. Dodge doesn't like people stealing his stuff either, and he's got a few things to say to whoever this fellow was."

"Ya mean you don't know?"

"Well, we know who he said he was—but we don't know too much about him. Mr. Dodge hadn't known him very long. And besides," Wyatt gave the boy a look of stern sympathy, "a fellow shouldn't have to sit still for having his bike stolen."

He described the violinist. The brother and sister looked blank.

"Never met anybody that looked like that," Ellie said.

"If anything comes up, or you think of anything—anything at all that gives any clues about what might have happened to this fellow—will you leave me a message at the South Hero store? There's someone from the island in there every day or so, checking for telegrams or mail. We're expecting more guests at the island soon, and we want to make sure things are safe for them."

"Ya think this fella might be comin' back to murder somebody else?" Ethan asked with unwholesome eagerness.

"I certainly hope not, but it pays to be careful."

As he headed back down to the shore, Mrs. Tarrant caught up with him.

"Mr. Wyatt—Ethan says he was a mite sharp when he found you and Ellie—"

"It's only natural he'd be concerned about seeing a stranger with his sister."

"He's real protective." She wiped her hands on her apron, a reflexive gesture. "And I don't mind too much, I guess. A girl that age—they get kinda secretive on ya. She used to tell me everything, and now I see her at church, makin' eyes at some of the young fellas an' all—"

"I suppose that's pretty natural at her age." Wyatt hoped fervently that the secretiveness extended to the state of undress in which Ellie had found him. "Give her a few years, after she's married and settled, and she'll be back to telling you everything, I dare say. Besides, if it was my daughter and she turned up with a strange man from a boat, I guess I'd be concerned. Good thing I'm old enough to be her father."

"Aw, no, you ain't," said Mrs. Tarrant.

CHAPTER 26

"It's gotta have been the fiddler, then?"

Germain helped Wyatt tie up the skiff at the dock. He had taken the rental back to Keeler's Bay and rowed *Merganser* back to the island.

"Can't see how it could have been—ah, anyone else." Wyatt hung the oars up in the boathouse and followed Germain up the elm avenue to the porch of the guest cottage.

Germain leaned against a porch column and folded his arms. "You thought it might be Jeremy, didn't you?"

"I had to rule him out. But there's no way he could have swum from Paradise Bay around into Keeler's Bay in the time he would have had—"

"If he'd killed Van Dorn and taken the skiff."

"—given what we know about when Van Dorn died."

"Mr. Dodge'll be happy to hear about you putting his family in the clear. But there's still Amy," he said with mock seriousness.

Wyatt ignored the sardonic note. "I suppose she could have pushed him off the cliff on a birding walk. And she was up and about pretty early that morning. But Van Dorn was a lot heavier than her—unless she led him down a path he didn't know, to the edge, and stepped back just before he lost his balance—"

Germain broke into a laugh. "You're having to work pretty hard at this."

Wyatt sat down on the top step of the porch. "More to the point, there isn't a shred of motive that I can think of, can you? Not that I'd expect Dodge to tell me if he knew of one—"

"—blood being thicker than water, *hein*? Still, you can't let your kids go around bumping off houseguests—lowers the tone of the place. Can't imagine why Amy would have had any reason to hurt Van Dorn. Seemed to me she was fond of him."

"They had met before?"

"Several times. Miz Dodge dragged her along on afternoon calls, the Van Dorns came to dinner—she and Mr. Van did talk about birding a bit, now I think of it. So, now, what about this fiddler and the boat?"

"It seems he took it, ditched it on the shore below a farm-house, stole the farm boy's bicycle, and headed for—I'm guessing—the railroad station."

A thought occurred to him suddenly. "Germain—do you think Mrs. Van Dorn knew any of the musicians in the quartet?"

"That'd be slumming for her, seems to me. Opera tenors would be more in her line. Famous ones at that. Why'd you ask?"

"Just a thought. At any rate, my next move is to find the bike."

"Your next move is to change for dinner, *mon ami*. You can look for the bike tomorrow, but first you gotta be sociable. And don't mind my saying so, but you look like a dog's breakfast."

Wyatt rose but halted on the top step of the porch. "I'm back to thinking the violinist must have been from New York after all. What I'm still having trouble figuring out is, what got the fellow here. Onto the island, I mean, with murder on his mind. Any ideas?"

Germain furrowed his brow. "*Alors*—his English wasn't so good, right? So, maybe somebody from the Webbs'—some Italian he knew from the household staff—told him something about Heron Island. Taking the quartet along for entertain-ment—a visit—somebody mentions the President, how he's in-terested in birding."

Wyatt's thoughts raced ahead. Roosevelt had just created a national bird sanctuary in Florida, to protect the pelicans from plumage hunters. Heron Island's northern neck, the anarchist hears, is a "bird sanctuary"—and there is a visitor—the anarchist has never seen Roosevelt in person, of course; this man is older, stouter than he is pictured, but it must be he—there is talk of birding in the morning...

"So they're heading for the island," Germain went on, "and the other fellas in the quartet say, they might not tell us if the President was coming. Wouldn't be discreet to ask, we gotta play our best in any event. So he gets up before dawn, prowls the shore, and there's his man—he thinks—with the mustache and the little gold glasses, and a pair of binoculars around his neck."

Wyatt picked up Germain's thread. "And the anarchist points to the skiff and says, 'You wish to see birds? I will take you out, come with me. I like birds also, very much. Is easy, in boat—'"

"Must've seemed like a great stroke of luck to this Rossi," Germain said, "for Roosevelt to come on a visit so soon after his own arrival at the Webbs'."

Blunderer or not, Wyatt mused, Rossi had accomplished his mission—as he thought—and got clean away. His cadre, wherever it was, would soon have realized the blunder when they saw the obituary of a prominent New York banker, dead by accident on an island in Vermont.

Would they try again? Would they learn of Roosevelt's real visit? Perhaps. Wyatt had better assume as much. And certainly the Barre anarchists, Abate and Galleani and the rest of them, would now be looking for gaps in the President's official calendar.

Germain interrupted his thoughts. "Oh, yeah, forgot to tell you. Mr. Armbruster's here, from the President's detail."

"The visit's still on, then?"

Germain smiled. "TR always travels armed, Mr. Dodge says."

"So, most of the guests will be here only for the day." Armbruster nursed a brandy with Dodge and Wyatt on the Camp's verandah. Fireflies blinked and crickets trilled in the warm dusk.

"They're coming in private rail cars, for the most part," Dodge began ticking groups off on his fingers. "There's a contingent from the Adirondacks, taking the *Maquam*—the lake steamer—to join the Fisks at Isle La Motte. Another party from Newport, coming by train to Burlington. Webb will bring them over on *Elfreida*, along with the President's party. The Webbs themselves, and the Fisks, of course, who'll pick up the Newport travelers from the South Hero station on their yacht. My older son Chip—uh, Gardiner, his wife, two young children—they'll stay the night. I've asked Willem Van Dorn to come. If he does come, I doubt he'll stay over—"

"The son of the fellow who drowned?"

"It'll be a boost for him, to get out and meet the President," Dodge explained. "Mourning is all very well, but a man must get back into the world. Mrs. Van Dorn won't be coming, naturally."

It occurred to Wyatt that Mrs. Van Dorn would welcome the chance for an airing and a social gathering far more than her stepson. He did not envy her, swathed in crape and immured in a stifling New York townhouse in the height of summer with only the servants for company. No matter how much wealth was hers to control, she could take little advantage of it at present.

"Will Webb's musicians be coming back?"

"We've checked them out good and proper now," Armbruster said. "Foreigners, except the first violinist there—Perlstein, was it? That second fiddler's gone without a trace—we've had the Pinkertons out looking for him, and Macalester's had Sergeant Petrosino's people out as well. By the way, I stopped in to visit Mac on the way, and he said something about you owing him a report—"

"I told him I'd see what I found on the lake." Wyatt explained his discovery of the missing skiff.

"So the fellow hopped a train, you think?"

"Probably southbound. If he'd gone north, there might have been difficulties at the border. I'd been thinking someone could have picked him up from the island, until I found the boat. That makes it more likely that he was acting on his own, at least in this instance."

"If he did go south," Armbruster rocked gloomily in his chair, "he could have melted into the city, or even gone to Washington—who knows where? We've circulated his description to all the major cities along the seaboard—even the constabulary of Oyster Bay, if you can call it that. He could have shaved off his beard, dyed his hair by now."

"I'll feel more sure of all this when we find that bicycle. If our theory is right, it should be somewhere near the South Hero train station."

"What about the Barre crew?" Dodge interjected.

Armbruster nodded at Wyatt. "That's where we're counting on you. You know what they look like—the ringleaders, anyway. We thought of alerting Chief Brown, but from what I've heard, the Barre police department has more leaks than a sieve. Could let the cat out of the bag and defeat the whole purpose."

Dodge rose and turned towards the verandah door. "Did you think of stationing anyone in Keeler's Bay?"

Armbruster shook his head. "Why not Burlington, or the Milton shore, or one of the other islands? You have more miles of shoreline than you could possibly cover. A boat could set off from anywhere."

The household had retired. Germain and Wyatt sat together on the verandah, sipping iced bourbon from Germain's private stock. The white wicker of their chairs glimmered faintly in the half-moonlight. Wyatt finished his story about meeting the Tarrants and finding the missing skiff.

"Lucky for you you're a good-lookin' man." Germain said. "If you'd been plug-ugly, that gal would have turned and run home to her mama as fast as she could."

Wyatt waved a dismissive hand. "Curiosity's a great thing. They don't get many visitors around the farm, she's a lively girl, it's only natural."

"You'd brought your bathing-costume?"

"Um, no."

Germain rocked with laughter, setting the ice tinkling in his glass. "I see what you mean about curiosity, then. Where you going to start looking for that bike?"

"I figure I'll scour all the roads around the south end of the island. He might have gone cross-country for a bit, then got back on the road somewhere else—or headed across the Sandbar towards Burlington. That rail line's new—maybe Rossi didn't know the trains run right through the islands now. Might've thought he had to go to Burlington to get one."

"So we're back to the fiddler." Germain stood up and laid a hand on Wyatt's shoulder. "Time for me to turn in. If you want some company on the bike hunt, I got the afternoon free."

"Armbruster's joining me for the morning. If we haven't found it by noon I'll take you up on that. How's your tolerance for brambles?"

"I'll bring a basket," Germain paused with his hand on the screen door. "Cook has a nice touch with a jam."

Wyatt sat in the warm darkness, letting his mind drift towards sleep. Summer was on the turn in Vermont; the grass was damp with dew, the air whirring with crickets. He tossed the dregs of his drink in the grass and walked down the long, sloping lawn to the shingled west beach. The half-moon, high now, plated the black water with a streak of pale gold. Out of the trees behind him a bird whistled, realized its mistake, and fell silent.

Another call answered it, prickling his scalp and setting his heart racing: a deep, rasping squawk, almost a human sound. The blue heron, he realized, letting himself breathe again. They had night-vision, like owls. He walked in the direction of the sound, but it eluded him. He wondered if in his drowsy state he might have imagined it, but then it came again out of the darkness. Marking off its territory, he supposed, but who was there to challenge it at this time of night, except himself? Gerald Van Dorn had been excited about the chance to see one at close range; he'd said so to Dodge on the verandah, before that last dinner. Dodge had told him about the heron who fished at the base of the south cliff. The musicians were nearby. Had the violinist heard?

His mind was drifting again. This time he let it go, slipped back in the side door and down the hall to his bed. His hand registered the crisp nubbles of the hobnail bedspread, the smooth white sheets enveloping him.

CHAPTER 27

Afternoon clouds thickened overhead, threatening storm. The sun eddied through like a sleeper trying to untangle himself from dreams. Wyatt and Germain tramped through dry daggers of grass that rasped against their trouser legs. Gnats circled their sweaty faces, landing occasionally and getting stuck before hands could slap them off.

The morning search with Armbruster that dragged on past noon had failed to turn up the bicycle within a half-mile radius of the station, and no one who had seen a man on a bike that whole day, never mind early morning.

"I was out in the field all day," one farmer had said, sweeping a hand towards the neat furrows around him. "We was pickin' strawberries, me an' the boys here. They're ripe you gotta pick 'em, Sunday or not. Field's right by the road—straight shoot to the station, half a mile west. We didn't see nobody on a bike all that day, you can take that to the bank. We'd'a seen that for sure. If I wasn't right out there, onea the boys was."

They had been bushwhacking along the road from Paradise Bay to the South Hero train station since landing in the Tarrants' cove after lunch. Armbruster had stayed behind to 'recon' the island, as he put it. Ellie had greeted them shyly, in contrast to her frank manner when she and Wyatt had met. She must never have met a colored man before, Wyatt thought. She seemed fascinated and intimidated at the same time.

"We mean to find Ethan's bicycle," he had told her.

"There ain't no call for you to do that. It was an old thing anyways. Looks like he's got another one lined up, same fella he got that one from—"

"It might be important."

"Oh—you mean, on accounta the drownin' an' all?" she lowered her eyes.

"If he left anything else with it, it might tell us something."

They had walked briskly to the train station and begun sweeping opposite sides of the road, fifty feet in on either side. Germain had given Wyatt a basket and they picked blackberries as they went, pausing at intervals to free their clothes from thorns. By three o'clock they had covered three-quarters of the distance back to the Tarrant farm, without result.

"This isn't making sense." Germain wiped his face with a crumpled handkerchief. "What would've been the point in taking the bike, if the man had ditched it this far back? He might as well have walked the whole way."

Wyatt took off his straw boater and dashed sweat from the brim-line. "You know, it might make more sense now to look on the north side of the railroad station. He could just as easily have dropped it there."

Germain glowered at him, then grinned.

"Okay. But then we stop in at the Station Inn, and you buy me a cold beer."

"Blackberries are good in beer," Wyatt observed.

On the west side of the railway station was a cornfield, stalks towering over them, tassels full and the ears almost plump enough for picking.

Germain's body drooped. "Land's sake—how are we going to make any headway through that?"

"He wouldn't have put it in here," Wyatt said after a moment's pause. "Back then, this would only have been a foot high, two at the most. Those woods over there, maybe, but we needn't concern ourselves with the cornfield."

Germain raised his eyes heavenward. "Thank God for small mercies."

They had left their berry baskets in the waiting room at the station, which smelled of dust and ink-pads. Thunder was growling overhead when they returned, empty-handed, from searching the woods to the west. A sharp ozone smell filled the air. As they opened the door to the waiting room, a train whistle sounded in the distance. The ticket-man straightened behind his cage.

"Train's at Allen Point," he said cheerfully. "Be here in twenty minutes."

Wyatt frowned at him, puzzled. "But it's only a couple of miles to there."

"Got to slow way down crossing the causeway. Practically comes to a stop there, where it meets the Point. Not much reason to speed up—you'd just have to slow down again to come into the station."

"That true both ways?" Germain said sharply.

The man looked startled. "Sure," he said hesitantly. "Goin' south, you mean? Yeah, you have to be mighty careful goin' back on to the causeway."

"Would you keep an eye on the berries a little longer?" The clerk nodded and Germain turned to Wyatt. "There's one more place to look for that damn bike."

The rail embankment fell off so steeply that they had to tramp along its course in the ditch-like depressions that edged the neighboring fields. Above them, the train puffed north with a doleful clank of its bell. Wyatt looked up at the passing carriages. At the end of each a door led onto a narrow platform, a dozen compartment windows between.

"If we could get up there, it would be easy enough to jump on, at the speed she's going," he said after the train had passed.

"I was thinking that," Germain said. "But not along here. Bank's too steep."

They tramped the four miles to the southern tip of the island, through mostly flat farmland planted to wheat, corn, and beans. Gray-brown clouds piled on and the air continued to thicken. At last the fields gave way to patches of sharp, slender grasses and limestone outcroppings. The embankment tapered down to a foot and a half at the shoreline. On the east side, fifty yards off, was a mixed clump of hardwoods and hemlocks. Germain struck out for it, Wyatt following. Ten feet into the woods, off a small path, a stray sunbeam caught a glint of metal, half-smothered in dirt and dead leaves.

Wyatt reached into the leaf-pile and pulled out the missing bicycle by the handlebars. "I'll be damned."

"Shoulda thought of that road." Germain began brushing leaf-mold off the bike's hubs with his handkerchief. "South Street. Runs a quarter mile east of the track, due south of the village. We couldn't see it from the angle we were at. But it makes sense now I think about it—fellow steals the bike, heads south where the Paradise Bay road meets the main road—which is why no one between there and the train station saw him. Then south and west over the back roads till he picks up South Street. Goes as far as he can, walks the bike into the woods—"

"—waits for the train, and jumps on it as it's coming off the causeway," Wyatt finished.

"Or going onto it, more likely. There's one going south too, early in the morning."

Wyatt looked thoughtful. "Our man knew the territory pretty well."

"Wouldn't have had to. Long as he knew there was the point at the south end, where the train would have to slow down."

"There's enough woods to hide in and listen for the train coming either way," Wyatt added. "Why didn't you tell me about the road?"

"He could have ditched the bike anywhere along the rail line, for all I knew. And he might not have known the embankment was too high to climb, except at the southern end—and near the station, but he'd have wanted to avoid being seen."

"Still, it's surprising no one remembers seeing him," Wyatt said. "He must have been in a state when he got on the train."

Germain splattered a mosquito that had been feeding on his forearm. "Maybe he cleaned himself up in the lake a little bit.

You telling me you never hopped a train for a free ride? Easy enough to dodge the conductor, if you're quick on your feet."

"I was a God-fearing, stay-at-home farm boy," Wyatt said. "I guess you weren't."

They bent to examine their prize. The bike had been covered with a thin, patchy layer of dead leaves and stray bits of tree branch, which they brushed carefully aside. The weeks' rains had pock-marked the fenders with rust spots.

Wyatt shook his head. "Ethan will have a job getting this back in shape."

He knelt and dug around in the dirt near the bike. Something else had gleamed from a small patch of pine-needled earth near the bike: a gold watch-chain. He pulled it out and a dirt-covered disk came swinging up with it, spattering gray-brown humus. He put it on his handkerchief and brushed away the mud from its case.

"Let's get it out here in the light. There's something on here, but I can't read it." They moved out to the path, splotched with a dappled patch of sunlight. The something proved to be only a feathery pattern of chasing, but when he had cleared the mud from the watch-stem, the case popped open. On the inside, in engraved script: *To my darling Gerald from your own Malvina, June 12, 1879.*

"First wife?" Germain asked.

"Probably. Will would've been born in, what? '82? A wedding gift, maybe."

"He stole the man's watch. That's low."

Wyatt brushed away the rest of the dirt. He pulled the stem gently, set the time, pushed it in and wound it. The watch began to tick smoothly and quietly.

"Why didn't Rossi take it with him? You'd think it would have fetched a good price. The cover's solid gold, and so is the chain."

"Now that is a mystery," Germain shook his head. "Maybe the fellow's got a few scruples. One thing to kill a capitalist enemy of the people, another to covet his goods."

"Maybe he figured with the inscription he'd be taking too much of a chance trying to peddle it."

"A regular thief would know somebody who could mill that out. But I doubt our man's connected that way."

"Even so," Wyatt wrapped the watch and put it carefully in his pocket. "It's odd."

"Think he might try to come back for it?"

Wyatt shrugged. "It's not out of the question. You know, this is the only link we have to him—the man seems to have come and gone, nobody knows him, no one on the train crew remembers him, the anarchist crowd in New York never heard of him, or at least not Czerny and his friends—"

Germain's brow darkened. "What gets me about those anarchists, they think they got some kinda solidarity with people of color. Hell, there wouldn't be a colored man alive in the South if the anarchists took over there. Look what's happened since they lifted martial law—lynchings are family outings for white folks, God's sake."

"It's the kings and dukes the anarchists should be after. I don't think they grasp the implications of overthrowing an elected government." Wyatt steadied the bike. "At least we know for sure who we're after now."

"Flip you for who rides that thing back," Germain said.

Mrs. Tarrant bustled out to greet them when they arrived at the farm's dooryard. Ellie came out behind her mother, wiping floury hands on her apron. When she saw Wyatt wheeling the bike, she started and flushed pink.

"Where'd you find it?"

Wyatt introduced Germain to Mrs. Tarrant. "Miss Tarrant and Mr. Germain met earlier," he added. Germain bowed. Ellie recovered herself, came forward and gave Germain her hand, which he brushed with his lips. Her color deepened to fuchsia.

"We found it in a grove of trees on the south end of the

island," Wyatt said. "Whoever took it ditched it there, with some leaves and dirt over it. I'm afraid the rain has got at it—"

Ethan came out of the barn, flecks of straw and hay sticking to his green overalls. He blinked in the sunlight, his face brightening as he came forward.

"Hey, ya found my bike!"

"It's been lying in the rain and dirt for some time." Wyatt watched Ethan's brows furrow as he ran his hands over the wheel casings. The boy plucked thoughtfully at the strands of his mustache.

"Aw, hell, it was worse'n this when I got it." He caught a frown from his mother at the profanity. "Sorry, Ma. I can fix it up, though. Nothin's bent, anyways. That'd be a lot of work."

"D'you know who took it?" Ellie asked.

Wyatt smiled inwardly at the tone; she still had a child's intense curiosity.

"Not really. We know who he said he was, and what he looked like—I told you about that the last time we were here—but not much else. And we have no idea where he's gone."

"So you ain't any further along," Ethan concluded.

"Not much," Wyatt admitted, "except that we know how he got away, and that he can row a boat and ride a bike."

"Which, when you think of it," Germain said as they rowed back in tandem to the island, "is more than you'd expect from a poor starving immigrant."

"And plays a pretty good violin, too," Wyatt called back over his shoulder. "I'm guessing he's one of those ruined aristocrats you get flocking into steerage these days. Like Zabielski from the quartet, remember? Except he's some younger son who won't inherit the family estate, well educated, resentful. Turns his personal frustrations into a political cause—"

"That doesn't get us any farther looking for him, does it?"

"Maybe we won't have to. Maybe he'll come back, when the President's here."

Wyatt felt the weight of the watch in his pocket. It seemed

right to have one there again, though to own one like this would be beyond his wildest imaginings.

Germain pulled back on his oar. "We'd best keep a close eye on the Burlington Grocery men. 'Case any of your old pals turn up."

"Calcagni would let me know," Wyatt said. But he wasn't altogether sure of that.

CHAPTER 28

Inspector Macalester, in his shirtsleeves, snipped the string from a small brown parcel on his desk with a pair of rusty scissors. Inside the opened box was a letter from Wyatt, identifying the contents and the circumstances of its finding. *It has been left as we found it,* the note said, *in the event of your wishing to subject it to laboratory analysis. That done, may I request that you have the timepiece cleaned and returned to Mrs. Van Dorn.* So Wyatt had ruled out the Dodge boy as the killer and learned how the violinist had got away. It was a start.

He made a note to ask Petrosino to send his detectives back among the known anarchists of Little Italy to search for traces of the fellow, since Wyatt thought it most likely he would have headed for the City. So did Macalester, but he had little hope of progress. His Italian-speaking detectives, gathering evidence in another gruesome killing thought to be the work of the Black Hand, had a lot more on their plates than the ambiguous death of a banker in Vermont. The others wouldn't get far with a clannish group of immigrants whose English came and went at convenient intervals.

Once the laboratory work was done, it occurred to him that a conversation with Mrs. Van Dorn might be productive. He dressed in a businesslike gray suit and alighted from the Fifth Avenue trolley on a sultry afternoon. The Irish maid who answered the door showed him into the small morning room, protesting that "the Missus" was indisposed but obeying his injunction to fetch her down presently, it being a police matter.

Mrs. Van Dorn came down twenty minutes later, in a dark gray tea-gown trimmed with black Brussels lace, which dulled her rosy complexion and chestnut hair. She greeted Macalester with cool reserve, but led him into the library and rang for tea.

"You have—news concerning my late husband, Inspector?"

"Not precisely, ma'am. But I'm afraid there's little doubt now that he was the victim of foul play."

She colored and her hand went to her throat. Macalester withdrew the watch from his vest-pocket and dangled it between them. As if mesmerized, she reached slowly for the case and cupped the gold disk in her hand.

"Why, this looks like Gerald's, it was his first wife's wedding gift—" a little cry broke from her and she covered her mouth with the back of her hand.

"Open it, please," said Macalester, expressionless.

She popped the case open and looked at the engraving. "Yes, of course, it is—I knew it right away. Where did you find it?"

Macalester told her. "So, someone took it from him, and got that far with it, and then left it. He may have been afraid that he wouldn't be able to fence it, d'you see—"

"Fence it?" she looked at him, eyes wide and China-doll blue. A pretty pair, pretty enough to make a man do something daft for her—was that what had ensnared Gerald Van Dorn? And whoever killed him?

"Sell it to a dealer in stolen goods." he said curtly.

"Oh, dear, how dreadful—to think of poor Gerald's watch—it was precious to him, I didn't mind, even though it was from his first wife, but then she died so long ago, and—it could have ended up in the hands of some—it doesn't bear thinking of."

The maid brought in tea with lemons and lump sugar. Macalester noticed the soft swelling of Mrs. Van Dorn's belly under the loose folds of her gown, unmistakable now.

"May I ask if you have been keeping well since—since the tragic events?"

"As well as can be expected, I suppose," she smiled bleakly. "You are kind to ask," she added, turning the blue gaze full on him. "I must say it has been rather confining—" he looked at her sharply.

"I mean, the strictures of mourning—one cannot leave the house, except in a closed carriage, and I so greatly feel the want of fresh air—Gerald and I used to take the victoria through the Park—it was so pleasant, even on warm days, the breeze on one's face—oh, but pray don't think I complain, one must do what's right, but—"

"I quite understand," said Macalester, his natural kindliness awakened. "But I must say it seems an awful shame, to mure yourself up like a servant of the old Pharaoh—surely we can do honor to the dead without havin' to be cut off from the light and air? I can't see Mr. Van Dorn, from what I've heard of him, wishin' that on his wife."

"I've tried to tell Will that too—but it would be unseemly, he says."

"Your stepson? And how does he, pray?"

"Oh, he's well," she said airily. "He's been occupied, of course, with seeing to the settlement of the estate—so much time with lawyers! And—"

"Will he be going back to college, d'you think?"

"He feels he should not, for the present. He feels his place is with me, till—" she broke off. Macalester let the silence hang between them.

"—till things have settled down," she finished in a constrained voice.

"And what do you think he should do, ma'am, if the question's not too impertinent?"

"Oh, as to that, I've tried telling him I think he should finish at Yale. Jeremy's company would be a comfort to him, I'm sure, better than hanging about this old mausoleum. It's different since Gerald died, he'll certainly never need to work unless he wants to, but still, an education, that's a great thing, and I know his father would—well, you understand—"

"Quite." Macalester wondered why he'd raised the topic. "If I may change the subject, Mrs. Van Dorn—did your husband wear his watch as a regular thing?"

She smiled reminiscently. "He was never without it. I remember when he first showed it to me. He looked at it so fondly, and he said, 'You know I will always adore you, my dear, so I hope you will not mind that I keep this about me, in memory of Will's mother and the happy days of my youth.'" Her eyes spilled over, and she reached for a pocket-handkerchief trimmed in black ribbon.

"And would he have carried it even in his dressing-gown, d'you think?"

"Why," she blew her nose vigorously, "it was never far from him. But I'm not sure—"

"I wonder no one thought of its being missing—after he was found," Macalester rose and paced towards the window, "especially as it meant so much to him." He turned back to look at her, saw her flush slightly.

"Indeed, but one was so distressed, so taken aback, one could hardly think clearly in the circumstances—" she took up her teacup and put it down again with a clatter.

"Quite so. It is amazing, really, how the human mind reacts in such situations. For instance, this fellow having had the presence of mind to recover the watch. Knowing to look for it, for that matter."

"Recover it? I assume Gerald must have dropped it on the island, and this violinist, whoever he was, was found and took it—"

"There was evidence of water seepage," Macalester went on, relentless. "He took it from wherever he drowned the man. Mrs. Van Dorn, we need your help. Who might have had reason to kill your husband?"

"Oh, dear God." She covered her face with her hands and sobbed aloud.

The library door opened to admit Will Van Dorn, resplendent in a cream linen suit, his mustache now grown thick and lustrous. He stood silent for an instant, taking in Mrs. Van Dorn's shaking shoulders, the policeman, and the tea service.

In two steps he was kneeling at her side, his face full of concern, a hand on her shoulder.

"What has happened? What's the matter?"

She shook her head and continued to sob.

Will rose and glared at Macalester, angry now. "What have you done? What have you said to distress her so? Why are you intruding on a house of mourning?"

Macalester picked up the watch from between the teacups.

"I was returning an item of stolen property to your stepmother," he said, noting how Will paled at his words. Will seized the watch from him.

"What are you doing with this?"

"It's an odd thing. A piece of this value—solid gold, and no one reported it missing."

"Missing? Stolen? What are you talking about?" Will rang for the maid, who entered and hurried over to Mrs. Van Dorn's chair. "See Mrs. Van Dorn up to her room. And in future remember my instructions that she is not at home to visitors. Now, sir—"

"Inspector Macalester, of the Central Detective—"

"I know who you are," Will cut him off. "You were investigating my father's death, as I requested of the Commissioner. Was it necessary to distress his widow in that fashion?"

Macalester felt his own color rising. "It was an item of evidence, for one thing. And a thing of value, for another. I made the assumption that she'd wish to know of its discovery, and to have it back. Which I would say she did—having it back, at least."

"Who found it?"

"I'd have thought you'd be more interested in where it was found. I told Mrs. Van Dorn the whole story, and I'll not waste your valuable time by repeating myself. I needn't distress anyone further at present." Macalester crossed the room and reached for the derby he had left on a small table by the door. "But I will say this, though I realize it's none of my business. It can't be healthy for the lassie to be cooped up in a stuffy house in this heat, mourning or no mourning. If I were you, I'd see that she got out for some fresh air. Good afternoon to you, sir."

The gold orb twisted on its glittering chain in Will's hand. "I wish you had—" his voice faded through the closing door.

Macalester kept walking and let himself out. A cheerful-looking young man in a silk suit was approaching on the sidewalk, carrying a large bouquet wrapped in green paper. He scanned Macalester's face with a mixture of hope and puzzlement and tipped his boater, revealing a head of wavy red hair, neatly parted and smelling of pomade.

"Good afternoon, sir." The accent was foreign—Italian, perhaps.

"And to you." Macalester tipped his own hat in turn.

"You have been to visit Mrs. Van Dorn? Have you seen her? Is she well?"

Macalester stared at him for a moment without replying.

"I am sorry. You do not even know me. Permit me to introduce myself. Signor Eduardo Romano, at your service. An old friend of the lady's." He bowed slightly.

"Macalester. Inspector Macalester, of the Central Detective Bureau."

The young man's face clouded and assumed a look of—was it fear? Not the first man to react that way when Macalester announced his profession. *Did tremble like a guilty thing surprised*, was that the phrase? Perhaps it was only concern.

"Oh—has something happened?" The bouquet drooped in Romano's hand.

Macalester looked at him keenly. "Yes. I should say that something has definitely happened. You wouldn't by chance know anything about the death of Gerald Van Dorn, would you?"

"Me, *signor*? Why would I—?"

"No reason. Unless you were up on Lake Champlain in the middle of June."

"But I was, as a matter of fact. I was staying with my friends the Van Sicklens, on Abenaki Island. The large one, next to the island where—at the time I did not know the Van Dorns were there. I should certainly have gone to visit. Also, my hosts are acquainted with the Dodges. But in the event, I left a few days before—ah, the tragedy occurred."

"Indeed! And where did you go then?"

"To, ah, visit some other friends. Upstate. But, Inspector, you are not thinking that someone killed Mr. Van Dorn?"

"I'm quite sure of it, as a matter of fact."

"But such an amiable gentleman—who could possibly want to kill him?"

Macalester eyed him keenly. "Who indeed? Someone with designs on his widow and his fortune, I shouldnae wonder."

"Oh, *dio mio*, poor Millicent—how terrible—she must be—"

"Distraught. She is, rather. I've just left her in the care of her lady's maid. I wouldn't bank on being admitted just now. She's not at home to visitors, according to her stepson."

Romano's nostrils flared and he threw up his free hand. "Again. Each week I come, I leave flowers, I hear nothing. She is shut away like—like a princess in an old fairy tale."

"Fairly typical by American standards of mourning, I gather." Macalester shook his head ruefully.

"It is like that in the old country. But I had thought Americans more modern in such matters."

"You might as well leave the flowers," Macalester said, fingering a cluster of sweet-smelling pinks in the bouquet. "I've no doubt they're a comfort to her."

Romano beamed gratitude at him and mounted the steps. Macalester walked on, pausing half a block away to stare back thoughtfully at the man on the doorstep.

He turned south down Fifth Avenue and onto the side street where the maid had told Wyatt to find Dr. Tinmuth's office. The doctor's name was engraved on a discreet brass plate. A pasty-faced young woman answered Macalester's ring.

"The doctor is with another patient at present. Since you have no appointment, you may have some time to wait."

"I'm not a patient." Macalester flashed his badge. "This is a police matter." The woman looked at him and pursed her lips. "Please inform the doctor that I will wait on him at his earliest convenience."

She showed him into a white-tiled room that smelled sharply of rubbing alcohol. Ten minutes later, Tinmuth was glaring at him, drying his hands on an immaculate linen towel.

"On what subject did you wish to confer with me, Inspector?"

"You were in attendance on Mr. Gerald Van Dorn, I believe?"

"The late Mr. Van Dorn, yes." The doctor hung the towel neatly on a glass rod. " I was his physician for the last twenty years of his life."

"And Mrs. Van Dorn?"

"She has her own physician—my associate, Dr. Venables. Though I have been called in on occasions when my colleague was not available. Inspector, my patients are in the most exclusive ranks, if I may say so, of New York society. You will surely understand that I am not at liberty to disclose any matters touching on their—private conditions—"

"We're investigating a murder, Doctor."

"A murder! I was not aware there was evidence to conclude—"

"There is now."

"What on earth do you think I can tell you about that?"

"How far advanced is Mrs. Van Dorn's condition?"

"How far is—? Whatever are you—"

"Mrs. Van Dorn's pregnancy is quite apparent," Macalester said grimly.

"You have seen her?"

"I was admitted, yes. To return an item of evidence. Now, just how far along is she?"

The doctor told him.

"Doctor Tinmuth, was Gerald Van Dorn fully functional?"

"Whatever do you mean?"

"I mean, capable of consummating the act of marriage."

"Obviously so." Tinmuth's tone was incredulous. "Why on earth do you ask? What a thoroughly improper question."

"It stands nonetheless. Did he ever consult you on such matters? A lively young wife, he so much older—gentlemen have been known to experience—difficulties."

The doctor flushed and looked away.

"Oh, come, Doctor, we are men of the world, are we not?"

Tinmuth took a deep breath. "He had—ah—come to me some time ago. Asked me if I had any powders or pills, monkey glands, that sort of thing—I had little to offer him. It's really not in my line, nor am I acquainted with persons of that stripe—"

"So you did nothing for him?"

"I gave him some powders—a vasodilator, thought to be helpful in some such cases."

"And was it?"

"He said it gave him headaches. Didn't ask about it again. I thought either matters had resolved themselves, or he had decided to live with it."

"Were you surprised to learn of Mrs. Van Dorn's condition?"

"Mildly so, but then I reasoned that things must have taken care of themselves. They often do. 'Mind over matter, my dear sir,' I said to him at the time, 'it's often simply a question of mind over matter!' I assumed he had taken my words to heart. What a shame he should not survive to see the birth of his new heir—such an amiable gentleman—" the old soldier seemed momentarily overcome.

Macalester ignored this. "Indeed. And what does the present heir think of all this?"

The doctor cleared his throat and recovered himself. "Willem? I don't know if she will have told him. Ladies of my acquaintance are reluctant to discuss such matters with anyone but their husbands, and perhaps a confidante or two—"

"It must be obvious to him before too much longer."

"Quite so. And I must say the young man is extremely attentive, and protective—as if she were his own mother. Naturally she has sent him away when Dr. Venables has called."

"Becoming delicacy of feeling," Macalester murmured. "By the bye, are you acquainted with a Signor Romano?"

"Not personally. But there is an Italian singer of that name, I believe." The doctor's nose wrinkled with distaste. "I am told he has come to call at the Van Dorns' on numerous occasions. A persistent fellow, as—such people are wont to be. My associate found him at the door on one recent occasion with a bouquet of—ah, vulgar dimensions."

"And was he admitted?"

"Not since Mr. Van Dorn's death, of course. That would be highly improper. He is evidently an old acquaintance of the lady of the house. When Mr. Van Dorn was alive, I believe he was received. But, there, Inspector, have I told you what you came for?"

"You have. It will be treated with the utmost discretion. I don't mean to tell you your business, Doctor—but I do think the lassie would be better off with a wee bit of fresh air, and even a bit of mild exercise."

"One puts aside normal activities to honor the departed," the doctor replied stiffly. "That is what mourning means. Why, Mr. Van Dorn—young Mr. Van Dorn—will not hear of her leaving the house, even if she did feel otherwise, which I am sure she does not. He has, I may say, a finely developed sense of propriety. Clearly a young man of good breeding."

"It sounds like punishment to me."

"Perhaps customs in such matters are different in your country."

"This is my country as much as yours, sir," Macalester shot back. "But, yes, I'd say a bit more common sense would be applied in my former country. I'm sorry to have disturbed your consultations," he added, putting his hat back on and opening the front door. "Good afternoon to you."

CHAPTER 29

A dowdy parlormaid at the Dodges' town house, clearly resentful at having been left in the city, informed Macalester that her employers had returned to Heron Island. The President's visit was going forward, then, despite Rossi, gone without a trace and plotting who knew what for an encore, and the Barre anarchists, presumably still as hell-bent on their wee natter with Mr. Roosevelt as Warren Dodge was on his. Well, the President's security men would be on the alert for intruders. And Wyatt, capable and devoted despite his cageyness around policemen, would be helping them.

His clerk brought him a mug of tea and a pile of letters when he arrived back at his office. "Commissioner wants you to look in before you leave for the day. Nothing urgent, he says."

"Miss Templeton, does the name Romano—Eduardo Romano—ring any bells?"

"Romano? No, sir. Should it? Is he a criminal?"

"I don't know. See what we've got for that name in the records."

He gulped a mouthful of lukewarm tea and slit open a letter from Dr. Caron, Town Health Officer for the town of South Hero, Vermont.

...I have personally examined the report of a postmortem examination on Gerald Van Dorn prepared by Dr. W. Seward Webb. As you are aware, I was out of the country when the death occurred. In accordance with Vermont law, Dr. Webb signed and presented a certificate of death to the South Hero Town Clerk, who issued a Certificate of Permission for transportation of Mr. Van Dorn's remains.

In my professional opinion, Dr. Webb's decision to conduct the examination, though somewhat beyond the bounds of accepted protocol, was not unreasonable in the unusual circumstances. The examination appears to have been conducted in accordance with professional standards.

Although the circumstances of Mr. Van Dorn's demise were certainly unusual, I am inclined in the absence of substantial evidence to the contrary to accept Dr. Webb's opinion of accidental death. I trust this will be helpful to your inquiries...

Medical men were worse than thieves for sticking by one another. Macalester wondered what the good doctor Caron would think of the gold watch. Officially, the letter should close the matter. He should be spending his time helping Petrosino on the Black Hand case. But his colleagues didn't call him the Scotch Terrier for nothing, and he wasn't going to let this Van Dorn business go now. He consulted a train schedule and confirmed the departure time for the overnight Pullman service to Vermont.

The telephone on his wall rang, startling him from his thoughts with its shrill, insistent clang. Infernal machines. There'd be no peace anywhere soon. He took the conical earpiece from its cradle and bellowed into the receiver. "Macalester here."

"Inspector. Sergeant Petrosino asked if you'd meet him right away at the Grand Street El station. Something's come up on the Black Hand case. He says it's important." The voice was vaguely familiar, with a slight accent, but he couldn't place it. One of Sergeant P.'s immigrant patrolmen, no doubt.

Macalester was already reaching for his hat. "Tell the sergeant I'll be there presently. Oh—hold on a wee minute. Northbound or southbound side?" But the line had already gone dead.

"Petrosino's looking for me. I'll be back in a bit," he told his clerk. He trotted down the great staircase and south on Mulberry Street, crossing over to the east side to avoid the blazing afternoon sun. He slowed to catch his breath after a couple of blocks, which allowed the man in shabby overalls and cloth cap who had detached himself from the shadows of an entryway to keep him easily in his sights.

Wyatt scanned the passengers alighting from the morning train at the South Hero station. No sign of Macalester, and no message there or at the telegraph office about a change of plans. The train station had a pay telephone for hire, and he asked the attendant to dial the main number for the NYPD headquarters, which Macalester had given him. The woman collected a dollar fifty from him before making the final connection.

"This is Dade Wyatt calling long-distance from Vermont." He tried to speak clearly but resisted the urge to shout across the hissing, crackly line. "Inspector Macalester was due in on this morning's train—"

"Macalester! Hold on a minute," an Irish desk sergeant said. A woman's voice came on the line. "Mr. Wyatt?"

"Yes. I'm looking for Inspector Macalester—"

"This is Miss Templeton, his clerk. Are you his friend in Vermont? The Van Dorn case?"

"Uh—yes, I am. We were expecting him on this morning's train—"

"Train...oh, dear! Then you haven't heard about the accident—"

Wyatt felt his stomach drop and a chill run down his back. "What's happened? Is he—"

"He's alive, but he's unconscious—he may be in a coma, they say. They took him to Bellevue, after he—" she stumbled, gasped for breath and went on. "After he fell onto the tracks. The El tracks, I mean. At the Grand Street station, when the train was coming in. The brakeman saw him lose his balance at the edge of the platform. He managed to slow the train enough to keep it from running over him. But it caught him right on the head, bounced him a bit and carried him a few feet on the fender, somebody said. There are broken bones, and some internal injuries, they think, and they don't know if he'll—" a sob caught in her throat. "If he'd hit the third rail, he'd have been killed outright. As it is—"

Something cold prickled across Wyatt's scalp. "Where was he yesterday?"

"I don't know. A number of places. He told me on his way out he was going to meet Sergeant Petrosino—"

"Was Petrosino at the El station?"

"Uh, well—no one mentioned seeing him. And I haven't seen him since then myself. But he'd phoned and asked him to meet him—Oh. Oh, dear."

Wyatt tried to keep his voice even. "Miss Templeton. Please ask Petrosino about that phone call. I suspect he never placed it. And my guess is Macalester was pushed."

A gasp on the other end turned into a whispered conversation. The desk sergeant came back on the line.

"Mr. Wyatt. Are you tellin' me you think somebody tried to kill the Inspector?"

"There's a good chance of it. Is anyone with him at the hospital?"

"A patrolman went with him on the ambulance—but I doubt he's still there."

"Please—put a guard on him right away. Around the clock. And if he wakes up and is able to talk, it'll be important to catch whatever he has to say. He may know who did this to him."

"It'll be one a them dagoes he was after, d'you think?" the sergeant sounded intrigued.

"Maybe. He's also been, ah, assisting the Secret Service with an investigative matter. How involved was he in this Black Hand case, do you know? Enough so some of those fellows would see him as a danger?"

He could almost hear the sergeant scratching his head. "I wouldn'ta thought so. I'd'a thought more likely they'd be after Petrosino himself. Inspector Mac's just been in the background of it, like. But it was right there in Little Italy, see, so that makes me wonder. Hold on—Miss Templeton's got something for you."

"I was just looking at his desk calendar," she said breathlessly. "Just a couple of scribbles, but one looks like "Mrs. D" or—there's a squiggle in front of it—v? vD? and the other says Dr T. I don't know what that might mean."

Returning the watch, Wyatt guessed. And, since he was in the neighborhood, reassuring Dr. Tinmuth that Wyatt's motives when he attempted to revive the swooning Mrs. Van Dorn had been honorable. There must have been something else, somewhere else…maybe not yesterday, but recently…

"Did he say anything else about where he'd been or where he was going? Please try to remember. It might be important."

"Well…just before he left, he asked me to check the files and see if we had any records on somebody. What was the name now—Ro-something—Rosario?"

"Rossi?"

"That might have been it. I didn't write it down, I'm afraid, and somebody else asked me to do something, so—at any rate, I haven't looked him up yet. After we heard—"

Wyatt wondered what could possibly be in the files about Rossi that Macalester wouldn't have found already. He left the train station's number and asked to be notified of any change in Macalester's condition. After a moment's hesitation he placed another call to his landlady, Mrs. Baird.

"I thought you'd want to know," he said after explaining what little he'd learned. "He hadn't mentioned any family in the area, and I wondered if you might—"

"I shall go down to Bellevue at once," Mrs. Baird interrupted him. "And I'm obliged to you for letting me know, Mr. Wyatt. He's all alone in the world, as far as I know, and I dare say he'd be glad enough to see a friendly face when he—if he—"

"When he wakes up," Wyatt said gently, "it'll be very important to see if he knows who did this to him. If you're there when he's up to talking, you might ask him. I don't believe for a minute it was an accident. But you'd best be careful—whoever was after him may try to finish the job."

"Not while there's breath in my body," Mrs. Baird said stoutly. "He's an old friend and dear to me. I sha'n't leave his side."

"Best tell them you're his sister, then, so they let you in." Wyatt doubted anyone at Bellevue would distinguish between a Highland and a Lowland accent, as different as they sounded now to his own ear. He paused on the train station steps, wondering what else Macalester had been doing that day. Something that had led him, at last, to Van Dorn's killer?

Wyatt came around the Camp from the dock and found Armbruster and a newcomer testing out a circle of odd-looking chairs on the sunlit lawn. The chairs sat low to the ground, seats sloped downwards where they met the backs, which were slatted in a fan pattern, with flat arms splayed wide enough for a book and a drink. The wood was still yellow, as yet unsilvered by wind and weather.

"Some friend of Mr. Dodge's that runs a resort on the New York side had them made and sent over. Westport chairs, he calls 'em. Wants to know what we think of 'em." Armbruster

292

poured Wyatt lemonade from a green glass pitcher. "Here you go, you look hot. This is Brigham, from the White House detail."

"How do." The slight, rat-faced man in gray stood up and shook hands. His whiskers twitched and Wyatt felt the keen eyes assessing him with a quick once-over. He perched on the arm of an empty chair and filled them in on the news about Macalester. Armbruster brooded, his head resting on a meaty hand. He shook his head slowly.

"Glad you thought of setting a guard on him. Though that mightn't stop the Black Hand, from what I've heard."

"I doubt he's the one they'd be after," Wyatt insisted. "He's been far in the background on that case."

Brigham looked skeptical. "So who else would want to do him in?"

"It may be the man who killed Van Dorn. Or some confederate of his. I tried finding out where Macalester had been the last few days, but they don't keep track. He evidently took the watch back to the widow and visited Van Dorn's doctor, but that's about all they know at his office."

Armbruster sipped his lemonade. "And you're thinking he stumbled on something that led him to Rossi?"

"Could be, but we won't know unless he wakes up and tells us."

"I don't like it. So many unknowns. We've got the fellow's description, but he may send confederates, or have changed his appearance—"

"We'll be checking everyone who tries to set foot on this island." Wyatt refilled Armbruster's lemonade. Sweat-lines rolled down the globe of the pitcher.

Armbruster sipped absently. "This fellow got away at the crack of dawn, or not much past. He can make his way back—even in the dark, I suppose."

"There are a lot of submerged rocks on the way out. You

have to know your way. Besides, we'll be out there around the clock—"

"We can't be everywhere," Brigham broke in. "It only takes a minute."

"How much is the press likely to know?" Wyatt settled himself into the chair, which proved more comfortable than it looked.

"Nice thing about Sagamore," Brigham said, "is you can just run a sailboat over to the Connecticut shore. They haven't caught on to where we keep the Express. They think we have to take a train back through the City, instead of Hartford up to White River and then west."

"But they'll figure out he's not there, won't they?"

"We don't let them anywhere near the grounds when he's at Sagamore," Armbruster said. "In any event, there will be a couple of them on the island—as guests, not reporters. Riis is coming—he's summering at Lake George—Fox from the *Tribune*, of course, Miss Pearle from the *Post*—she's a great friend of the Princess—"

"Code name for Miss Roosevelt," Brigham added, straight-faced, in response to Wyatt's raised eyebrow. "They might write about the party afterwards, but not till it's well over. What've we got for entertainment?"

"A couple of opera singers—they're guests, but I understand they can be persuaded to sing for the First Lady—" Wyatt stopped. "—that reminds me. Did one of you check up on Eduardo Romano?"

"Did that one myself," Armbruster said. "Why'd you ask?"

Wyatt's mind flashed to something Germain had said, when they talked about a possible connection between Milly and someone in the quartet. *Opera tenors would be more in her line. Famous ones at that.*

"Go on," Armbruster said. "Why'd you stop?"

"Oh—nothing. Just that—Van Sicklen, who owns Abenaki

Island, mentioned that Romano was visiting there in June, not long before the—Van Dorn's death. I'm wondering where he went after he left Abenaki."

Brigham frowned. "You'll talk to him?"

Wyatt nodded. "Also, the Webbs' quartet will be back. They got Czerny to come back for a few days—the Met's not into full-blown rehearsals yet."

"The one you told me was an anarchist?" Armbruster said sharply.

"I'd stake my life he's not a violent one. He has a wife and child—it's really more of a study group of sorts. It puts out a broadsheet once in a while and cloaks itself in mystery. They don't even advocate violence—"

"Despite the way they roughed you up on the street?"

Wyatt smiled ruefully. "I had my doubts at first, I have to admit."

"What about this crowd from Barre, though?"

"After they, ah, grabbed me, I told them we'd cancel the President's visit, but I doubt they'll believe that we did. They'll at least look for gaps in the President's schedule. We should plan on their making a try to confront him while he's here." Wyatt wondered suddenly what had happened to the photographs the anarchists had used in their blackmail attempt. He felt himself reddening.

"It doesn't do to be soft with such people." Brigham seemed to read his thoughts.

"Granted," Wyatt's tone was almost irritable. Did anyone in this idyllic retreat have a clue how "such people" had to live? He doubted it. "We'd all feel safer if this visit had been cancelled. But the President made the decision. Talk to Czerny yourself when he gets here."

Armbruster stood and swigged the last of his lemonade. "We did our own recon of the island while you were over in South Hero."

"Everything under control?"

"Pretty well. There are really only two good places to land, the dock and the beach there." Armbruster's arm swept towards the edge of the lawn. " I think we can keep those pretty well covered." The three men ambled back towards the dock.

"What about checking in the guests?"

"That's where we'll need you. Um, maybe you could have a word with Mr. Dodge. He's none too happy about the intrusions. Seems to think you and he could handle any problems that came up."

"You men don't work for him," Wyatt grinned. "He has a hard time with that. I'll talk to him."

A clatter of hard-soled shoes on the path announced Amy's arrival on the dock, breathless and stopping at Wyatt's feet just in time to avoid bowling over Brigham.

"You're back. I'm so glad. Mother's in a tizzy about the linens, and Father's—did you catch him yet? The one who did it, I mean."

Brigham looked at Wyatt, his whiskers twitching.

"Miss Dodge was—ah, among those we questioned after Mr. Van Dorn's death. She was most helpful on some matters of timing, since she'd been out early that morning. It wasn't Jeremy," Wyatt added, turning to Amy.

"Oh, wasn't it? Well, I never really thought it was. He wouldn't have had the nerve. I've been helping Mr. Armbruster—showing him all the places there are to hide, or land a boat, if you were really bent on coming in unseen—"

"Miss Dodge has been most helpful." Armbruster's tone held no trace of condescension.

"I may show him the cormorants' chicks, mayn't I?"

"Can't imagine why not. There'd be no stopping him from going once he hears of them. He's quite the birding man."

Dodge, in shirtsleeves and an open waistcoat, strode down the elm-lined path to meet them. "New telegraph works fine. I got a wire from Will Van Dorn. He's decided to come for the reception. Be good for him to get out."

"Will he be staying?" Brigham asked.

"I'd said we'd put him up overnight, but I think he's going to leave with the rest of the reception crowd."

"I should think the place would have bad memories for him—meaning no disrespect," Armbruster said, nodding in Dodge's direction.

"More so for his stepmother, I dare say. It was all over by the time Will got here. He's a practical sort of fellow. He'll need to be, to manage all he's been left with." They reached the screened verandah, where aromas of baking pies wafted on the still air.

"Hot day for baking," Brigham observed.

Jeremy emerged from the cool darkness of the house, carrying an easel and paint box. He blinked in the sudden light and caught sight of Wyatt.

"Oh, it's you."

Wyatt considered a tennis invitation and decided it would keep.

"Van Dorn's coming," Dodge turned to his son. "You'll share a room?"

"You sure you should trust someone with my murderous tendencies?" Jeremy scowled from his father to Wyatt.

Wyatt's face darkened. "We'll talk later." He walked past Jeremy into the house.

Armbruster followed him into the bunk-room. "We'll meet at the guest cottage in half an hour. The two bunks on the right are free—unless Fiorello's bagged one already. Our third man."

"He's here?"

"Sprucing up, I was told. He's particular that way. I'd like

297

to talk things over with your man Germain. I understand he more or less runs the place?"

"Absolutely. Both Dodges defer to him on all household matters."

Germain appeared in the doorway of the bunkroom. "My ears were burning. Sorry we can't put you gents up in more comfortable quarters."

"I've been in a lot worse." Armbruster advanced and extended his hand. Surprised, Germain took it.

"Mr. Roosevelt drink iced tea?" he asked Wyatt.

"He prefers lemonade," Armbruster said, "and the colder, the better."

"We got in a new shipment of ice," Germain replied to Wyatt's unasked question.

CHAPTER 30

Fiorello was olive-skinned and lithe, with a long aristocratic nose and protuberant blue eyes that seemed at odds with his Neapolitan origins. His long-fingered hands, quick and graceful, would have suited a concert pianist. An American for most of his thirty-five years, he spoke with a jerky Brooklyn honk that reminded Wyatt of the heron's squawk in the night. In fact, most of Fiorello resembled a heron, down to the blue-gray of his immaculate silk suit. Wyatt took him around the island on the morning the President was due to arrive, pointing out cliffs and landing-places and clumps of shrubbery where even a large man might conceal himself.

"We'd best keep an eye on the northern extension," Wyatt was saying when they passed the tennis courts. "It's a tough place to land, but it's the one spot where you could get in without being seen—a bit of a climb up the rock face, but not impossible for a fit man, especially if he knew the place at all. I've done it myself. And our fiddler, if he decides to come back, might have had a chance to check it out when he was here."

"Think it was him that killed that banker guy?"

"It fits with what we know. But I confess it's not making a lot of sense to me. If he was smart enough to worm his way into the Webbs' confidence, it's hard to imagine him mistaking Gerald Van Dorn for the President, if that's what happened."

"Any other reason he could've killed this Van Doawan?"

"Damned if I can think of one," Wyatt shrugged. "Unless he was one of those bomb-throwing types you hear about, like that fellow Henry who wrecked the train station café in Paris a few years back."

Fiorello looked polite but puzzled.

"Emile Henry. When the judge asked him how he could kill all those innocent people, he said no one was innocent. The bourgeoisie was as guilty of oppressing the masses as the capitalists, because they went along with it all."

"Ah! I see whatcha getting' at. Who's more of a capitalist than a banker?"

"I've never understood that," Wyatt shook his head. "Killing on principle, in cold blood. Bad enough in the heat of battle, or a jealous rage or some such, but just to up and kill a man because you don't like what he stands for—"

Fiorello looked away.

"You worked for McKinley too," Wyatt realized. "I'm sorry."

"Man wouldn't'a hurt a fly." Fiorello's voice was choked. "You shoulda seen him with his wife—she'd get these fits, and he'd just hold her, you know? And talk to her till it passed. That was the worst of it , her left alone like that. We got along pretty good, her and me. I wanted to do that Buffalo detail, but Gallagher pulled rank on me. Maybe if I'd been there—"

He stopped, realizing that Wyatt had been there and hadn't been able to stop it. There was a moment of awkward silence.

"It's all right," Wyatt said. "We've all got to live with our regrets."

"Anyway, I'll be damned if I let anything happen to this one. That's why these things scare me. And he's just not careful. He's got this he-man thing—"

"I've seen it," Wyatt said. "Followed him up Kettle Hill in '98. I remember thinking, this is crazy. But he gets you caught up in it. Running straight into Mauser fire, and you're having fun."

They followed the slope of the lawn to the edge of the southern cliff.

"That's where we found Van Dorn." Wyatt nodded towards the wavelets winking in perfect innocence on impenetrable deep blue.

"What's the shore we can see from here?" Fiorello nodded to the west. "Is that where we came in on the train?"

"Grand Isle, yes. We found the boat over there, in South Hero." Wyatt pointed farther southwest.

Fiorello pulled a crumpled paper out of his breast pocket. "This is the composite they've got of your violinist."

It could have been anyone with curly hair and a beard. You could tell the really skilled portraitists—Jeremy was one—because they could draw mouths. The police artist got something, but it wasn't the mouth he remembered on the fiddler. That had been fuller, more sculpted. And the nose had been rendered too bulbous.

"It's not much like him." He handed the paper back. "But it's not much not like him either, from what I remember. It's not specific enough. This could be a lot of people."

"He'll probably look pretty different by now anyway," Fiorello sighed and folded the paper away. "I was him, I'd'a shaved the beard first thing."

"That's why we have to focus on the landing-spots. If it's anarchists we have to worry about, they could send anyone. And after dark is when we have to be most concerned."

Fiorello squinted and shaded his eyes. "Here comes a boat."

Wyatt raised his binoculars. "It's Dodge. *Calliope.* Best refer to it as a yacht, if you want to stay on his good side. I've got a good fix on the people he's bringing, so why don't you tie up and help the ladies up onto the dock and so forth, and I'll—"

"Tie up?" Fiorello looked alarmed. "I don't know any of that sailor stuff. I'm a city boy."

They trotted across the lawn to the north end and the dock. "It's simple. You just grab the line when they throw it to you, pull the boat in, wind the line around the cleat a couple of times, finish it with a thumb knot—never mind," Wyatt said, noting Fiorello's wide eyes. "Just don't let anyone off till we're all tied up."

Armbruster was hurrying over the grass to intercept them.

"I'll give you a hand tying her up. Greg, watch me on this. He's a quick study," he added to Wyatt. "Time the next boat comes in, he'll have it down. Forgot this is his first summer on the Sagamore detail."

Armbruster shaded his eyes and peered out to the boat. "We should be all right for this crowd. The overnighters. A dozen besides the Dodges—well, there's Gardiner Dodge and his wife and kids, so that's actually eight Dodges and six others, including Mademoiselle Marchant, as she insists on being known—"

"The soprano?" Fiorello's eyes lit up.

"She herself. The Mrs. is a great admirer, and TR is coming around."

"We'll have two opera singers," Wyatt told Fiorello. "Signor Romano will be here as well."

"Who's he?"

"Up-and-coming baritone at the Met," Armbruster said.

Wyatt pointed north. "He's been staying with the Van Sicklens off and on this summer. At Abenaki, the next island over."

"We can have duets!" Fiorello grinned happily.

The yacht sailed towards them, massive but graceful under its broad spread of sail. Not much wind to catch today, the air warm and moist. Wyatt began to make out faces along the rails, the ladies re-pinning their elaborate hats, removed for fear of being caught and carried away on the breeze of the yacht's passage.

There was Augusta Dodge, like a figurehead, in peacock crêpe de Chine with an ivory lace bodice. Amy buzzing around her in white dotted swiss, her hair still tied back by a bow, not yet put up. Wyatt found himself relieved at this. A russet-haired man who looked like a younger, taller Warren Dodge, a sweet-faced, plump woman at his side in striped rose taffeta: Mr. and Mrs. Gardiner Dodge, whom he had met in New York. Beside them, a solemn-faced little girl in a white dress and crimson silk sash, a smaller boy in a sailor suit. Odd to think of the vigorous Dodge as a grandfather.

"There's Signor Pellegrino." Fiorello lowered the binoculars and pointed towards a tall, lean man who bore himself with that mix of affability and reserve that marks the career diplomat. "Seen him at Sagamore a month ago—he's been at Newport since then. And his wife—she's a looker, ain't she?"

The looker was a fine-boned strawberry blonde in her thirties, wearing a flower-dotted taffeta dress the color of fresh butter. She stood by the port rail straining eagerly towards the shore, clasping her hands and talking with Augusta Dodge, who was pointing something out to her. Beside her was a younger woman in poppy red, dark-haired and full-lipped, her exquisite Grecian profile turned towards Signora Pellegrino.

A boatload of flowers. The deep green of the yacht's hull, with its cream stripes below the rail, set them off perfectly. The men hovered behind them in suits of tan and olive green, their boaters at jaunty angles. He heard Dodge shouting commands to Jeremy and Gardiner, which they obeyed out of long reflex, as the yacht furled its sails and drifted in towards its mooring. A small skiff, newer than the lost boat and freshly painted, waited at the mooring buoy to serve as a tender.

Wyatt wondered how much the anarchists acted out of righteous anger at all this privilege in the face of mass misery, and how much out of sheer envy. Perhaps it was beauty, available in such abundance to the rich, that the poor missed most, not just the abundance of food, the roof over the head, security. *The poor you will always have with you.* That one had never sounded right to him, a mistranslation perhaps. Sell one of these yachts, and you could...

The woman in poppy silk must be the opera singer, only twenty-two and already an acclaimed interpreter of Puccini on the great stages of Europe and America. As much a coup for the Dodges to have snagged her as TR himself. And when they presented her to the Roosevelts—well, that would be a culminating moment, a family legend for the Dodge posterity.

Warren Dodge's father had left his childhood home in a dirt-poor Pennsylvania mining town and made an odyssey north to a paper mill in the wilderness of Groveton, New Hampshire where he started as an operative. His ideas for improvements in production impressed the owner, and he quickly became the plant manager. Before he was thirty he had persuaded the aging owner to sell to him on favorable terms, doubled the plant's profits and laid the foundation for the empire of pulp mills and paper plants his son would later build across the northern forests. Now that son was playing host to the President of the United States, and one of the old Dutch aristocracy at that.

Wyatt's musings did not divert his gaze from the yacht and its occupants. Will Van Dorn, minus hat and jacket, shinnied down the stern-ladder and dropped gracefully into the skiff. He untethered the boat from its mooring in one smooth, swift motion, took up the oars, and brought the boat alongside the yacht, where a solid-looking wooden ladder had been let down on the port side. Augusta Dodge descended first, followed by Amy. Will offered a hand to Signora Pellegrino. He rowed towards the dock, pulling with little strain despite the load. A natural athlete, Wyatt thought, his body coiled and dense in contrast to Jeremy, who was all languor and looseness except on the tennis court.

The guests came in, in small batches, Signora Pellegrino and the young diva next with Mrs. Van Sicklen from the neighboring island. He watched their descent from the yacht into the skiff, had ample time to scan each face and match it to a picture in his memory, like the Bertillion cards the New York police were beginning to replace with finger-prints. Wyatt wasn't sure he believed in finger-prints.

Armbruster had been right. Fiorello was a quick study. He secured the boat line quickly enough to combine it with flashing dazzling, shy smiles at the disembarking ladies and greeting Signora Pellegrino in her native tongue. They dimpled and smiled in return, except for Augusta Dodge, who disapproved of the whole security plan and shared her husband's theory that the family could have handled matters quite well by itself.

Will Van Dorn handed up the last of the women and found himself face to face with Wyatt.

"Glad to see you back, Mr. Van Dorn."

"Thanks—it feels a little odd, I must say. Perhaps it wasn't such a good idea."

"I'm sure it's hard not to associate the place with—with what happened."

"Yes. But Mr. Dodge is right." Will gave him a rueful smile. "We must get on with life, mustn't we."

"May I ask how Mrs. Van Dorn does?"

Will blinked, his face darkening for a moment before it cleared. "Well enough, I guess. She's not recovered her health as yet, and of course, she is still in deep mourning. I think she will be fine, given enough time. Thank you for asking," he added after a pause. "I must take the boat back for the others." He waved a hand towards the green yacht, resumed his rowing stance and pulled away from the dock. Wyatt heard a step behind him.

"How's the little mama doing?" Germain stood tall and polished in an embroidered silk vest and knife-pleated cream trousers.

"Still in purdah, from the sounds of it."

"That's got to be hard on a woman like her. You want help with the luggage after the next crew comes in?"

"I don't recall baggage-handling being part of the deal."

"No room for lady's-maids on this trip," Germain said, "'cept for the First Lady's, of course. She'll help out with Miss Roosevelt too, I understand."

Wyatt glowered. "I'm not helping anyone with corsets."

Germain retreated up the path, chuckling to himself.

The skiff returned, full of men this time. Will Van Dorn now had help from another rower, a pink-cheeked young man a few years older than himself, a headful of bronze curls popping up despite the obvious application of macassar oil. Where had Wyatt seen him before? The photo, yes, but in person somewhere…flowers. A near-collision on the Van Dorns' doorstep, a muttered apology. Only an instant.

Warren Dodge sprang out of the skiff, took the line from Fiorello and made the boat fast. He presented Wyatt to a smooth-haired man with cheeks like polished apples.

"I think you know my associate Mr. Wyatt, who's been helping us with arrangements—Jacob Van Sicklen. Our neighbor from Abenaki Island," he added for Fiorello's benefit. "And his guest," Dodge went on, giving a hand up to the curly-haired young man, "Signor Eduardo Romano, who I trust will join Mademoiselle in a song or two for us this evening."

"So pleased to know you." The young man had an accent to match his name. "but I could not possibly—" he turned back to Dodge, "she is, a, you know, the best—the toast of New York, as you would say—she would hardly wish to sing with me!"

"I already talked to her. She's looking forward to it."

The young man put his hand over his heart. "Such an honor!" he effused. "And the President too—I am terrified!"

"You'll do fine." Dodge led him and Van Sicklen up the path. Wyatt and Fiorello turned back to scan the lake.

"If he's Eyetalian, I'm a Hottentot," Fiorello said. "I doubt he's ever gotten closer to Italy than Grand Street."

"Sings well, what I hear."

"Is that Fisk's boat coming around the point?"

The *Marmorean Angel* glided to its mooring in a blinding spread of canvas and white-painted wood.

Wyatt drew in a sharp breath. "God, that's beautiful."

"They don't get much prettier," Germain said. "Don't stare at it, though—Mr. Dodge'll get jealous."

"His is nothing to sneeze at. There's just something about all that white on a day like this." The air was clear, the water ink-blue and sparkling.

"Yeah," Germain said. "Shame we have to work, isn't it?"

Fisk had dressed in white to match his yacht, Wyatt noted when he handed up the last of the *Angel's* passengers. This crowd had been trickier; he didn't know any of them by sight except for the feline, whiskered face of Jacob Riis, whom he recognized from the frontispiece of his book. Its photographs of desperate New York slumdwellers had shaken Fifth Avenue's complacency, for a little while.

The other passengers tended towards the average of New York's upper strata, the men corpulent and good-natured, the women controlled, confident, magisterial in ornate, mountainous hats, their bosoms spilling cascades of lace. As instructed, the men gave Wyatt their names and presented their invitations. The women fluttered and rustled out of the skiff and up the avenue of young elms, parasols popping open to protect fair complexions from the sun. One or two bestowed idle, curious glances on himself and Germain before consigning them to the servant class.

Fiorello had been escorting passengers up to the Camp, depositing them in wicker chairs on the lawn and in rockers along the verandah. The housemaids moved among them with trays of iced lemonade. Fiorello helped himself to two glasses, winked at Bridie's glare, and made his way back to the dock.

"Just checked the perimeter with the big fellow," he told Wyatt. "*Elfreida*'s about two miles south, I'd say. Twenty minutes, maybe. Want some lemonade?"

"So TR's finally going to set foot on Heron Island." Wyatt drained half the glass in a swallow and handed it to Germain, who finished it. "I'm glad for Mr. Dodge. They've wanted this for a long time."

Fiorello shot a finger at him. "See you don't let us regret it. Wilkie wasn't at all happy about this, nor was Armbruster, but the chief wouldn't hear anything about it. He likes these folks, and he's after bird sightings."

"Everybody settled up there?" Germain asked.

"Sorry—I didn't introduce you gents yet," Wyatt said. "This is Mr. Fiorello, of the President's detail. May I present Mr. Germain."

Fiorello, who had observed the shared lemonade glass with mild surprise, shot out his hand.

"Yes—you're the steward, aren't you? Pleased to meet ya. You got a nice setup here."

"We do all right. Heard your boss likes lemonade. Think this'll suit him?"

"Better than Sagamore's. This isn't too sweet." Fiorello replaced the glasses on Bridie's passing tray and earned another glare. They watched the prodigious but graceful *Elfreida* inch her way into the channel between the moored white and green yachts. On the foredeck they could see two small figures, sunlight glinting off gold-rimmed lenses: Dr. Webb and Theodore Roosevelt, hands waving in animated conversation.

Webb was directing Roosevelt's attention to the northern headland. Roosevelt raised field-glasses to his eyes and peered around in jerky half-circles. On the port side towards the stern, uniformed men were lowering a small boat to the deck.

"They brought their own tenders." Fiorello shook his head in wonder.

"He calls it a yacht, but it's really more of a small steamer," Germain said. "You could sail the Atlantic in that thing."

"We won't need the skiff, then." Wyatt hauled it up onto the bed of flat rocks next to the dock. The elm path came alive again in ripples of muslin and summer silk, women streaming down from the house to the dock to greet the guest of honor, followed by embarrassed-looking men.

"Couldn't keep 'em up there once they heard the yacht coming in," Fisk leaned over Wyatt and Fiorello from the path. "Hope it doesn't disrupt your arrangements. Hello, Wyatt. Good to see you under more pleasant circumstances."

Wyatt had a brief vision of Fisk's lanky body hunched like an interested vulture over Gerald Van Dorn's corpse in the icehouse. He shoved the thought aside.

"Governor Fisk—Mr. Fiorello of the President's staff." The two bobbed their heads slightly, like a stork being introduced to a heron.

The string quartet disembarked first, rowed by a hairy-handed giant in summer whites. Brigham, now standing next to the President on the foredeck, spotted Fiorello and raised an arm. After the musicians came the Webbs' son Watson and his wife and two younger couples Wyatt did not know, the wives plump and complacent, the men lean and driven.

"Good thing Brigham's vetted this lot. I don't recognize half of them."

"Anywhere else he went, there'd be a brass band," Fiorello said. "He eats 'em up, too. Can't get enough of 'em. But I must say it's a nice change not having to stand through 'Hail to the Chief' and 'Stars and Stripes Forever'." He bent to tie up the line from the tender. "I'm getting good at this thumb-knot stuff."

Wyatt saw Germain starting back for the house and called after him.

"Where are you going? The President's coming off in a minute. You said everything was in hand."

"It is. But if I don't send Cook and the girls down here to see him come off the boat and get themselves glad-handed, I'll never hear the end of it. Cook 'specially. The girls and I will have lots of chances while he's here, but she'll be stuck in the kitchen."

"Decent sort of fellow, for a colored man," Fiorello said after Germain had left. "Was he here when—"

"When Van Dorn died? He's always here when the family's up. Helped calm things down considerably. He was with me when we found the bike."

"The one the murderer stole from the farm?"

"They found the skiff he'd taken on their beach. The bike was gone from behind their barn. We found it in the woods along with Van Dorn's gold watch. If theft had been a motive, seems he'd have taken that."

"No sign of him since—?" Fiorello stopped and nodded towards the steam-yacht. "Look, there's the Princess—"

Alice Roosevelt, in one of her signature blue gowns, was being helped over the side of *Elfreida*—or, rather, she was fending off helping hands and making her own way, seating herself with a flounce of skirt and a careless sweep of the head. Three strands of pearls circled her exquisite throat. The hairy boatman gawked at her in undisguised admiration, which she rewarded with a seraphic smile.

"She looks like trouble," Wyatt said.

"You don't know the half of it," Fiorello sighed. "She's worse than TR for taking chances in public places. I have these nightmares about her getting kidnapped and held for ransom. Could see her bribing the crooks not to let her go, just to keep things stirred up. I'd bribe 'em myself if it weren't for all the fuss it would cause."

"Why'd she come along on a jaunt like this?"

"They don't like to leave her alone too much. She's probably not real happy about it. So she'll get back at them by making eyes at every male that comes along."

"There may be more benefits to this assignment than I'd thought."

"I wouldn't if I were you," Fiorello said. "I'd hate to have to kill you."

When the tender docked, Wyatt hung back to let Fiorello offer the Princess his hand. She stepped onto the dock, dazzling Wyatt with a gas-jet gaze. Sweet and twenty...no. Twenty and beautiful, but nothing sweet about this one. Elizabeth Fisk stepped out of the crowd of ladies and swept her up the path to the avenue of elms. They turned to watch the President's arrival, the one small, round-faced, motherly, the other all the soft angles of marble carved by a master. This, Wyatt thought, could be Fisk's Marmorean Angel. A woman who might desire—the blue flame of it was in her eyes—but never love. And who might in turn be desired to the point of obsession, but never truly and generously loved as mortals love each other...

The tender's third trip brought Theodore Roosevelt and his wife Edith, a gentle-faced woman who appeared to have been brought into the world to balance him out. Flashing teeth as white as his immaculate suit, he talked and gesticulated to the boatman and the Webbs, Edith sitting beside him in a simple dress of white lawn, smiling gently, still as the eye of a hurricane.

Brigham was in the boat with them, his rat-whiskers twitching at some Presidential witticism. The Webbs sat facing them in the prow like a matched set, Lila cool in summer white, animated Dr. Webb directing Roosevelt's attention to a pair of teals flying overhead. The guests on the shore lined themselves up along the path from the dock to the elms, like an honor guard or spectators at a parade.

"We should have got flags for them," Wyatt observed.

Fiorello grinned. "Most of these folks have known him since he was a pup. That's one reason Wilkie and Arm-buster went along with this. The older ladies still call him Teedie in private. They remember him when he was still in knickers."

The tender reached the dock and Wyatt caught the line thrown by the hirsute oarsman. The Dodges, in perfect rhythm like the head couple in a reel, paced down the path cleared by the guests and stepped onto the dock. Roosevelt handed Edith up to Warren Dodge, who took her hand long enough to guide her firmly onto the dock, then let it go, stepped back and made her a gentlemanly bow with a flourish of his Panama hat. The President scrambled up behind her, not waiting for help, with Brigham fussing behind him. The crowd cheered and clapped. Roosevelt swept off his own Panama, held it to his chest and bowed towards them before grabbing Dodge's hand and pumping it.

"Dee-lighted to be here, old man. Ain't this a splendid little spot! What a find! Three years you've had it?" He bowed to Augusta, took her by the hands and pecked her on the cheek. "Dear Mrs. Dodge! What a pleasure to be here at last!" Augusta blushed and dimpled like a maiden. Nelson Fisk made his way down to the dock.

"Why, it's Fisk!"

"Mr. President," Fisk bowed with his boater over his heart. Roosevelt clasped him by the arms. Behind the tiny glasses, the President's eyes filled.

"Lot of changes since last we saw each other, eh?"

Behind Fisk, Alice Roosevelt took Amy by the shoulders and shoved her into the President's path.

"Here's someone who wants to take you bird-watching, Papa." Amy shrank back, but Roosevelt stepped forward and took her by the hand.

"You must be Miss Dodge. I hear you are the ornithologist in residence here. Deelighted to meet you at last!" He gave her the full spread of his toothy smile. "And will you really take me out to look for nests?"

Amy paused, swallowed, smiled crookedly back at him. "I'll be dee-lighted to!"

"Well, that'll be just bully!" The crowd broke into laughter.

Wyatt helped the Webbs onto the dock, exchanging a look with the doctor that spoke of their shared history, the events of the ice-house, the still unsolved riddle of who had killed Gerald Van Dorn and where he had gone. Roosevelt moved through the crowd, shaking hands and exchanging genialities.

Cook and the maids, hovering at the back, were pulled forward for introductions. "Dee-lighted!" Roosevelt whooped.

Augusta and Warren Dodge preceded the Roosevelts up the path, pointing out the guest cottage where they would stay, newly repainted and furnished in rustic luxury for the occasion. The rest of the party followed them into the Camp, to the great screened porch where Germain had arranged chafing dishes and platters piled high with flaky pastries, pale green crescents of honeydew melon, red and purple mounds of berries amid massive bouquets and ice-sculptured swans.

Elfreida's engines churned back into life, the crew back on board and headed for anchorage in Burlington to await their scheduled return in the evening. Wyatt helped Brigham shoulder carpet-bags and leather valises up the path to the guest cottage.

"I don't like it. If we had to get him out of here in a hurry—" Brigham shook his head.

"We have the telegraph line now. Next to Germain's room, off the kitchen. We could get *Elfreida* back here from the Yacht Club pretty fast if we had to."

"And there's a doctor in the house," Fiorello added, coming up behind them with a belting-leather suitcase.

"Didn't do much good the last time," Brigham grumbled.

"Van Dorn didn't have you fellows watching him around the clock," Wyatt said.

"Chief won't this time either, if he's in his usual form. He loves to give us fits. It's his idea of fun."

"Is he reckless?"

"Oh, I don't think you could go that far, Brig," Fiorello demurred. "He was pretty spooked after the Buffalo business. I don't think he'd put himself in real danger, do you?"

Brigham snorted. "You see him with that herd of bison last year?"

"No, but anything here should be mild compared to that."

They climbed the porch steps of the guest cottage, where a rank of deep green rockers on the open Southern verandah invited occupants. Thyme flowers, tiny yellow stars, flecked the grass that surrounded it and kept mosquitoes at bay.

Wyatt took his load into the main bedroom, newly furnished with an oversized double bed framed in cedar logs, its headboard inlaid with contrasting barks of white birch, beech and cherry. In the far corner stood a large dresser with a twig-mosaic trim and birchbark door panels, a side table nearby with a base made from an up-ended yellow birch trunk, its branches lopped off evenly at floor level. It made Wyatt think of an octopus in rigor mortis. This elaborate rusticism, all the rage among the fashionable families of the Adirondacks, seemed mannered and self-conscious when he thought of the deal table and plain wood chairs of the Tarrants' kitchen on Grand Isle.

"That bed doesn't look so comfortable." Brigham sat on the patchwork quilt and bounced. "Good firm mattress, though. Wouldn't surprise me if he grabbed a pillow and blanket and went to sleep under the stars."

"He hasn't got any guns with him, has he?" Fiorello said anxiously. "It'd be too bad if he mistook one of us for a bear prowling in the night."

"City boy," Brigham snorted.

"I think they cleared the bears out a while back," Wyatt said.

"No, but you know how it is when a fellow wakes up, isn't sure where he is at first—"

Wyatt made a mental note not to stumble over any sleeping Presidents while on night patrol. "How early will he get up?"

"The question is, will he go to bed at all," Brigham said. "He'll be up half the night talking politics with the men, till they all drop from exhaustion but him, then up at first light to go birding with the young lady there—"

"By the way, who's covering that?" Fiorello asked.

"We checked it over yesterday," Wyatt said. "The northern extension is the only place you could make a surprise landing. I'll get out in one of the skiffs at first light and patrol that headland. It's almost impossible to land and climb up there in the pitch dark—it would be too dangerous, especially if we get rain. But if you had a little daylight—it's steep but it might be done. For today, we'll keep checking in there and around the shoreline as long as there's still light. After dark, we'd spot anyone trying to get near it—they'd have to have a light."

They unpacked valises as they talked, arranging linens in drawers, hanging dresses and suit-coats and trousers in a tiny cedar-lined closet.

"First time in a while he hasn't had Rufus with him," Fiorello said to Brigham.

"He'll manage. No collars after today, he said. He's just here to relax."

314

"Germain can help him out if he needs a valet," Wyatt said. "He'd do it for the President. Mrs. Roosevelt's sharing her lady's maid with Miss Alice?"

"It's a holiday thing they do. I think she looks forward to it," Brigham said.

"They get along?"

"Mrs. R.—she's a class act. If you can't get along with her, there's something wrong with you. There are a few eligible men in the crowd, right?"

Fiorello frowned. "Mostly couples."

"There's the opera singer," Wyatt said. "Don't know much about him, though."

"Armbruster filled me in. You were right, Greg, the Italian accent is fake, but he really is from an Italian family. Spoke it at home as a kid."

"He from the City?" Wyatt asked.

"He lives there now, but he grew up around Albany. Made his debut at the Troy Music Hall back in—'97, '98, somewhere in there. What's that opera, Greg—you know, the one where the valet's trying to keep the Count from making off with his girl—Figaro? Yeah, that's it. He was the Count. Real musical family. Five kids, and they all played an instrument of some kind."

"He play too, or just sing?" Wyatt kept his tone casual. Somewhere in the back of his brain, a faint alarm bell was going off.

"Plays a little violin, what I remember," Brigham said.

"And he lives in New York now?"

"He's been up here a lot this summer. You didn't meet him at Abenaki?"

"He'd just left when I got here, that time in June."

"He came back up a couple days ago. Must like the place."

"Know anything about his politics?" Wyatt asked carefully.

"Politics? He's an actor. Or a singer, same thing. What else you got for eligible men?"

Wyatt shrugged. "There's Will Van Dorn."

"The fellow who—wasn't that his father who—?"

315

"Was drowned here. That's the one. Rich, good-looking, respectable—Yale man—and far as I know, eligible."

"The one that rowed people in from Mr. Dodge's boat," Fiorello added. "Healthy specimen, too. Might be a little short for the Princess, though? He's not in politics, is he?"

"A pair of them lift shoes would fix him right up," Brigham said. "She'd never know the difference. Maybe I'll give him a tip."

"Well, if matchmaking's part of the job—" Wyatt raised an eyebrow, "there's Jeremy Dodge, too. He's taller than her, even. But she'd eat him for breakfast."

"We're on our knees night and day," Brigham said, "praying for somebody to take her off our hands. We caught her smoking in the Blue Room one day."

"What happened?"

"Her father said she couldn't smoke under his roof," Fiorello sighed. "So she climbed out onto the roof of the White House and smoked there."

Germain's head appeared around the bedroom door.

"You gents all set in here?"

"Looks fine," Wyatt said. "Maybe you could send Bridie—uh, Bridget down to unpack Miss Roosevelt's things."

"If I can get her feet to touch the ground. The President shook hands with her. She says she's never gonna wash that hand again." Germain gave a dead-on imitation of Bridie's Kerry lilt. "'Oh, an' the lovely blue eyes of him!'"

"It'll be all over County Kerry in a week. How's the Continental breakfast going?"

"Should've had more of the *croissant*. The chocolate ones are going well. And the raspberry Danish-pastries too." Germain allowed himself a complacent smile.

"We're missing this?" Fiorello looked alarmed.

"I held back a few. I guess they can move on to the apricot if they run out."

"Mr. Germain, you seen Miss Roosevelt?" Brigham asked.

"Last I saw, she was working on getting that young Jackson

away from his wife—that junior guy from Morgan's, used to work with Van Dorn—"

"Land's sakes." It was Brigham's turn to look distressed.

"We're thinking we should steer her in Will Van Dorn's direction," Wyatt told Germain. "Keep her occupied."

"Will's with Jeremy somewhere. Two for one, she could take her pick. I'll get Mr. Dodge to do the honors."

"Much obliged," Brigham said with relief. Germain disappeared.

Music broke through the murmur of the crowd: the string quartet's introduction, followed by a soaring soprano like a peal of bells in the summer air.

Brigham's whiskers bristled. "What's that?"

"That," said Fiorello happily, "is Rossini. 'Signor, perdona' from *La Cenerentola*, to be precise. And *that* is Mademoiselle Marchant," he sighed, "of the Metropolitan Opera. Getting the President here was a piece of cake compared to this. Oh, he will be pleased."

"He didn't know?" Wyatt said.

"Politicians don't like surprises, as a rule, but we figured we could let this one go. Even old Arm-buster—" Fiorello ignored Brigham's glare—"said it was all right. Shall we go have a look-see?"

"You go," Brigham said. "I want to give this place one more going-over."

"Your bed's in the cellar." Wyatt pointed towards the stairs. "They chased the raccoons out just for you."

"Bed!? Who's going to sleep on this job?"

"Four-hour shifts, Armbruster says," Fiorello told him. "He wants us alert on the night watches especially. In case anybody tries to land."

"Makes sense, I suppose," Brigham conceded. "But I'm still worried about that northern end, even in the dark. The bird-roost there? *Almost* impossible, you said."

"We'll keep an eye out for anything on the lake. I think that's as much as we can do."

Wyatt and Fiorello walked back around the lawn and slipped into the crowd on the west porch, where Mademoiselle Marchant was nodding and smiling to rapturous applause. Roosevelt was on his feet, his face pink with delight.

"*Brava! Brava!*" he boomed. "By God, Dodge, I wasn't expecting this."

The singer motioned them to sit with a graceful drop of her hand and launched into 'Quando m'en vo," Musetta's waltz from *La Bohème*. She strolled as she sang, flirting, lightly touching the men's shoulders—she could act, too, Wyatt saw. She had the room in her hand, even Alice Roosevelt who stared at her, mouth half-open in some combination of wistfulness and envy. *When I go out alone in the street…*—that's how it started, he remembered, he had gone to see the opera with the Dodges out of some self-punishing impulse, and how did the song end? *I know well: you don't want to say it, but you feel as if you're dying.* As he had, then. And now the singer stopped in front of him, lifting his chin with an enameled forefinger, stripping his soul with her huge dark eyes, uncovering the pain he had sealed away, realizing it, discomposed for an instant, recovering, smiling, turning away, moving on around the circle. He felt the heat in his face, a great lump in his throat that had to be swallowed, shoved back where it came from. He caught his breath, took three slow gulps of air. He was all right. He would be all right. It had been a mistake, he'd known it at the time, but Dodge had talked him into it, his new box in the Met's Diamond Horseshoe, Augusta regal and smiling in the crimson silk and pearls in which Sargent would paint her.

And then the heartbreaking music, their story, his and Rose's, that had played itself out in the backstages of the National Theatre instead of the garrets of Paris, but the same in its essentials. Love, alienation, irrevocable loss. *Mimi!* Rodolfo's last despairing cry had unmanned him. He'd left the box without a word, wandered the winter streets of Manhattan until he was numb with cold, finally reached his door at 107th Street, closed it behind him, lain on the bed for what seemed like days, purging his grief till it was all out of him.

Or so he had thought until now, until the voice took him back to that stage, that night. Other stages, other nights. Rose in Ophelia's mad scene, trailing dead flowers, a ghost in white gauze, her eyes fever-bright, cheeks scarlet, going on night after night because that was all she could do. She would die if she stopped, she said, she had no faith in rest cures, so she died anyway, a pulmonary haemorrhage, one night not long after he had come back from the war. A night he had gone out with Dodge. Starting to learn, he thought, to live without her. And when he came to the theater to look for her, the janitor was cleaning up the last of the blood and told him where they'd taken her. He got there just before, had a moment when he thought she recognized him, he'd never be sure, his face already full of grief and remorse, hers unreadable, a faint, enigmatic smile, already passing into distance. He had felt her squeeze his hand once, or perhaps it had only been a death spasm. Then she was gone.

Dodge had found him three days after the opera, came to his apartment to apologize. *I never made the connection. I'm thick that way, sometimes.* Something Warren Dodge had never done for anyone in all the time Wyatt had known him.

Dodge was too occupied now with this culmination of his hopes to have noticed the pain that engulfed Wyatt's face and was snuffed out by a great effort of will. And it was all so long ago, surely. He scanned the crowd—that was what he was here for, after all. There was the young baritone, his bronze curls bobbing in time to the music, his expression part awe, part envy. Augusta Dodge, as unaffectedly happy as he had ever seen her. Edith Roosevelt smiling, lips slightly parted and cheeks flushed, ecstatic, Roosevelt himself transfixed. The soprano ended her song to another tumult of applause, paced lightly over to where Signor Romano was standing towards the back of the crowd. She whispered something in his ear. He blushed, smiled and nodded, made his way over to the quartet, bent to speak to Perlstein, the violinist, who nodded in his turn. Romano joined Mademoiselle Marchant in the center of the room.

"Sank you so very much for your warm welcome," the soprano said, the delicate French phrasing only adding to her considerable charm. "As you know, I 'ave been privileged to sing wit' the Metropolitan Opera these past three years. I would like to introduce to you a young member of our company—zis will be his secon' season only—I 'ave asked him to sing wit' me, since I know we will be 'earing much more from him in the future. Signor Eduardo Romano, ladies an' gentlemen!" Polite applause rippled as the violins struck up the introduction to a duet from *L'Elizir d'Amore.*

"Romano did this last season," Fiorello hissed in Wyatt's ear, startling him. "Dr. Dulcamara, the snake-oil salesman. Not a bad role for a newcomer."

"Isn't he a little young for that character?"

"They had him in whiskers and padded him up a bit. His own mother wouldn't have known him."

The soprano line carried most of the song, but the male part called for vocal swoopings and dartings that would have challenged Jean De Reszke himself, Wyatt thought. Still, not a great showpiece for the male voice; rather, the baritone line served to punctuate the soarings of the soprano. The song ended, cheers mingling with the applause this time. Then the soprano said something to the young man, who looked at her in surprise and shook his head with an oh-no-I-couldn't expression. She nodded vigorously, smiled and turned to the musicians, who began the introduction to "Deh, vieni alla finestra," plucking the violin strings in creditable imitation of Don Giovanni's mandolin. The young man was left alone at center stage. It was a baritone's aria, a moonlight serenade, and he did it full justice. Though not so fine a voice as the diva's, Romano's was rich and full, the song seemingly effortless. The listeners, led by Roosevelt, applauded with enthusiasm. The young man bowed and made his way back into the crowd, where he was greeted with claps on the back from the men and clasps of the hand from the ladies.

Mademoiselle Marchant returned and began to sing "Porgi, amor", the Countess's lament for her husband's lost love from *Figaro*. And at last tears were not only permitted but expected. They glinted on Roosevelt's pink, shiny cheeks, on the exquisite bones of Signora Pellegrino—even, Wyatt was surprised to note, on the smooth olive profile of Germain, who had paused with his hand on the door to the kitchen.

She was done. Applause like an explosion in a firecracker factory, roars of *"Brava! Brava!"* She advanced to the President, made a slight curtsy. He took her hand and kissed it.

"Ravishing," he murmured, his cheeks still wet. "Utterly ravishing!"

Germain signaled to the kitchen, and the maids appeared with silver trays bearing flutes of champagne. Dodge took two and handed them to Roosevelt and the diva, who drank each other's health, haloed in their mutual celebrity. More applause, and the string quartet struck up selections from opera overtures while the guests broke up like summer clouds, dissolving in white and pastel patches onto the lawn and into the gardens.

Augusta Dodge, glowing with delight and pride, advanced on the young diva and drew her to a rocking chair in the midst of a knot of admirers, including Signor Romano, who kissed her on both cheeks. The younger people of the party had joined him: Jeremy Dodge looking rapt and adoring, his brother and sister-in-law, Alice Roosevelt broken clean out of her self-absorption, plying Marchant with questions, she answering in her charmingly fragmented English. Will Van Dorn was there too, looking sad and abstracted, his attention drifting and returning like a tethered balloon.

Perhaps, Wyatt thought, it had been too soon to expect the young man to be sociable. Bad enough years later, when the loss would come on you strangely out of the clear air, knocking the wind out of you as it had just been knocked out of him. He thought of Milly Van Dorn, immured in the luxury of her Fifth Avenue prison. She would have reveled in this—even if her grief over Gerald were sincere, which on the whole Wyatt doubted. Far better for Will to shut himself away, Milly turned loose to recover amid flowers and summer silks and champagne. She would not be a widow past the bounds of propriety—or not unattached, in any case. And who was the father of her child? That was still a puzzle. Wyatt found himself gazing at the barely tamed mop of bronze curls next to the diva. Signor Romano. Who was not altogether what he seemed. Who had visited the neighboring island, and left just before Milly Van Dorn had arrived here. Who came from a musical family and played the violin…so well disguised in his opera role, Fiorello had said, that his own mother wouldn't have known him…

He would take it slowly. It was too soon to disrupt the proceedings. Taking advantage of Will Van Dorn's wandering attention, Wyatt caught his eye and jerked his head towards the screen door that led to the lawn. Van Dorn rose and unobtrusively followed him out.

"Mr. Van Dorn, forgive my disturbing you—"

"It's no trouble. I was looking for an excuse to get up. What can I do for you, Mr. Wyatt?"

"There's something I wanted to ask you—have you ever seen Signor Romano before?"

Will looked back towards the verandah, his face clouding with distaste. "Yes, I've seen him. Mrs. Van Dorn was gracious to him after one of his performances last season, and the fellow seemed to take it entirely the wrong way."

"Indeed?"

"He had understudied for Don Giovanni, and the principal was ill that evening. He did it reasonably well, I'm told. Anyway, Father said she insisted on going back to tell him how well he'd risen to the occasion. It's like her, isn't it? Well, after that he came calling, bringing her flowers, staying to tea and so forth. The fellow's utterly presumptuous, if you ask me."

"Did she, ah, return his attentions?"

Will's frown deepened. "She was kind to him. As you may know, she takes a great interest in the opera—"

"Had they known each other before?"

"Lord, no, I don't think so."

"Your stepmother was at one time a singer?"

"Yes, but she was a cut above the likes of that fellow. He's a fraud, you know. He's no more Italian than you or me—born and raised upstate, I'm told."

"Seems a reasonable enough baritone."

"Oh, he sings well enough." Will's hand waved dismissively. "Do you know, I had to have him turned away from the house. He actually came to call a month after—after Father's—tried to make his way in with a couple of ladies from St. Thomas's Memorial Committee. In fact, now I think about it—it was the day you called to ask me about Jeremy, and I met you at the Union Club—"

Wyatt had another flash of memory, of a young man with copper hair and a disconsolate expression coming down the steps of the Van Dorn's townhouse.

"—Fortunately, I had alerted the staff, and they headed him off. Why are you asking about him?"

"Oh," said Wyatt idly, "he looked familiar to me from somewhere, but I couldn't place him. Perhaps I saw him at the Met. But I'm keeping you from lunch."

Roosevelt came down the steps with his arm around Dodge's shoulder. Augusta began shepherding guests towards the marquee on the southwest lawn, where round tables draped in snowy linen had been set up for the formal luncheon. Amy had hand-lettered the place cards in a graceful chancery script, refusing all assistance or supervision, the cards edged with embossed roses.

"His name means rose-field," Amy had informed Wyatt. "Mother's harvested a few acres of them for the luncheon."

The tables were heaped with Bourbon, moss, damask and Jacqueminot roses, headily scented, in colors that drifted from cream-white through pale apricot to scarlet and fuchsia. With the party tucking into terrapin soup, Wyatt went out to walk the shoreline, encountering Armbruster by the ice-house.

"Everything all right here?"

"I sent Brigham out to chase off that little yacht—" Armbruster pointed east, "—it's getting closer than I'd like. Fiorello's gone to the north end. Brigham's going to row around it on his way back. From here we'd see anything getting within range of it, though."

"Anyone on the west side?"

"Other than all the guests and the entire household staff, no. That would be the best area for you to concentrate in, since you're the known quantity in the group. Let's walk over that way while we talk."

"I've picked up something interesting about one of the guests—nothing to do with a threat to the President, as far as I can tell, but it may pertain to the prior, uh, episode here." Armbruster listened with furrowed brows as Wyatt described his conversation with Will Van Dorn about Signor Romano.

"It would just about fit, wouldn't it. Maybe a little investigation would reveal whether Signor Romano and—what was her name then?"

"Milly Dawkins—"

"—had ever shared the stage at the Troy Music Hall."

"Romano was a guest at Abenaki Island in June," Wyatt said. "He left about a day before the replacement fiddler showed up at Shelburne Farms."

"And Fiorello's seen him perform at the Met?"

"Said he disguises well," Wyatt said. "Maybe we've found our anarchist."

CHAPTER 31

"He may be your man for Van Dorn's murder," Armbruster said after further discussion, "but that doesn't mean the President's safe—from him or from any genuine terrorists who might decide to take advantage of a sitting duck situation like this."

Fiorello joined them and absorbed the new information quickly. "Maybe it's just me, but I have a hard time figuring how this Italian-American-whatever-he-is would've managed to fool everybody into thinking he was Italian for real."

"Nobody here spoke Italian, far as I know."

"But young Will there, Mr. Van Dorn, spent a summer in Siena," Fiorello said, "studying music, two years ago. Got that from our Yale contacts. He might have caught the fellow out."

"No reason for our man to have known about that. And Will wasn't on the island when the Italian was here."

"Lucky thing for this fellow, if it was him." Fiorello flicked a speck of dust from his cuff. "So, how should we proceed here? Make a nice, quiet arrest, you thinking?"

Armbruster shook his head. "What do we have to go on, except young Van Dorn saying the man came around the house? Granted, the description's pretty close—height and physique and so on—and the timing's suggestive, so odds are he's our man. The whiskers were false, naturally, and he'd have got rid of them in the lake on the way back to the mainland. But if we collared him now, he'd have every right to say there's not a shred of evidence tying him to Van Dorn's death. Which there isn't."

"I doubt he's a threat to the President," Wyatt said. "If he is a murderer, his motives were personal and particular. And what if he has an iron-clad alibi for the days when the substitute violinist was with the quartet? In which case we've still got the wrong fellow."

"You could take him aside discreetly and ask him a few questions, as someone who knew the Van Dorns," Armbruster said. "If he's known to the police in any way, he's more likely to talk to you than to us. See if he'll admit to knowing Mrs. V. in her maiden days. And you might winkle out of him what he claims to have been doing after he left Abenaki Island."

"What about sending a telegram to Mulberry Street?" Fiorello suggested. "NYPD might have some records on him, if he did have any connections with that anarchist lot."

Wyatt thought of Inspector Macalester, drifting in some timeless dream in a hospital bed, and wondered what he would have to tell if he ever woke again.

"Sound thinking." Armbruster's voice broke in on his thoughts. "Let's keep a close tab on this fellow. Wyatt, will you mention it to Brigham?"

"I'll do that. Oh, and one more thing—hide the *Merganser* in the boathouse."

"Why?" Fiorello asked.

"Far as our man would know, the boat should still be back on that beach in Paradise Bay," Armbruster explained, "since nobody at the farm would've known where it belonged. If he sees it here, he's likely to get the wind up—figure we've found out something that could tie him to Van Dorn's death. Tell the Dodges not to mention to anybody that the boat was found."

Completing a circuit, Fiorello and Wyatt crossed the narrow neck from the bird sanctuary to the main island. Fiorello stopped, sniffing the air.

"It's pretty nice here. Even the grass smells different. What is that stuff?"

"Thyme. They use it a lot in French cooking. Germain's an expert with that."

"What's the story with him? You don't see too many colored up here."

"He's a Creole from New Orleans. A quadroon, he tells me. Damned if I can figure out how a fellow can be three-quarters white and still classed as colored."

"His skin's no darker than mine, you get right down to it. How'd he end up here?"

"He met Warren Dodge. The timing was good." Wyatt told Fiorello about disfranchisement in the South.

"They're not even letting 'em vote down there any more? What did that war get fought for, anyway? What was the sense in it?"

"As much sense as any of them." Wyatt picked a stem of thyme and crushed it in his fingers.

"You were in Cuba, weren't you? With the Chief?"

"I still haven't figured out why."

"Help 'em get loose from the Spanish Empire, I guess."

"Why do we still have Porto Rico, then? And what do we think we're doing in the Philippines?—" Wyatt heard his voice rising and broke off. "I'm sorry."

Fiorello laid a hand on his shoulder. "Hell, it's not like we agree with everything he gets into. That's not our job."

"I'm going to take out the Adirondack boat." Wyatt bent to untie the line. "I'll be circling towards the north end— Brigham's got the south. Give a shout if you need anything."

"You got it. Don't be surprised the ladies start asking you to give 'em rides."

The other winced. "Last time I did that, her husband was dead the next morning."

"Think there's a connection?"

"No!" Wyatt shoved the boat off from the dock.

He made leisurely circles around the island, keeping a half-circle out of phase with Brigham's orbit. He scanned the horizon with some lower part of his brain, ruminating on the possibility that Milly Van Dorn herself might have been involved in her husband's death. The more he learned about Signor Romano, the more it seemed possible the murder had been a collaboration. Milly might have lured her husband outdoors to the spot where the killer had struck the fatal blow—a variation, Wyatt realized, on Amy's theory of a conspiracy between Mrs. Van Dorn and a mythical young lover.

He was passing the west beach, paddling north, when he spotted the singer strolling with Karel Czerny, the second violinist from the string quartet. With a stab of pain and anger he remembered Rose's gift, his poor silver-gilt watch, which Czerny had taken from him as an object lesson in the redistribution of wealth. No time for that now. He took a breath and let it go. He pulled around to the dock, tied up the boat and ambled towards the pair.

"Mr. Wyatt!" Czerny's greeting bore an unmistakable air of relief. "It's good to see you again. I didn't get a chance to say hello when we docked. How lovely everything is—the weather is perfect, yes? You have met Signor Romano?"

"I enjoyed your performance very much." Wyatt bowed towards Romano.

"You are very kind!" The young man looked at him with bright eyes and bowed in turn. "I was hardly prepared—"

Czerny laughed. "But surely you knew they would ask you to sing?"

"I understand you sang Dr. Dulcamara at the Met this season," Wyatt said. "I'm happy I was able to hear you today, since I missed it."

The young man beamed. "Why, yes, I did—a most enjoyable role. And the chance to sing with Mademoiselle—ah!" His fingers came to his lips and arced away.

"I wonder if you play tennis, Signor? There are a pair of fine clay courts here—I'd be glad to show them to you, if you'd like."

"I should indeed like to see them. That would be most kind of you—you will excuse me, Mr. Czerny?" They parted with mutual bows, Czerny giving Wyatt a grateful smile.

"You are also from New York?" Romano asked politely.

"Yes—I'm a business colleague of Mr. Dodge's."

"I love New York so much," the young man said fervently. "I have been so happy since I came there! For so long I wondered if I would get the chance—I began in Troy, you know—an excellent house, but the audience, she is so—provincial!"

They reached the tennis court, where Jeremy was playing with Signor Pellegrino, his fast, aggressive game checked by the older man's smooth strokes and unexpected reach. On the other side of the court Signora Pellegrino sat with Mademoiselle Marchant, their skirts mingling like cream-splashed strawberries, lacy parasols at casual angles, hands waving in animated conversation.

"Troy?" Wyatt sat on a wooden bench and gestured for Romano to join him. "I met a lady here earlier this summer who came from Troy. Mrs. Van Dorn—"

Romano's face clouded. "Poor dear Millicent! I have known her for some time—we were acquainted there. I knew she had come to New York, when she and Mr. Gerald were married, but I did not know where she was living until she came to see *Don Giovanni.* It seemed so providential—the principal was ill that night, and I had to sing—God was with me, I think, for I sang quite well—"

"If you sang 'Deh, vieni' as well then as you did today, your future is assured."

"You are too kind, Mr. Wyatt! She was Miss Dawkins when I met her. A sweet voice—a little light, but that is all right for a woman, no? I think that is what made Mr. Van Dorn fall in love with her. And she was so very kind to me, so—encouraging!"

Encouraging was a word Wyatt could certainly associate with Milly Van Dorn.

"You visited them afterwards?"

"I called in the afternoon, yes, on several occasions. Mr. Van Dorn was at his bank, of course. *La signora* was kind enough to invite me to tea. Mr. Wyatt, were you here when—when the tragedy occurred?"

"I was, I'm afraid."

"Do you know what happened? It seems so strange."

Wyatt let his gaze drift and fix on the tennis players. "I guess no one's really sure."

"I understand there was some suspicion that—that it might have been murder," Romano said hesitantly. "But who could have done such a thing? He was such an amiable gentleman. Ah—there is his son, who rowed us in today."

Will Van Dorn and Alice Roosevelt were walking towards the west beach, Will pointing out something in a tree, a bird, perhaps, the Princess chill and smiling, inclining an ear towards him. Theodore Roosevelt tramped about in shirt-sleeves and a battered Panama hat in the middle of a knot of men, Dodge and Fisk and Webb and two others from the Fisk boat.

"He seems to have taken a dislike to me." Signor Romano nodded towards Will Van Dorn.

Wyatt raised an eyebrow and looked at him inquiringly. "How so?"

"I wished to pay a—how do you say, a condolence call on Mrs. Van Dorn. Only a brief one—I know the proprieties, though he thinks I am an ignorant dago. I gave my card. This was, I think, a month after the funeral. I merely wished to see if, you know, she was all right. I was concerned for her."

"Naturally." Wyatt let the silence hang for a moment.

"I was told she was not at home," Romano went on, "but two ladies who arrived just before me were admitted. I believe this Mr. Van Dorn was responsible. Tell me, was there anything improper in my calling on her?"

"It's quite usual for bereaved ladies to sequester themselves for some time, I understand," Wyatt said. "though in general if a lady is at home to one visitor, she would be at home to another. To make such an obvious distinction among them—that is unusual, I believe."

"Have you seen her? How is she? I think she was perhaps unwell. At the funeral, she looked so pale."

Wyatt could detect nothing in Romano's tone but anxiety for a old and valued acquaintance. He must indeed be a cool customer if he could have murdered Milly's husband and so successfully impersonate a disinterested friend of the family. He decided to push things forward.

"You were in the area yourself, I believe, around the time of Mr. Van Dorn's death."

"Oh, no—I had gone by then. I felt so badly afterwards—I had no idea the Van Dorns were staying here. I did not realize this island was even inhabited, until my hosts—you have met the Van Sicklens?—mentioned it to me. And of course my hosts did not know the Van Dorns, so they could not have told me they were visiting. I would certainly have wished to come and see them, if I had known."

"When did you leave the island?" Wyatt hoped it would sound like an offhand inquiry.

"Ah—it was perhaps a week before the unfortunate event. I had to go back to Albany—my family lives there now, you see, my mother's birthday, an important one—"

"You're not a native of Italy, then?"

"No," the young man confessed with a sheepish grin. "But my family spoke only Italian at home, when I was a small child. And it does give one a certain—air, you know, if one is a singer—"

"But surely it's the voice, the talent—"

"There are many aspiring opera singers in the world, Mr. Wyatt," Romano said ruefully. "Whatever one can do to gain a little advantage, to add a certain dash, an air of romance— well, it does not hurt anyone."

"No. Of course not. So you stayed at Albany for some time?"

"Just a few days. I went on from there to see some friends at Newport, where I heard of Mr. Van Dorn's death. So I came down to attend the funeral, and then back to Newport."

"How I envy you," Wyatt said airily. "Other than my short visits here, I've been stuck in the City all summer."

The sun was beginning to slant, but the breeze was still fresh, the sky deep blue, almost autumnal, decorated with baroque puffs of cloud. Wyatt was glad for the Dodges. Things had gone so perfectly, the luncheon dishes by chance including a number of Roosevelt's favorites—though now he thought of it, it would surprise him if Germain had had not had informants at Oyster Bay or in the White House kitchen. Mademoiselle Marchant had charmed the President speechless and promised a duet or two before dinner with Signor Pellegrino, an amateur of opera like so many of his countrymen.

The diva spotted Romano and waved him across the tennis court. Wyatt continued his perambulations. Romano's story of having left Abenaki for his mother's birthday party could be checked quickly by telegraph. And, in any case, he was leaving with the Fisks for dinner and an overnight stay at Abenaki Island.

Wyatt caught up with Armbruster in the perennial garden, where the big man was inhaling the fragrance of a mass of pink and purple phlox with appreciation.

"Anything back on your wire to New York?"

"Not a thing yet," Armbruster grumbled. "Did I see you with our *signor*, over by the tennis courts?"

Wyatt related the conversation. "The Albany City Clerk might be able to confirm Mr. Romano's story about the birthday dinner. How are you with that telegraph equipment?"

Armbruster stripped a stalk of lavender and held the tiny blossoms to his nose. "Even if his mother's birthday did occur when he claims, it doesn't mean he was there."

"No, but if it *wasn't* in the last week of June, we'll know we have something to worry about."

"Best do it right away, then. I haven't known too many municipal employees disposed to linger beyond quitting-time. And it's getting late in the afternoon."

"We may not get an answer till tomorrow at this point," Wyatt said. "But Romano will be on Abenaki Island with a good-sized group tonight, so I doubt he'll have much chance to slip away and cause trouble, assuming he's inclined to."

All they had to do was keep watch along the shore for boats that shouldn't be there. Easy enough while there was still light, and even in the dark, someone on guard should hear the splash of oars or paddles. The only spot that concerned Wyatt—and really it was a remote, abstract concern—was the northern headland where the birds nested.

"I'm going to take a skiff around and just see how much work it takes to get up the cliff on the north end. "I don't think there's much chance, but—"

"Fine with me," Armbruster said. "This is a good time, with everyone pottering about at one thing or another. There's something about an island—I don't know, you should feel safer there, I suppose, but it feels exposed to me, somehow."

Wyatt pulled away from the dock and headed north along the east shore of the headland. Absolutely no place to land a boat or climb—the cliff was low, no more than fifteen feet, but sheer, not a toe-hold for the smallest creature there.

Nor along the narrow north face, where the cliff hung cantilevered and the heron fished in its shade. But just past there, the cliff fell away at a more stepped angle, and there was barely enough sand to beach a small boat and fasten it to one of the scrubby firs nearby.

He nosed the skiff in and tied it to a sapling that grew almost horizontally from the cliff. His dress shoes were thin-soled, but he made his way, hand over hand, up the bare cliff face. He almost fell twice, but if he had fallen he would have bruised and skinned himself, no worse. The drop was gradual. He reached the top and found himself just shy of the narrow loop path where Amy would bring the President to see birds in the morning.

They would have to station someone below in a boat. He walked back to the neck between the lobes of the island, to the dock where Armbruster was waiting for him.

"You were right, then."

"Afraid so. We should keep someone in range."

"I didn't hear you coming until the last fifty feet or so."

"I was trying to be quiet, to see how long it would take," Wyatt said. "We need to worry about the bird watching."

Armbruster shook his head. "I was hoping he'd forget about that."

"Because of the safety risk?"

"No. He'll want to take eggs home, and then we've got to find straw, and packing-cases—"

"I doubt he'd find anything rare enough for that."

"But the thing about Te—the President—is he likes to collect things," Armbruster said in long-suffering tones.

"What happens to them?"

"It's getting to where we can't look Mr. Langley in the eye. TR summons him to the Mansion, all excited, and hands over his latest finds—last time it was a pair of bustards he shot in Texas, and a clutch of their eggs—"

"The Smithsonian already has an ample supply, I take it." Wyatt tried without success to keep a straight face.

"Lord, yes—any number of 'em."

"He's not planning on shooting anything here, is he?"

"I don't think so—but he's often armed. For a long time after the Buffalo business, he carried a revolver under his jacket. Wilkie lived in dread of his pulling it out and frightening the voters."

"So part of your job is—"

"Protecting innocent wildlife from the President." Armbruster rolled his eyes.

"Amy won't let him shoot anything. They're all her birds, you know."

"No, I dare say she won't. Seems a rather strong-willed young lady. Reminds me a little of the Princess."

"Who is where, by the way?"

"She seems taken with your young Mr. Van Dorn there. The grieving son? Sees it as a challenge to cheer him up, is what it looks like to me. She may have got him onto the tennis court by now, if her father's done beating up young Dodge."

"Does he like you to let him win?"

"No, and he gets pretty steamed if he thinks you're trying it. I had a word with Jeremy before he got on the court."

"The boy's good," Wyatt said. "Only time you see the Dodge blood in him. He plays as if his life depended on it."

"The chief will have had a good time, then. Where's the moon at this stage, by the way?"

"About three-quarters full. Enough light to row by, if you were sharp-eyed and pretty well knew where you were headed."

"Duly noted," Armbruster said.

CHAPTER 32

The light of a perfect late summer day deepened from white to pink-gold. Wyatt tallied the departing guests along with Brigham and Fiorello, while Armbruster continued his patrols. Horsetail clouds were moving in from the west; the air felt warmer. In the barometer by the kitchen door, the mercury was falling. There might be rain overnight, or even early in the evening if the weather system moved fast enough. Clouds didn't so much move in as condense, Wyatt thought. They thickened from wisps into billows, then darkened with the weight of rain until they couldn't get any heavier and shed their load.

The Fisk party embarked first, around five o'clock. A half-hour's sail would take them to Abenaki Island, where they would spend the night as guests of the Van Sicklens. The *Marmorean Angel* spread her wings and glided majestically north in the dying breeze, Fisk himself and several eager male guests hauling at the sheets. The Fisks and Webbs had been gracious in ceding pride of place to the Dodges on this occasion; Roosevelt was an established guest with them, would no doubt be so again. Wyatt stood on the dock watching them round the northern headland, then noted a distant plume of gray: the returning *Elfreida* and her crew. The Webb party would have a speedy journey back to Shelburne Farms.

Footsteps behind him, and a tap on his shoulder. He turned to find Karel Czerny.

"Did you find him?" The violinist asked without preliminary.

Wyatt wasn't sure how to answer this truthfully. "No. But we know what to look for now, so if he tries to come back—"

"He killed the old gentleman?"

"We're pretty sure of that now. Van Dorn wasn't that old, you know."

"What a dreadful thing. Dreadful—and to claim to be one of our—our—"

"Brotherhood?" Wyatt offered.

"Yes—it goes against all our beliefs, you know, we are not like that fellow, the one who killed McKinley. He had nothing to do with us. True anarchists abhor violence—it is just another kind of power by which one man controls another," Czerny said fervently.

"That's what I told the Webbs."

"I know—and I am so very grateful to you—I feared I was to be cast out, you know, deported, and now I have my job at the Opera—you have heard, yes? It is very exciting—you must come and see us—I shall get you tickets myself, it will not cost you—"

"You are very kind," Wyatt said, "but I have heard you play, and it would be a pleasure to pay for the privilege."

"You are a gentleman, Mr. Wyatt. But I almost forgot—I have something I must give you." Czerny reached into his pocket and drew something out, enfolded in his palm. He seized Wyatt's hand and dropped something into it. The silver-gilt watch.

"Sometimes—ideals are one thing, humanity another. They should always be the same. I am sorry."

Wyatt felt a constriction in his throat and his vision blurred. "Thank you."

"And now, I must shake your hand and pack my things to go."

A thought struck Wyatt. "Mr. Czerny—had you met Signor Romano at the Met?"

"Not until I came here. He sings well, yes? I think he will be a success. We had a long conversation. But as you saw, I was glad of the interruption."

"How so?"

"His talk was—strange. Disturbing. Do you think he knows of my—affiliations?"

"The brotherhood, you mean? I can't imagine how, if you'd only just met. What made you think that?"

"He spoke of our new century, and how it would be a time of change—of social revolution. In the coming age—what was it he said? The old standards and institutions will fall. People will be free to love one another as their hearts move them, and not according to the dictates of class, or convention, or even religion. Did I not think that would be a fine thing?"

"What did you tell him?"

"I did not know what to say. Some of our institutions have worth, I said. I am blessed in my marriage and my child, for instance. It was then that you appeared. I wondered if perhaps he might be a, you know, provocateur. Or perhaps he was trying to let me know he was one of the brotherhood."

Thoughts raced across Wyatt's mind. Was it possible that Romano was not only Milly Van Dorn's lover but a genuine anarchist as well? If that was so, then the President might be in danger after all…

"I'd have thought he'd want to talk music with you," Wyatt said carefully.

"He was admiring my instrument after the concert, and Perlstein's also. Mine is a Brandl—he had a famous workshop in Pest, and worked in the style of Stradivari—he played a little himself, he told me—"

"Czerny!" a voice called from the north porch. "Get a move on! We leave in ten minutes!"

"I'll see you in New York," Wyatt said. "Give my kind regards to your family." Czerny flashed a luminous smile and ran up the path to the Camp.

He was beginning to take some satisfaction in the imminent resolution of Van Dorn's death. How easily ideals became convenient covers for desires, he thought—Romano lusting after another man's wife, justifying the man's death on the basis of his being a member of the oppressor class. It sickened Wyatt to think of it—the false sense of righteousness, the smug self-deception as to motive, the enjoyment of the spoils, all neatly packaged. Kill the oppressor, however benignly or neutrally he might behave towards you, and consider the appropriation of the thing he held most dear as no more than just reward for your labor on behalf of the oppressed. He would enjoy that moment of confronting Romano with his crime, of forcing him to face the moral enormity of what he had done.

Watching *Elfreida* steam away, he tallied the island's residual population: eight Dodges, three Roosevelts and their lady's-maid, the Pellegrinos, Mademoiselle Marchant—and Will Van Dorn, who at Jeremy's urging had decided to stay overnight. Himself and the President's three men; Germain, Cook, the two Irish housemaids. He had declined Dodge's invitation to join the dinner-party. Jeremy and Will were on hand to balance the unmarried ladies, except for Amy, who was lecturing on natural history to her wide-eyed niece and nephew on the balcony but would join the diners when the younger ones were put to bed.

Germain found him on the edge of the dock. "Well, that's another load off my mind." He nodded towards *Elfreida*. "Rate those folks were eating up that crab salad at lunchtime, I was afraid we'd run out."

"The President had thirds, I noticed."

"That man can eat. Does he do anything in moderation?"

"Drinking," Wyatt said. "No one's ever seen him drunk, so far as I know. I've noticed—he seems to live near the edge, but he always stays in control."

"I don't guess you'd end up President otherwise. Well, I take that back. There was that Johnson fella, way back. After Mr. Lincoln. People say he was drunk as a lord half the time."

"But he did get impeached," Wyatt said. "Speaking of—was that a crate of fresh peaches I saw you unloading yesterday?"

"All the way from Georgia, just as ripe as can be—and no bruises," Germain smiled. "Don't know how they managed it.

I aim to combine them with a brandied blackberry coulis and vanilla ice cream—"

"*Pêche Marchant?*" Wyatt guessed.

"Right the first time. In honor of her black hair and dark eyes. And that creamy voice." Germain folded his arms and scanned the horizon. "All quiet on the shoreline?"

"So far. I'd be happy for it to stay that way."

"That true?" Germain said. "Man like you seems to crave a little action now and then."

"I can do without it when there's a President involved. By the way, when do we go back to Mrs. Beaudoin's?"

"Next time we're both in the City. But you don't need me for that."

"Nice to have your company for the supper part." Wyatt walked to the end of the dock and caught the line Armbruster tossed to him.

Brigham sniffed the air. "Think it'll rain tonight? Feels like the air's thickening up."

"Good chance of a storm," Wyatt said. "The glass is still dropping."

"That should keep intruders to a minimum." Armbruster laid the oars carefully in the skiff and stepped onto the dock.

They gathered on the west lawn, listening to Mademoiselle Marchant's lovely clear tones floating out on the warm air. There was barely any light left; fireflies winked on and off, hovering low on the grass. Amy was doing a creditable job of accompaniment on an upright piano that had been wheeled onto the porch. After much begging, the diva had consented to perform the Queen of the Night's aria from *Die Zauberflöte*— "Mozart, 'e loooves to torture sopranos!"

Wyatt didn't care for the piece particularly—it seemed to him to have more to do with testing the limits of the form than melodic beauty—but she performed it with lightness and grace and not a hint of strain. You had to admire that.

Amy, at the piano, was hard pressed to keep up, but she managed. Looking onto the porch where oil lamps glowed like haloes in the dusk, Wyatt could see her smile, mingled exhilaration and relief, as the soprano caught her hand to make her join in the bow while Roosevelt rose to his feet once more, his meaty hands pounding together. When the applause had died down, Germain's voice announced that dinner was served.

"What do they see in that stuff?" Brigham grumbled, his whiskers twitching.

"They spend a fortune on it, too," Armbruster said. "I'd rather go to the races. But she does have a fine voice, if you like that sort of thing."

Fiorello strode across the grass from the south cliff. He stopped in front of Armbruster and looked down in dismay at his shoes.

"Grass cuttings. There's dew now. I just polished these before I came out. Stuff's stuck all over them."

Armbruster suppressed a smile. "Anything to report?"

"Not a thing. Lake's empty as far as I can see. You got somebody on the north end?"

"Just got back," Brigham said. "It's getting too dark to navigate the paths on the headland. Thought I'd best be out before I broke my neck. Nothing to report there."

"All right, then, here's the drill. You two—" Armbruster gestured at Wyatt and Fiorello, "—go get some dinner from the kitchen and then catch some sleep in the guesthouse cellar. Brigham, you'll wake 'em up at one-thirty. You and I will split up. Start on the beach and work your way clockwise. I'll be coming in the other direction. When you get to the north headland, take a lantern and go around the main path, but don't try the smaller paths to the edge of the cliff. Keep an eye on the water as much as you can, and keep your ears open. But get some food first."

"There's something you should know," Wyatt recounted his conversation with Czerny. "I don't know why on earth

Romano would be so open about it—his anarchist interests, his knowledge of the violin—"

"Didn't think it would get back to anybody," Brigham said. "He wouldn't know we'd had any dealings with Czerny."

"Well, it wants care," Armbruster said. "He's only a mile away by boat. And even if it ends up a filthy night, a fellow that had designs on the President could just be crazy enough to chance a landing."

Wyatt wasn't tired yet, but Armbruster's protocol made sense to him. He joined Fiorello at the kitchen table for a slice of game pie and a half-glass of Chateau Petrus which, as Germain had predicted, paired with it nicely.

Germain came in with two empty bottles of port. "Don't miss the Stilton. I saved some for you in the pantry."

"Tomorrow night," Wyatt said. "We're on guard duty in a few hours."

"Who's gonna come out on a night like this? It's bound to storm. Wind's starting to come up already."

"Nobody, we hope," Fiorello said. "You got oilskins, by the way?"

"Downstairs, near the woodpile. You'll have to dust 'em down. Dodges aren't much for boating in the rain."

Wyatt lifted the bulkhead door in the corner of the kitchen and climbed down to the wood-room. He retrieved a bundle of yellow oilskins, smelling of fish oil and sticky with cobwebs, came back upstairs and dumped them on the bulkhead. Germain handed him a damp sponge.

"Ah! Just what I was looking for." Armbruster covered the kitchen in two strides and snatched up an oilskin. "No point in getting soaked to the skin."

A beep from the alcove between the kitchen and Germain's room signaled the beginning of a telegraph message. Armbruster went to it and sat on a cane-bottomed chair below the shelf where the machine had been placed. He tapped back and waited. The beeping resumed, and he wrote rapidly in a ruled notebook. The others stopped eating as if under a spell and waited till he tore the page from the notebook and returned to the kitchen.

Fiorello caught Armbruster's grim look. "What's it say?"

Armbruster threw the paper on the table. ARTEMISIA (GAGLIARDI) ROMANO BORN FEB 18 1851 PER MARRIAGE LICENSE STOP LOCAL HERO IN TROUBLE? STOP KELLEHER ALBANY MPD.

"He lied about his mother's birthday," Wyatt said. "Which means he probably didn't go to Albany after his last stay with the Van Sicklens."

Armbruster drew in a sharp breath. "I'm glad you suggested that wire."

CHAPTER 33

W yatt felt a hand on his shoulder, bouncing him gently in a web of dreams. Theater dreams, he realized, the old actor's nightmare of going on stage without a costume, without knowing what play you were in or what your lines could possibly be. He came awake and focused on Brigham bending over him, light and shadow playing on his rat-whiskers from the lantern that swayed in his hand.

"One-thirty. Time to trade places." Brigham's voice was a hoarse whisper.

"They all asleep?" Wyatt sat up in the bunk and reached mechanically for his trousers.

"The chief turned in an hour ago. I walked 'em to the guest cottage myself. He'd have been up later if Mrs. R. hadn't pointed out that everybody else was asleep on their feet. But once he's down, he's out like a light."

"At least we don't have to worry about stumbling over him in the dark."

On the bunk across the room, Fiorello stirred and groaned. "Put that damn light out—oh, it's you, Brig," he said, coming fully awake. "One-thirty already? Seems like I just closed my eyes." He swung his legs over the side of the bunk and began pulling on his trousers, which he had folded carefully on the headboard. "Anything happening?"

"Quiet as the tomb," Brigham said. "Here and in the guesthouse, anyway. Wind's come up. Whitecaps on the lake, and the trees are starting to blow. Smell the ozone too."

"I'll go and find Armbruster." Wyatt was on his feet now and fully awake.

"There's coffee in the kitchen. I left the oilskins there. Too

344

hot to walk in unless it's actually raining."

Fiorello straightened the bedclothes on his bunk. "All yours," he gestured invitation. "Sweet dreams."

"Nah. I'll be in the cellar at the cottage," Brigham said. "Handier if anybody got through. But I don't imagine you'll get much action out there."

"I don't mind." Fiorello straightened his jacket collar.

Wyatt left the bunkroom by the north porch and walked east around the house with a stiff tailwind behind him. He climbed the kitchen stairway to let himself in. Popple-leaves rattled in the quickening wind. The wind caught the screen door and he seized it just in time to keep it from slamming against the wall. He took a thick mug from a hook in the pantry and poured himself coffee from a blue speckled pot. Hot and strong, chicory-laced, just the way he liked it. He put on an oilskin and went out again with an oil lantern, closing the door carefully behind him.

He put the lantern down and tried to accustom his eyes to the near absence of light. Whitecaps shone phosphorescent, and every now and then the moon broke through the clouds. It flickered eerie light on Calliope, tossing as if in troubled sleep off the east shore, and on the silvered boards of the dock. Wyatt's night vision was acute after years of negotiating dark backstages, and he set out along the narrow path of the bird sanctuary, checking his footing carefully at each step and looking out over the water for any sign of a boat. When he reached the edge where the cliff sloped down to the tiny landing area, the lake to the north lay empty, dark except for the billowing froth of whitecaps. The wind was growing stronger. He made his way back to the causeway and almost collided with Fiorello at the dock.

"You went out there in the dark? What are you, crazy?"

"There's a space you could land, if you meant to. It's unlikely, but it's the only place you could count on not being spotted right away."

"I'll leave that to you cat-footed country types," Fiorello said. "I don't figure I'll do anyone any good by breaking my neck."

Half an hour later they crossed paths with Armbruster on the western beach. Lightning began to flash in the west, followed a few seconds later by low growls of thunder.

"Two or three miles off," Wyatt said. "Over Grand Isle at the moment, I'd say." Great drops of rain splattered on their oilskins. The flashes illuminated a veil of rain coming right at them, obscuring all distinction between lake, sky and land.

"I don't see much point in staying out in this," Armbruster said. "Think I'll head for a bunk."

"Go ahead. I'll go in in a minute." For conscience's sake, Wyatt took one more look over the lake to the west. The lightning came and went like the flickering Vitascope images of a vaudeville show. The movement of the water looked jerky and disconnected, a confusing sequence of black and white and then—something blacker, a solid, rounded mass, with something else solid, lighter, in it. Were his eyes playing tricks on him? He stared out. No, there it was again, perhaps a hundred feet offshore. *No light, but rather darkness visible.* Where was that from? *Paradise Lost?* The *Inferno?* Some hellish image.

A boat, he saw now, a small pea-pod of some sort, pulling hard against the racing waves, a rowing figure swathed in something light—yellow oilskins like his own, most likely. Making its way north, from the looks of it. And then the veil of rain descended, and the thunder roared overhead as if a freight train's wheels rolled over him, and the lightning flashed on a curtain of white. He stood rooted for a moment, shivering, bareheaded, the rain pouring down his neck from where the oilskin gapped. Why hadn't the boat landed on the west beach? Was it heading for the dock? If the oarsman had rowed straight in, he would have got his feet wet, but he could have landed safely. Surely wet feet would be the least of his worries at this juncture.

Wyatt looked around, regretting that he'd sent Armbruster in. Where was Fiorello? Probably in too, by now. No one but a lunatic would be out on the lake in this…or a fanatic. The anarchist? Romano, or a confederate? Surely not even he—and the boat was coming from the south, not north where Abenaki Island lay. But it could have been blown south by the gale, gusting stronger now. Romano might have set out not knowing or heeding the weather signs. But this rower handled a boat capably; Wyatt could see that even in darkness and at a distance. He ran towards the dock. He would get there before the boat. He felt the bulk of the revolver in its holster under his arm—an unnecessary precaution, he had thought at the time, but Armbruster had insisted. He'd hide behind the boathouse, wait till the boat landed, take the boatman by surprise. No time to go back for the others.

The storm roared on, seemingly stalled overhead, splitting the sky in two. Wyatt huddled under the shallow eave of the boathouse, barely inside the drip-line. From somewhere behind him came a crash and a roar. One of the elms hit, he thought. He stared towards the dock. He could barely see all of it, its end obscured in the veil of rain. But he'd see the boat when it came in, he'd hear it, he couldn't miss its landing.

He waited half an hour, wondering more than once if his watch had stopped. No boat, no sound, no sign. Had it foundered on the rocks around the north headland? If so, the oarsman might have swum onto the tiny patch of shore, or been carried in by the waves. He ran back to the west beach. Nothing there. Back to the dock. Nothing.

The northern landing. Maybe the boat had made it there, the rower, intent on concealment, deciding to wait out the storm. If it was the anarchist—Romano, he was nearly sure now—he'd have had the chance to reconnoiter the place on his first visit.

In his haste, Wyatt had dropped the lantern at the beach. It would have been hard to keep lit in this rain in any case. The light-colored oilskins would make him conspicuous when the lightning flashed, so he opened the boathouse window and stuffed them in. Then, relying as much on touch as sight, he started onto the path around the northern headland, brushing aside the soaking branches that shed water onto his dark clothes. The rain lashed down like metal-tipped scourges, the sky fizzled and crackled, the world rumbled. Insanity to be out on such a night. His quarry would be armed, but Wyatt would have the jump on him, if he could move quietly. If he could just get to the top of the cliff-path, knock the man backwards into the lake—it would be better to take him alive, of course, find out who had sent him, how they were organized, root out the whole nest of them. And confirm the man's connection to Milly Van Dorn.

His thoughts blurred into the sensations of shivering cold from the onslaught of rain, the squelching mud of the path underfoot, his arm trying to protect the gun in its shoulder holster. He tried to quiet his breathing, though he was almost panting from trying to breathe what was more water than air. His shoes stuck to the path, making sucking sounds as he forced his legs forward. He pulled a stray branch from the brush and used it as a blind man would a stick, to feel the edges of the path, the steep slide of the cliff falling away to the north. Lightning broke the sway of leaves and branches into jerky bursts. The air was full of growls and roars and the snare-drum rattle of the rain on the roof of the boathouse. He wondered how many of the household would sleep through this—but they were snug in dry beds, with closed windows, someone warm to hold…

He rounded the headland, starting back south. The path even closer to the edge now. He'd had nightmares like this as a child. The apex of the cliff-path lay thirty feet ahead, he thought. He dropped to his hands and knees. His clothes were ruined. He crept forward, keeping his head below the tops of the shrubs and brush. Ten feet, and he looked over. The pea-pod boat, empty, tossing and tumbling on the rocks below. Something light-colored inside it, a cloth—a yellow oilskin, like the one he had discarded.

He heard sounds. Gasping, grunting, sobbing. Tearing sounds. Someone was scaling the cliff-path. Closer still, and he heard the ragged drawing-in of breath, the slip of a boot on the soft stone, a curse. Soundlessly he drew his gun. He did not pull back the hammer. He inched closer on his knees, crouched just beyond the crest of the cliff-path. The breathing was a gasping wheeze now, the climber almost to the top, the sounds of feet losing purchase, tearing roots. A hand appeared above the path, then a head, hidden by a tight hood. Wyatt stayed crouched. The figure pulled itself the last few feet to the top of the cliff and lay sprawled for a moment on the narrow trail, began to straighten.

Wyatt sprang forward, both arms closing around the climber's neck, the gun-barrel stuck in the cheek he could feel beneath the hood. A slender neck, he realized. A woman's.

A ragged, female half-scream, a half-familiar voice. "Oh, jeezum cripes!"

He loosened his grip as the figure twisted to face him. A flash of lightning illuminated the corpse-white face of Ellie Tarrant.

"Oh, Jesus God! Mr. Wyatt!" She clutched his sodden shirt. "Don't shoot me!"

CHAPTER 34

Wyatt and Ellie slogged their way back along the trail, Wyatt half-leading, half-dragging the shuddering girl. The rain had begun to ease off, the intervals lengthening between flash and rumble. They stumbled down the slope of the headland onto he causeway by the dock, so preoccupied with keeping their footing that they didn't notice the drawn guns of Armbruster and Fiorello pointed at their chests until they almost walked into them. The two agents looked like monks of some sinister order in their hooded oilskins.

"What've we got here, Wyatt?" Armbruster asked easily.

"Young lady of my acquaintance," Wyatt gasped, motioning the two to put their guns away while Ellie clung to his chest, sobbing with fear. "What she was doing out in this, I've no idea. She's half-dead with exposure. Will one of you wake up Germain and ask him to meet us in the kitchen?"

"I've seen better-looking drowned rats," Armbruster said. "What happened to your oilskins?"

"Long story." Wyatt's breath came fast and ragged. "Let's get us inside and dried out first."

"I'll go back to patrolling," Fiorello said. "There may be accomplices."

"I don't know what we're dealing with here," Wyatt said, "but I'd lay odds we won't have any more surprise guests tonight."

Ellie sat with her feet drawn up, convulsed with shivers in a kitchen chair till Germain arrived with Bridie, bearing thick towels. Armbruster, never taking his eyes off the girl, hung his oilskins on a peg by the kitchen door. Bridie, who was about Ellie's size, carried dry clothes and took her charge off to the bathroom adjoining the kitchen, where a bath could be heard running in the claw-footed tub. Bridie's voice floated out from the bathroom, its tone alternately soothing and scolding. "What on earth ye'd be doin' out on a filthy night such as this, miss, I can't imagine. Sure an' ya coulda been drownded out there an' not a sowl to help ya…" Ellie's only response was a series of ragged sobs.

The voices were lost in the closing of the bathroom door. Germain took a fresh pot of coffee from the stove and retrieved a bottle of Napoleon brandy from the pantry. Wyatt, who had traded his sopping clothes for Germain's dressing-gown and a pair of his trousers, toweled his hair and took a large swallow from proffered mug, his eyes widening with the burn in his throat.

"That'll take the chill right off," Germain said. "Now what in hell is going on here?"

"I haven't a clue. She came out in a pulling-boat, little pea-pod thing, got caught in the storm. Damn near drowned, near as I can tell, managed to land at the north headland—that spot I've been worried about. She could have pulled in on the west shore, or come around to the dock, but she went right by it—"

"You saw the boat?" Armbruster said sharply. "When?"

"I was just about to follow you fellows in. I spotted something out there. I thought it was our anarchist. Couldn't think who else would be crazy enough to be out there on a night like this—"

"I'd never have guessed anyone would," Armbruster said. "So she evidently didn't plan to be seen—you know this girl, you say?"

"You didn't meet the Tarrants when we were out together. She's from the farm where the missing skiff was found. What she's doing here, or what she has to say to us, I can't imagine."

Ellie emerged hesitantly from the bathroom, stocking-footed in a brown cotton dress with a high neck, her wet hair tied up in a ladylike bun. Germain handed her a mug of brandy-spiked coffee and Fiorello sprang to hold out a chair for her.

Ellie looked up at Germain. "You came to see us the other day, with Mr. Wyatt."

Germain nodded. "Drink that down. Do you good."

She drank, grimacing at first with the unfamiliar tastes. The four men watched her in silence. At a signal from Germain, Bridie reluctantly went back upstairs to bed. Ellie scanned the new faces as if to reassure herself there was no danger there.

"Boy, that warms your tummy right up. I can feel it goin' down my legs too. They're goin' all rubbery." She looked up suddenly, startled into recall.

"Mr. Roosevelt—he's all right, ain't he?"

Armbruster's eyebrows shot up. "Go wake up Brigham," he told Fiorello. "And check around the cottage, just in case. What have you got to tell us, young lady?"

Ellie shuddered and hugged her arms around herself. "My folks don't know I left. I had to wait till everybody was asleep, and wouldn't ya know it, Ethan stayed up late. I was hopin' it wouldn't storm—I thought I could get here an' back by first light an' say I'd just been out for a walk or somethin', if anybody saw me. They'll be frantic if they wake up an' I'm not there—"

"What on earth possessed you—" Armbruster began. Wyatt held up a hand and he stopped. Brigham came in, yawning. Wyatt sketched introductions. Brigham straddled one of the kitchen chairs, his beady gaze fixed on Ellie, his mouth crooked in an attempt at an encouraging smile.

"Go ahead, Miss Tarrant," Wyatt said.

"See, I had to get to you. There's somethin' I have to tell you. I'm—I wasn't as straight with you as I shoulda been, Mr. Wyatt. That time you came an' asked us about the boat. But I was too scared 'cause I'd'a had to tell my folks, or Ethan, same thing, and they'd'a had a fit, or my Ma would, anyways. I didn't think so much about it at the time, but then I saw him in South Hero yesterday mornin', at the train station. See, we'd brought vegetables in for the market, an' he was gettin' off the train from the

City, an' he was all duded up, not like last time. An' he was with some other fancy folks, an' they were talkin' about comin' here an' meetin' the President, an' all, so I figured that's where he was goin'. An' I started thinkin' about the old gentleman that got drowned an' I just thought, oh, Jeezum, maybe the guy's plannin' ta kill the President too—"

The men around the table looked blank. Wyatt blinked and shook his head. "Slow down, Miss Tarrant, we're not following you here. Who is it you're talking about?"

"Eddie," she replied. "Eddie's the fella that took your boat, the skiff, an' then got Ethan's bike."

"You saw him, then?"

"I couldn't tell my folks, see, they'd'a been so mad. I was down at the lake that mornin', skinnydippin', ya know, early—a little ways after six, I think it was. An' this fella comes rowin' round the point, and I kinda scramble out to get a towel around me. An' he sees me an' laughs, an' says, 'well, ain't this a lovely treat for a summer mornin', don't be in such a hurry', an' I'm thinkin', oh Jeezum, what if Ma catches me, so then he lands the boat, an' I've got my pinny on by this time, but I'm still kinda wet, ya know, an' he comes outa the boat an' comes up ta me an' puts his arms on my shoulders. An' he says—" she cleared her throat.

"He says, 'You're the prettiest thing I've seen all day.' An' then he puts his arms round my waist—an' he gives me a kiss, real sweet—" a pink flush bloomed across her face, "—an' then he says, 'so now we've both got a secret.' An' he says, 'I won't tell yours if you don't tell mine.' I shoulda told him off, I shoulda pushed him away, but ain't nobody ever talked so sweet ta me before, an' tell ya the truth, I wasn't thinkin' real straight. So he says, 'you promise you won't tell.' So I says all right, an' he says he's playin' a trick on his friend that's comin' in from New York on the train. He's supposed ta meet him at the train station, only he's rowed around from where he's stayin' somewheres north a' Kibbie Point, an' he's gonna turn up on the train an' surprise him. So he asks me if I've got a bike an' I says yes, only it was Ethan's but I didn't tell him that, an' he says 'can I borrow it an' I'll get it back to ya,' so I says all right, but you gotta bring it back. An' he says, 'Don't worry, I'll bring it back an' when I do I'll bring somethin' special for you too.'

"So I take him up to where the bike is. An' just before he goes he gives me another kiss an' says, 'I'll be back, don't tell anybody our secret, ya hear?' So I didn't. Only he never came back with the bike. An' I could just hear Ma, what do ya think's gonna happen when you let a boy take liberties with ya, there'da been hell to pay. So I couldn't say anythin' when you came round askin' about it. But then I heard about the old fella gettin' drowned and then you came by an' said the boat was from the island, Heron Island. An' I started to wonder. An' then I saw him again—Eddie, I mean—yesterday. An' I thought, what if he's onea them anarchists you hear about an' maybe he killed that fella an' maybe now he's goin' after the President?"

"How did you know the President would be here?" Brigham asked sharply.

"Everybody knew. People get invited to meet Mr. Roosevelt, they ain't gonna keep their mouths shut about it. Word gets around."

"So much for discretion." Armbruster's mustache twitched at the corners. "This—Eddie. What kind of accent did he have?"

She looked puzzled. "Didn't have much of an accent. Well—kinda upper class, I guess. New York, maybe. Like you fellas talk. Or the Dodges."

"It wasn't foreign?" Wyatt said.

"No." She looked puzzled.

"And you saw him in South Hero yesterday morning. When you said he'd got duded up, what did you mean? Had he shaved off his beard?"

She shook her head. "He didn't have a beard."

"Wait here," Wyatt said to no one in particular. He headed for the bunkroom and riffled through the package of photographs he had used to identify the previous day's guests. It seemed like years ago. He pulled out a photo and brought it back to the kitchen.

"What color was his hair?" Germain asked. "Kind of a coppery red, real curly?"

"More like blond, I'd say. When I first saw him, it was kinda wet, little curls stickin' up at the ends, so it looked dark. But yesterday when I saw him it was definitely blond. Slicked down, though, with brilliantine or somethin'. An' there was somethin' else different, but I can't remember it right now..." she was beginning to droop from the brandy and exhaustion and the relief of being safe.

"While you were out, she said the fella was about Brigham's height," Germain told Wyatt. "What are you, five feet seven?"

"Five feet eight," Brigham replied with asperity.

"I thought our violinist was closer to five-ten or eleven," Armbruster said.

"Miss Tarrant, will you take a look at this?" Wyatt handed over a publicity photograph from the Met, featuring Eduardo Romano as a pensive-looking Valentin in Faust. "Is this the man you met on the beach? The man who took Ethan's bicycle?"

Ellie stared at the photo and slowly shook her head. "He didn't look nothin' like this," she said. "That's not him." The four men looked at one another.

"Did he tell you his surname, by any chance?" Wyatt asked.

"He did say somethin' about that. Oh, yeah, King. Eddie King..." Her voice drifted away. "I remember now. The thing that was different. When I saw him yesterday, he'd grown a mustache. But I'm sure it was him." Her head slumped onto her chest.

Wyatt stretched out a hand to Ellie. "Gentlemen, I suggest we allow Miss Tarrant to get a little sleep and continue this in the morning."

"It *is* the morning," Brigham pointed out.

Germain looked an inquiry at Wyatt, who nodded. He murmured something to the girl and picked her up as gently as a mother cat, carried her out and up the stairway to the servants' loft. They heard him speaking in low tones to Bridie, who had evidently not gone back to sleep, and he returned alone.

"Kid wouldn't've made it up the steps."

Wyatt rose and opened the kitchen door. His bare feet hit the cold wet of the landing. The storm had passed. It was still dark, but the warm wet-earth smell that rose up promised light soon. He rested one arm on the railing and rubbed his face with the other hand.

Eddie King. *Oedipus Rex.* A son who killed his father and married his mother...it couldn't be right. The alibi had been checked and rechecked...they had ruled him out almost before anyone else. Something was wrong somewhere. Behind him, he heard the beep-beep of the telegraph machine.

"I'll get it," Armbruster's voice said.

One thing Wyatt was sure of now. If Ellie Tarrant had spoken the truth, the President was in no danger from the man who'd killed Gerald Van Dorn.

Armbruster came to the door. Wyatt turned and came inside.

"What've you got?"

"A reply from Mulberry Street. They had a quiet night, evidently, so the D.O. did some homework." He showed Wyatt the telegraph message.

EDUARDO ROMANO ARRESTED FEB 21 RAID ARISTON BATHS STOP CHARGE DISMISSED STOP NO OTHER RECORD STOP D S CLIFFORD MBP

"What would the charge have been?" Wyatt asked.

"Sodomy, most likely."

"Which rather suggests—"

"—he's a fairy," Brigham said.

Armbruster scowled at Brigham. "—that he's not likely to have fathered a child on Mrs. Van Dorn."

The sucker-punch Wyatt had received from the granite-man in Barre hadn't knocked the wind out of him as surely as this. Homo-sexual acts didn't mean a man couldn't and didn't lust after females—especially when money was at stake—but in this case Wyatt knew better, and knew that he'd known better all along.

In his drive to find an answer, any answer, to this impossible business, he'd seized on Romano as a dishonest scientist seizes on the data that suit his hypothesis—letting emotional investment substitute for the clarity and integrity and—yes, he had to admit it—dull, hard work of empirical observation. He thought of Romano's clear eyes, the face so full of goodness and boyish cheer, of innocent affection. And it came to him that he'd been ready to pin the crime on Romano because he envied him that innocence, that unwoundedness, that assurance that everything would turn out beautifully. Envied those things because he wanted his own life back, before all that had happened between him and Rose. He wanted love and he wanted youth, and he couldn't have them.

All this flashed across his mind between Armbruster's words and his own reply. "And the story about the trip to Albany for his mother's birthday was probably a cover for illegal activities—but not the kind that result in fatalities. Macalester's people checked Will Van Dorn's alibi, right?"

"They did. A conductor at Grand Central remembers his valet coming on with his valise, placing it in his Pullman berth, handing over the ticket—"

"But does he remember Will?" Brigham asked.

"Well, he didn't see him then. But he had the ticket, which the conductor punched and put in its slot, and went on about his rounds. Mr. Van Dorn had a call to make, the valet said, and would be boarding the train at the last minute. When the conductor came back, the door was closed with a do-not-disturb sign on it."

"Did anyone talk with the valet?" Brigham persisted.

"Didn't seem to be any need for it. Happens all the time with the first class passengers, I'm told."

"What I'm getting at is—no one actually saw Will get on the train."

"Well, the conductor saw him come out of the Pullman berth when they pulled in at South Hero," Armbruster said, "which would suggest he'd managed to get in there somehow."

"Where is Will supposed to have been the week before his father's death?"

"At a hunting retreat in Maine, with a couple of school chums.

Deep in the back woods—incommunicado, it's a good thing it didn't happen then, or you'd have been days finding him— oh." Realization dawned on Armbruster's face.

Fiorello came up the back stairs and through the kitchen door. "It's starting to get light. What's with the young lady?"

"What time will the Roosevelts be up?" Wyatt asked.

"Amy and the President are going birding at six," Fiorello said. "So I guess people will start trickling up after that."

"Let's let Ellie sleep till eight, then bring her down and let her have a look around. The house staff already knows she's here, but don't tell anyone else."

"I take it you don't doubt her story," Brigham said.

"I know it must sound foolish after her lying to us," Wyatt said, "but I'd stake my life on that girl's honesty. She put herself at risk of a nasty demise to come and warn us as she did. The President's not in danger—or not directly, anyway. But you'd best warn him and Amy about that path around the northern neck. It's slick with mud and there's not much of a margin for error."

"You know it better than anyone," Armbruster said, "since you've done it twice now in the dark. Clean yourself up, take a nap and report here at six."

Wyatt pretended to scowl. "You'd think I worked for you."

"It could be arranged."

CHAPTER 35

He was back in his apartment, in his own bed. His hand moving under the covers, up the curve of a woman's naked back, smoothing a tangle of curls. It was Bella Duvalier he was holding, a soft breast in his hand, the flesh a little damp with warm sweat where he held it, a scent of some exotic flower—frangipani? in the soft space between her throat and the mass of dark curls. *Comme t'es gentil*, she whispered, turning into his embrace. Her moist breath on the angle of his jaw. A rough hand shaking him awake, blinding bright light, a bunk-bottom above his head, a face looming over him. Macalester.

Macalester?

He sat up abruptly. Was he still dreaming? "What in God's name are you doing here?"

"Good to know you're so happy to see me," the Scotsman said, despicably hearty and cheerful and altogether real. "Time for your stint, I'm afraid. Mister Roosevelt's been up this past hour and more."

"How did you get here? We heard you were in a coma—"

"'The report of my death was an exaggeration,'" Macalester grinned. "My head, though bloody, is unbowed." He caught Wyatt's glance at the cane that was bearing his weight on the left side. "Oh, I got knocked about a bit, but it'll take more than that to put a stop to a laddie from the Gorbals."

Wyatt blinked inquiry at him.

"Slums of Glasgow. Makes your Lower East Side look like Fifth Avenue on a Sunday. Anyway, I made them turn me loose from Bellevue and took the night train up. Hired a boat to bring me over and here I am."

"What happened to you?"

"I'm sorry to say I don't remember a thing of the actual event. Last thing I recall is running up the stairs of the El station. They tell me I lost my balance and fell in front of the train."

"That seem likely to you?"

"No, it does not. And Miss Templeton tells me you thought I'd been pushed."

Wyatt sat up in the narrow bunk and rubbed a hand over his face. "My guess is the pusher had something to do with our inquiries in the Van Dorn matter. Says you'd asked her to look into something about Rossi. Don't suppose you brought me any coffee?"

"As a matter of fact, I did." Macalester handed over a mug. "I'm surprised the smell didn't wake you. Your man Germain's a dab hand at the beverages, I must say—though his tea could be a wee bit stronger. So's you could trot a mouse over the top of it, like."

Wyatt grimaced. "Can't stand the stuff at any strength."

"It wasn't Rossi I'd asked about," Macalester said. "It was Romano. Met the fella on the street at Mrs. Van Dorn's." Wyatt was about to speak, but the Scotsman held up a forestalling hand. "Not to worry, the President's men have brought me up to date on all the doings. Do you aim to accompany Amy and Mister R., or patrol from a boat?"

"The boat. They don't need one more person up there crowding the path and spooking the birds. I'll just make sure nobody else tries Ellie's trick. She up yet?"

"Sleepin' like a wee lamb upstairs in the maids' quarters," Macalester grinned. "Her parents will be thinkin' she went off for a rondy-vooz with some young fella. And they'll be right, of course, in a way."

"Where's Fiorello?"

"He'll be at the dock. He picked his way out there, along the headland, just as if he was walkin' on eggs at every step, to make sure he knew where all the pitfalls and hidin' places were.

Got squawked at a few times for his pains, by the sounds of it."

"The creak of new leather from his shoes would've given him away." Wyatt yawned and pulled up his suspenders. The morning light drew harsh lines on the Inspector's bruised face, the bandage around the head, the hand leaning on a cane. Macalester looked older than he'd remembered.

"Inspector—I am glad to see you up and about." The depth of his relief surprised him. Mostly he'd thought of the man as a nuisance.

A twinkle in the Scotsman's eye acknowledged the concern. "And on the verge of solving this wee business, as I understand."

"We almost missed our man. It never occurred to me—that degree of disguise. Accent, height, beard, everything. If we're right, crimes don't get much more premeditated than this. But at least the President's not in danger. Amy even gave me the clue early on—he was in the Yale Dramat, she said."

He walked out into the cool, rain-washed air of the north verandah. Macalester hobbled after him, leaning heavily on the cane.

"A bit misty out yet," Macalester said. "A touch of autumn in the air."

"If he hadn't left that one loose end, we might never—they've got the house covered, right?"

"Aye, the agents are all up now—and dyin' to know how this is goin' to come out."

"We'll find out after breakfast. Make sure Ellie stays upstairs till the President's back and they've all eaten—they're waiting breakfast, I assume?"

"Well, no, they're following country-house rules, I'm told. Catch as catch can, with chafing-dishes on the booffy," Macalester said. "Germain doubts anybody but Amy and Mr. R. will be up before eight in any event."

"Good. Keep an eye on them if they are. We have a couple of problems here. One is corroborating evidence—physical evidence, for example. All we'll have is the girl's statement placing Will on the lake just after his father's death, in possession of a boat from Heron Island. If he denies everything, where does that leave us? Which brings me to the other problem—jurisdiction. We haven't involved the Vermont police—"

"Perhaps Mr. Fiorello can enlighten us on that point," Macalester gestured towards the slim, tailored figure walking towards them. They dropped off the verandah to meet him.

"Oh, that presents no difficulty," Fiorello told them. "You found the body in the water, am I right? Now, the thing about Lake Champlain, it's a federal waterway. Boundary between two states an' all. So the Service has automatic jurisdiction. We can always arrest on felonies anyway," he added cheerfully, "but then, so can either of you."

"I'd really rather not," Wyatt said.

"As to your first point, Wyatt," Macalester gestured towards him with the tip of the cane, "There's a way to do it—a bit chancy, but if the girl has as much pluck as she showed in gettin' here last night—"

"—put her into the skiff and use her as bait," Wyatt said. "Arrange for him to spot her in some quiet place, no one else around, see what he does."

"Otherwise you've the risk he'd just deny ever havin' met the lass, and say she's mistaken him for somebody else."

Fiorello looked alarmed. "What do you think he'll do?"

"Try to sweet-talk her into taking the skiff back, and arrange to dispose of it later," Wyatt said. "And if that doesn't work, he may—"

"He might try to do to her what he did to his father, is what you're saying," Fiorello said. "Whack her on the head and shove her overboard. What are you, crazy?"

"Very little chance he'll be armed. Especially if we catch him after a tennis-game or some such. And we'll be watching and listening, on shore and on the water. We'll have a boat just out of sight, but Ellie will know it's there."

Behind him, Theodore Roosevelt bounced off the verandah, binoculars swinging from his neck, flashing his toothy grin. "Morning, fellows. What a day, eh? Nice and cool. Little bit of mist to keep the birds hunkered down. Splendid! Ah—here comes my young lady."

Amy looked scholarly in a cotton dress of soft olive green, with a birding guide tucked under her arm and field glasses around her neck. Her hair was pulled back into a long, tidy plait. Roosevelt swept her up by the arm and they ambled across the neck to the headland, at home with each other like lifelong friends.

"Time to go." Wyatt strode towards the dock. Fiorello sketched a salute at him. He swung himself into a skiff and cast off, nodding back towards the President's agent.

"Those shoes could use a polish."

Fiorello snarled at him and followed Roosevelt's retreating back.

Wyatt pulled around the east side of the headland, scanning the cliff for movements. Rustles in the scrub-firs and young popples and a low murmur of voices let him trail the birding pair as he circled. Scarves of mist floated low over the mirror-still water. The mist would lift and the day would end up hot, maybe more humid than yesterday. For now, the sky was a dull white. No danger of rain, though.

Already one or two rags of red leaves in the maple saplings that shared cliff-space with the firs and popples. Too early, surely. Vermont summers were so short they made you melancholy. He'd slowed down now that he was around the northernmost of the island. His heart clenched for a moment when he looked south, down the island's west side, and saw a boat floating fifty feet out. Then he realized it was Ellie's, adrift since it foundered here last night. He pulled out towards it.

The lake around him was otherwise empty. No boats, no signs of life on Abenaki Island; Fisk's *Angel* would have docked on the north end, out of his line of vision. It would be a languorous late-summer day, a day for strolls on the shore, a tennis game, perhaps a lazy swim, drinks on the verandah, portly but insubstantial novels left open on wicker chaise lounges—not the sort of day on which to bring a murderer to account. Except that it would have to be.

He spotted a glint of light at the top of the cliff. Roosevelt, following something with his binoculars, gesticulating to Amy. Wyatt raised his own glasses and followed Roosevelt's gaze. The blue heron in its balletic flight, wheeling in for a landing, gliding down the west shore of the island to its fishing spot under the south cliff. The spot where he had found Gerald Van Dorn.

Lust and greed, Warren Dodge had once said to him. *The only two reliable motivators I know of.* Passion might be a better word in this case, perhaps even love. It would all be clear soon enough. The actor in him couldn't help but respect the performance the murderer had put on to accomplish his goal. And berate himself for not spotting it. But acting was a collaboration in which the audience accepted a set of given circumstances, and would do so indefinitely as long as the actor did not break character. Even then, he might have got away with it, if Wyatt hadn't been stubborn or lucky enough to push his search for the missing boat farther south than made sense.

Quietly and carefully, so as not to disturb the birds or their watchers, he rowed over to the little pea-pod and attached it to his own boat with a tow-line. Amy and Roosevelt looked down at him from the cliff above. Amy leaned dangerously over the cliff-path to talk to him.

"We found swallows' nests, lots of them," she hissed.

"The birds have flown, of course," Roosevelt said. "But they do make such a nice little nest—like pottery, didn't you think, my dear? Did you see that heron, Mr. Wyatt? It was splendid—quite splendid! What a bully spot for bird-watching, Miss Dodge."

"Were the gannets there?" Wyatt asked in a stage whisper.

"We saw them," Amy said. "And we were very quiet, so we got to watch the mother bird feeding them. But Mr. Fiorello came along behind us and almost stepped in the nest—what a fuss she made! She was pecking at his trouser-legs!" she giggled. "Perhaps we'd better go in now, Mr. Roosevelt. Breakfast will be ready, and I'm starved, aren't you?"

"Famished," boomed Roosevelt, "absolutely famished!"

Wyatt rowed back in leisurely pulls that took him to a partially built jetty, the future landing for large yachts and small steamers. Fiorello helped him portage the boats across the narrow causeway to the dock.

"When do the fireworks start?"

"Directly after breakfast, I should think. I mean to have Miss Tarrant in the *Merganser*—the skiff he took and left on their beach—and arrange for him to see her when no one else seems to be around. He'll probably try to head her off. We'll be tailing them as closely as possible, trying to hear what they say. If he says anything that confirms he's the one who left that boat, it places him on the island at the time of Van Dorn's murder."

"That gonna be enough?"

"You're the law enforcement expert," Wyatt said.

"What if he pretends not to recognize her?"

"If he were in company at the time, that's what he'd do. But if he's alone, or thinks he is, he's likely to be shocked by the boat's reappearance. There's no way the other Tarrants should have known where it came from, so I think he'll want to talk her into getting it out of sight."

"Or whack her on the head, maybe."

"He won't do that unless he thinks he has to," Wyatt said. "And even then, he'd still have to deal with the boat, which as far as he knows has just reappeared. Of course, he may not be thinking that clearly, so he may do something desperate if she doesn't cooperate. We're planning for that."

CHAPTER 36

He circled around the house and climbed the outside steps to the kitchen door. Germain was in the pantry, icing down white wines in the copper cooler for luncheon, which was to be served on the lawn. Wyatt pulled him aside.

"Where's Mr. Dodge?"

"Playing tennis, I think, with Signor Pellegrino. You need him?"

Wyatt told him why.

"*Saint-Dieu*," he said. "You stay here and I'll go and get him. Are you sure?"

"Pretty sure."

"Do me a favor and finish icing down those wines, will you? Though after this, I don't know what will happen to our lunch plans."

"We'll try to keep it clean. But you never know." Wyatt felt an unreasoning anger washed over him towards the man who had brought murder to this peaceful retreat, whose apprehension might now ruin his host's gift of that peace and privacy to the President. He smiled at himself. A social transgression. Surely that was the least of it.

Dodge arrived, his high-boned face flushed and sweating from his tennis game. He dropped his racquet in a corner.

"This damn well better be important."

"We've got a young woman here who's identified Van Dorn's murderer," Wyatt said quietly. "She's upstairs with Bridie. When I bring her down, we're going to set some things in motion that will end with his arrest."

"He's here? Where? Who—you mean the anarchist?"

"In a manner of speaking." Wyatt told Dodge what had transpired the previous night.

"Dear God. You're sure, aren't you."

"If it goes as planned, we'll have one of the President's men make the arrest. That will avoid jurisdictional questions when it comes to trial. We're hoping to do it discreetly. There will have to be handcuffs for the boat ride, I'm afraid. But we'll be armed and there will be an escort boat."

"So Roosevelt's men are in on it. Have they told him?"

"We don't think that's necessary just yet. If you and Mrs. Dodge can contrive to keep the other guests busy at something a man in mourning might decline to participate in, that would be helpful."

"You think I should tell Gussie, then."

"I think it would be best."

"What if we have Jeremy do an *impression* of the party in the perennial garden?"

Wyatt smiled. "That should work. I'm betting that Will will excuse himself. If he doesn't initiate it, you might suggest it."

Ellie Tarrant, wide awake and trembling, walked slowly down the elm avenue towards the dock like a doomed aristocrat approaching the guillotine. She had refused breakfast after Wyatt had explained the plan to her, for fear she wouldn't be able to keep it down.

"It's real pretty here, ain't it?" Her voice was high. "Ethan came here once in the winter, before they built the house—the lake froze real hard an' he snowshoed over. Wasn't much here then, he said."

"Let's sit down here for a minute." Wyatt gestured towards the dock.

"Good choice," said a voice from behind him. Ellie started and let out a little cry.

"It's only Mr. Fiorello. You met him last night, remember? Mr. Armbruster's here with him too."

"How do, Miss Tarrant," the latter said.

367

"Tell ya the truth, I was in such a state I don't remember much of anythin' from last night."

"But you're sure about what you told us? About the man you met?" Wyatt said.

"I only wish I wasn't. Do I really hafta do this?"

"It's the best way to catch him," Fiorello said. "See, all we've got now is your word against his that he's the fella from the boat. No physical evidence like parts of his disguise, or finger-prints on anything."

"Finger-prints?"

"The modern thing," Macalester said, coming around from the tennis-courts. "It turns out that no two sets of finger-prints are quite alike. So if we know what a fella's finger-prints look like, and we find them on a murder weapon, say, then most likely he's the killer. We've just adopted the method in New York."

"Not everyone has faith in that method, Inspector," said Brigham, who had followed him to the dock. "And in any case no one thought to preserve any evidence that would have allowed us to check for them. Miss Tarrant, you and your brother had taken the skiff out once or twice, I think?"

Ellie nodded.

"So that would have contaminated, possibly wiped out any prints we could have obtained. And of course you can't ask someone to submit to finger-printing unless you're charging him with a crime, which gives the game away in a case like this."

"Self-incrimination is our best hope at that," Macalester said.

Ellie gulped. "So, what d'ya want me to do exactly?"

"Paddle around until you spot him. Get him out in the boat with you," Armbruster said. "Keep the boat in close to shore. Row around to the north headland where he'll feel safe from detection—watch out for those submerged rocks. Two of us will be on the headland—we'll be hidden, but we'll be there. Wyatt here will be out in this blue dory here, around the other side of the cliff. Macalester and Brigham will be patrolling out of sight, but if you get him up that way they'll head for this—" he indicated a green-painted skiff tied up to a ring on the half-built jetty, "—and come around to box you in on the other side. Try to stay close enough in that we'll be able to pick up your conversation."

"So, what's her story?" Brigham said.

"You're doing this Eddie a favor—bringing him his boat back," Wyatt said. "You saw him with the crowd getting on the yacht to come here for the President's reception. So you decided to come and bring him the boat—it gave you an excuse to try and see Mr. Roosevelt up close. What girl wouldn't jump at the chance?"

Ellie took a deep, ragged breath. "All right. I'd best get goin' before I change my mind."

"You're a good boatswoman, we know that," Wyatt said. "Just try to stay calm and remember, we'll be nearby."

Half an hour later, the only sign of life on the west side of Heron Island was a blond man in tennis whites crossing the lawn from the Camp towards the tennis courts, head down and racquet dangling at his side as if in deep thought. The *Merganser* stood at the south end of the west cove, Ellie Tarrant trailing its oars in the water. When she spotted Will Van Dorn, she began to row towards the shore. She waited till he came within hailing distance.

"Hey, Eddie! Eddie, it's me! I brought your boat back!"

Startled, Will Van Dorn looked up, taking in the sight of the *Merganser* and the gap-toothed farm girl. Lying flat in a stand of scrub-pines just south of the beach, Brigham saw him flush and drop his racquet. Will looked wildly around to see if anyone else was in sight. She continued to row towards the shore.

"What are you doing here?"

"I came lookin' for you." She shipped the oars. "You never came back for the boat, then I saw you yesterday at the train station, with all them fancy folks headin' over here. Figured I'd row over this mornin', get ya the boat back an' maybe get a look at the President."

Will hurried towards the beach to intercept her. "That's, uh, not a good idea. He has guards—they're ordered to shoot intruders—look here, you'd better get out of sight. Really, you'll be in big trouble if they find you here. Take the boat back and— uh, I'll come and get it tomorrow."

"Ethan's pretty mad about his bike," Ellie said. "He was goin' on so bad I finally broke down an' told him I let somebody take it. So he wants me to get it back. If you got it here, I could take it with me."

"No, it's not here. Look, you really have to go—" Will startled at a clatter of pots from the Camp kitchen.

"Come on out an' talk ta me for a minute," she wheedled. "I've been waitin' for ya to come back all this time. Been lookin' forward to it. You said you'd bring me somethin' nice, remember?"

Somewhere in the Camp a door slammed. Ellie beached the boat and began to climb out onto the shingle. Will looked wildly around again and went towards her.

"No, no, look, someone's bound to come out, you need to get away. I'll come with you but for heaven's sake hurry!"

He helped her push off the boat and they jumped in, Will grabbing the oars. His powerful arms took the boat north in long, swift strokes.

Macalester was in a clump of birch trees between the tennis courts and the lake, counting on his light-colored suit to provide camouflage. He watched the boat pull past him, heard Ellie's voice, high and trying to conceal fright.

"It's nice a you to worry so much about me, Eddie. But they ain't really gonna shoot somebody unless they was tryin' ta hurt the President, are they? I think ya just don't want anybody else ta see me with ya." Her tone was as close to flirtatious as she could make it. "Who's your tennis date with? Miss Alice

Roosevelt? I'd sure love ta meet her. Imagine livin' in the White House an' havin' folks waitin' on ya hand and foot."

"It is with her, actually, and I haven't got much time…" Will's voice trailed off as he pulled out of Macalester's hearing range.

"See, Eddie, the real reason I came over is I gotta ask you somethin'," Ellie's voice floated up the cliff to the bird-watching path on the headland, where Amy and the President had greeted Wyatt earlier that morning. Armbruster was there now, lying flat on his stomach, concealed from sight below by a screen of scrub-firs and popple saplings. He went dead still, listening. The rowing stopped. Will shipped the oars.

"Thing is, that mornin' you came over, that was the day Mr. Van Dorn—that was his name, wasn't it?—got drowned on the island here. An' they said there was some fella that had been on the island, but he took one a the boats an' got away. An' they figured this fella had somethin' to do with the man that drowned. So I got wonderin', 'specially after I found this stickin' ta onea the seats—"

Fiorello, further down the cliff-face, saw her dip into a pocket and pull out a bundle of fine, reddish fiber. His eyes met Armbruster's in alarm. This wasn't in their script.

"See, they said this guy had red hair an' a red beard."

Will Van Dorn stared at Ellie's hand.

"What do you want from me?" His ice-blue eyes chilled her in their gaze.

"I don't want nothin'. It's just, I gotta get Ethan's bike back."

Wyatt, his own boat bobbing on the waves just around the headland, felt a cold fist squeeze his heart. Ellie had Will Van Dorn in a trap for which there was only one exit.

"What exactly did you tell—Ethan, was it?" Will made an attempt at lightness.

"Oh, I didn't tell him nothin', 'cept it was probably one a the hands from Phelps's that had been out sparkin' down to Allen's Point with his lady-friend, an' had ta get back in time for milkin'."

"Good thinking." Will relaxed a little.

"But Ethan said he could tell I was lyin'. He'll get it outa me, sooner or later. I know him."

"Ellie," said Will smoothly, "did anybody see you leave this morning?"

"Aw, no, it wa'n't even light yet. They weren't even up for first milkin'."

"So, for all they know, you could have left last night?"

"Well, I guess so."

"But of course, you'd never have gone out in that storm," Will's voice drifted around the headland. "Unless you were crazy enough to try to sneak over to see the President..."

Wyatt felt for his holster, gripped the oars. He saw Armbruster pop up, hold up a finger like a starting gun.

"But what you were crazy enough for, was to come looking for me," Will was saying. "Come here, Ellie. I wanted to come back. I couldn't. But I couldn't stop thinking about you. You'll let me kiss you again, won't you?"

Fiorello watched Will take Ellie's chin in his hand and pull her towards him. With one smooth motion, his hand was over her mouth, his other hand reaching for an oar, pulling her up with him. Armbruster's finger dropped like a starting-flag. Wyatt shot around the point just in time to see Will raise the paddle-end of the oar, his left hand still clamped tight around Ellie's mouth, stifling her terrified sobs.

"Stop right there!" Armbruster yelled. Will looked up, the momentary distraction enough to allow Wyatt to close the distance between the two boats. He reached out and grabbed the *Merganser*'s gunwale and pulled. Will lost his balance and toppled over, dropping the oar off the skiff's port side, pulling Ellie down and backwards with him. His fall cushioned Ellie, who twisted out of his grasp, scrambled to the stern of the skiff and made a shallow dive into the water.

Will's body lurched over the bow and he fell head-first into Wyatt's dory, tearing open a cut over his left eyebrow. Wyatt had dropped his oars and was reaching for his gun when Will righted himself like a gymnast, seized one of the oars that had caught on a rock, and stood up, swinging it at the side of Wyatt's head. It connected with a crack. The blow was glancing, but it threw Wyatt off balance and dazed him for a moment. He slumped and fell heavily backwards, bracing himself on his wrists to break the fall against the floorboards of the dory. Fiorello was stumbling, half-falling down the cliff-path but keeping his balance, Armbruster close behind.

Brigham and Macalester closed in, pulling the green boat to where Ellie gasped and bobbed in the water. She clutched at the gunwale and held on. Will leapt back into the *Merganser* with the oar from Wyatt's boat, seized the oar he had left in its oarlock, and started to pull away from the melée down the east side of the island. Ellie let go of Brigham's gunwale.

"'S'all right, I can swim," she got out between gulps of air. " Go get 'im."

Brigham nodded, pulled out his revolver and aimed it at the retreating *Merganser*. Macalester began rowing.

"Don't lose that oar!" Wyatt yelled to no one in particular. Ellie swam towards Will's rapidly retreating boat, jack-knifed below the surface like a seal and came up with the oar Will had dropped from the *Merganser*. Wyatt grabbed it from her and made his way back to the thwart of the blue dory. Fiorello braced his hands on the gunwales and started to jump in.

"Don't," Wyatt said. "One-man boat—too heavy. Fellow rows for Yale. You and Armbruster follow in the Adirondack. It's tied up at the dock."

"He'll be in Canada by then." Fiorello looked ready to dive into the water and swim after the retreating skiff. "Why didn't we just shoot him when we had the chance?"

"Don't have to," Wyatt spoke rapidly, blotting the gash on the side of his head with a handkerchief. "Better if we don't— he's not armed. If he heads south, we'll be right behind him. If he turns north, he's got to go past Abenaki and we can round up some more boats there. But go! Now!"

"Brigham, you and Mac head that way as fast as you can," Wyatt pointed south along the island's west shore. " More likely he'll keep heading south—if you hurry you can cut him off at the south end." Brigham frowned for a moment, nodded once and holstered his gun. Macalester pulled on the oars and shot away.

Armbruster was already scrambling back up the slope. Fiorello came forward to give Ellie a hand out of the water, but she shooed him away and he clambered up the cliff-path after Armbruster. Wyatt pulled his dory out around the curve of the headland and started down the east side, in the lee of the northern neck. On the cliff-top, the pounding of the agents' feet back down the path to the dock produced a chorus of angry squawks and flappings.

The morning mist had cleared and the sun glared into Wyatt's eyes. Forcing them down to lake level, he spotted Will Van Dorn's boat two hundred feet ahead and redoubled his efforts at the oars. They had lost precious minutes in the struggle. No sign yet of Brigham and Macalester's boat. Will kept heading south, close to the shoreline, focused on gaining headway rather than leeway from the island. Wyatt's head throbbed where Will's oar had struck it. He thought of Gerald Van Dorn. He hoped the poor man had felt nothing after the blow that knocked him into the lake. The bleeding had slowed, but it was matting his hair and trickling down his cheek. He checked the urge to take his hand off the oar to wipe it away.

Will skimmed rapidly past the dock, pulling in long, even strokes, his head down, giving no sign he had seen Armbruster and Fiorello launching the Adirondack boat. They shot out fifty feet ahead of Wyatt, Armbruster rowing with his broad, powerful back to Fiorello who was in the bow, handling the sneak-paddle with a practiced air. Will's white face looked up and registered the two boats bearing down on him. Almost reflexively he altered his course slightly eastward. The

Adirondack was better built for speed than the *Merganser,* and Roosevelt's men began gaining slightly on him.

Van Dorn's only hope, Wyatt realized, was to get the skiff up one of the swampy river-mouths or inlets on the Vermont mainland, far enough in to find dry footing and head out cross-country, losing his pursuers in the process. There was an inlet just north of the Sandbar bridge. Wyatt had noted it when he took Milly Van Dorn to her rendezvous with the Webbs, so very long ago now. It ended at the edge of the highway half a mile inland on the Milton shore. From there, Will could go on foot, find a bicycle in West Milton or Checkerberry village, make his way to the Central Vermont rail line, catch a northbound freight…

His mind raced with possibilities as he rowed. Runnels of sweat set up a maddening itch along his back, which he tried to ignore. Will was approaching the southernmost point of the island—he would clear it in another minute—

And no sign of the green skiff that held Brigham and Macalester. Will might just outrun them all; he was young and strong and desperate, and he'd rowed for Yale. Then something new popped into Wyatt's line of vision, a boat approaching from the south, a few yards ahead of the *Merganser.* A wide-bottomed canoe of some sort. Two figures, their paddling rapid and smooth. Fishermen?

"Hey!" he yelled. "Stop that boat!"

Startled, the men looked up, saw the three boats bearing down on them: *Merganser,* the Adirondack boat, Wyatt's blue dory. They stopped paddling, exchanged quick, startled looks, began paddling furiously backwards, heading south the way they had come, opening up a gap for Will to shoot through and make his escape. They thought they were the ones being pursued, Wyatt realized. His vision focused on the man in the bow, something familiar about him—

Carlo Abate.

The anarchist from Barre. And someone else, who knew who. But it didn't matter.

"Fiorello!" Wyatt roared. The agent's head jerked back. "Call that boat! It's the Italians—from Barre. They think we're after them. Tell 'em we're chasing Van Dorn's murderer and they have to help us block him in." Fiorello looked stunned.

"Trust me, damn it! Do it now!"

Fiorello turned and hailed the canoe with a rapid stream of Italian. Wyatt caught the words *uccisore*, which he thought meant murderer, and *auito*, help, and Van Dorn.

"*Porca miseria!*" He saw Abate's face go from bafflement to fear to clarity and resolution. He said something in rapid Italian to his companion and they began paddling rapidly northward towards the *Merganser*, directly into Will's path.

"Get out of my way!" Will's voice was a hoarse scream.

Will steered to outflank the canoe on the east side. It kept after him. Frustrated, he sped up and went straight at the lighter craft as if expecting it to pull back. The canoe kept coming at him. The *Merganser* rammed it at full speed, flipping it over from the port side and tossing its occupants into the lake. They went under and came up coughing and spluttering, hanging onto the overturned canoe. Will angled the *Merganser* east again, heading for the open lake to the south. But the green skiff, Brigham kneeling alert in the bow with his revolver drawn, doughty Macalester pulling on the oars for all he was worth, had popped out from behind the south headland of Heron Island and was closing fast. Carlo Abate, of all people, had bought them the time they needed.

Will tried to dodge left, but they were upon him now, blocking his progress. He turned the boat due east, but the Adirondack boat had gained enough ground to lock him in on that side. Wyatt himself was coming up fast from the north. Will was surrounded by boats on three sides, by the mass of the island on the fourth.

The Adirondack glided within range of the *Merganser*. Fiorello dropped the paddle with a clatter, knelt on the caned bow-seat and pulled out his gun. Armbruster shipped his oars and unholstered a revolver. Brigham motioned to Macalester to stop rowing and pulled out his own Colt. Wyatt completed the circle, blocking Will's exit to the north and shipping his oars. Will Van Dorn's head swiveled, staring down the barrels of four guns. He raised his hands and his lips formed a bitter smile.

"I guess I gave you a run for your money, didn't I?"

"You're under arrest, Mr. Van Dorn," Armbruster's voice was polite and icy-calm.

What happened next was a blur in Wyatt's memory. Will Van Dorn muttered something—"not like that," he thought he heard—and sprang towards Fiorello across the narrow gap between their boats, head-butting him in the gut and knocking him off his feet, twisting the revolver out of his hand, pulling him on top of himself into the *Merganser*. The tangle of their bodies prevented anyone else from getting a clean shot at Will, who wrestled Fiorello out of the skiff in a ju-jitsu motion. He spun back towards the enemy boats, the *Merganser* bucking under him in the shock wave of Fiorello's fall into the water, with Fiorello's revolver cocked in his hand. In the slow crawl of microseconds before anyone else could react, he turned the gun to his own chest and fired. He collapsed onto the boards of the skiff in a slow half-spiral.

Fiorello surfaced, gasping, and grabbed onto *Merganser*'s gunwale.

"It's all right," Armbruster said. "He's done for." Will Van Dorn lay face up, a dark stain spreading on his white tennis sweater. As if he'd been carrying a leaky pen in his pocket, Wyatt thought absurdly. Will tried to speak.

"Please—" he croaked. The other boats bobbed around him, the men straining to catch the words that came and went with the ragged intakes of his breath.

"Please—Milly—she knew nothing. She—had nothing to do with—It was all my—please—take care of her—take care of our child—tell her I—tell her—" His head lolled to one side, the blue eyes half-lidded, staring up into emptiness, the arms going slack. Abate and his companion—Wyatt was not surprised to recognize Luigi Galleani—clung onto the rocking hull of their canoe, their faces full of shock and wonder. The men in the boats lifted their gazes from the lifeless boy and stared at one another, heedless as yet of the horrified knot of men in linen suits and pastel-clad women on the south headland by the flagpole. A light wind from the south drifted the cluster of boats towards the shore.

Jeremy Dodge, palette still in his hand, broke through the little circle on the cliff and froze in horror at what he saw.

"Will! Dear God—what happened? What have you done?"

Augusta, white-faced, rounded up the wives and children and led them towards the Camp. Warren Dodge made his way to his son's side, put his arm around Jeremy and began to lead him away, murmuring explanation in his ear. The President was staring in fascination, wordless for once, at the bloody chaos on the water. Tearing his gaze away from the scene, Carlo Abate raised his eyes and spotted Roosevelt on the headland.

"*Ecco!*" He loosened the grip of one hand on the canoe, nudged his companion and pointed upward.

Dazzling in a white tennis costume with a sailor-suit collar, Alice Roosevelt turned to her father with a gelid smile.

"So much for my thinking Vermont was irredeemably dull."

CHAPTER 37

On the water, no one moved for a few long moments. The boats bobbed on the waves, the sun shining indifferently through a light haze. At length Abate and Galleani, still clinging to their canoe like a pair of shipwrecked sailors on a spar, looked inquiry at Armbruster and Brigham, whose guns had now swiveled in their direction. Fiorello, too, clung on and bobbed with the motion of *Merganser*, his eyes fixed in fascinated horror on Will's blood-soaked body cradled in its hull. Wyatt caught Brigham's glance, nodded and gestured downward with his hand, palm and fingers flat. Brigham and Armbruster holstered their guns.

"Somebody get me outa here." Fiorello's voice quavered with cold and shock, his hands blue-white on *Merganser*'s gunwale. Armbruster steered over to him and flopped him into the Adirondack boat like a landed game-fish. His suit was ruined, Wyatt reflected irrelevantly.

"Please. It is cold. You will help us turn over our canoe?" Abate inquired, as politely as if knocking on a neighbor's door to borrow sugar.

Wyatt started back to alertness. He rowed the dory towards the canoe, shipped his oars and grasped the overturned stern while Abate and Galleani held onto the dory's gunwale. Macalester steered the green skiff to the other end, Brigham seizing the canoe's bow. He and Wyatt heaved it upright and it splashed violently back into place. A large wicker picnic basket drifted away on the shock wave, tilted sideways, and sank slowly into the lake. Abate and Galleani made their way hand over hand from the dory to the canoe and climbed in, their shoes squelching on the boards.

"Our paddles are gone."

Fiorello tossed the Adirondack's sneak-paddle to Abate. "That'll get you in. Head back around to the dock—" he jerked a thumb northward, "—and wait there till we get back. We need to talk to you." Abate nodded.

Germain, one arm around a shivering Ellie Tarrant, met the flotilla at the dock with a tarpaulin. Armbruster had taken *Merganser* in tow, and the skiff eddied and drifted on its tether while they tied up the Adirondack. He took the canvas from Germain without a word and laid it out flat on the dock. Wyatt and Macalester tied up the boats while Armbruster and Brigham lifted Will's body from the skiff and laid it, almost reverently, on the tarpaulin. Without being asked, Abate and Galleani stepped forward. Each took an end of the wrapped bundle and helped the two agents carry it towards the boathouse.

"You got some dry clothes?" Germain asked Fiorello, who was dripping and shivering on the planks of the dock.

Fiorello's nostrils flared. "I always travel prepared."

"Go get yourselves dried off and changed," Armbruster said over his shoulder. "You too, Wyatt. Tell Mr. Dodge what's up and have him keep everyone up there for now. Meet back on the cottage verandah in fifteen minutes."

It was an odd little assembly, Wyatt reflected: three Secret Service men casually leaning on the verandah posts, the grizzled Scots police inspector sitting in a green rocking chair next to a pair of Italian anarchists in some old clothes of Jeremy's, and a trembling Vermont farm girl in yet another borrowed dress. Like the introduction to a long, bad joke.

"Well," said Fiorello, who as if by magic had reappeared in an immaculate poplin suit, "where do we go from here?"

"Suppose these gentlemen introduce themselves and tell us what they were up to in that canoe." Armbruster nodded towards Abate, who bristled, whispered indignantly to Galleani in Italian, then rose and bowed to Armbruster with an expression of icy politeness.

"Carlo Abate, sculptor and publisher of Barre, Vermont, at your service." He gestured towards his companion. "Mr. Wyatt I already know. This is Signor Giovanni Pimpino, my editorial assistant. He speaks no English."

Wyatt eyed the tall, horse-faced man with the drooping eyes. Galleani, no doubt about it. His eyebrows went up but he said nothing.

"That answers the first part of the question," Brigham said.

"We came to see the President. We heard he was here."

"And just how did you hear that?" Macalester put in.

"That is not important now. But you will agree that our arrival was—what is the word? Fortuitous?"

"Give you that," Armbruster said. "You know what happened out there?"

"You found the man who killed Van Dorn. And we kept him from getting away from you. Who was he?"

Wyatt rose from his rocking chair. "His son."

Abate took a sharp breath. "*Dio mio.*" He turned to the man he called Pimpino. "*Su figlio.*"

Galleani's great eyes widened in horror. "*Vero? L'uomo che assassina—*" Abate nodded. "*Per qualo...?*"

Abate shook his head.

"What was in that basket?" Brigham demanded.

Abate lowered his head for a moment, then looked up, laughing ruefully. "I am sorry. It is just that—after all this... we brought a picnic. And now it is lost. A fine basket, too, borrowed from my landlady. Some good things that we make in Barre. Wine from my neighbor, sausage, a little *castagnaccio*... chestnut cake...an offering."

"For the President?" Fiorello said, incredulous.

"*Si, si*—your friend Wyatt there would not believe us, perhaps, but so it was. As I have said all along, we wanted only to meet him, to look him in the eye—"

381

"Look, then."

Theodore Roosevelt stood in front of the verandah. The rocking-chairs emptied, pitching wildly as their occupants— even Galleani—straightened up and stared at the President, who had materialized from nowhere, Amy Dodge at his heels, the field-glasses still around her neck. Armbruster, Fiorello and Brigham reflexively interposed themselves between Roosevelt and the anarchists. He waved them away.

"Good to know I've still got the old hunter's stalk. Didn't hear a thing, did you? Look here, the ladies are having conniptions up there and it's not fair to keep 'em in the dark about this. Now, who are these men and what happened out there? Young Van Dorn's dead?"

"Yes, sir," Armbruster said. "After more or less confessing to the murder of his father." He sketched the situation quickly, ending with Ellie's arrival the night before and her rendezvous with Will in the *Merganser*.

"You men should have told me about this. Dear God, child, you might have been killed." Roosevelt clasped Ellie by the hands, blinking indignantly from the agents to Wyatt and Macalester. She blushed and looked at her feet, biting her lip and swallowing hard. Amy went to her on the porch and, wordless, put a protective arm around her.

"We thought we had matters well in hand, sir," Brigham ventured. "We didn't want to ruin your visit if we didn't have to."

"And these gentlemen from the canoe? How did they happen to be by?"

Wyatt took a deep breath. "The anarchists from Barre, sir. The ones we, uh, were telling you about. Back at Sagamore."

Roosevelt blinked again. The sun glinted off his gold-rimmed lenses.

"Anarchists, eh." He let go of Ellie's hands. "Wanted to have a look at me, did you. Well, let's make it mutual."

Cautiously, Abate and Galleani descended from the verandah and stood silent, face to face with the President for what

382

could only have been a few seconds but felt to Wyatt like a quarter of an hour. He remembered that piercing look of Roosevelt's, inspecting his men before that insane afternoon charge in hundred-degree heat up Kettle Hill, missing nothing. Galleani's eyes burned into Roosevelt's face. Neither flinched.

"So! Are you philosophers, or criminals?"

Abate relayed the query to his companion, who smiled sardonically and gave a brief reply.

"Revolutionists, Mr. President," Abate said. "We hurt no one. We seek only for justice for the poor and the workers of this world."

"Well, I'm all for that too. And I hurt no one either. Not if I can help it, anyway. But anarchists, that's what you call yourselves, isn't it? No government at all is what you're after. So, who'll protect the weak from the strong in that set-up, I'd like to know?"

"Who protects them now? No one," Abate shot back. "Mr. Darwin makes the rules in America."

Fiorello and Brigham exchanged a frown and Brigham started forward.

Roosevelt waved an impatient hand. "Let the man talk. It's a free country, for all he says."

Brigham glowered but took a step backwards.

"And what do you suppose would have happened to that man who killed Mr. McKinley if there hadn't been a rule of law—if you anarchists had had your ideal world? Why, I'll tell you. He'd have been ripped limb from limb on the spot by the good citizens who witnessed his horrible deed. Only the police power prevented that—"

"—So that they would not be denied the privilege of killing him themselves," Abate broke in.

"So that justice could be done by the man," Roosevelt went on, relentless. "We have laws in this country, sir, so that we don't have mob rule—so that you and your ilk may speak freely without fear of retaliation—which, I assure you, wouldn't be long in coming if the law did not forbid it."

"You argue that this is a just society? You who have seen the worst slums of New York, the dying children, the workers enslaved by—"

A slicing motion of Roosevelt's hand silenced Abate. "Yes, by God, I've seen all that, and I don't like it a bit more than you do. Mr. Riis, who was here earlier," he gestured back towards the Camp, "was good enough to take me along on a few of his investigations. I don't mind telling you I was appalled. But it's the rule of law that will fix all that, Signor Abate, not your anarchist ideas, and not his—" he pointed at Galleani, "calls for assassination and bomb-throwing. And I don't mind letting you know, either, that I aim to fix as much of it as I can. But if I succeed, there'll be no thanks due to any assassins or subversives or other criminals of that stripe." He paused for breath at last, red-faced, while Abate translated rapidly, Fiorello listening keenly to make sure the translation was accurate.

He's wrong about that, Wyatt found himself thinking. McKinley had been a good and decent man in private, but he hadn't been a reformer. Like almost all of his predecessors in the last half-century, he'd equated the success of American business interests with the progress of the nation, while waves of immigrants became downtrodden and exploited workers, corporations dumped poisoned wastes into the shining rivers of the continent, and children died gasping for air in filthy slums.

An assassin's act had given the country the man who now stood before him, a man who for all his patrician upbringing and his corporate connections cared passionately about economic justice, about preserving the beauties and wonders of America, about breaking up the corporate giants that stood in the way of both those ideals. To say that Czoglosz had done the country a favor would be going too far, but still…

Galleani leaned over and said something softly to Abate, who turned back to Roosevelt with a smile that was equal parts irony and respect.

"You are an honest and honorable man, Mr. President. We are agreed on that. *Cronaca Sovversiva* may have taken note of the heroic actions of the honest men who have killed—and died—for our cause, but it has never called for an assassination—nor will it ever do so in your case."

"Murder's murder," the President snapped. "It's not made a whit better by the claim that it's committed on behalf of a cause. In fact, what your 'heroes' do is far worse, because they negate the free choice of the people. And you see where such thinking leads—you see what happened here. A son killing his own father—no doubt finding some perverse justification for it in his mind."

"Mr. President," Abate ventured, "there will be many things on which we will always disagree. Parricide is not one of those. And in that spirit of agreeing when we can, we wish to invite you to come to Barre and speak to the people of what is in your heart."

Roosevelt's face softened momentarily in surprise, then the mighty jaws clenched. "I thank you for that. But I will not set foot in that town so long as that man—" he pointed to Galleani, "is there and hiding from a just examination of the violent events in which he played a part. When he is gone, then I will come to Barre."

"We could arrest him, sir," Fiorello put in, trying to be helpful.

Roosevelt shook his head. "No. Not here, not now. We'll give them that much in thanks for what they did out there. But if you hear of any further criminal activity that can be traced to him, well, that will be a different matter."

"We broke no laws in coming here," Abate said. Roosevelt looked inquiry at his protectors.

"He's right, sir," Armbruster said at length. "If they had landed here without permission, the most we could charge them with was simple trespass, and then only if they refused to leave after being asked."

"As it is, of course," Fiorello added, "they only landed because we told them to."

"Of course, if they'd come after you directly and tried to hurt you—"

Abate held up his hands in protest. "There were no weapons in that basket. No guns, no bombs. And none on our persons, as you know."

"That part's true enough," Brigham said. "I frisked 'em myself. Who knows about the basket, though. On the bottom of the lake by now."

Roosevelt stared into Abate's eyes. Abate looked back, direct and earnest, and shook his head firmly.

"I believe you," Roosevelt said finally. "And I know what I saw out there."

Warren Dodge came up the path behind the President, breathing hard but managing to mask whatever emotions roiled in him. He took in the sight of Amy's arm around Ellie with a sharp glance. "Things all right here, Mr. President? Anything we can do?"

Roosevelt turned and grinned, slapping Dodge on the arm. "Between my men and Mr. Wyatt and the Inspector, I think we've got the hurly-burly under control."

Dodge couldn't quite contain himself. "Who are these men?" He gestured towards Abate and Galleani. "How did they get here?" No one spoke for a moment.

"They happened to be passin' by when we were chasing young Van Dorn," Macalester said. "We might've lost him without them."

"Mr. President, I wish to—" Dodge began. Roosevelt cut him off with a gesture.

"Nothing to do with you, old man. Only thing you could have done differently was not to have invited Will Van Dorn— which you did out of generous sympathy to one bereaved. Who could fault you for that?"

Dodge opened his mouth to say something and thought better of it.

"I'm only sorry Edith had to see that," the President went on, "though she's tougher than she looks. But that man dug his own grave. He's responsible for all this, not you. And from what I hear, this young lady deserves a commendation, putting herself in danger to bring us word because she was afraid the fellow was out to hurt me. I'm obliged to you, Miss—"

"Tarrant," Fiorello offered helpfully.

"Miss Tarrant. We are all obliged to you." Roosevelt clasped Ellie's hands again. Her lingering fear and troubled look dissolved into a sunny, gap-toothed smile. "These good fellows will take care of it all. Let's go back and explain matters to the ladies, shall we?"

Dodge didn't look as if he felt at all obliged to Ellie Tarrant. After all, Wyatt reflected, the party would have gone off without a hitch if she hadn't shown up to deliver the bad news about Will. And a man's murder would probably have gone unavenged or been blamed on the wrong man. Well, killing the messenger was a venerable tradition, though hardly an honorable one.

"We'll get Miss Tarrant home," Fiorello said.

"Not until she's had some luncheon," Amy said firmly. "You haven't eaten all day, have you?"

"Oh, no, I couldn't—" Ellie demurred. But she allowed Amy to lead her up the avenue of elms towards the house, past her frowning but speechless father.

"Mr. Wyatt has told us all about your farm…" her voice drifted back from the verandah.

Carlo Abate cleared his throat. "May we borrow a set of paddles?"

There would be hell to pay, Wyatt reflected, the first time Warren Dodge got him alone. On the theory that diving into a breaker was better than letting it knock you from your feet, he sought out Dodge in the quiet hour before dinner when the ladies were resting and the men strolling about quietly. Dodge was alone on the south headland, staring moodily into the dark blue water which gave no hint of the two violent deaths that had happened there.

He turned when he heard Wyatt's approaching step. "I can't see how this place will ever feel the same." The sun's lengthening rays caught his cheekbones in high relief. He looked gaunt and tired. "All I wanted was a place—to get away from things, where we could come and relax and entertain our friends, a chance to give the President a quiet few days, and along comes some farmer's daughter and a couple of terrorists invading our privacy and everything goes to hell in a hand-cart—"

Wyatt couldn't believe what he was hearing. He felt anger boiling up and over in him like water in an unlidded pot. He shoved it down with a great effort.

"They didn't hurt anybody," he began very quietly. "If they hadn't shown up, Will Van Dorn would have gotten away. And you're more upset about them showing up and 'invading your privacy'—" he heard his voice rising but couldn't keep it down, "than the fact that your friend was murdered by his own son, who tried to pin it on people like them, counting on our prejudices against foreigners and immigrants and people with the bad taste to go out in the streets and demand social justice. And he almost got away with it—would have if it hadn't been for the guts of that young farm-girl who took her life in her hands to come and warn us about him. For no gain to herself."

Dodge opened his mouth and held up a hand, but Wyatt had built up a head of steam and it had to go somewhere. "The reason I've worked for you these past years is that you're a fair-minded man. I don't know how you treat all your employees but I know how you treat me and the ones I've seen. If you're really going to stand for Congress it might do you some good to pay attention to how people live out there. Not everyone in your district lives in a Fifth Avenue mansion—"

He wondered if he'd gone too far. Dodge had reddened as he spoke, his lips tightening.

"Maybe you didn't know that your friend Van Dorn was a partner in the most notorious slumlord firm in the City," Wyatt pressed on. "Plaster falling off the walls and stinking privies and rats running everywhere. And little children, for God's sake, dying from untreated consumption and heaven knows what else. A child of seven and his sister's selling herself to get him medicine. Now what did that child do to anybody to deserve to die that way in a place like that?"

Dodge stared at him for a long moment, arms folded, and took in a deep breath that was almost a snort. "Are you done?"

Wyatt nodded and stared back.

"So what exactly have you done about all this?"

It was Wyatt's turn to stand speechless and open-mouthed.

"You've been in hiding for five years, Wyatt. Understandable up to a point. But losing your wife gave you an excuse, didn't it? To disengage yourself from the world?" He watched Wyatt recoil as if he'd been struck.

"You've avoided connection to anything and anyone in all that time. I don't say I don't understand it—Lord knows how I'd be if I lost Augusta—but I'll say to you what I said to—to young Van Dorn there. A man's got to get back into the world. Talk is cheap. Easy to prick another man's social conscience. But what about your own?"

Wyatt blinked but managed a smile. "I feel like a man who should have known better than to pick a fight with Jim Corbett."

"You and TR are going to turn me into a damned social reformer before you're done." There was a slight upward twitch at the end of Dodge's mouth. "I had to listen to the same damn lecture from him before he'd agree to back me for that House seat." He sighed. "Look, you're right and so is he. Will's the one responsible for all this mayhem, and he's paid the price. I guess we'll all get over it in time. Now, this boy you're telling me about. Find him and I'll see he's taken care of."

"That's a good start, Warren," Wyatt said, feeling the tension ease out of his shoulders. "But there are thousands like him."

"Well, what do you want me to do about it?"

"You might talk to Mrs. Van Dorn. She's inherited some real estate I suspect she'll be happy to get rid of."

Dodge gave a short laugh. "I'll think about it. Go get yourself dressed for dinner."

CHAPTER 38

Germain's long legs stretched out of a wicker chair that glimmered in the gathering dusk. "You got some ingenious ways of wrecking a house-party."

"Poor Warren," Wyatt sipped at his Scotch. "It meant so much to him, getting the President here. And then we go and foul it up going after a murderer."

"I wouldn't worry too much about that. Mr. Roosevelt said he thought it was a bully little island and he'd be delighted to come back next summer. Good practice for the boys, he said—what if Will had been a real anarchist? Only sorry he wasn't invited in on the action himself. And he's asked the boss over to Oyster Bay in a couple weeks to talk some more about the House seat."

Wyatt shook his head slowly and smiled. "What about the Princess?"

"That's one cold-hearted woman. I don't envy the fella that ends up with her. Most fun she's had all summer, she told Mrs. Dodge. Shame about Will, she said—waste of a good-looking young sport. But catching a murderer—well, that beats an ice cream social on the White House lawn any ol' day."

"It's so quiet now they've left." Wyatt listened to the trill of crickets and the soft lap of waves on the shore. The moist night air carried the slight chill of early autumn.

"You think he really loved her?"

"Milly? To madness, I think. You know the Greek myths?"

"I thought of that. What'd he call himself, Eddie King? Oedipus Rex—"

"—who killed his father and married his mother," Wyatt said. "That was the loose end that Ellie finally gave us."

"Least Oedipus waited till after Daddy was dead to get his *maman* in the family way."

"They knew the child couldn't have been Gerald's. Gerald would've known too. And it wouldn't have taken too long for him to narrow down the possibilities," Wyatt went on, as if to himself. "And then Will thought his father was going to sell the old country place—"

"Where he'd spent time with his first mama," Germain said. "Who's that German fellow I was reading about, talks about how we're all in love with our own mamas when we're what— five, six?"

"About the age Will was when the first Mrs. Van Dorn died. He's from Austria, the fellow you're talking about. Freud."

"Think Mrs. V. was in love with Will?"

"I'm not sure. Macalester talked me into going with him when he goes to break the news to her. Mrs. Dodge is coming too—she's getting ready now."

"You believe what he said, about her not knowing?"

Wyatt gave him a bleak smile. "I'm sure he didn't tell her in so many words. But I won't believe she didn't know. I'd best get my things together."

"They'll be here for a week or so after Mrs. Dodge gets back," Germain said. "Just quiet family time, the boss says. But she'll be after him to get on to Newport. They're invited to the Belmonts' for the Labor Day week, then he's due back in New York for some big board meeting—"

"—and life goes on," Wyatt said, the warmth coming back to his smile.

"Your young farm-lady friend? Spunky little gal."

"She is that. They had the good sense not to let her see Will's body up close. She was crying and saying it was all her fault—"

"Man tried to kill her, for God's sake."

"Women are funny that way. He's still the man that gave her her first grown-up kiss. Fiorello took her home and he was going to explain everything to the Tarrants."

"That's why he put an extra polish on his shoes before he left."

"Her mother must be wondering about this string of good-looking men she's been bringing home—present company excepted, of course," Wyatt grinned. "More excitement than they've had in their whole lives, I dare say."

"That little gal'l be a good wife for somebody."

"She'll find something interesting to do before she settles down," Wyatt stood and stretched. "She was asking Mac if they had police-women in New York City."

"Lord help us," Germain said. "And what about you, *jeune homme?*"

"I was thinking I might pay a visit to Mrs. Beaudoin's."

"Give her my regards."

Wyatt and Macalester, dressed in somber black despite the late summer heat, shifted uneasily in their leather chairs. The great vase of lilies on the library table had been replaced by bronze chrysanthemums. Their bitter-edged fragrance lay heavy in the still air. Augusta Dodge had gone upstairs with the maid to assess Milly Van Dorn's condition before bringing her to the library.

"I've never seen such a tomb-like place in all my—" Macalester began when the door opened. They scrambled to their feet, Macalester leaning heavily on his cane.

Milly Van Dorn passed in, pale but smiling, Augusta Dodge rustling close behind her in a light black silk. Milly's pregnancy was unmistakable now. She wore a loose dress in dove-gray, trimmed with black ribbon. Wyatt found himself relieved that the growing life within her had been released from its prison of whalebone. She gestured for them to sit down, spreading herself out on an embroidered loveseat while Augusta Dodge hovered behind her.

"Mrs. Dodge tells me that my stepson—has died," she choked slightly on the last words but maintained an eerie composure.

"And that you gentlemen could tell me more of the circumstances. There was an accident with a gun, I understand?"

"No more of an accident than your late husband's death—forgive me, ma'am, for speaking so bluntly."

Wyatt looked at Macalester in surprise. The Scotsman's directness was almost aggressive. Milly let out a little gasp, and her knuckles flew to her mouth. Macalester cleared his throat and began again more gently.

"I am sorry. As you know, we considered the circumstances of Mr. Van Dorn's death—the elder, that is—highly suspicious. He was not known as an outdoorsman, other than for a bit of birdwatching. For him to have been out of doors in his dressing gown at such an hour, and in the water—and then a boat missing, and the Italian fiddler gone—"

Milly Van Dorn held up a hand. "I am sorry, Inspector—I don't follow you. You thought the violinist might have killed my husband?"

"We did, ma'am, but there were two difficulties. One being that the fiddler had disappeared along with the boat. We found the boat, but never a trace of the fiddler— violinist, I should say. He disappeared as if he'd never existed."

"And the other difficulty?"

"The violinist, so far as we knew, would have been unknown to your husband. But it seems that someone he did know woke him that morning, got him out into a boat, and—"

"How? I would surely have awakened, if there had been a noise—"

"A bird call, ma'am—the call of a bird that he had perhaps longed to see. Mister Wyatt here tells me your husband was most curious about a great blue heron which had been described to him. It has a call which is perfectly possible for a human being to reproduce with some degree of accuracy."

Wyatt studied Milly Van Dorn's face. There was something veiled in it, something fearful and cautious despite the light of frankness in the china-doll eyes. She was pale again, and there was a slight tremor in the fingers that stretched in seeming languor across the back of the love-seat. Perhaps it was just the first manifestation of grief.

"So you think this Italian fellow lured my husband out with a bird call, persuaded him to get into a boat, and—"

"And drowned him, ma'am, after rendering him unconscious with a blow to the head. From an oar, most likely. But, no, we do not think an Italian did it. For some time our primary suspect was a young man who I believe is known to you. Signor Eduardo Romano?"

"Eddie? But, how absurd. Eddie is an absolute lamb—"

"Harmless enough, as it turned out. He was not altogether truthful in his account of his whereabouts in the period leading up to your husband's death. However, we now know that after he left Abenaki Island, he actually went to stay with a group of—ah, friends near Saratoga. Friends whose private activities are the object of some interest to the local police, but which in my own view are harmless enough. And at length a witness came forward who was able to identify the murderer. Your stepson, Willem Van Dorn, his actions confirmed by his own dying words—"

"He confessed?" she gasped in horror. "He—he told you that he killed his father?"

"Did you know about it, Mrs. Van Dorn?" Macalester asked, ruthlessly. Augusta went to her friend and put a protective hand on her shoulder.

"What did he tell you?" Milly's voice shook, her face flushing a deep red.

"Did you know about it?" Macalester's blue eyes narrowed to ice-chips.

She took a deep breath.

"Of course not. I am shocked—I am horrified—I cannot tell you how distressing all of this is! Gerald gone, and now Will! How could you think—" Her chest heaved and she buried her face in her hands. The three watched her sob for what seemed a long time, as if observing an experimental subject. Augusta looked from Wyatt to Macalester and back again.

"I will ask the maid to bring a *tisane*," she said in a neutral tone. She left the room, but returned quickly. Milly looked up at last, wiped her face and drew herself up.

"He came to see me on the island. It was he, the violinist, as you thought."

Wyatt interrupted. "Mrs. Van Dorn, you may wish to have an attorney present—it is your right—"

Macalester glared at him but Wyatt stared back and the Scotsman nodded, his palms upturned.

"I think it only fair that you should know," Wyatt went on, "Will said you knew nothing—I assume he was referring to his father's death—"

"What else did he say?" she was dry-eyed now.

"Things of—of a somewhat private nature."

"They cannot be private if he said them to you." She swept a cold glance from one man to another.

"Very well," Macalester said. "His words were these. 'She had nothing to do with any of this. Please take care of her, he said. Of her and'—" he broke off.

"She might as well hear it now," Wyatt said. "'Of her and of our child,'" he finished. "And he began to say, 'tell her I—' but he was unable to finish. I do not think much imagination is required to know what he meant to say. His last thoughts were all of concern for you."

"Do you bear Willem's child, Mrs. Van Dorn?" Macalester asked.

"I really think—" Wyatt put out a restraining hand.

"Yes," she said abruptly, through clenched teeth. "Yes, I do, and I wish to God I did not. I did not want it then and I certainly do not want it now."

"Milly, for God's sake, what are you saying?" Augusta Dodge seized her hands and sat heavily down beside her. "Pray stop now. You are grieving—in no condition—"

"I'm not the one who killed him," Milly snapped. "It was only later I realized what he must have done. He went to the Webbs, you see—he was an excellent violinist, he arranged to take the place of the Hungarian fellow, he had spent a summer in Siena once, with friends of Gerald's, studying music, and he was so clever with languages. And he knew by then, you see, about the child, and how Gerald must know, and would find out—" She rose and walked heavily over to the window, parting the heavy curtains and staring out into the street.

"My mother, when I was growing up—she always said to me, 'better to be an old man's darling than a young man's slave.' Advice I took to heart. When I met Gerald—I had not many more years before my voice and my looks would fade—but I didn't know how hard it would be," she turned to them with a look almost of pleading, "to live without passion—passion and stimulation. Gerald was kindness itself, he was so fond of me, but he was so often away, so devoted to Mr. Morgan and all his business. And Will—oh, there were handsome men around, in plenty, but I'd never have chanced it. Gerald's pride, you know, and he was so good to me, and I knew he could be vengeful if he were crossed, he'd told me of several instances, in his business dealings. But then, Will—" she stopped, drew in a deep breath, let the drape fall, supported herself with her hands on the edge of the window-seat.

"The foolish boy fell in love with me. It was madness and I told him so, but it only made him more ardent, it seemed. He would bring me little presents—some things I had to hide, some I could wear—these earbobs—" a hand fluttered to her ear, where a cluster of small garnets dangled, and she let out a little half-sob.

"You didn't tell your husband, I take it," Macalester growled.

"Of course not—how could I? And then one day, in the upstairs salon—early March, and so dark and dreary—it was sleeting, no one was going out. And Gerald had been gone for days, and I had absolutely nothing to do. And then Will came in, and came to me and seized me in his arms—oh, it was all quite romantic, and—"

"*That day we read no further,*" Wyatt murmured. "You fell in love, then?"

"Well, no. He did. I, for my part, did not. Oh, he was certainly handsome enough, and—quite virile, you know, and we had a great deal of—fun, but as time wore on he became much too intense, and possessive, and he quite began to frighten me. Every chance he had to come home from college, sometimes with Jeremy, sometimes not, but always he found occasion to—come to me, and I didn't know what to do then—I tried to tell him we were being foolish, we must stop, Gerald was bound to find out—"

"And then you found yourself with child," Macalester said. "What did he say when you told him?"

"Oh, heavens," said Milly, some of her old sprightliness returning as she warmed to her narrative, "he was over the moon. Ecstatic. We'll run away together, he said. We'll sell some of your jewels, and go off to South America and live in a little cottage by the beach—well, I must tell you that didn't interest me in the least! I told him I wanted to get rid of it—and he was horrified, he wouldn't hear of it, but then, I asked him, what else are we to do? Your father will know, he'll ask questions—"

"'You must trust me,' he said, 'I'll find a way.' He got very quiet and serious then. Will's quite a planner, you know, when he sets his mind to—" she broke off and her eyes welled up for a moment. "So he said, 'Don't worry, I'll take care of everything with Father, just go to the island and enjoy yourself, and I'll come and see you there, perhaps I'll spirit you away in the night.' So I thought he was arranging for a, you know, an operation. And then I realized he'd come up with this scheme, this musician business—"

"Did you know it was him?" Macalester said.

"Not at first," she laughed. "He certainly did a good job, didn't he? He even wore lifts in his shoes, he told me, to heighten the illusion. Did you know he was one of the leading men in the Yale Dramatic Society? But then, once the quartet came to the island, I noticed the violinist staring at me, and I recognized his eyes, and he saw that I'd seen him, and he just shook his head, just a little, to warn me not to say anything. It made me anxious, I can tell you, knowing he was there—I was afraid he would try to come to me again, and I didn't want that at all, so I tried to keep from being alone, and mingle with the other guests, until Gerald got there, but then I had started feeling quite unwell in the mornings, as you unfortunately saw—" she gestured towards Wyatt, "and Will didn't seem to be making any progress in resolving our dilemma, just this silly disguise business, and we hadn't a moment alone, really, before—"

"I can understand your distress in the circumstances," Wyatt said, "but when we found Mr. Van Dorn, you told us—"

The blue eyes widened. "—that he had quarreled with his father over Blauwberg."

"Why did you tell us about that, Mrs. Van Dorn?" Wyatt asked.

"Well, I truly didn't think he'd have—I thought it must have been an accident," she said. "And the thing is, and I'm sure you'll think this is hard to believe—he really did care for his father, in his own way."

"Were you surprised to see him when he arrived with Jeremy?" Wyatt persisted.

"Oh, I knew he and Jeremy had arranged for him to come," she said, "but, of course, then there would be no opportunity—they'd be sharing a room, you see, and—"

"So you thought he had just adopted this disguise so he could be near you, and slipped off to get rid of it so he could arrive officially?" Macalester said.

"Something like that, I suppose." The eyes china-doll wide, a pretty shrug of gray-clad shoulders.

"And you honestly never thought he'd had anythin' to do with Mister Van Dorn's unnatural and untimely demise?" the Scotsman glowered, half-rising from his chair.

"No, I did not," she replied primly. "Will said so himself, didn't he?"

"What about afterwards?"

"Mrs. Van Dorn," Wyatt said, "I really think you should—"

"We never spoke of it. We were in mourning, of course, I was in seclusion for some time—it was so tedious! Will was with the undertakers, and then with the lawyers, seeing to his father's affairs, and, frankly, he seemed rather cut up about it all. And I didn't like to ask—"

"You didn't like to ask," Macalester said, incredulous.

"Only, then, a week or two after the funeral, Will came to me, in my salon. He made sure the servants overheard him saying we had much to discuss, in confidence, concerning the settlement of his father's estate, and he—he said he was so happy now, we could be together for always, us and our child. But of course I would have to be in mourning, I must stay in seclusion, until the child came, no one need know, and after a suitable time, we would marry, and he would adopt the child as his, the child everyone would assume was his father's—"

"Legally, the child will be Mr. Van Dorn's heir, will it not?" Macalester said.

"Yes—that's so. Mr. Pendergast explained the terms of the will to me—he did not know of my condition, of course."

"And now you and the child will inherit Mr. Van Dorn's entire estate," Macalester said, "after a suitable period of probate—"

"Oh, no," she said quickly. "Will told me he changed his own will, so that everything he inherited from his father would go to me in the event of his death. Including that vile old estate on the Hudson, which I shall certainly sell at the first opportunity." Her face brightened at the thought.

"When young Mister Van Dorn put this proposition to you—" Macalester began.

"Oh, I was horrified—horrified! To be mewed up in four walls like—like a Carmelite, or some such. But not a nun! That certainly wasn't his idea. But what could I do? He knew

I wanted to be rid of the child, so he didn't want to let me out of his sight. And he pleaded with me. He said, you'll come to love it in time, it's the—the fruit of our love, that's what he said. And then he—he came to me, and he was very ardent, and so happy, but I was miserable, and it's been so hot and stifling, all shut away. Every day, every afternoon, he came to me, even though I was growing bigger, my waist getting so thick. He said I was blooming, I was like a flower opening, he wanted to touch me, to taste my body—oh, how I grew to hate it! But the more he came to me, it seemed, the more he wanted, and I couldn't go out, I couldn't get away—I felt so trapped! So suffocated! And if anyone did come to call, he made me put on those dreadful mourning-weeds, so confining, I couldn't get a breath of air, and finally he had the servants tell everyone I was ill, that I wasn't receiving—"

"The child needn't have been his, after Mr. Van Dorn died," Wyatt said gently. "Could you not have decided then to break with him? You could have sent him to live at Blauwberg, Mr. Van Dorn had left the house to you—"

"Oh, you don't know Will," she shook her head. "He frightened me so! He had a gleam in his eye, a wildness to him—I found it attractive at first, I confess, but later I grew afraid. I didn't know what to do! I thought my life was over, and now—"

And now I have it back, Wyatt finished silently. *And beauty still, and a fortune, and any number of ways to temper the inconveniences of motherhood.*

"I have said far too much," Milly Van Dorn suddenly drew herself up into a semblance of Fifth Avenue dignity. "I am sorry for Will's death. I am even sorrier for what he did. My husband was a kind and good man and did not deserve to die in such a dreadful fashion. But now justice has been served and we will have another funeral and perhaps it can be given out that Willem died in a hunting accident."

"That would hardly reflect well on the Dodge household," Wyatt observed drily.

"I trust further that since there are no criminal matters to concern you here, I may rely on your discretion as gentlemen to say nothing of what has passed within these walls," Milly turned to Augusta Dodge. "And I know I may rely on your goodwill, my dear."

Augusta rose. She looked at Milly with barely concealed distaste.

"You may say whatever you wish. For my part, I will have nothing whatever to say of the matter, and I trust that no one will have the incivility to ask. And now, if you will excuse me, I must attend to matters for my return to Vermont." She swept from the room in a rustle of black silk. Wyatt and Macalester looked at each other. Macalester pushed himself up with his cane.

"It seems, Mrs. Van Dorn, that matters have resolved themselves rather favorably, on the whole—excepting, of course, for the two unfortunate crimes that have been committed. For self-murder is still a crime. But you are quite right. There is no evidence to implicate any survivors in any criminal activity. I will therefore take my leave of you, wishing you comfort in your bereavements—and joy of your fortune."

"Thank you, Inspector," she rose and started to put out her hand. Macalester ignored it and brushed past her. He bowed as he opened the door. "Good afternoon, ma'am," he said, and was gone.

She looked pleadingly at Wyatt, the bright blue eyes soft, searching in his face for sympathy. "It's all so very tragic."

"Dying for love, or killing for love?"

She looked at him, silent, open-mouthed, as if he had struck her, reminded as he had intended of their conversation in the boat, that first day, when he rowed her to meet the Webbs.

"I played Hippolytus once," Wyatt said, reminiscent, "in *Phaedra*. Except in that story she loved her stepson and he didn't love her. You're right, though—it's tragic all the same. Good day to you, Mrs. Van Dorn." He followed Macalester out the door.

CHAPTER 39

Wyatt affected a casual air, not an easy appearance to give while walking down a narrow street with a huge and expensive bouquet of flowers. The fragrance of musk-rose and carnation wafted into his face when he stopped in the warm evening to look at house numbers. At last he walked up the steps he was looking for, rang and was admitted. Mrs. Beaudoin greeted him in the flower-carpeted parlor.

"Ah, Monsieur Wyatt, you honor us with your presence again. *Mais où est votre ami?*"

"Germain's still in Vermont, getting ready to move the household on to Newport. But I thought I'd come and pay a visit to Miss Duvalier, if I might."

Mrs. Beaudoin's welcoming smile faded to sadness. "Oh, *quel dommage!*" Her eyes lit on the bouquet, in which orchids and lilies predominated. She fingered an exquisite, creamy white blossom. "Ah, *belles fleurs pour la belle*—I am so sorry to tell you, Bella has left us." She gave him a look that stopped just short of pity. "Though I should not be sad—she is very fortunate. She had an admirer, a wealthy gentleman, of Dutch family, I believe—he came here often and always asked for her. Then just last week he arrived, and brought her a ring, with sapphires, you know, and diamonds, and took her away to live with him in Albany. They will marry, she says."

Wyatt had felt the color rise in his cheeks while Mrs. Beaudoin was speaking. Her practiced eye took this in, noted how the color heightened the symmetry of the long lines between cheekbone and chin. The face of a Norman knight on a tomb effigy she remembered from a cathedral in childhood, and with something now of its bleak gravity.

"Does she love him," he asked, his throat dry.

"Love?…ah, *oui*, she is fond of him, 'e is very kind to her, and so generous—who knows what is love, Monsieur Wyatt?"

I did, once, he said to himself. *Or thought I did.* He forced a smile. "Is he a handsome man, would you say?"

She laughed, a warm rippling sound like a summer stream. "I think you would say not. Per'aps not extraordinarily ugly, and you know, portliness is still the fashion for the gentleman, is it not?"

Wyatt rose. "I'd best be going now."

"Come back again, Monsieur Wyatt. It will always be a pleasure to welcome you."

"Maybe one day. Please give Mr. Germain's regards to Miss D'Arbanville—and mine also."

He walked all the way home, north across Manhattan in the gold evening light. It was dark when he let himself in, and then Mrs. Baird was just inside the door, scanning his face with concern and something like joy in seeing him again.

"It's time ye were back, Mister Wyatt. Between you and Macalester, I've been in a state these last few weeks."

He took in the wrinkled, homely face, thought of the hours she'd spent by Macalester's bed in the hospital. The meals that had appeared outside his own door in the weeks following Rose's death, when he'd lost interest in eating or forgotten to eat. Faithful friendship, not to be taken lightly.

He handed her the bouquet. "These are for you. To make up for all the worry we've been causing you."

"No need for that," she said gruffly, but she stuck her nose in the fragrant blossoms and sniffed appreciatively. " Such bonny flowers…they must've cost you a fortune. I've a nice bit of bacon put aside for the morning. Come down and have your breakfast with me. You'll not have anything laid by yourself, being gone so long."

Wyatt thanked her and shut the door. A new pile of mail waited on the side table. It could wait a little longer. Rose smiled wistfully at him from her portrait. The image seemed to have faded somehow, and he felt a vague regret about that. He undressed and lay down on the bed, letting the street sounds float in on the warm night air until his mind drifted away.

The blue heron began its slow, silent flight across the landscape of his dreams.

THE END

Historical note: Vermont, 1903

Most Vermonters in 1903 worked in granite quarries, textile mills, hardscrabble farms and factories that offered equal parts danger and misery, while wealthy and powerful urbanites escaped city summers among the state's lakes and mountains, enclaves of beauty and ease. Luigi Galleani, the leading thinker of the Italian anarchist movement, and Theodore Roosevelt, twenty-sixth president of the United States, two of the most influential men of their time, inhabited these parallel worlds for a while, each leaving his distinctive mark on the State's history.

Fleeing indictment for his role in a New Jersey strike that had turned violent, Galleani made his way to Barre, a booming granite town populated by immigrant stonecutters, many of whom were openly anarchists. There he collaborated with the sculptor Carlo Abate on a new Italian-language anarchist journal, *Cronaca Sovversiva* (Subversive Chronicle), first published on June 6, 1903. Sold widely in the U.S. and Europe, *Cronaca* became the most influential voice of anarchism in the Italian-speaking world.

At the turn of the century Theodore Roosevelt made several visits to socially prominent friends at their summer retreats on Lake Champlain. On September 6, 1901, as Vice-President, he was giving a speech at the Isle La Motte home of former Vermont Lieutenant Governor Nelson Fisk when he received word of President McKinley's shooting by the anarchist Leon Czoglosz. In 1902, the new President's political swing through the then-stalwart Republican state took him to Rutland, Montpelier, the state capital near Barre, and Burlington. After a speech there, he sailed on the yacht *Elfreida* to Shelburne

Farms, lakefront estate of railroad magnate Dr. William Seward Webb and Lila Vanderbilt Webb.

Details of Roosevelt's other, more private visits to Vermont in this period have been lost to history.

In October 1903, a confrontation between Barre's anarchists and socialists turned lethal with the shooting death of the anarchist granite sculptor Elia Corti at the Socialist Labor Hall. The night's scheduled speaker, socialist leader Giacinto Serrati, was responsible three years later for revealing the whereabouts of Luigi Galleani to the authorities. Arrested and tried for his role in the Paterson strikes, Galleani was freed by a hung jury and returned to Barre, where he continued to publish *Cronaca Sovversiva* until he moved it to Lynn, Massachusetts early in 1912.

Carlo Abate formally established the Barre Evening Drawing School in 1911, where children of the granite shed workers learned sculpture and monument design with a view to escaping the fate of their fathers. At the end of the Great War, he had moved far enough into the political mainstream to be commissioned to design the horses for a war memorial.

Theodore Roosevelt returned to Vermont as a Progressive candidate for President in August 1912. Reflecting his populist political philosophy as it had evolved over the intervening years, he made Barre his one campaign stop in the state, speaking from his campaign car in front of City Hall. "I am trying to bring nearer the day when social and industrial justice shall be parceled out to all alike in this land of ours," he said in his speech.

In a speech given earlier that year at Sagamore Hill, he said, "This country will not be a good place for any of us to live if it is not a reasonably good place for all of us to live." A few weeks after his visit to Barre, his candidacy was effectively halted in Milwaukee when he was wounded in an assassination attempt by a deranged saloon-keeper, John Schrank—who, incidentally, was *not* an anarchist.

Acknowledgements

This book would never have come about without the hospitality of my dear friends Michael Burak and the late Mary Haas, who first invited me to what evolved into Heron Island.

My deep gratitude for their generosity, patience and honest feedback goes to my fearless readers: Mary Hays, Cathy Bennett, Don Rowe, Bob Swierczek, Catherine Hughes, Ginny McGrath, and Kit Ward of Christina Ward Literary Agency. Karen Lane, director of the Aldrich Library in Barre, Vermont, Marjorie Strong, Assistant Librarian at the Vermont Historical Society, and the late Professor Richard Hathaway provided expert advice and steering for my historical research. Their collective suggestions have improved this book immensely; errors and faults of content and style are my own.

I am indebted to the staffs of the Kellogg-Hubbard Library of Montpelier, Vermont, the Lower East Side Tenement Museum, New-York Historical Society, the Vermont State Library, and the Museum of the City of New York for access to places, photos and documents which were important underpinnings for scenes in the book.

Author and teacher Jonathan Strong helped me understand that the best stories are a journey of discovery, and the best mysteries are those the writer hasn't yet solved. Archer Mayor, Vermont's literary "crime boss," gave valuable leads on literary agents.

Boston's literary meeting place, Grub Street, is an invaluable resource for New England writers and proved so for me, as did Sisters in Crime, the national organization of women crime writers.

Although this work is strictly fictional, the following were important sources for historical context and such authenticity as it conveys:

Goodbye Highland Yankee: Stories of a North Country Boyhood by Scott E. Hastings, Jr. related a real-life incident that formed the basis for the grocery warehouse scene in Chapter 20. The writings of Mari Tomasi, author of *Like Lesser Gods* and *Men Against Granite*, and of poet Verbena Pastor helped me to understand the lives and challenges of Barre's turn-of-the-century granite workers. *The Vanderbilts and the Gilded Age: Architectural Aspirations, 1879-1901* by John Foreman and Robbe Pierce Stimson and *Anarchist Portraits* by Paul Avrich helped round out the characters at the societal poles of the era. *Vermont* magazine, 1901–1906, in the Kellogg-Hubbard Library Vermont Collection, provided a photographic and historic portrait of Nelson Fisk.

The following books and manuscripts from the Barre Historical Archives at the Aldrich Library provided invaluable historical context: the Ben Collins papers; George Ellsworth Hooker, "Labor and Life in the Barre Granite Quarries;" Paul Demers, "Labor and the Social Relations of the Granite Industry in Barre" (Goddard College BA Thesis, 1974), and William H. Jeffrey, *The Granite City, Barre, Vermont*, Rumford Press, 1903.

The University of Dundee Department of Forensic Medicine, "Bodies Recovered from Drowning," www.dundee.ac.uk/forensicmedicine/llb/water.htm, and forgotten-ny.com were particularly helpful websites.

I save my warmest thanks and deepest love for my husband, Wayne Fawbush, whose good heart, good humor, sharp eyes and unwavering faith sustain me on the great roller coaster of writing and of life.

About the Author

Roberta Harold is at work on her third novel, a re-imagining of the life of a Civil War widow. Her first two books, *Heron Island* and *Mortal Knowledge*, mysteries set in the early 1900s and published under her pen name of R.A. Harold, feature security agent and sometime Shakespearean actor Dade Wyatt.

A 2001 graduate of the Bread Loaf School of English at Middlebury College, she studied fiction writing with novelist Jonathan Strong and poetry with Paul Muldoon, winning the 1999 Poetry Competition there. She was a 2009 finalist for the Orlando Award in Short Fiction of the A Room of Her Own Foundation. She is a member of Sisters in Crime and of Grub Street, Boston's creative writing center.

A native of Scotland who emigrated to the U.S. at the age of twelve, she was among the first women graduates of Princeton University in 1973. She lives with her husband in Vermont and in Brooklyn, New York.

Coming soon from R.A. Harold:

Mortal Knowledge: the second Dade Wyatt novel

Breinigsville, PA USA
17 January 2011
253472BV00001B/1/P